Runes of Iona

Runes of Iona

▶▶▶▶

Robert Balmanno

A Caveat Lector Book

REGENT PRESS
Berkeley, California

ISBN 13: 978-1-58790-203-1
ISBN 10: 1-58790-203-6

Library of Congress Control Number: 2010927877

First Edition

0 1 2 3 4 5 6 7 8 9 10

Cover design/photos by S. R. Hinrichs

Manufactured in the United States of America

REGENT PRESS
www.regentpress.net
regentpress@mindspring.com

ACKNOWLEDGEMENT

To all those whose assistance, in various ways, contributed to making this book possible, the author expresses his appreciation and gratitude, with special mention to:
Phillip Balmanno, Janelle Gray, Becky Breitwieser, M.Y.Mim, Scott Hinrichs, Adele Horwitz, Ethan Place, and Kenneth Jacobs, for reasons known to each of them.

Introduction

Fifty miles beyond the start of her journey, Iona knew she'd have to enter the Forbidden Zone. It was an area picked clean, scoured-to-the-bone, bleached of all life. The Forbidden Zone was the grimmest place on the surface of the Earth.

There were piles of flinty scree, alluvial fans of gravel, biscuit pan, undulating expanses of sand dunes, and thirsty, dry creek beds. Thirty-five years before, water flowed freely, albeit sporadically, along the deeply fissured gulches; a desert made drier and more desolate by man's attempt to control the weather.

The zone had been created by an elite corps of engineers. Their experiments in weather alteration and climate change created an impregnable firewall, on a north-south axis. Intense heat and absence of water were the zone's most important hallmarks. Forming a critical link in what was envisioned as a world-encircling barrier, it stood as an impassable ring of fire separating the "sacred and privileged" climates of the north—from the "fend for yourself and good luck" climates of the south.

Iona was going to risk her life when she passed through the Forbidden Zone during midday when the hills and flatlands would be fiery furnaces with temperatures of 140 degrees Fahrenheit.

One hundred miles beyond that point—perhaps less, perhaps more, nobody knew for sure—Iona would reach the other side of the wasteland of the Forbidden Zone, and perhaps find safety.

But she didn't know what lay on the other side. A little better climate? A little worse? Survival at a minimal level? Of course, later on, the climate could only ameliorate, improve with time, but how long a time—that was the most disturbing question.

In the year 2070, at the age of thirteen and a half, Iona left Tom in their home, a home they had secretly shared as a sanctuary clandestinely created by Iona's deceased father, the eminent world scientist Regis Snow, during the time he had been chief engineer of the government's global weather control system. As the one surviving daughter of Regis Snow, it was untenable for her to stay. To avoid detection, Iona's survival depended on her traveling alone to a destination in the south. It was for her safety that her parents had planned this leg of the expedition. It was for her survival that she was setting out to do what she had been selected to do, all in line with her parents' dying—and now almost completely suppressed—rebellion.

Later, subsequent aspects of Iona's mission would be revealed to her, but only when she needed to know.

So, Iona set out on her adventure to preserve her life and to do whatever else she might be able to do for humankind.

So, only fifty miles south of her home, on the edge of the Sonoran Desert and the great Western canyons and inviting caves of the Sierra Madre Occidental Mountains of north-central Mexico, the Forbidden Zone beckoned her. Alone, on foot, Iona headed south. She would have to travel twenty-five miles a day if she were going to have the slightest chance for survival.

Intuitively, Iona knew what her odds were. Analytically, she knew what she was up against.

Tom, the pessimist, had given her a chance of one in sixteen. Iona, the optimist, had made it one in four.

But what did one base the odds on, really? There wouldn't be a repeat performance. Just one roll of the dice.

With steps taken with neither daring pride nor bold experimentation, but with stillness, patience and nerves-of-steel composure, in the context of the next forty-five years, large doses of stillness, patience and nerves-of-steel composure were exactly what it was going to take to keep herself alive.

So Iona stepped into her future.

Chapter One

A FTER WAITING three and a half years, Iona received her wake-up call—the long-expected news from her mother, September Snow, one of the four prominent leaders of the rebellion against the Universal State Gaia-Domes—that the time had come for her to leave. She dressed in two moderately thick layers of clothing as a make-do toga, made of home-spun fiber that Tom and she had combed and carded from the cotton they had grown in their garden. With two long lengths of fabric, one nine feet long, the other sixteen, she wrapped herself from head to toe, including her face, dressing in the manner of the Tuareg of the Sahara Desert, effective prevention against dehydration.

But before she covered herself, she filled four three-quarter gallon water sacks and hung them down her back with grass-woven thongs. She attached them, side-by-side, next to her bare skin, resting them from the top of her shoulders to the bottom of her hips.

Hidden carefully inside her wraparound clothes, the four sacks otherwise looked like four elongated sausages, or four long water balloons, nineteen to twenty-two inches in length—the shorter ones on the inside, the longer ones on the outside—so as to snugly fit the contours of her back down to the small of her back. Under her clothes, they were strapped to her skin. Thus they rested in a semi-flat position, pressing against her body.

On the outside of her clothing, Iona carried her prepared cornmeal in a ten-pound pouch on her right. Her bow and arrows, her head and face protection cloth, her drinking cup, along with her combination digger spike and flint fire starter, were carried on her left.

At birth, Iona had a freckled face and her hair was strawberry-blonde in color. As a sixteen-month-old baby, she had "shining goldielocks of hair" that changed color as she grew. First, her hair went from blonde to a sandier washed-out hue. Then at the age of twelve, it had become a cross between dirty blonde and light-pale brown.

Iona's eyes changed color too. At birth, her eyes were blue, resembling her mother's. Twelve years later, they turned a greenish gray. The new color made Iona seem subdued, but also haunting, bewitching, even frightening, especially when viewed from an angle, with the sunlight glinting on their surfaces, her eyes appeared opaque.

But what was it that caused her hair and eye color to change so drastically? Was it due to the day-to-day changes in the fracturing of the sunlight? Or was it something else in the ruined environment. To the north, due to fluctuations in the intensity of ultra-violet rays coming from the sun, the scavengers' and cannibals' eyes—at least the eyes of the foolish ones who ventured out into the full exposure of the midday sun without wearing protection—had turned a burnt, mottled gray-bluish color. Some of their offspring, and more importantly, their offspring's offspring, had developed strange creases on their foreheads and wrinkles resembling gills on their cheeks. Many of them had lost their hair, or what was left of their hair had turned white. Plainly intense radiation had penetrated their skin, causing damage to the genetic material of their cells and corrupting their cells' programs. As Iona was growing up, she and Tom had always lived safely within the confines of Regis Snow's protective bubble, which had effectively shielded them from the most dangerous hazards of the sun's rays.

But all in all, in the end, it didn't matter because in terms of Iona's strength, undetectable to even the eyes of the most astute outside observer, she was strong, though not muscular, just angular, taut, lean. Physically and mentally, she was incredibly tough.

Iona and Tom faced each other. Iona viewed her old *teacher*, who had guided her for the last nine years—and it was almost as if Iona wanted some sort of blessing from the seventy-six-year-old man. Iona threw herself down on her knees. She averted her eyes away from Tom's downward stare. In a low voice, almost in a whisper, Iona murmured: "Goodbye."

Tom did not reply.

Iona felt a pang in her heart. She felt she had not done enough. She felt an urge to attempt one last stratagem, a final ruse. She decided she would remonstrate once more. She quickly thrust her arms out, stretching them out to their limit. She held out limp, trembling hands in supplication, as if she were holding two invisible begging-bowls, as if she were making a final plea.

Iona drew her lips together silently into a frown. She lowered her head and averted her eyes. In a rasping whisper, she said, "Please, Tom, please. I beg you. I implore you. Accompany me. I know you are able to. I know you can do it."

There was a moment of silence. Tom hesitated, but only an instant. "Can't do that," he said at last. He rotated his foot back and forth, like a haltered horse. He scuffed the bottom sole of his sandal on the turf of the desert.

"I'll hinder your progress. Impede you. You know that. That's for certain." Then his face broke into a charming smile. He appeared engaged, at ease, radiating a portrait of calm and serenity.

"I'm too damn old. Breathing down on seventy-seven. Too cranky, as well. Besides, with only one of us left, instead of two mouths to feed, I can survive much longer on what's left in storage. That's good. I eat little. I eat like a church mouse. You'll see. It'll work out for the best. I know this to be true."

Tom nodded his head. He was giving the best performance of his life.

"You'll do fine," he continued. "Go. You'll see. It's for the best. You mustn't delay. You know what your mother said about the timing. How crucial it is. Remember what she said about the attacks on the weather-changing machines. It was all planned so long ago. Timing is utterly important. That's why you must leave. Right now."

Iona abruptly rose from her knees and stood up. She was only an inch and a half shorter than Tom. The sudden spurt of growth—the last three and a half inches—had occurred only within the previous eighteen months.

"Very well," Iona said, speaking with a voice that carried a note of protest, but the protest was only half-hearted. Her face had the look of dejection and her eyes were downcast. Tom bent slightly at the waist, inviting a peck on his cheek. "Come on," he grunted, pointing his index finger to his right cheek. "Give it to me. You're not too old for that yet, even if you aren't a runt any longer, you pesky little rodent."

Without hesitation, Iona rose on the balls of her feet. Instead of a peck, she placed both hands on the sides of Tom's head, cradling Tom's head gingerly, as if she were grasping a rare dinosaur egg and kissed Tom squarely on both cheeks. Then she threw her arms around Tom and buried her head deeply in his left shoulder, weeping silently. Tom reciprocated with two quick mechanical pats on her shoulder. Iona was too self-disciplined to weep for any prolonged period of time, and Tom was also too self-disciplined to say or do anything that would induce Iona to continue to weep. They flirted with their emotions, but they were rarely seduced by them.

More out of suppressed sadness than outright anger, but out of anger too, Iona stepped back. She dropped her arms to her side—not casually or lackadaisically, rather in a stagy, choreographed, military-like precision. She raised her hands vertically—to both sides of her head—while at the same time staring fiercely at Tom. Tom returned Iona's look with a strange unflinching counter-gaze of his own. Only with his eyes, without even a nod of his head, Tom commanded her to go.

Iona barely nodded—so imperceptibly and economically, the gesture was barely noticeable. Using the ends of her cloth, she covered her neck, jaw, mouth, entire lower face, covering up to the middle of her nose. Then with the last long tuck of the cloth, she completely covered the top of her head: all of her hair, tying the ends in a knot, covering most of her forehead, leaving only a tiny gap, a small chink, so her eyes could peer out. With solemn, fierce eyes, almost as if they were the eyes of an animal, she turned three-hundred-and-sixty degrees and surveyed each part of the horizon. She took in each section separately, surveying each part carefully. Then, in a flash, she took in the whole. It was as if she were taking a picture of the place for posterity. She closed her eyes.

Tom spoke. "Try as I may, I can't be silent. What you're attempting—it's so important, it behooves me to say *something*. The brimstone in the Forbidden Zone devours everything. That's true. The fire there—it eats everything, corrodes everything, annihilates everything. The fire and the brimstone of the Forbidden Zone. What more can be said? *Almost* everything. What I mean is, it won't devour you. You'll be untouched. Why? Because you're too strong. You're tough as nails. No, tougher than the points of rusting iron. I pray that you will make it. Make it all the way to the other side."

What was the point of the pep talk, Iona wondered? *What difference could it have made? She had committed herself. That was that.*

Placing one foot in front of the other, Iona began her journey.

Tom nodded his head approvingly. Slowly, he watched Iona disappear into the mirage of the simmering heat of the desert. As Iona continued into the distance her body seemed to shimmer, break up, waver, break into bands, the bands of her body wavering and shimmering even more. The powerful illusion of a mist caused by the hot air arising from the desert floor—made her white-clothed image flit and flutter in unequal parts. Then her image was lost in the mirage. At last, she disappeared from his sight.

Tom could tell that once Iona had swung into her stride, there was nothing that was going to stop her, except of course if she ran out of water: the large *possibility*—the loss of potable water, the threat to life through thirst and dehydration; the number one bugaboo, the absence of water.

Iona refused to look back. She did not turn around and glance. All of her energy was directed toward one goal: walking as far south as possible, in as short a time as possible. Having left in the late afternoon, by nightfall she had covered eight miles. As the sun sank below the western horizon, she rested for fifteen minutes and watched it. As if she were in a hypnotic trance, she gazed dreamily at the horizon. It was a view that was terrifying and moving at the same time. During her rest, she touched not a drop of water nor ate a morsel of food. As darkness fell, she rose and continued to walk at a clip of just under three miles per hour. She kept this up with only one forty-minute rest-stop just after midnight—until two hours before sunrise. Then she stopped walking. Instantly, without wasting time, she commenced a search for water and food. She found a deep narrow canyon on the edge of the desert and climbed down into it. With only two hours left before sunrise, she found cactus and yucca plant and after eating the edible portions, she busied herself by digging for water. She found that, too—in the spongy roots of a dying plant that had sunk its roots deep into the clay bottom at the base of two towering granite boulders wedged in the side of the steep canyon. She dug out the roots and drank the water that remained in the empty hole where the plant had been, then she squeezed the remaining moisture out of the roots into her upturned mouth, drinking in the last, tiny drops of the dewy moisture.

Just after sunrise, she covered herself in a deep crevice in the rocks, using one of her rolls of cloth as a canopy to provide complete shading. She slept peacefully until an hour and a half before sunset, resting a full eight hours. After she woke, she drank two meager mouthfuls of water, ate no food, and set off walking.

She had covered almost thirty miles the first night and planned on doing the same the second night, maybe, with luck, adding a mile or two.

She walked methodically, maintaining her brisk pace. Three

hours before daybreak, however, after having taken her usual two breaks, she reached what she presumed was the dry riverbed of the Yaqui River. She had never before ventured this far south, so she was traveling on oral instructions from rote memory.

Even before the big climate change, Tom had taught her that the river sometimes flowed underground during the dry season. She decided to stop for the rest of the night, even though she could have continued walking. Stopping prematurely reduced her progress to a bare twenty-five miles for that night.

She found a few desert plants to eat, one of which was almost delicious, and she began to dig. For four hours, she dug nonstop in the ravine of soft clay. Three hours before sunrise, she finally found water. During that last hour, she could feel the heat rising from the ground as if triggered by a blast of fire from the rising sun above. As the sun rose, degree by degree, the mercury soared. As Iona diligently worked, she felt the heat on her back, then the nape of her neck was wet. She began to sweat; the most dangerous of all occurrences because even a small amount of sweat signaled body-liquid loss which would have to be replenished. The only source of water she'd soon have was the water she was carrying on her back. Luckily, she found plenty of water to replace the loss, five feet down beneath the river bed.

By the time Iona found this water, she was utterly exhausted. Her arms, shoulders and back ached. They were as tired and sore as her legs and feet had been. The water source was nothing more than a tiny well-spring, but it seeped up for two and a half minutes, gurgling for a minute, then stopping. Enough water formed in the clay basin so she could drink more than her fill. She scooped the water up, cupping the palms of her hands together so she could bring it to her mouth. The water tasted sort of *off*—there was a touch of bromide and the taste was slightly saline—but she knew it was entirely safe to drink. It was tepid water, brown in color, almost the color of a strongly-brewed tea. There was enough left over to thoroughly wash her face and hands. After she had slept for most of the day, there was an extra bonus: more water seeped into the basin and she was able to drink her fill again: replacing all of the water that she had lost from sweating during the strenuous digging. She had been incredibly lucky. She was proud of herself. Finding water: hardly an exact science, rather a slap-dap, hit-and-miss, pragmatic, more-an-art-than-a-science sort of task. Fortunately she had picked the right spot. She could have dug forever (twenty hours, thirty hours, who knows?) and found nothing. She smiled inwardly, with a profound sense of contentment. She knew that Tom would have been proud of her accomplishment. She imagined Tom smiling at her with a delightful expression of approbation gracing his old, lined face. The thought of his approval gave her a feeling of comfort, lifted her spirits, and encouraged her to travel on with a renewed vigor.

She covered herself with her long toga and slept reasonably well during those day-time hours. She was lucky again. This day, the temperature rose to 112 degrees Fahrenheit. As there was still water left at the bottom of the hole, she gorged herself almost as if she were a camel, managing to soak up and store another two quarts of water. But she only had barely an hour left before sunset, so she immediately continued on her walking trek.

The first leg of her journey proved to be easy. It was almost too good to be true. Iona managed to walk across the desert in two nights, all fifty-five miles. The remaining part would be over foothills and mountains. Even better, she had been successful at foraging off the land. From her own provisions, she drank only a rare mouthful of water and consumed a small handful of cornmeal.

She had made a good start.

What surprised her, though, was that she had traveled across so much of the desert, and there was no sign of the beginning of the Forbidden Zone. Only that consideration caused her a little concern.

Iona walked twenty-seven miles the third night, with a tiny sliver of moon showing over the foothills. Iona knew how to navigate by the stars, checking the position of the Big Dipper and the North Star every hour. She walked due south, occasionally making an easterly adjustment to travel parallel to the contours of the Sierra Madre foothills as they slightly curved eastward. She never had to worry about cloud cover obscuring her celestial guides; there were never any clouds, not this far south of the protected zone. But there was no sign of the edge of the Forbidden Zone either. Although she was able to forage for the little food she required, the terrain was tougher and wilder, more scant in vegetation, more arid. There was no place to dig for water. She had to break into her reserves. On occasion, she experienced intense thirst. She sat down and drank almost a pint of water. Her body had become dehydrated. She needed water badly and she needed rest as well. The temperature that day rose to over 133 degrees Fahrenheit, and without drinking another pint of water on top of the first pint she had drunk, she could not have slept at all, much less with a modicum of comfort.

On the fourth night of her trek, Iona set out as usual. The moon, only a thin sliver showing, rose earlier than the previous night, but the night seemed all starry including a few shooting stars. But here was the trick, as Iona understood it: Six hours before, she had endured temperatures in excess of 132 degrees. During the cruelest part of that day, she could not move, she had to lie perfectly still, moving an arm or a leg was painful, just opening and shutting her eyes used energy she would have preferred not to expend. Iona knew that if she could somehow survive two hours of that roiling heat, and the temperature dropped to 125, then an hour after that, 115, she could use her muscles. She could lift her arms and legs a little. Her joints would become supple and limber again. The temperature finally dropped to 110 about an hour before sunset and she was almost in her comfort zone again. The heat was *tolerable*. She started walking. Six hours later, just after midnight, the temperature dropped to 104 degrees, and it *felt cool,* but only comparatively speaking, of course, for ironically, it was still in absolute terms, hot.

By morning, she reached a dry riverbed, probably the former River Mayo. There was no water to be found, only a collection of pebbles, rocks, and dust. Two hours before sunrise she began digging for water but before she had dug three feet, she stopped. She *knew* there was no water to be found, certainty no water close enough to the surface for her to find by digging with her digger stick and her bare hands. Was it a sign that she was close to the Forbidden Zone? She didn't waste any time shifting priorities. She needed to study the terrain ahead in order to obtain a much better overview. Even with the most sensitive eyes, there's only so much one could see in the dark, especially for purposes of choosing the best route. She needed to reconnoiter. She climbed to a point that was fifteen-hundred feet up a hillock, reaching the top of a scrabble of rocks, at about the same time as the sun rose over the Eastern horizon and the light began to filter in. She had already traveled fifty-five miles farther south than she deemed necessary to arrive at the edge of the Forbidden Zone, yet she had not seen any evidence of it, except for the indirect evidence of the growing wildness of the terrain and the diminishing water resources.

Then Iona saw what she had been searching for. The skinny tree she was clutching literally snapped in half as she squeezed the trunk, just as the sun lit the land. The bark of the tree was dry and brittle; it reacted to the light pressure of her hand as if it were decaying paper.

She dropped the upper trunk of the tree on the ground. It crumbled into powder before her eyes. Iona realized that she was on the very precipice of the Forbidden Zone. At first glance, she hadn't realized it. She just needed a little more sunlight to see "it."

The "it" in question couldn't have been anything other than the Forbidden Zone. From the second moment she gazed, it took on the qualities of a beast. From one point of view, the Forbidden Zone was strictly a mineral-geological phenomenon (at least that would have been Tom's scientific-observational way of describing it). But to Iona, it was alive, in the same fashion that the Earth was alive.

It was like her own beating heart, and it didn't involve practicing philosophy, as in Tom's strange way, where reason did not bend to, or recognize, a higher authority. He had described it as a skeptical way of thinking. Rather, for Iona, it was a matter of thinking pragmatically, about what she must believe, in order to struggle with life.

As far south as she could see, the Forbidden Zone was red and undulating. In the rising heat, it looked unfocused, wavering, *as if it were a predator*. Also, it was like an open and vivisected wound, a wound that had ruptured, without indicating any signs of healing.

"The Beast" (Iona had resolutely decided to give it that name) even compared to the unworldly and weird terrain she had traversed, looked like a nightmarish place. She imagined that it was from the planet Mars, mostly because of the red tone. Not a fleck of green was evident. As far as the eye could see, there was no evidence of any vegetation whatsoever. It looked ruddy, red, vermilion, with a mix of gray. But, at least until the sun was high in the sky, there were tiny traces of shade here and there.

Seeing that, Iona let out an audible sigh of relief. The idea of shade gave her cause for optimism, even if it was a false or illogical optimism. She didn't care if she was hopelessly deluding herself. She was willing to grab onto any straw that would allay her fears. And if shade was all she had to grab onto, she would grab onto that ethereal thing, too.

But the other problem was that she did not know how far the Forbidden Zone extended. One hundred miles? A hundred and fifty? Farther? Had she not already misjudged the distance from her home to the northern edge of the Forbidden Zone by a good fifty-five miles? Iona knew that another error like that would cost her her life.

She descended down the hill speedily with a sense of urgency. At the base of a slightly overhanging crop of rock, she quickly dug a smoothly hollowed pit. She literally burrowed herself into the earth, as if she were burrowing into the rectum of a long intestine. She worked fast. She molded the cavity to fit the contours of her body. There was no time to spare. The sun was rising fast. Again, she had to drink a half pint of water. She sensed that her body was starting to experience the early signs of dehydration. She worked fast because the temperature was rising fast. Once she had completed the digging, she burrowed inside the cavity that she had formed in the dry, crusty earth. It was amazing how small she could make herself by bending at the waist, shoulders and knees. The pit that she had dug was small. With barely an inch or two to spare, she fit in snugly. She fell asleep immediately. But later on, she nodded off and on, between alternately restful and fitful spasms of sleep. She didn't know how hot it was outside, but she knew that it was hotter than it had been on the previous day. Inside the burrow it never rose above 102 degrees.

Now came the real test that Iona had been preparing for. The total absence of movement—unless movement was absolutely necessary—that was the test of survival. Iona remained perfectly still, her breathing shallow, as close as possible to complete inertia. In her imagination, she saw herself as a lizard or a rat; better yet, an insect, or better still, a specially-adapted desert scorpion. Now that was truly the best of all! The desert scorpion was arguably the toughest terrestrial creature on the surface of the planet. It didn't need water. (Iona remembered Tom's lecture on that most incredible of all incredible creatures: He had explained that it got all its water from food. No matter how dry the food, there was always enough moisture to provide for its bodily needs. It conserved its bodily fluids so assiduously it never drank, absorbing sufficient water from the flesh of its prey. It also had an extraordinary capacity for eating: It could gain up to thirty percent of its body weight in a single meal. Tom had once described such a feeding "as the direct conversion of prey biomass into scorpion biomass." Afterwards, the desert scorpion would then appear horribly swollen, but it could then survive for up to a year before another feeding. However, there were no specially-adapted desert scorpions living in the Forbidden Zone, because there was no food available. There was nothing—*living*—out there, to eat or to be eaten.)

Iona told herself she was going to have to do better than the specially-adapted desert scorpion. She must cheat the Forbidden Zone, fool it at its own game.

When she began the fifth night of walking, she waited till the sun had set this time. No walking the first hour or the first two hours before sunset, as she had done before; it was just too hot during all of the daylight hours now. She finished off the first of her three-quarter gallon sacks of water. It was refreshing. It was luxurious. *The temperature finally dropped to 116 degrees Fahrenheit. It was hot, but at least no longer in the killing zone.*

Now she had only three three-quarter gallon sacks left. Until she crossed over to the other side, with the water that remained, she was going to have to be even more frugal. She was certain that no water was going to be found anywhere in the Forbidden Zone. What she carried with her would have to suffice. But she now had less to carry, and the lighter load raised her spirits.

How would she survive? Her sole traveling companions: solitude, absolute aloneness, perhaps also the so-called "God" in the formation of a Universal Gaia would accompany her. Tom had argued not that Gaia was unknowable, but that Gaia's unknowability was the most profound and illuminating thing humans could know about Gaia.

She was beginning to understand.

Chapter Two

I T WAS HARD TO SEE AT FIRST, but Iona soon realized that
the trail she thought she was forming, creating—by the occasional dragging of her feet—in the first section of the Forbidden Zone, was actually already there. She was, in fact, following the
faint existing path marked by the slight indentations of a stranger's
footprints.

"Ah ha!" She took note. "And there!" she nodded. As she continued Iona discovered another. Then another. Finally another! Little by little, the footprints became increasingly evident. They formed
a pattern creating a portraiture in sand. Such huge footprints they
were too. Heel to toe, they were massive in size. They measured over
fifteen inches long and four-and-a-half inches wide. The boot-prints
left deep impressions and the balls of the feet tucked inside the boots
left impressions, especially in the sections of the path where there
were pans of soft clay. Even though it was night, aided by the light
of the moon and the brightness of the stars, Iona was able to make
out the prints—read them, as it were. She could also analyze them,
and study them.

Clearly they were the footprints of a fully grown man, a big
man, someone weighing nearly 300 pounds. The prints were fresh,
or, at the least, relatively recent. In Iona's opinion, derived from her
childhood experience of tracking still hot or already cooled paths
of scavengers and cannibals—those who occasionally strayed from

their normal hunting grounds and ventured too close for comfort and security, the man's prints were about six months old. Iona semi-successfully suppressed a guilty smile, then a gloatingly smug grin quickly made its appearance and passed, but after a moment's reflection, there was left a mischievous twinkle in Iona's eyes, because, after a brief period of time Iona had deduced a number of things about the man just on the strength of her examination of his footprints. Although well shod, indeed, he was wearing expensive footwear—a special kind of boot—the man's feet were tender and he clearly was unaccustomed to walking distances of any length. By adjustments in his gait (and the absence of a noticeable lilt, or a staggering lilt—to be more accurate, disclosed the maturity of the man, he was older—probably in his late fifties, if not that, then perhaps even a few years older, maybe 60), Iona could detect that he was developing blisters on the balls of his feet, and on both the inside and outside portions of his heels. The discomfort caused by these expanding, developing—ever-growing blisters, caused the man to walk even more splayed-foot than usual.

This man had a different life, involving aspects of privilege and luxury, where exercise was infrequent and shunned. Therefore, when the forced-walking tour was imposed on him, it undoubtedly generated a side effect in the form of a kind of shock to his system. Iona wasn't able to prevent herself from being drawn into speculation about the nature of the world this man had inhabited before his mishap. At the very least it was clear that—as worlds go—it was a place that was profoundly different from the Spartan-like regime that Iona had grown up in. Had the mysterious man been rich? Was he an idler? Perhaps he had been rich and an idler? There were other possibilities. Had he worked all his life behind a desk? Was he a high-level commander or some type of paper-pushing administrator, new and unacquainted to the hardships of travel and the unappealing, drudgery aspects of field-work? Had he been a helioplane pilot, or at least a passenger, perhaps even an important or celebrated passenger?

And how did he get there? Had he dropped from the sky, parachuting from an aircraft in the middle of flight? Had he survived a crash of a helioplane or some other type of aircraft? What else could have brought him to the Forbidden Zone but a strange and tragic accident. There was no evidence of any aircraft wreckage located in the vicinity. Of course, that in itself didn't prove anything. The site of the crash could have been located on the other side of the mountain, or many miles away. Iona realized that she could speculate endlessly on that subject without getting any closer to a satisfactory answer.

By the end of the fifth mile (at least as far as Iona had been tracking), the mysterious man's blisters had grown appreciably. By the end of the eighth mile, they had firmly established themselves as being in need of being lanced. Less than ten miles farther on, the blisters were on the verge of rupturing into boils and some of them, if they hadn't been lanced soon, would have prevented the man from being able to walk at all.

There were places where the man had fallen and his hands had stirred the soil as he braced himself for his fall—and he rose quickly too, because the ground must have been fiercely hot, and would have burned his ungloved hands. (The disturbing of the soil also provided evidence that the man had been traveling in a stupid fashion—namely during the hazardous early and late *day-time* hours.) Iona knew what Tom would have said about the blisters on his feet. Tom would have described the blisters as: "one at least the size of a quarter, the other a Susan B. Anthony."

Iona hadn't a clue what a "Susan B. Anthony" was—or the meaning of a "quarter." Several decades before the Eleven-Years-War, 40 years prior to Iona's birth, they had been terms for purposes of exchange, that much Iona knew. But what was that? *Money? Mediums of exchange?*

Iona remembered that Tom had taught her the first presidential profile to appear on a piece of United States coinage was a likeness of an Abraham Lincoln.

"Lincoln penny" had been an expression employed by the endearingly knowledgeable and occasionally humorous Tom, along with other sayings he had a fondness of using when they shared their home, the Regis Snow-created protective bubble on the edge of the Sonoran Desert.

With Tom's panache for spell-binding erudition and wit, Iona remembered the occasions of speechifying and some of Tom's repeat performances, too. For Iona, these colorful screeds, diatribes, and incidents of storytelling involved archaic expressions that had a thrilling cachet and striking allure, but they described an unknown world, an alien living structure encircled by myth and fantasy, the world of Tom's childhood, youth, and manhood.

From Iona's memory, weird phrases kept popping into her head. They also simultaneously fitted into her delicate mood of nostalgic yearning. *Iona missed Tom badly—that's why she'd been momentarily bitten by that peculiar bug known as "homesickness."*

Along with "Susan B. Anthony" and "quarter," there were other Tom favorites that stuck in Iona's mind: "Totally," "sweet," "far out," "awesome," "dude," "punked"—most of these coined 70 to 80 years prior to Iona's birth in 2057 A.D., before the time of Tom's birth in 1994 A.D. Tom had salted his conversation with a rich supply of terms. ("Burn-out," dating back—what—95 years? had been one of Iona's all-time favorites, along with the peculiarly elusive: "haul ass," "flat as a pancake," "go for broke," and "there's still gas in the tank.") In a flash, Tom's employment of expressions surged back into Iona's mind, along with phrases that were weirder, as "behind-the-times" as 130 years earlier, 140 years earlier—*ANCIENT—according to Iona's perspective!*

When Iona was a child—six, seven, eight, nine, ten—and Tom was correspondingly in his late sixties and seventies—not yet too old to occasionally play the spirited role of buffoonish clown—it was a role that delighted Iona.

Thinking back in time with nostalgic indulgence, Iona imagined Tom's head bursting into an eruption of infectious laughter. Tom's rascal-like face related story after story. Some of Tom's stories were colorful. They touched on youthful flings, acts of wanderlust, before the beginning of the cataclysmic Eleven-Years-War. What a hoot!

Just inside the Forbidden Zone, soon after Iona had picked up the man's tracks, without a doubt in her mind she decided to follow them. Traveling inside the folds and contours of a tapering, narrowing, cul-de-sac-like valley, his trail led due south, with only an occasional twist to the east, matching an adjustment in the twist to the terrain. The prints were headed precisely in the direction she wanted to travel anyway. *Where would they lead, she wondered?*

Because of the frightening, life-threatening, searing heat during the daytime hours, Iona walked during the night hours only, the light emitted from the stars and the moon serving as her visual guide. Unlike her disadvantaged "on foot" traveling predecessor, Iona's superbly honed night-vision and seeing-at-night powers allowed her to make out not just shadowless areas, but also shadowed regions as well. Even without a moon, just the canopy of stars overhead, Iona still managed to see in the dark, that's how trained and focused she was.

Iona covered the distance of twenty-seven miles on that fifth night of travel, an extraordinary accomplishment considering that the Forbidden Zone was next to impossible to cross during the day, and *absolutely impossible* to cross during the hottest hours of the midday: Iona estimated that to mean, according to Tom's "wristwatch-time," between eleven-fifteen in the morning, and four in the afternoon.

Once at midday, she awoke in an unsettled state due to a disturbing dream. In fact, she had experienced an unseemly nightmare—producing a sleep that did not refresh. Abruptly opening her eyes, she trembled at first but possessed enough good sense to keep herself from thrashing about in a spasmodic manner, in other words, she didn't do what she instinctively was inclined to do: panic. Rather, she kept still. She didn't disturb her fragile environment with an exaggerated movement of arm or leg, thus shielding the membrane of her "cave," her only protection against the searing heat outside, indeed, at that time of day, lethal-in-nature—roiling blast of heat—what with the air quality in the Forbidden Zone at that time, between two-fifteen and three-thirty in the afternoon: the hottest point—and most dangerous time of the day.

The nature of Iona's nightmare? Iona dreamt that her hands were bound and tied in twelve places. Then her legs were bound and tied in twelve places. Finally her mouth was sewn tightly shut, using needle and thread—twelve stitches all told.

(What was the meaning of the recurrence of the number twelve—or did the recurrence of the number have any meaning? Iona wondered.)

The needle and thread pierced through skin—according to the dream—administered by a doctor with a manic expression on his face, dressed in a blazingly white surgeon's smock. But only after the doctor had shoved wriggling insects into the cavity of Iona's mouth did he apply the final stitch work. And the surgeon then sliced Iona's eyelids off with a razor blade for good measure.

The dream was so realistic! *Iona's mouth smarted and her eyelids stung too!* She couldn't swallow. The muscles of her throat seemed to contract. Iona needed to regulate—normalize—her breathing patterns, and she was experiencing effort in doing so.

Naturally having woken from such a dream and realizing the limitations of movement in the "cave," this incubus coming from the unconscious mind left Iona for a few moments in a state of barely controlled disquiet.

Assuming there is such a thing as a dream having symbolism—or significance—it didn't take long for Iona to divine the meaning of her dream. Iona knew she was in great need of giving herself a respite, a temporary suspension—from the boring routine of *waking, walking, returning awkwardly to sleep; waking, walking, returning awkwardly to sleep—over and over, with scarcely a mouthful of cornmeal on occasion to diminish her growing pangs of hunger.*

Having awakened and more or less recovered from her reaction to the nightmare, Iona decided to indulge in a frivolous and costly exercise before trying to return to a state of sleep, just because she felt intuitively that it was the right thing to do (only *apparently* frivolous, not *really* frivolous). Iona reckoned that the action might help in dispelling the lingering effects of the dream. For several reasons, it was an extravagance she could ill-afford, but she did it anyway.

Iona took three tiny handfuls of water, an amount roughly equivalent to less than half a pint. She carefully splashed her face, gently dabbed the back of her neck and hands, and applied the third portion to her feet. Having done so, she rubbed the moisture into the pores of her skin, applying special attention to her toes and insteps.

Iona was troubled by an instance of doubt. She remembered Tom's solemn commandment: all water shall be for purposes of replenishing precious bodily fluids, no other purpose allowed. Alas, SHE HAD ALREADY DONE IT!—she had already parted from Tom's explicit instructions.

Less than a few seconds after she had administered the dabbing, she closed her eyes. She instantly felt as if she had been transported to another place, a better place. She was experiencing the thrilling sensation of a powerful ecstasy, as if she had entered a blissful state of heaven-like pleasantness, a sublime transport into a realm of comfort. Although the air was motionless and hot, Iona continued to keep her eyes closed. In a way she was able to fabricate a fiction that there was a breeze blowing through her "cave."

Luxury! Worth it, too!

Even though this state of bliss lasted only for a short while, as her legs and arms settled snugly inside her confined space, what a thrill this experience was. Iona positively sighed.

After Iona fell asleep again in the tight wrap of her cocoon-like world, added to her occasionally lucky dreams of imagining rivers and streams was a refreshing dream of another theme: cool wind blowing through her hair, caressing her lips. And no nightmare came to haunt her this time. Up until now, Iona had experienced not so much as a *breath* of air, much less wind.

(There was no wind in the Forbidden Zone, not a hint of it, yet another reason why the place was so ghastly.)

Now Iona experienced "it." Because of Tom's preaching-like

pedagogy, Iona knew that the Greek word for *breath,* wind, was synonymous with the word, *spirit.* And she felt it too—*spirit.*

When Iona had a sleep day of good dreams, she also slept deeper, more effectively. And when she slept more effectively, she had more energy for her next evening of walking. Thus, reckoned according to a larger scheme of things, placed in a measurement of that balancing act, the otherwise wasteful use of water refreshed her, lifted her spirits and probably hadn't been such an ill-advised exercise in extravagance after all, when you consider the extra energy it gave her after she had slept soundly. It also had the effect of taking the bad taste of the dream out of her mouth. Psychologically speaking, physically speaking too, it was priceless.

So, by the end of the day, Iona still had to drink a half pint of water and eat a half-measure of cornmeal, but by the beginning of the night, the rising moon was almost half-full; and now Iona had the added advantage of being able to see well at night, the light from the reflection of the moon improving her night vision significantly.

The first thing Iona observed along the trek on that sixth night under the milky-bluish moon-glow were articles of discarded clothing strewn here and there by the large, mysterious man. The first garment she saw was a light coat, then an indistinguishable piece of clothing, a formless, curving head-piece, perhaps the remains of what—a soft, felt hat? These were followed by other articles: a torn shirt, a pair of underpants, then not one but two pairs of socks with the remains of faded, coagulated blood stains covering parts of the material. An hour later, Iona found a discarded water canteen. Empty. Shortly after that, she came upon a loaded laser gun, a standard Gaia military issue. A little farther on, she found lying in the sand, next to each other, a ratchet key for a helioplane door and an ignition key for a helioplane starter-engine. A quarter of a mile farther on, she saw two large fistfuls of gold and silver coins sprinkled carelessly over the sand. Finally, there was a single sixty-ounce bar of gold bullion lying partially buried in the sand—presumably to have been used for purchasing purposes, if one had nothing else of value to use as barter.

Years previously, Tom had done a remarkable job of teaching Iona what he knew about the old customs of money and banking. The international Gaia system had issued only special commemorative gold and silver coinage to special outlander couriers because 99.999 percent of all international business transactions employed huge webs of computers. There was very little paper or plastic money in circulation. Everyone, except the magisters, was paid with digital tokens, starting with Suits, Middle-middles, and Upper-Minds, right down to the lowest level of workers in proltowns (all slaves and domestics, of course, were exempt—they were paid nothing—being not figuratively, but literally, slaves). Tom had also explained to Iona that the actual workings of the international Gaia system was the biggest, closed secret of all: The only illumination he could provide was that the Gaia-Domes were a vast network of putatively theocratic-operated city-states which rose up in a war-torn world a year after the end of the Eleven-Years-War. Through their extensive web-like power, these Domes controlled virtually all of the urban world and most of the rural, agriculturally viable land: with the exception of the remaining rebel bases, the ocean-going pirates, a few isolated, primitive outcasts here and there, and at the bottom of the bottom, the biological mutants, the scavengers, and the cannibals.

Iona was amused as she tried to imagine the wretched man, obviously from the pattern of discarded effects a crash victim attached to a special Gaia outlander courier service, walking into and chancing upon the presence of a group of unsuspecting and perhaps slightly startled biological mutants, or scavengers, or cannibals, and then trying to barter *something* for purposes of trying to save his life, by brandishing nothing but a sixty ounce bar of gold bullion! She knew that he would have just as effectively impressed those heathen haters of cleanliness by brandishing a one-pound bar of soap!

Clearly the man had shed everything that was useless for his crossing although hardly in the order that Iona thought suggested wisdom, much less, common sense. She already knew that the man was, effectively, a walking dead man.

The physical evidence of the pilot's demise came soon enough, another twenty miles farther on when Iona found the body. The corpse was lying face down with his arms and legs outstretched. The body had shriveled somewhat, giving what was left of his clothing a decidedly ill-fitting look. Iona deduced that he had died from extreme fatigue and heat exhaustion rather than dehydration, and that he had drinking water with him until near the end because a second empty canteen lay near his body. She didn't waste more than two minutes examining his remains. The body had baked in the sun for anywhere from 140 to 180 days, and for almost two hours on each of those days at 140 degrees Fahrenheit. The corpse had lost much of its form and a large amount of its moisture. Under such harsh conditions, in three years, the body would resemble a mummy, with a few square inches of tattered clothing stitched together here and there to cling to the shrunken flesh. What was left of the uniform covering the corpse confirmed Iona's suspicion all along that he had been a Gaia courier. Iona was neither disconcerted nor depressed about finding the corpse. She felt a certain sense of relief and buoyancy that came from knowing that another had, also, tried to walk in the same direction as she, even if his ill-fated trip was doomed to failure.

The only useful thing she found with the corpse was an army field compass and a few drops of water left in his discarded canteen. She drank the water down greedily. His large, oversized boots were intact but Iona had absolutely no use for them. The compass was incredibly lightweight, weighing only an ounce and a half. No Gaia Global satellite navigation system, she wondered? Perhaps the compass was an heirloom, kept by the owner for no other reason than for its sentimental value. Iona took the compass (in spite of its age, it was shiny, rust-free and in fine working order) thinking it might come in handy if the clouds ever returned—which would mean that her mother, September Snow, would be successful in destroying the weather-changing machines.

In the fullness of time, rain would then return to parts of the world from which it had been stolen, including the Forbidden Zone.

The destruction of the climate-changing machines would also destroy entirely the Forbidden Zone, Iona reasoned, and that thought made her heart leap with hope, too. Wouldn't it be wonderful, she thought, if she actually had to use the compass to find her way—because of cloud cover, or because there was rain falling. She had dreamt of rain falling many times, when she wasn't dreaming about cool rivers, streams, and cold wind blowing.

The next five nights of walking were all the same and passed without serious incident. Iona walked under a growing—waxing—three-fifths, two-thirds, three-quartered, then seven-eighths gibbous moon that made the Forbidden Zone look less and less like a Marsscape and more and more like a bluish, ghost-like moonscape: as if Iona were seeing everything through a luminously milky filter that changed its tint a little with each passing night of the slowly waxing moon. She drank a pint of water at the beginning of her day, and another half-pint at the end; in between she ate a handful of cornmeal. She was now passing through the heart of the Forbidden Zone and all she wanted to do, now, *was get through it.*

From the beginning, Iona had been realistic and matter-of-fact about her circumstances. She never expected to see a living tree or a clump of grass in the Forbidden Zone. But what she hadn't expected was the absence of a single stick of dead wood or a single strand of dead grass for a hundred miles, and she had already traveled more than a hundred and twenty-five miles and saw nothing living or dead except for the remains of the courier.

By the end of the tenth night Iona finished drinking the contents of her second water bag and by the end of the thirteenth night, there was only the fourth water bag left, plus approximately two quarts from the third bag. While sleeping, Iona occasionally was lucky enough to dream of rivers and streams. These were happy dreams of course, but all the same she felt depressed immediately after reawakening. When the temperature dropped to 95 degrees Fahrenheit in her makeshift "caves"—then and only then, she felt better, a little more relieved, a little more upbeat, instead of experiencing what was increasingly becoming the norm; a stifling, unsettling condition of hopeless lassitude and listlessness. No doubt about it, the scorching, pulsating heat of the merciless sun, like a hammer pounding relentlessly on an anvil, was getting to her.

Something was wrong, Iona was realizing, something was out of kilter. The crushing monotony of Iona's Forbidden Zone experience was intensifying her original, harder-than-ever-now-to-suppress anxieties. And slowly, in spite of the concocted rationales she continued to foster and employ in order to boost herself, she was starting to lose heart. She was beginning to harbor doubts about the efficacy, indeed the sanity, of her mission. How did she know that the Forbidden Zone didn't continue on forever, that there wasn't another side to it, and that her end was not going to be the same as that of the ill-fated, overweight courier pilot? To have even the smallest chance of survival, she needed to tap into some extraordinarily deep reserves.

Iona remembered something that Tom had once said to her: "The lure and the terror of the desert is that the *isolato,* the solitary loner, may find himself not free of self, but, on the contrary, full of himself. By virtue of that, he may find himself less in the company of angels and more in the presence of devils." Or as Iona remembered Tom was so fond of repeating: "The devil has his contemplatives, too. *Oh yes, he does!"*

Then Iona remembered what her mother, September Snow, had told her, when she last saw her—when she was nine years old. This memory came back to her now, almost as if it were a dream. She remembered that her mother had given her special instructions; instructions that she had been ordered not to divulge to Tom. She had been given directions about where to go and what to do when she approached the boundary of the other side of the Forbidden Zone. She was to locate two large mountains, each almost 11,000 feet high, a good 2,500 feet higher than any of the surrounding mountains, and thus relatively easy to find. These mountains were less than thirty miles apart, on a line running almost in an east-west axis. When she found them, she was to find a cave among a series of caves on the western slope of a long, narrow, and winding valley between the mountains. She was to remain in one of the caves (it didn't matter which one) until clouds passed overhead, signifying the destruction of the climate-changing machines and thus the destruction of the man-made climate structure. She was to gather all the dead wood she could find and build a huge bonfire. After the very dark clouds had passed overhead, she was to wait one day, and then ignite the fire so it could be seen from a distance of many miles.

After starting the fire she was to return to the cave, after leaving a trail of rocks leading up from the bonfire to her cave, guiding someone who would come and find her and take care of her.

In the cave, Iona could live on a half pint of water per day, perhaps as little as a third of a pint of water per day, if she was careful and limited her activity to only the bare essentials.

September told Iona that walking alone through the Forbidden Zone would not be her big test. Hiding alone, inside the cave, perhaps for as long as two weeks, that was going to be the greater challenge.

And that was why her mother told Iona that the real lessons about learning to live, to survive in the cave—lessons taught by the old blind man, the 102-year-old Indian *brujo* of the *Raramuri*—would be of such importance, even though Tom, himself, would never be able to understand it, and for that reason, Iona was never to discuss her cave experiences with him.

And Iona remembered September's famous last words: "I'll never see you again, my love, for I am...in effect...already dead. It's already happened. It was inevitable, you see. Don't grieve for me. Don't mourn either. It isn't sad, my passing. Because my love for you is timeless—deathless. My love for you will never cease. My love for you will go on, forever. It will not diminish over time. In fact, it will grow deeper and richer."

September instructed Iona never to tell Tom about the cave, although Iona was never given any reasons for the necessity of the heightened sense of security.

Repeatedly, September had made Iona swear solemn oaths of silence over the matter, and if there was anything that September had effectively taught Iona how to do, it was how to follow orders.

Unbelievably, everything started to go right for Iona towards the end of her thirteenth night of walking. With the aid of the nearly full moon, she sighted two, towering, 10,500 foot mountains, and having found them felt more than lucky, she felt actually touched by a divine spark of grace. Her night vision, with the aid of the almost full moon, was almost as good as her day vision. And she was so happy when she found the mountains that her vocal chords tightened, rendering her speechless, strangely mute but deliriously happy.

When Iona reached the northern end of the winding valley between the high mountains, an unexpected and miraculous thing occurred. As Iona took her first steps into the valley, she realized that she had just stepped out of the Forbidden Zone. Of course there were no signs posted anywhere announcing a border, she just felt it instinctively, mainly she felt the euphoric sensation inside herself. The air was not so brimstone hot nor was there that sharper-than-dry-as-paper-burning-pine-needles-flying-in-the-air feeling. She could breathe a little easier and her chest wasn't so tight. Not a living thing was around her, true, not a trace of green, but there was some dead wood lying around and a few clumps of dead grass, all blazingly visible under the silver sheen of the cool light of the full moon.

Fourteen miles farther, she fully realized she was truly on the other side of the Forbidden Zone. So under the euphoria-inspiring moon, she jumped up and down in a frenzied celebration. Her heart thumped rapidly. She beat her thighs with the palms of her hands in a state of rapture, shouting whoops and other child-like cheers. She literally danced a victory dance, stamping the ground hard, shedding tears and crying that tight cry that came from inside her chest and in the upper part of her throat, then unable to suppress any longer what she wanted to express: shouting and exclaiming in happiness: experiencing the greatest pleasure that a thirteen-and-one-half-year-old could possibly have known all alone: relief, not-a-return-to-home-kind-of-relief, but a return to a home-like, safe place that was from now on going to be the closest thing to "home" to her.

Under the full moon on the thirteenth night, Iona spent a full twelve hours gathering wood which she turned into a huge fifteen foot stack—so that later—she would light it and thus create a huge bonfire—just as her mother had instructed her to do three and a half years earlier. Less than three-quarters of a mile from the site, she found a large open-mouthed cavern that went one hundred yards into the side of the mountain. At the end of the cave she discovered an upper room with a thirty-foot-high ceiling. In a couple of days she discovered the temperature was cool, 67 to 70 degrees Fahrenheit during the day, 66 to 69 degrees during the night, remarkably constant and invariable: maybe not paradise on Earth but as close to comfort as one was ever likely to find. The only problem was that Iona had only one three-quarter gallon size bag of water left to meet her water needs and there was no water to be found within many miles of the cave.

However, with open arms, she welcomed the solidity, the stationary-ness, the safe-haven-ness of her cave.

Chapter Three

ON DAY FIFTEEN, at high noon, Iona emerged from her cave. This was the first time Iona had exposed herself to the sun's punishing rays—to direct midday sunlight—since she had left the protected bubble of her now lost home. Understandably, in anticipation of what she would experience, she was filled with a feeling of dread and suffered from a slight attack of nerves.

Upon emerging from the mouth of the cave, she shaded her eyes with both hands as she expected to be dazzled and perhaps even blinded by an engorgement of light and swept away by a roiling blast of heat, but instead, she experienced something unexpected.

To her surprise, and to her relief, she discovered the temperature was relatively temperate, hovering in the low 90s. More importantly, the sky was blanketed with mysterious-looking, brooding, dark, thick clouds. Initially, Iona was astonished and bewildered by the sight of these strange clouds, shapes and sizes she had never seen before. But the clouds were exactly the sign that she had been instructed by her mother September to be waiting for.

These were high-altitude clouds that she was staring at, almost as black as pitch, all of them well above fourteen thousand feet altitude. The entire sky, to the horizon, was darkened by them. There was not a patch of blue to be found, and all of the clouds were moving quickly, in a southerly direction.

Iona craned her neck back and looked straight up, directly into the underbelly of the high clouds. In the mass of black clouds, she barely made out explosions of a fireworks display of light and thunder. However, there was not a drop of rain falling.

Although the clouds were heavily laden with moisture, they were too high up and moving far too rapidly to allow for any possibility of rain in the form of ground-level precipitation. Iona realized that this configuration of dark clouds constituted something that did not exist within the range of what was considered to be *normal phenomena*. She was witnessing something unique, in fact, it was something that would happen only once in her life-time; indeed, once in a thousand years.

Iona shook her head in puzzlement at this phenomenon until she realized the reason for what was happening. The Forbidden Zone was a man-made bubble. Since she was in a cave only fourteen miles from the edge of the zone, she was still within a diminished influence of the Gaia-Magistrate distant weather-changing apparatus, which, at least, was still in operation.

As Iona's mother had predicted, once the climate-changing machines were rendered inoperable, the weather-changing system would disintegrate and the heavily-laden clouds drifting fifty miles south of the Forbidden Zone would swoop down and the man-made system would collapse. *That's what she was observing!*

Gazing at the clouds made Iona yearn for rain. It had been many years since she had seen and felt drops of rain, so many years in fact that she had to remember back to a time before she lived in the desert, back to when she was living with her mother and father on the island of St. Helena in the south Atlantic Ocean, where the nuclear-powered wind machines manipulated the weather to suit the magistrate's programs. That was when she was three and one half years old.

That occurred two years before Iona was placed under the guardianship of Tom. She only remembered one or two of these events directly, that is to say, she did not consciously, truly remember the total portion of these early events.

Now, in the deep recesses of the more recent memories formed from earlier retold stories, did it come flooding back to her: she had been told that she had lived until the age of three-and-a-half like a princess in the grandest Dome of them all. Her father, Regis, was then the greatest and most highly honored scientist in the world and he effectively oversaw the operation of the climate-changing machines. Her mother, September, had been an important leader in the Gaia Magistrate Government on her own (before she disappeared and re-emerged years later as a leader of a rebellion and an adversary of the government). That was the last time Iona "remembered" seeing such thick clouds with the portent for luxuriously heavy rain and flooding.

Iona remembered the last day she saw her father alive. It was from her direct memory. She was sitting on his knee, and he was reading poetry to her. The last lines of the poetry were still clear in her mind:

> *All that we see or seem*
> *Is but a dream within a dream.*

The lines were taken from a poem written by Edgar Allen Poe. Iona remembered the lines clearly because her father had asked her to repeat them over and over. She remembered that he drew enormous satisfaction from her recitation of those peculiar lines. Then she recalled how she smuggled the sixteen long scrolls of thick paper that he placed in her panties, arranged and fashioned and "pinned in" to resemble the form of a diaper, which was not totally incongruous for a three-year-old child to be wearing, though Iona had been toilet trained many months before.

After Iona escaped, with the help of the pirates of the underground rebellion—the rebellion her mother had joined years earlier—her mother told her when they were united that her father, Regis, had been executed six weeks after she escaped. His crime was refusal to run the climate-changing machines any longer. The scrolls he pinned on Iona contained poems that were, in effect, secret-coded instructions that could be used to render the climate-changing machines inoperable.

Iona surmised that her mother and father had been successful

in making the climate-changing machines inoperable, and they ultimately must have destroyed them.

The Domed-city Gaia Magistrate System may have still been as
powerful and invincible as it was when September and Regis con-
spired to rebel against it many years before, but, at least, with the
climate-changing machines destroyed, that had been a major accomplishment.

It also confirmed that Iona's mother, September, had joined Regis in death. Iona understood this, too. For, in the act of destroying
the climate-changing machines, she invited certain death. It had been
explained to Iona, when she was younger, that although the rebels
may eventually succeed in destroying the climate-changing machines,
above and beyond that important and critical service to the cause for
the liberation of the eco-damaged Earth, the rest of the goal, the liberation of the masses, toilers of the earth, was either, at worse, a goal
that was ultimately doomed to failure, or, at best, a goal that was to
be hopelessly postponed until some faraway distant time.

Yet her own physical survival—and indeed her own well being—
was all she felt she could afford to place in her focus.

Iona got as cozy as she could in the cave, waiting for the clouds
to pass, waiting for what their mysterious presence would bring later
on. After the sky was clear she waited the prescribed twenty-four
hours, then she lit her bonfire. The fire burned brightly, producing
waves and waves of dense smoke, lasting many hours before it finally
died down.

Then Iona scattered the ashes, went back to the cave, and rested.

Each day, as she rested and waited, she slept longer hours,
counting the days by cutting a little notch in the strap of the leather
corn storage pouch where she stored her dwindling supply of cornmeal. Days and nights passed. The moon waned until it completely
disappeared from the sky. Almost a week went by before the moon

reappeared. On that night, Iona was down to her last pint of water and one and a half cups of cornmeal in her pouch. It was day thirteen since she had entered the cave, day eleven since she lit the bonfire, twenty-seven days since she left Tom and had begun her ordeal. Iona was emaciated and had become abnormally thin due to several weeks of restricted rations and was terribly thirsty from being limited to a half-pint of water during the first day in the cave, then a third-of-a-pint a day after that first day.

She decided to pull out all the stops. One more healthy, more-than-ample meal and the remaining water, then she would rest and not move again. In the lining of her pouch, in reserve for a desperate situation, she kept four long strands of squirrel jerky that she extract-ed and ate with the remaining cornmeal. It was the most nutritious meal she'd eaten since leaving home. With every bite, she chewed each mouthful forty times so as to obtain the maximum break-down of the protein before it entered her stomach and thus allowing a maximum mixture with her saliva. Eating in that way, she spent over two hours consuming the meal. She ate more at that one seating than she had eaten over the previous three and a half days and nights combined, but she knew exactly what she was doing.

Now she slept for even longer periods, up to eighteen hours a day (she could sleep easier and more soundly on a full stomach). When she was awake, she lay very still, not moving so much as an inch.

For two days she went on like this. However, by the beginning of the third day, she knew that time was running out. Even though she was experiencing hunger pangs, it was not a serious problem. Iona wasn't going to die from starvation. The more serious problem was dehydration.

She could survive for another day, but before the end of the day, she knew she would lose consciousness.

She had to act quickly. She had to time what she was doing ex-actly right.

She knew what she had to do. There were no choices. After using a fire to sanitize the cutting edge of her digger spike, she cut an incision into her forearm, opening a large vein. In no time, she squeezed a pint of blood into her cup, drinking it as she released the blood so that it had no time to coagulate. It was extra hard to swallow the blood because Iona had hardly any saliva left in her mouth. Even worse, due to her acute dehydration, the blood was thicker than normal, but she managed.

She almost fainted before staunching the flow of blood and closing the wound, using a hem of cloth torn from her toga to wrap around the wound. She formed the tailings of the cloth into a knot by holding the two loose ends between her teeth, then nimbly tying the knot with the fingers of her trembling hand. Immediately, after finishing, she curled up on the cool cave floor and fell into a deep sleep.

Before losing consciousness, Iona reckoned she would be found in one or two days, maybe three. Even then, it would require three large jugs of water and a miracle to revive her.

Her last thought was: *What else can I do?*

Iona knew that if her mother and father were still alive they would have been very proud of what she had accomplished. That thought comforted her. Iona was still their little girl—at least in her eyes she was. And the old and stubborn Tom, Iona's beloved teacher, if he had had any way of knowing what she had done, would have been more than flattered: he would have been beaming with pride.

It was only during the final days of crossing the Forbidden Zone that it dawned on Iona that she never fully realized the reason why she loved her deceased mother September so much. She found that elusive key to her understanding. It was the *not-knowing part:* the emotional part, prevailing over the *conscious* part: mysteries abounded in the world, beyond the grasp of her comprehension, not provable in a scientific sense—what mattered was what you believed in your heart, that's what mattered. She realized she didn't need any external validation for that belief either. Believing in it in itself was enough.

"Am I dying?" Iona barely managed to ask herself.

Sleep? Will it come? At last?

Sleep came.

Chapter Four

IONA WAS FOUND FINALLY by a forty-seven-year-old seasoned rebel officer. This officer was also a seasoned army corps
doctor. The doctor had been sent by Iona's mother, September
Snow. She was supposed to have arrived three days earlier. She knew
how dangerously late she was.

The first thing the doctor noticed was the sheen of Iona's skin.
It had a glassy, porcelain look. There was gooseflesh on Iona's arms
and legs. Even from a distance, the doctor could see that Iona's
physical constitution was strong, but her stomach was caved in, her
jaw-line was sunken, and her eye-sockets looked gaunt.

Upon closer examination, the doctor surmised that Iona had
been unconscious for at least three days. It was clear that Iona had
not ingested solid foods or liquids for well over three days.

Iona was on her back reclining on the smooth stones of the
cave floor. (That was good, since the air was permanently cool in the
cave and circulating well.) Her hair was fanned out on either side,
resembling neatly ironed plaids of cloth. Iona's eyes were closed, as if
she were reclining in a state of serenity. Actually her eyes were rolled
toward the back of her head because she was in a coma.

Upon closer examination however, the condition of Iona's lips
was the doctor's more immediate concern because it told a more
precise and accurate tale, especially the upper lip. It was lacerated
and frayed. It had receded and shriveled almost to the base of her
nose, exposing her front teeth, giving her the appearance of a cross

between a beaver's mug and a mummy's mouth.

The doctor didn't waste any more time *just* observing. She hurriedly opened her bag and at the same time firmly clasped Iona's wrist, seeking a pulse. Finding one, she smiled, but the smile was tentative. The doctor discovered the pulse was weak, an indication of a barely beating heart.

Iona's condition was far more critical than the doctor had first presumed.

The doctor's diagnosis was that Iona had about fifteen hours left to live. The trick was to revive her without shocking her extremely frail, delicate system, causing her heart to fail.

Fortunately, the doctor had brought with her her medical equipment: syringes, rubber tubing, nutritional potions needed for related procedures. She rigged a stand to hold the liter bag and secure the plastic tube. She jabbed a 16 gauge IV needle into a vein at the bend of Iona's left elbow, and in three and half minutes, the doctor pumped a liter of five percent dextrose in water (D-5W) into Iona's long depleted system. After a while, she saw the first contractions, the involuntary relaxations and contractions of Iona's muscles, so she rigged another liter of D-5W and repeated the procedure.

When the doctor saw that the treatment worked, the solution took, she emitted a sigh of relief. She knew she dare not risk injecting more than three liters on the first day because it was already almost too heavy a burden to place on Iona's extremely fragile system. The doctor found a good, level place on the cave floor, put a blanket over Iona's legs and finding her own spot instantly fell asleep. During the night, Iona apparently gained strength and grew stronger, but still didn't come any closer to regaining consciousness. Iona's situation was still very critical, but it had apparently stabilized.

By the end of the third day, Iona temporarily regained consciousness. She moaned and groaned for a few moments, talked gibberish for a short while, then relapsed into a coma. Thirty-six hours later, Iona regained total consciousness. Now Iona took her nourishment orally by drinking cups of water and sipping bowls of watery soup. For the first time in eleven days, she was able to get up and pee. At the beginning of day seven, Iona was able to stand up, walk outside, but only with the doctor's assistance, supporting her by holding her arm.

Iona was bursting with questions, aside from Tom, her mother, and the two old blind Indians, the doctor was the first person she had an opportunity to talk with, since she had been five-and-one-half-years-old.

"It's actually a miracle you're alive," the doctor said at last, breaking the long interval of silence. She drew herself up to the child. She spoke with an emphatic note, with the felicities of a mother, a sister, indeed, a friend.

"What you've been through must have been sheer hell," the doctor said, eyes swimming with sympathy and even deeper pools of compassion.

"I can only guess what it was like," the doctor said. She stopped herself short, shaking her head politely. "No, I don't know. No, I don't know what it was like—mind you, but I can guess."

The doctor smiled. She reached around and gave Iona a thumping slap on the back. The pat was not intended to be interpreted as an act of patronization or condescension, it was more like a friendly coach giving a favored athlete a much deserved compliment after having run a magnificent, next-to-impossible-to-accomplish, race. "You're plucky, you know," the doctor said, placing her index finger under Iona's chin. "Believe me," she said, nodding her head, "I know."

"Couldn't be helped," Iona said in a weak voice. "There was nothing else to do."

The doctor was touched.

As a way of introduction, the doctor said, "I'm from the Fifth Army of Irregulars, or what's left of it. We're the last of the rebel armies operating between the Forbidden Zone and South America. For a long time we were called the 'torrid teasers,' because we were the last organized rebel force operating in the zone between Central America and southern Mexico. They shouldn't have even called us an army after a certain time, since our numbers had dwindled over the last six years to ten thousand. Before that, we managed to make enough trouble to be called an army. Six years ago, we earned the nickname 'torrid teasers,' a name that has since become very apt as we are now so weak that all we've managed to do lately is 'tease' the enemy. The only reason we've managed to survive until today is that when things really got tough we were able to hide in the Sierra Madre Oriental and the plains between Tampico and Vera Cruz, just below the southern rim of the Forbidden Zone. The people who lived there liked us. The campesinos took us into their hearts. They protected us. They weren't afraid of reprisals from the magister's army. But..."

The doctor paused.

"We were permanently pushed out of that region several years ago, just as we were pushed out of Chiapas province and the Yucatan before that. We've never been able to go back, not even for provisions. Your mother contacted us via satellite communication two months ago while we were still on the run. She gave us instructions about you. I was chosen to carry the instructions out. My commander ordered me to contact you as soon as possible, after you sent up the smoke signal, which you did immediately after the dense cloud formation passed overhead. A forward scout, who knew where to search, saw the smoke through a telescope. By the way, those clouds didn't produce a drop of rain anywhere near the southern rim of the Forbidden Zone, but it did unleash torrential rains causing full-blown flooding fifty miles south of here. Eighteen inches of rain fell in five hours in one area. By now, there's standing water less than fifty miles from here. Within six months time, rain will fall here. In five years time, rain will even fall in the Forbidden Zone. In thirty years time, there won't be a Forbidden Zone. Nature will reclaim what man had destroyed. The climate-changing machines have been destroyed or disabled, all of them, that much is certain. I was immobilized by the flooding for three days after the storm, but that's not the only reason why I was late. I was unavoidably detained for other reasons."

"What's your name?" Iona asked the doctor.

"I'm under the strictest orders, given to me by no one less than your mother, never to reveal my real name. Just call me 'the doctor'."

Iona covered her mouth with her hand, giggling. "'The doctor'?" Iona asked. "But why? How silly. Such a formal name?"

"For security reasons," the doctor replied with a shrug of her shoulders. "After I set you up and brief you about the directions you're to follow, you'll never see me again. By the way, where we're going, you'll be able to use your bow and arrows for hunting if you travel enough distance to find game, and the cave where you'll be living is inviting—at least *it will be inviting,* once some of the natural climate is restored. In your case, climate restoration will occur sooner than in most locales. There'll be water there too, but only from a hidden spring inside a cave. Otherwise, the place is appallingly desolate, completely lacking in water. That should prevent outsiders from becoming too curious. No one but you will know how to survive there. You won't have to worry about intruders interrupting your life too often. If one should wander in, you should be able to scare him off with a few arrows or wait for him to leave on his own accord. Your father, Regis Snow, may he rest in peace, was a genius. This splendid set-up was, for the most part, the result of your father's secret work."

"Restored climate?" Iona asked doubtfully, uncertain as to what exactly the doctor meant. "You mean, the way it was before?"

Why keep her in the dark? the doctor wondered. She decided Iona deserved a more thorough explanation than she had originally intended to give.

"About fourteen years ago," the doctor began, "let's start then, shall we? Well actually, Iona, the climate wasn't the same as it was—until you go back to before the Eleven-Years-War, which began in 2040 A.D. Even then, it wasn't the same as it was before—*really.* You have to go back thirty years before that, or so I've been told. I was born in 2023. Some of the old-timers say you have to go back well beyond that. I don't understand this stuff very well. Even among the rebels there's a lot of confusion and controversy over this matter. Your parents started planning this, your survival, when you were only two-and-one-half years old. Understand?"

"You talked to my mother?" Iona asked.

"No, not personally, of course," the doctor replied. "Only my commander did. The conversation lasted forty-five minutes. However, I learned a lot about you—*from my commander.*"

There was a short pause because Iona didn't know what to ask the doctor next. Then it occurred to her exactly what the next question should be. "Why did it take you so long to find me?" Iona asked. "I did everything correctly. I followed all of the instructions. My location between the mountains, the bonfire, the cave, the timing. Everything!" Like a torrent, the words gushed out. Now, her fear was returning as she recalled what she had been through.

"Ah, that," the doctor sighed deeply. "I've been expecting that question." Although the expression on the doctor's face was diffident, the tone of her voice was reassuring. "Unfortunately the answer is complicated. I'll give you a full explanation later. But for now, my child, you must rest."

"Okay," Iona replied.

"Can you really hunt animals with your bow and arrows?" the doctor asked, smiling. Her expression changed. Now she spoke with lightness and tenderness. The doctor had the gift of putting Iona at her ease by diverting her attention from her problems. "Can you hunt even in the dark?" the doctor then asked.

"Yes," Iona replied. She was grateful to be asked about her skills and talents. "Not even in the dark," Iona replied, "but *always* in the dark. I am exclusively a nighttime hunter. I've hunted since I was five years old. I've only hunted small animals, squirrels, hamsters, even mice. Only small animals. That's all there was to hunt—where I was living."

"That's good," the doctor said. "That's awfully good." She spoke with emotion. "It's always good to start with really small things. Some day you may be able to hunt during the daylight hours, too. Perhaps even larger game."

In a lapse of politeness, Iona looked sideways at the doctor. She gave the doctor a penetrating glare. Underlying that look was deeper anxiety and deeper uncertainty. What Iona harbored inside was a basic and fundamental fear of an abyss from which there was no return, born years after the end of the Eleven-Years-War and the subsequent world-wide ecological apocalypse.

In an instant, the doctor understood the look. She nodded her head knowingly. She had seen the look in the eyes of many, in the eyes of the adolescent recruits to the rebel army, in the eyes of the famine victims all over the world, *it was the look of the times.*

"You're a clever girl," the doctor said in a faint voice. "Don't worry. You're courageous. You're a big girl. You'll see. Everything will be all right." The doctor wanted to comfort Iona.

"You're as tough as they get," the doctor added in a soothing voice. "Don't be afraid."

The doctor placed Iona's head on her lap and stroked her hair. Iona closed her eyes, as if she welcomed her caresses, then held the doctor tightly, surrendering to the doctor's overture of intimacy and friendship.

Iona felt as if she were being covered in a security blanket of comfort and warmth. She felt *loved*. Then the doctor used her own comb to carefully brush out Iona's hair, until it fanned out and lay smooth as it shimmered in brownish-blonde waves.

"There," the doctor said.

"You won't have to be any tougher than you already are, Iona, sleep, rest, save yourself for later," the doctor intoned in a soothing voice, "save yourself for tomorrow."

The doctor repeated the words again, using the same sequence, chanting the words as if they were a song or a poem. She began to weep. "Save yourself for later." It was as if she were the child that she was holding, their identities had somehow merged and had become fused into one.

After Iona was asleep, the doctor waited a short while, then carefully extricated herself from beneath the young girl's head. She rose to make preparations for their departure.

Chapter Five

WHEN IONA WOKE several hours later, the doctor was rearranging her equipment. When she saw that Iona was awake, she stopped and walked over to the girl.

"We're running out of supplies," the doctor said. There was a new directness in the doctor's manner. "We must leave now. We can't wait longer. We must leave before sunset. Understand? Come. Help me pack."

Iona nodded.

After they finished, Iona lay down to rest. The doctor went into a squat position and began to perform exercises. She placed her hands on her hips and arched her back. She held her arms in front of her, and performed some calisthenics, moving from a crouched position to a standing position, repeating the motions several times.

After completing these exercises the doctor grunted a note of satisfaction and rose to her feet.

"This is what happened, Iona," the doctor said. Her voice sounded weighty and solemn.

"This is why I arrived *almost too late* to rescue you," the doctor said. "I already mentioned the flooding. But there's something else. We were attacked."

"Attacked?"

"We were attacked by the enemy," the doctor said. "Those Gaians deployed bio-technical weapons. Most of my comrades are dead. There are probably six or seven hundred survivors, out of an army that originally numbered 10,000."

"How did you survive?" Iona asked.

"Fortunately, before the fighting started, I was deployed in the rear."

"What are bio-technical weapons?" Iona asked.

"Well, to be specific, anthrax. They dropped canisters of anthrax mixed with chemical agents and laser enhancers. Incredible technology." The doctor looked down. "I didn't panic when the first attack came."

"Anthrax?" Iona asked. "Isn't that a disease that kills cattle? It's highly contagious, isn't it?"

"Yes. Anthrax. Extremely contagious. But *partially* controllable. That's the point. The ability to keep contamination localized is the key. They were able to keep the airborne poison from being dispersed in the wrong direction. It's a suped-up, genetically engineered multi-strain of anthrax which is far more lethal than the standard issue. Some of our troops trapped outside of our underground shelter suffered for three days before dying. One of the symptoms of anthrax poisoning is mental derangement. Disease attacks the brain. If we had even let just one of them in, though, we would have perished. The contagion worry. So we had no choice. We had to shut them out."

"Must have been awful," Iona said.

"Yes. We had to sit on our hands and wait passively for our comrades to die—the very ones who fought so gallantly to save our lives in previous battles. How cruel a punishment that was."

"How long were you stuck inside the shelter?"

"Three days," the doctor replied. "We had to wait for the anthrax to completely dissipate before we dared come out."

"Then you came to rescue me?" Iona asked.

"Straight away. I didn't waste any time. Took me three and a half days. I traveled the first one hundred miles by burro, the last nine on foot."

The doctor then said, "We must leave now. I'll take you to a crossroads. I'll give you directions on how to find the right place to find permanent shelter. There are caches of food and water hidden along the route. There'll also be caches of food and water, and planting seeds, awaiting you, at your final destination. Many years ago, your mother and father carefully planned a future for you down to the tiniest detail. They loved you, child. They were looking out for you. *Way back many years ago.*"

Iona nodded. Since the wound on her arm had completely healed, she took the torn piece of cloth she had wrapped tightly around it and tossed it into the fire.

The doctor nodded. "You drank your own blood, didn't you? I noticed. You were desperate?"

Iona nodded in agreement.

"Dangerous trick," the doctor said in a scolding voice. She shook her head in a disapproving manner. Her voice carried an added tone of worry. Then she shook her head even more vigorously. "Luckily, somehow, it worked. But it could just as easily have backfired. Stealing from Peter to pay Paul is all right in the short run, but in the long run it turns both Peter and Paul into paupers. Same is true when it comes to your body. Don't do it again. Agreed?"

"Agreed," Iona replied.

The doctor reached into her pocket and produced a lightweight mini-compass that could be attached to a belt or an armband, or dangled freely. "Here," the doctor said, presenting it to Iona. "It's yours. A gift, from me to you. A compass is old-fashioned, but good for use."

Iona carefully examined the object dangling in front of her. "Thank you, but no," Iona replied. She studied the object again and smiled, then refused the gift by shaking her head politely. "Isn't necessary. I don't need it."

"Is that so!" the doctor said in a testy voice. She bit her lip. She was disconcerted by Iona's reaction. The doctor was expecting acceptance—more than that—a token of gratitude. She tried persuasion. "It could come in handy, you know. Where you're going? Who knows? You may need it. You're going to be there all alone—for a long, long time." The doctor tried to press the gift into Iona's hand but Iona refused it.

"I already have one," Iona said. She dove into her satchel containing her bow and arrows and pulled out the dead courier's compass. "See? I have one."

Then Iona explained how she had acquired it. She explained how she left the laser gun lying in the sand and took the compass instead.

"An interesting choice," the doctor said, nodding in approval. "A wise one, too. But why didn't you take the laser gun? Was it charged?"

"Yes," Iona nodded, "I believe it was. But no, I would never take the gun with me. I wouldn't dream of it."

"Why not?" the doctor asked. "Laser guns are very valuable. They can be fired many times before they must be recharged. They're very powerful. Not just for defense purposes, either. True, they're a little heavy and a little cumbersome to carry—especially if you're traveling light."

"That's not the reason why I left it behind," Iona replied, "or, at least, not the main reason. If you fight the other side in accordance with your enemy's rules, you'll lose. That's one of the things my mother taught me. I know it's true, too."

"Smart," the doctor grunted, but she was only partially mollified. She weighed Iona's words carefully. "So, once you've emptied the laser gun you'd have no way of recharging it, right? Am I right? That would have made it eventually totally worthless to you. There had to be other reasons, too? There had to be more to it than that. You were thinking of all the angles, right?"

"No," Iona replied simply. She thought carefully in a methodical way before she replied. Her heart was pounding. She was momentarily aching with shame because she was tempted to tell a lie but she quickly changed her mind. She felt an implacable need to hold steadfast to what she believed to be the truth. "No, there were no other angles. Only the one I just mentioned."

"No other angles?" the doctor asked. She could not believe Iona's reply. She was disappointed. She could not believe that Iona could be so naive.

"You don't get it, do you?" Iona said in a petulant voice that sounded almost shrill. "You can't win when you use the magisters' army methods—period. That's all there is to it. You have to come up with a new and better strategy than they use. You have to come up with methods that they would never think of—never occur to them—methods that would galvanize our strengths and maximize our advantages and neutralize their weapon superiority—their troop strength—their control of the skies. Even if it means sitting in caves for thirty years to figure it out, to devise a revolutionary new strategy, that's what we must do. That's what my mother taught me. That was her most important lesson. After all, she used their methods. Look what happened to her? She's dead. That's all there is to it. That's why I left the laser gun where it lay. I'd do the same again if I had the choice. You know yourself. You know it's finished. The rebels have lost. Another famous history lesson—as my teacher Tom would have said it."

"Okay, okay," the doctor replied. "Goodness! I won't argue with you, child. I certainly wouldn't dream of arguing with the memory of your blessed mother. No one can win that argument."

The doctor looked carefully at Iona. The expression on Iona's face was filled with innocence and a striking absence of guile. It caused the doctor to dig deeply into her own memory. Iona had almost fully recovered. She no longer looked emaciated or even haggard. But she still had an air of extreme lightness and leanness.

Iona went to the other side of the cave.

The doctor thought back to another time, twenty-five years earlier. "Those were better times," the doctor thought. She nodded to herself as she reflected on them. The Gaia regime was two decades away from becoming firmly entrenched. Beginning its fourth year, the Eleven-Years-War was still raging. The ozone layer had not yet been disrupted. The environment, although far from perfect, was still, more or less, intact. At the age of twenty-two, the doctor was a youthful pioneer. She was a bright, idealistic medical intern working her first assignment in a refugee camp.

She recalled the day after she had been there exactly one year. Foreign dignitaries and guests from different governments came in droves to visit the refugee camp. They traveled with legions of tele-communication armies attached to them like lampreys or barnacles, engaging in one more of their sordid feeding frenzies. The enter-tainment-cum-news industry, mercifully broke down in 2047, seven years into the Eleven-Years-War. (NO MORE NEWS! NO MORE NEWS! SENSELESS VIOLENCE, NIHILISM, CARNAGE, CHA-OS, ALL THAT'S LEFT TO REPORT.) For their sake, at the time, the government's humanitarian gestures were a much needed respite from the reports of a stalemated war-front where none of the bellig-erents could seem to prevail—much less win—what was increasingly becoming a deeply unpopular war. Constant stalemates were the or-der of the day. As time went on, the casualties of the Eleven-Years-War grew. Since civilian deaths were due mostly to hunger, humani-tarian gestures away from the front-lines became fashionable (for an entertainment-cum-news hungry public, it diverted viewers tem-porarily). Distinguished visitors all made the same pilgrimage, and when they did, they all made the same inaccurate observations when they came to see the twisted and emaciated bodies, the arms and legs looking like twigs, the bellies distended from eating a protein-less diet (grass, bark of trees) and drinking contaminated water. And the visitors always seemed to get it wrong. They saw the survivors as the losers, the ones who suffered the most, the bottom end of a nature-imposed triage system. But the medical intern knew better. After one year's experience, the young and overly-idealistic doctor learned the truth. The skinny skeleton-like specimens of humanity were in fact the best ones, the lucky ones, the *creme de la creme* of an unjust survival scheme. All of the sick, all of the infirm, all of the aged, all of the babies and toddlers, had died long before. Instead, those left were the hearty ones, the tough ones, the ones least afflicted by illness, disease, malnutrition. If you were still alive, it meant you had begun as the best physical specimen, best suited to endure the new environment, even though you *looked* skeletal after years of hardship, and trials of barely eking out a borderline-to-death existence. That's why bringing them back to life was so worth it for the doctor. They were the ones best able to recover and return to the regular routine life, if such a thing was possible.

This is what the doctor came to "know in her bones," based on her experience. But two singular images still haunted her: a young woman, a victim of famine, displaying a spread-eagled sleeping baby on her lap and a very old whiskered man, thin as a rail, shyly grinning from ear to ear, smiling like a half-wit: the old man looked as if he could not stop grinning, even if he knew he were on the verge of taking his last breath. That damnably stoical endurance of the hopelessly fatalistic! That archetype of character; the fatalistic victim, being almost worse that its opposite; the-groomed-and-growing-during-the-brewing-cauldron-of-an-apocalyptic-frenzy-of-unlimited-war: the firebrand and the fanatic, armed to the teeth, with nothing in his brain but hatred and an unlimited capacity for revenge! Being so young herself, the doctor couldn't *understand* it, or, *stand* it!

And that's exactly how the doctor felt when she discovered the nearly dead Iona in a cave fourteen days before. Memories of starving flesh flashed back to her as if they were photographs burned onto the retina of her mind, and the remembrances of them made her own flesh squirm. She hadn't felt that way in years, not since she started working in the infamous famine camps many years earlier, not since she received her first baptism in fire. The twelve through sixteen-year-olds then, she realized, were the toughest survival-fighters, the strongest survivors of famine and starvation. She remembered how spunky those adolescents were. Iona brought the memories of those youthful survivors back. The long repressed memories came flooding back. To have seen those teenagers miraculously recover, while practically everyone else in the camp who was younger or older than them perished, was for the doctor—almost, but not quite—a religious experience.

Iona's age group had been better suited to recover from the worst effects of malnutrition, starvation, and famine than any other age group in the camp. It was as if the strange transition from childhood to adulthood carried within itself a special survivor gene of its own.

"Let's go," the doctor said to Iona after it was obvious that Iona had finished packing her few remaining objects. Iona was still a little weak, but she had recovered sufficiently well so that she was able to walk without assistance—at least as long as she didn't have to carry much. The doctor was able to carry practically everything, including Iona's possessions. Except for a few small containers of rice and beans and some vitamin supplements, they had consumed everything. They were running low on water, too.

They walked the first three miles without difficulty. The long-unused deer trail which they followed, gradually rose as it ran south alongside the valley. But once they reached the end of the valley, they entered a box canyon, and the rest of the hike was more difficult.

Within less than a mile, they had to traverse some steep and rugged terrain. It involved climbing—hand over foot, then literally hand over hand—over rough ridges where there were scarcely any deer trails—not even a *phantom* of a deer trail. At the crest of the highest and sharpest ridge, the terrain was so rugged, only a mountain goat or sheep could have bounded over the rocks—but of course there were no goats or sheep, no animals at all.

Often, they had to climb over large, bare, smooth rocks and slide down the other side on their backsides. As long as they were able to take long and frequent rests, Iona was able to keep up. The doctor deliberately kept a slow pace. And whenever Iona began to lag behind, the doctor slowed more. They had timed their departure so as to walk during the late afternoon when the surrounding hills and mountains would provide shade and cover. In the event, they found to their delight that the temperature during the daylight hours remained relatively temperate, almost thirty degrees less than it recently had been. Temperatures at or below 90 degrees Fahrenheit were an added boon. Already, they were apparently reaping the benefits from the collapse of the global weather-changing nuclear-powered wind machines, although, from a strictly scientific point of view, it was much too soon to be certain that the change was permanent or just a momentary lapse or oscillation. Perhaps in a week or two, the temperature would shoot up again. Neither Iona nor the doctor knew for sure what would occur in the short run—although, in the long run—they knew that the results would be permanent, long-lasting, and certain. But how long must they wait for the long run to kick in? A month? Years? Decades? Would they live to see the changes? September had never discussed the matter with Iona, and neither had Tom.

"Probably within three or four decades," the doctor answered authoritatively when Iona asked her a second time, as they picked their way along the trail. "But that will be so only in certain places. Isolated locales. The Western Quadrant, for example! The Western Quadrant is an ideal place to make a quick recovery! In thirty years perhaps! That's the most expert estimate, which is based on the research your father conducted before he was executed. Where most people live, where the Domes exist, the recovery will take longer... *much longer.* For them, 300 years, 400 years, perhaps longer.

'With severe, unpredictable, and unexpected oscillations occurring before the permanent adjustment actually kicks in, gyrating and bouncing back and forth, perhaps in the form of great extremes in certain parts of the world—for a minimum of 35 years to a maximum of 500,'" the doctor added, apparently quoting directly from some document or briefing she had been given.

"I have one hell of a memory when I put my mind to it, don't I, Iona?" the doctor added, laughing.

"How do you know all this?" Iona asked.

"Let's just concentrate on getting to the place where you belong, okay, Iona?"

"Sure," Iona replied.

When they emerged on the other side of the sharp, high-rising hills just after dawn, they not only had no difficulty in finding the first hidden cache of food and water, but just two miles further on they found the doctor's burro. The animal was alive—and he looked not only healthy but also wholesome. The burro had been tethered to a spot where the doctor had left him sixteen days earlier and the doctor made sure he had enough water and forage within his reach to sustain him.

But it was more than food that kept the burro in place. It was immediately apparent to Iona that the burro had acquired a long, sentimental attachment to the doctor. With long lashes and brooding eyes, almost as if he were crying, the burro looked at the doctor and winked shyly—as if to say, "Where have you been? Are you surprised to see me? I've been waiting patiently. Just waiting...patiently. Yes, grazing and drinking too. A long time. Alone. Alone."

The doctor dropped her pack. Reaching out, she placed her arms around the burro's neck and gave him a kiss, feeling the hard, large bones of his mandibles. Patting him gently, she caressed his neck and shoulders. She ran her hand along his lightly curved back until she came to his hindquarters. She felt like singing. Like crying. Like dancing. "There you are," she cooed.

Iona viewed the surrounding scene. They were now at least thirty-five miles from the edge of the Forbidden Zone. The ground was covered with old dead grass, but there was nothing green for the burro to eat.

Iona asked the doctor: "How did the burro survive feeding only on old, dead grass? I can't believe it's still here!"

"Cotton seeds," the doctor muttered laughing. "Simple."

Less than ten feet from the tethered burro there was an opened, half empty burlap sack lying on the ground. Cotton seeds were spilling out of the bag.

"The cotton seeds are rich and nutritious," the doctor offered. "As good as, or better than, the sweetest alfalfa. Besides planting the cotton seeds, there's not much else you can do with them, they're totally unfit for human consumption, but they serve as a kind of super-high-octane fodder for animals. They have the added benefit of not being bulky, or too heavy to carry. A forty-pound sack will suffice for a long time, up to two months, if it is supplemented with a diet of dry grass."

"You grew cotton in Mexico?" Iona asked.

The doctor smiled. "You must understand Iona that the rebel army was rarely settled long enough in any one place to farm for any extended period of time—a rebel army rarely does. But some of the small peasant bands several hundred miles south of here grew cotton. We bartered with them for burros, cotton seed, food. And in exchange we gave them tools, laser guns, other war materials, and taught them how to defend themselves around their farms."

"Then there are still peasants and there are still cotton fields?" Iona asked in astonishment.

"Of course there are," the doctor replied. "But not as many as before. Cotton farming is a rarity. Scattered here and there, much farther south, three hundred miles—even farther—south of here, there are thousands of small bands of peasants who are very successful and resourceful. They manage to survive among the deep *barrancas* and the old, inactive volcanoes. Unlike here, the soil is very rich down there, very loamy, very fertile. Two and a half years ago, they actually had a bumper crop. They were even able to grow cotton, along with their food. But ordinarily, it's rough and tough, getting rougher and tougher all the time. For every good farming season, they'd have two or three bad seasons. What am I saying? There aren't any *real* seasons anymore—at least in so far as we're able to compare present circumstances with the past. Over the years, the weather had become increasingly unpredictable. The farmers could not depend on rain with regularity. The climate-changing machines saw to that. Plenty of man-caused starvation—plenty of sweat—then crop failure. Believe me I know. Practically all of the beneficial rains fell thousands of miles north of here. It was planned that way. From the beginning, most of the moisture in the south was literally sucked to the north. Later, even more shifted. Even the richest of soils couldn't make up for the climate change, ever since your father installed the wind machines."

"Otherwise known as climate-changing machines," the doctor continued, "they were first installed by your father in an attempt to return the weather patterns to the way they were before they went haywire during the Eleven-Years-War. Eventually, around the time you were born, the Gaia Magistrate Government operating in Gaia Domes took control of the climate-changing machines for their own selfish purpose and forced your father to operate them *their* way. So as to oppress people."

"But with the destruction of those machines, that's all changed now?" Iona asked. "Right?"

"Maybe, my dear," the doctor exclaimed in an exhausted voice. "Like I told you before, apparently you don't listen. *I don't know.*"

Iona smiled.

The doctor loaded the burro with all their remaining supplies and they headed off. But they didn't go south or east. Instead, they headed west.

"Where are we going?" Iona asked in an anxious voice. "We're heading back towards the desert," she said frantically. Her face was ashen. "*I've been there already. I don't want to go back.*"

"That's what you think," the doctor replied. "You still have things to learn, don't you? We are going to follow the southern rim of the edge of the Forbidden Zone as far west as possible, then we'll dip down to a special hiding place. To be sure, it's a barren and desolate place. In fact, nobody lives there now. But with your provisions and secret water source, you'll be okay. You'll be able to make for yourself a new life."

Chapter Six

THEY HEADED WEST. The burro carried all their supplies so they were free to walk unencumbered. Along the way, they talked. They traveled one hundred miles west, before turning south, then headed into some extremely dry-looking mountains.

Looking up at the desolate, barren peaks, the doctor stopped. "I can go no further. This will be your new home. This will be your new base. I am giving you a map so you can locate your supply caches and an inhabitable cave yourself. It is important that I don't actually see the place with my own eyes. In fact, I have deliberately not even so much as glanced at the map that I'm giving you now so that I will remain totally ignorant of the specific location of your new home. Once you have firmly established your base, you will be free to roam, as far north as the Forbidden Zone, and as far south as one hundred and seventy-five miles, as long as you stay away from the rolling flatlands, and as long as you stick to the higher mountainous areas. Just as you were safe on the edge of the Forbidden Zone *to the north* for the last eight and a half years; you will be safe on the edge of the now disintegrating Forbidden Zone *to the south*, pretty much for the same reason. In case one of us was captured and/or tortured, your mother wanted to make sure that no one on the northern side knew anything about what happened to you on the southern side, and no one on the southern side was to know anything about you on the northern side. That's why I never asked you who your protector was on the other side. Or even the person's name. That's also why I never gave you my name and why I can't accompany you to your new home."

Iona was speechless. She tried to express herself, but couldn't.

"I met your mother once, you know," the doctor said at last. "Ten years ago. It happened on the Yucatan peninsula. I was able to learn a little of what she was like even though I barely spent three hours with her."

"What was she like?" Iona asked.

"Strong," the doctor said without faltering. She nodded very carefully. "I know she wished that she could have been more of a mother to you, circumstances being different of course. But she was very tough. She had to be—circumstances required it. Don't you see?"

The doctor handed Iona her possessions and her share of provisions.

"Good luck," the doctor said smiling. "You have come out of the nightmare. You'll do fine."

"Where are you going?" Iona asked. She wanted to weep at the doctor's leave-taking, she had become so attached, but another part of her wanted to remain stoic. She decided to follow the emotionless path towards aloneness and self-reliance.

"Where I'm going, no one can follow," the doctor replied. "No one can follow. It's the path to certain death." The doctor did not show any defeatism or fatalism, much less morbidity. Iona could see she was at peace with herself. She had successfully concluded her most important mission. "Adieu," she said.

Iona watched the doctor dig her heels into the burro's underbelly. The doctor then waved the riding crop over her head as if it were a wand, and with her left hand she tugged hard on the left rein and prodded the beast into turning around. The doctor shouted "away," then "away-away!" When that didn't have the intended effect, she leaned forward and whispered something into the burro's ear. It was a real earful. The burro tensed up, bolted and took off running down the hill. The doctor grabbed her hat as she seemed to rocket away.

Waiting until the doctor was completely out of sight, Iona looked at the desolate, barren mountains. From her imagination, Iona pronounced some words—as she stared at the naked mountains. She said the words as a mantra, as a song: "I love the river—I love the river—I love the river."

She repeated the words: "I love the river—I absolutely adore the river—I love the river." She shouted the words out to the imperturbable firmament above and to the empty landscape below.

And she did love it. With all her heart. But it was a river that only existed in her imagination. Nevertheless, it flowed swift, clear, and clean-tasting in her mind, in her dreams. It was the invisible river that flowed through the desert. It was the current of her future. It was her river. It was the river of her life.

Caught between two eternities—and two abysses—the past and the future, Iona needed to find her bearings to make a new direction. Four weeks shy of her fourteenth birthday, she was going to take a totally dry environment and turn it into a safe haven. She was going to make it her new home.

BUT TO DO SO ALL ALONE.

PART TWO

Chapter Seven

"What is Gaia? It's the Earth healing itself. Simple. The bigger question is: Why do people believe in it? That's harder. That's a slippery slope. Having turned Gaia into a religion, one can then subject the otherwise healthy scientific aspects of Gaia to abuse. People justify that by saying that the religion of Gaia is a force against evil. I wonder where is the devil in this scheme? He's up to his usual tricks, no doubt. Our clerks and clerics, claiming to be serving Gaia, may be doing the exact opposite. They, too, may be agents of the devil."

— Clive Dumond, sub-magister

I T WAS COOL OUTSIDE, but warm inside, a room-temperature warmth, electricity coupled with the tingly smell of ions, found in a septic-sealed environment—underneath the giant, hemispherical glass-dome that enclosed the number-two-in-command, sub-magister, Clive Dumond's villa.

The sub-magister's villa was located on the wind-swept island of St. Helena. St. Helena was a tiny isle, located south of the equator, the lonely spot in the Atlantic Ocean where Napoleon was exiled.

The hemispherical dome served as a shell protecting four large villas and ten smaller ones. Under the protection of the glass enclosure, these grandiose villas were the luxurious homes of the top, *the creme de la creme, the apex of the high elite*—160 people.

These were the ones who enjoyed the good life. They were the ones who were protected from the danger of the sun's radiation.

Under one large dome to the west were small residences, about half of which were really just glorified dormitories, that housed the 700 Suits, Middle-middles, and Upper-minds.

Shoved into isolated corners scattered about the island—most of them Quonset huts left over from the Eleven-Years-War—were the quarters of the technicians and semi-technicians whose numbers fluctuated between 1500 and 3000, depending on the time of year, and the maintenance requirements of the nuclear-powered, climate-changing wind machines. Beneath them, were the 120,000 slaves who directly serviced the machines.

The vast majority of the technicians and semi-technicians, and the slaves (excluding domestic servants) did not live on the island because there wasn't enough space on the small island. Instead, they inhabited hundreds of large offshore oil-rig-like platforms, located beyond the harbor breakwaters.

These rigs were scattered about, located anywhere from five hundred yards offshore to a distance of one hundred and sixty miles. Almost invariably, when slaves were assigned to a his or her rig, it was for life. They never returned to their place of origin—not even after they died. They did not even return to where they had been purchased from middlemen (60 percent were purchased outright from slave-traders, 25 percent were captives; whenever there were slave auction slowdowns due to piratical raids or other disruptions, the last 15 percent of the aggregate slave population consisted of slaves brought in as confiscated war booty taken in sudden, surprise military reprisals). Few slaves lived more than ten years after the first plutonium-run nuclear generator cores were installed, expelling not just heat and energy, but also deadly radiation.

The fate of Kull's family was typical. Three years after they arrived, exposure to nuclear radiation, killed almost all of them. (Kull's eldest sister was the first to go, in under four years, and Kull's mother was the last, surviving an amazing nine and a half years.) Death rates accelerated after the plutonium-enriched nuclear reactors were completely operational. But it didn't happen to Kull. Unlike his parents and three older siblings, who were captured in 2049 on Mauritius Island in the Indian Ocean, he was actually born on the rig. His family was caught in the web of direct "slave" raids, still then called, from a legal point of view, not slaves, but "forced labor," under the *Officials' Emergency War Act*. In a series of steps, the World Gaia Federation took over control of the nuclear-powered wind machines and reclassified all working people in the weather-changing experiment from "forced labor" to permanent slave status. Kull was one of the first to be born as a slave in 2051. He had been fortunate in other ways, too.

In a metaphorical sense, he had escaped, but only barely, and not in the typical way that escapees escaped—in other words, through death. There had not been a successful slave escape, by the use of a surface watercraft, in the history of St. Helena Island, not a single one since the first experimental nuclear-powered wind machines were activated in 2050. Eleven years later, a sub-magister literally picked Kull off a "punishment rack" and saved his life. He took him into his own life, raised him in the bosom of his home, as if Kull had been his natural child, his own son.

The Dome under which the sub-magister's villa was located was fairly big, but it was not nearly as large as the Dome for Suits, Middle-middles, and Upper-minds, nor nearly as massive as the Superdome for the nuclear-power control center: (That Dome was fifty times the size of the sub-magister's villa's Dome.) Surrounded by thousands of miles of ocean, the island of St. Helena grew from being a modest way station into a primary nerve center for the world-wide nuclear-powered wind machine system that regulated the ocean currents and the rain—the weather in general. In the beginning, climate was controlled in some isolated pockets of the world, then later, in many parts of the world, and later still, in most of the world, with plans to regulate the entire world climate from a power grid base. Regis Snow was to oversee all of it, before his disgrace and fall from power.

Initially, by 2052, there were only ten wind machines in operation. The first foundation was poured in 2047 under the war-time code name: *Grand Coulee Dam*. These were followed by dozens more under an accelerated construction schedule. By 2055, the number of wind machines had grown to 50, the last 35 constructed at a breakneck speed. The magisters also started to build nuclear-powered wind machines at other locations. Eventually, by the year 2070, the number of wind machines in the greater St. Helena Island area was close to the goal of 400, with 1100 others completed worldwide, and another 300 under construction. Over the years, slaves were brought to St. Helena in increasing numbers, the numbers changing as the need arose. Men and women were kept segregated in separate press section gangs. No thought was given to keeping families together, in contrast to the earlier days when "forced labor families" were the norm. After the aborted South Pacific great slave mutiny of 2062 A.D. was cruelly put down, the steel-studded whip replaced the leather strap, and the garrote replaced the gallows. Seven-eighths of the mutinous slaves who surrendered were executed outright. From that point on, if a slave broke the law, he had at least a fifty percent chance of receiving the death penalty, no matter how minor the offense.

The closest land to St. Helena is the tiny island of Ascension, a volcanic plug located 700 miles to the northwest. The closest large landmass is Africa, 1200 miles to the east. South America is 1800 miles to the west. St. Helena is the peak of a tall volcanic cone rising up from the ocean floor (making the lonely island about as far out in the middle of the ocean as an island can be). On a floating platform rig, #12 rig, thirteen miles offshore, in 2051, Kull was born to a common-law "forced labor" husband and wife. There was no place to record the birth-date, nor was Kull allowed to acquire a Christian, Moslem, Hindu, Buddhist, or secular name. No Gaia "religious" family name either, just "Kull."

Three years later, his legal status as a slave had become formalized. But, at least, for the first four years of his life, he had been allowed to live with his parents and older siblings, and later, when that rule was changed, he was given the privilege of visiting them on occasion, until they died.

Though Kull was born under unpleasant circumstances, there were three factors that increased his chances for survival. The first factor was that from the time of his birth to the age of three, Kull was lucky not to have been subjected to nuclear radiation, since the rig didn't go totally "plutonium" until 2054. Also, between the ages of eight and eleven, he was safe from nuclear exposure because he was specially assigned to a staff laboratory that was protected from the effects of radiation, where he worked with highly skilled, professional, non-slave labor technicians. The second factor that increased his chance for survival was that he was one of the few to have been born on the rig, which meant that he had a special knowledge of the inner-workings of the rig. Thus, he had a leg-up on others who were brought in later and found themselves inadequately prepared to cope with their new environment. A third factor was that he was no ordinary slave. He was cunning, versatile, and precocious. He not only thrived, he almost flourished, in the closed conditions of what was essentially a floating prison. All of his attributes, including his charm (the non-slave labor technicians loved him, adored him, treated him as their mascot) were not enough in the long run. His condition changed for the worse at the age of nine when he suddenly shot up in height. He became too large to hide in the ventilator shafts or get into the vents, or tiny elevators that enabled him to ride to the top or the bottom of the rig. His small size had been his special pass. When he reached four feet tall, it was over.

Then, a year later, just as he was starting to get into serious trouble, fate intervened. An unexpected occurrence, a chance happening, that could have been seen as verging on the miraculous, literally saved his life. Not a moment too soon either. In the interim,

Kull grew another inch and a half, and continued to grow at a rate of two inches a year—making up for lost time—until he reached the age of nineteen.

Two years before this wondrous event occurred, a brilliantly successful sub-magister named Clive Dumond lost his entire family in a helioplane accident. The helioplane crashed over the middle of the ocean, at a time when his family was being transported from South America. There were no survivors. Those lost included both sets of his and his wife's parents, his wife, and his two children. The sub-magister's parents and his wife's parents were in their late seventies, and Clive's wife was dying of cancer. His eldest son, Hans, a ne'er-do-well drug-user perennially lost in a narcotic haze, was no great loss to Clive. But the loss of his younger son devastated him. Clive had pinned all of his hopes on the younger son, Alexander.

When the sub-magister received news of his family's deaths, he was filled with pain. But months later, instead of getting over his bereavement, he fell into even deeper despair. He often found himself unable to perform the simplest of tasks. He smoked and drank to excess. Although he improved later somewhat, he was still crushed by an inconsolable grief. The healing remedies of time, in fact, did not seem to work.

A change occurred by accident. Clive Dumond had a chance meeting. The sub-magister had been sent on a special tour. He had been ordered to visit five nuclear-powered wind machine rigs lying offshore from the island. It was a difficult tour, an errand requested by the superior of his boss, none other than the Grandmagister himself. Clive was indeed loath to perform the chore, but he was obliged to do so. By accident, during his rounds, he had been required to witness the punishment meted out to eight hapless slaves on rig #12. The first slave to step forward for his punishment was none other than Kull himself, a boy of eleven. Compared to the rest of the prisoners, he was not only small in stature, he was extremely puny for his age—not quite four feet, two inches tall, barely weighing forty-nine pounds. Fifty lashes was his sentence. How many lashes could Kull's tiny back take, the sub-magister wondered, as they stripped the shirt off his back. Kull had been caught in the act of stealing bread from the rig MX, but since the bread had been intended not for himself, but for others, older slaves, who were already on the verge of starvation, he was granted some leniency. Kull had been spared the death penalty. Because he was still an adolescent, he was given only fifty lashes with the old leather whip and not the new steel-studded model.

Kull was a look-alike, a dead ringer, for Clive's dead son Alexander. To be sure, the resemblance was not total. Kull's hair, though like Alexander's, was darker, kinkier, thicker, and his skin was several degrees darker than Alexander's, but other than that, he looked more like Alexander's identical twin brother than a close-to-the-same-age sibling.

But there was something about Kull's uncompromisingly regal stance, his defiant manner, his character, that reminded the sub-magister of his dead son. This non-physical resemblance was perhaps more important and more critical than the physical similarities. They would have been near to the same age, Clive figured. Kull obviously had no birth certificate, so there was no way to prove it one way or another, but there couldn't have been more than six months difference in age.

Clive Dumond also noticed something else that moved him. During the execution of the sentence, not a single tear rolled from Kull's eye, nor did he cry out, nor did he even so much as flinch under the brutal blows of the whip. From the start, it was obvious that Kull expected no mercy, nor did he debase himself by pleading for any. While on the punishment rack, Kull kneeled, his shirt stripped away from his back and his arms tightly lashed to the middle bore of the rack, his body-size so small a rack a third of the size would have been ample to restrain him. He kept his face lowered in a state of stony, cold resistance, his eyes glaring straight forward, as if he had positioned his stare on some imaginary fixed point. When they finished administering the sentence, they released his hands. He rose to his feet. He did not tremble. More importantly, Kull gave the impression of possessing an inner calm. *In the eyes of Clive, Kull's inner character was more revealing than his resistance to pain.* Kull seemed to possess an inner strength, "an inner spark," in the way he held his shoulders, not droopy or bent, but pushed back in an exaggerated erectness which indicated no fear in demonstrating his will and resistance.

Clive had been sitting so near the rack he could not help but notice the trauma to Kull's back. The heat was punishing, at least 100 degrees Fahrenheit. Kull's flesh was inflated and inflamed.

Kull's back was streaked with rivulets of sweat and blood, a few drops were clear, others were deep red in color. They were dropping on the deck from the ends of his pulverized flesh. His back resembled meat hanging from a butcher's hook. There were a couple of places where the lash cut so deeply that bare bone was exposed, especially at the shoulder blades, which looked like elongated half moons, shiny steel-rims—where the bone broke clearly through the surface of the mauled skin.

Then Kull did something odd. He smiled. Bloody and bruised, he behaved as if he were a grown-up, not a child. It was as if he had pulled something over on the guards, but it was his private joke.

He was laughing. But he'd be damned if he'd share his joke with anyone else. That was the meaning of his smile. It was an expression of a cheekiness in a waif who thought he could never be tamed, Clive thought. The look was beguiling and mischievous.

The sub-magister was awed by Kull's demonstration of control and mastery. What a find. To discover a prodigy in a world of floating rigs where a constant diet of suffering, humiliation, and death was normal in the course of a day. In the face of Kull's anguish, it was not the emotion of pity that the sub-magister initially felt, rather it was relief, in that he had found somebody he could actually look up to and admire.

more fanciful: Karl Marx. Clive had to shake his head in wonder. Although Kull admitted not being able to complete the two-volume set of *Das Capital,* not being able to plow through the second part of the second volume, partly because of what he called "the regurgitation of facts, statistics and trivia"—for example, how many pods of wheat were produced in the province of Galicia under Austrian-Hungarian imperial rule as compared to the eastern provinces of Poland under Russian imperial rule in the 1860s, as compared to production levels in the 1840s. Except for those who wanted to prove that the Russians were grimly inefficient agricultural administrators, Kull had to wonder who could possibly care.

Clive had to explain to Kull that his splendid seventeen hundred and fifty volume library, as marvelous as it was, did not include all of the thinkers of the past, just some, and perhaps not even the best. For example, his library was devoid of Aristotle, Lao-tse, Li Po, Xenophon, Dante, Goethe, Tagore, Tolstoy, Freud. Fortunately, Clive's collection did include Homer, Herodotus, Thucydides, Sophocles, Plato, Sun Zu, the *Tipitaka* of the Pali Canon of the Buddha, Confucius, Ovid, Milton, Defoe, Cervantes, Virgil, Juvenal, Horace, Shakespeare, Byron, Balzac, Dostoyevsky, Melville, Kafka, Carlyle, and on top of that, 40 percent of the most impressive novelists and poets of the late 19th, 20th and 21st centuries. But how many important authors were missing?

Clive wasn't sure where Kull picked up his facts, he must have "discovered" them in a book published in Antwerp (Antwerp was the city famous for inventing the first stock exchange and for publishing forbidden books during the Protestant Reformation), one of the last books that came out in 2054 A.D., before "final meltdown" (Antwerp until late 2054 published controversial, underground books) and so, somehow, one of the underground copies was smuggled out, and miraculously ended up in Clive's collection, the last book to enter his collection in fact, before the literary door slammed shut forever, and nothing new could be found on the black market—because there was nothing new printed. It was called: *More*

Lovely Lore About The New Age Gaia Gore:

> *"Whatever happens,*
> *we've got*
> *laser guns, anthrax, missile precision launchers*
> *and they don't.*
> *Whatever happens,*
> *we've got*
> *'bubbles,' amphetamines, opium, heroin, crack*
> *to make our boys fight like crazy-men and tigers,*
> *they don't."*

Kull learned from the book that the above was one of the favorite "doggerels" used by the hardened criminals and professional mercenaries employed by the nascent Universal Gaia State—as they mopped up pockets of resistance offered futilely by out-gunned, out-classed remnants of free armies operating in the marshes of North-eastern Europe, and in the Swiss, Italian and Austrian Alps in 2053-54. It was the same doggerel the Universal Gaia State troops were fond of using—eight, nine and ten years later, when they were in the process of destroying the much larger rebel armies operating in the western half of North America, in Central America, and in South America.

For all Kull's youthful flair, Clive realized Kull had an abiding faith in seeking the truth. After years of observing stupidity and blindness throughout the hierarchy of the Universal Gaia State, Clive thought he'd seen far worse in human nature than what he had seen in the development of the ex-slave-child.

While trying to teach Kull something about the past, Clive would shudder and ask him repeatedly, "Oh, what would we do, when we were not cowards, when we were still willing to risk our lives...before we let it all slip away?" And he would sulk, as if he were talking about a long-ago era, a long forgotten past, before the beginning of the New Gaia Age.

Yet, since he had grown to be "the ever wise and clever," "the gentleman-elder statesman," Clive Dumond had been a man of *not* a few words in his private life. In public, however, he was studiously and excruciatingly careful, in direct proportion to his private garrulousness.

Clive would preach, this time to Kull, his newly adopted. "People, even people with power, are scared. Frightened to death. When people are scared, such as occurs in these times, including people with considerable power, such as me, for example, they do exactly as they're told. Only that. No less, no more. For what reason? To survive. The result? Entropy. The process of slowing down. The eventual endgame being universal flatness and homogeneity. Entropy is the immutable law governing all of the Universal Gaia State. The idea of Gaia began as something that was valuable for humanity. In its origins, it was as pure as the driven snow. But over time, the original idea of Gaia was corrupted by the Universal Gaia State. Now it is thoroughly corrupted. Whenever the Universal Gaia State speaks of Gaia, it has become the opposite of what it was intended for. Instead of being a philosophy of wisdom and liberation, Gaia—as promulgated by the Universal Gaia State—has become a mechanism for repression and bondage. It is now the apologia for an assault on the Earth's true nature."

Within the public sphere, Clive was the absolute conformist, the staid establishment man, the cold-hearted careerist, in truth, the hopelessly superfluous yes-man; yet in private, he schizophrenically lived out the life of an armchair subversive and a neurotically charged, compulsive nay-sayer. He spent his nights in direct conflict with his days. He lived two radically separate and different lives, a man divided. He moved from one compartment that contained what he thought in private to another that held what he said in public.

The sub-magister could never legally "own" or "adopt" Kull, nor could he show him off to his elite Gaia society, not even pawn him off as a servant, serving the sub-magister's social equals, for example, at a function or party. No, when Clive entertained guests, Kull always remained out of sight in his secret quarters. It had to remain, forever and ever, a very special deep bond and a deep, dark, secret. Clive lamented the fact that although he had papers for his pedigreed dog, he could not produce papers for his "illegal" son.

In early 2070, to celebrate seven and a half years of their relationship, Kull being *approximately* 19-years-old, the anniversary was observed with a special gift: a thirty-six foot sailboat.

"I commandeered it from the harbor police yard's collection of confiscated boats," Clive boasted. "It was the only pirate boat available for an ambitious one-man expedition from St. Helena to elsewhere. So, by Gaia, when I saw the opportunity, I couldn't resist. I've waited years for a boat like this to show up for you. I knew you'd be excited to hear the news."

"I don't get it," Kull said. He was flabbergasted. He fell silent.

"What?" Clive said, mystified by Kull's reaction. "I thought you'd be beaming. It's a good boat! *Do you know how hard it is to find one? It's a bad omen when someone shows sadness when hearing good news for himself.*"

Kull smiled bravely. "How did you do it?"

Clive was all pumped up. "You see, for years, the harbormaster has owed me a favor. I've been waiting to find a way for him to repay it. I figured it out. The harbormaster and I go way back. Before the time of Regis Snow. Remember me talking about him? His eminence? The world's chief scientist?"

"Yeah, yeah," Kull said, "I remember."

"Well, anyway," Clive said, "I saved the harbormaster's life, then."

"How did you do that?"

"Oh, it was nothing at the time," Clive said dismissively. Clive took a fresh cigar from under his coat. Holding it between his fingers, he waved it in the air. He moved it back and forth under his nose to savor the aroma. "Ah," he said. He placed the cigar between his teeth and lit it. He sucked on it for a moment. Slowly, he drew in smoke. Then, once he had determined it was lit, he puffed on it contentedly.

"It wasn't a big deal at the time, but, over the years, well, we realized later, it was a big deal after all. You see, Regis Snow's three-year-old daughter..."

"The eminent scientist's daughter?" Kull asked. "Yes? Go on."

"You refer to him as an eminent scientist!" Clive guffawed. "*Regis ran the entire island!* Without him, your family would never have been transported here. They'd be back on the island of Mauritius, growing sorghum and peas in their family plot. Without him, I never would have become a sub-magister. I would have been back where I started, in charge of trainload shipments of plutonium from Africa. Regis brought me out of that place because he liked being surrounded by practical men. That was his principal reason for hiring me. Without Regis, there never would have been a weather-changing system. In the early days, when Regis had more power and authority, he could stand up to the Gaia authorities. He did. He'd stand up to them, and say, 'No!' That's right, he'd bellow out the word: 'No!' He had guts. Anyhow, through a dereliction of his duties, the harbormaster gave the appearance of letting Regis's daughter slip away. All hushed up afterwards. I saved the harbormaster's career. That's why, after all these years, he has owed me a favor."

"The boat is for me?" Kull asked in astonishment.

"Yeah, of course, it is, you dummy!" Clive shouted. "Who did you think it's for? The man in the moon?"

Unable to suppress his gloating, Clive shouted, "Boy, do I have plans for you!" He laughed jollily, with a look of contentment.

"But, I don't like the sea," Kull said.

The words just popped out. Kull did not want to sound ungrateful. He did not want to sound as if he were not impressed by the magnitude of the gift, either. "Believe me, excuse me, Clive, I am grateful for what you are trying to do for me, believe me, I am. But if the truth be known, as you well know, Clive, *I hate the sea.* You weren't born in a diseased rat-hole of a rig, bobbing up and down, like a ship going nowhere, on the roiling surface of the ocean, as I was, so you don't understand what I grew up with. The sea holds terrible memories for me. When I gaze out at it, I pretend that it's something different than it is. I pretend that it is a painting on the wall. True sailors take to the sea. I'm not one of them. I'm not a sailor. The sea is treacherous and pitiless. It is alien to me. In any event, it is not my home. I don't have a permanent home. I hate to say this, but I must, because it is the truth."

"I know, I know," Clive replied. He nodded. Clive loved Kull. He looked at Kull with sympathy. "I understand. I do. But it will be the way to bring you back to your home."

"But, I don't have a home," Kull repeated. He wasn't complaining, much less whining, nor was he ungrateful at the magnitude of the gift. In his heart, he felt something akin to happiness. Kull was only trying to be realistic in his thinking, in sharp contrast to Clive's more recently displayed tendency toward effusion and excessiveness.

"Without sounding dramatic, Clive," Kull said, "whether I like it or not, I've become the original Flying Dutchman. I don't have a home. My sister died seventeen years ago, my mother died nine years ago. My whole family died the day they were placed in captivity."

"It'll be the way for the Flying Dutchman to find a home," Clive said in the most agreeable voice he could possibly muster. "A true home for you. You'll see. Trust me. It'll work. You'll see. A boat is the only way to get off of this island. That's the only way you are going to get away from this infernal place. Whether you like it or not, even if you hate the sea, even if you loathe it, the sea is your only road to freedom. You must understand this. You must realize this, for what it is—the truth. And there's more..."

The sub-magister paused for a moment before continuing, but whatever hesitation he may have harbored originally, it was gone now. "On this island, the security that surrounds all air traffic control and all large boat transfers is not just thorough in the extreme, it is watertight. There's no manner in which you can escape on a helio-plane—it's impossible. The passenger rosters can not be changed or

altered, not even by a Grandmagister. And besides, if the impossible
occurred and you somehow managed to sneak on board a helioplane, once you arrived at your destination, what will you do? Security at the port of entry is even tighter than at the port of departure.
You'll be caught. And if you aren't caught, by chance, or by some
miraculous occurrence, there will be no place for you to hide in the
Gaia-Domes. Once you're in, you can't get out. They'd hound you,
until you are caught. You'll be hanged."

Kull nodded. The hard, tight knot of realism, which was the
inner core of Kull's soul, the hard, tight knot of pragmatism, which
was the inner core of his character, turned together in sequence, in
his very thought process. They combined in a compelling way to
make him see that it was futile to argue with Clive's logic. Upon
reflection, Kull could plainly see that Clive was correct in advocating
this course of action.

"The boat's in okay shape," Clive continued, "but it'll need
work." He smiled his infectious smile. He drew contentedly on his
cigar. "Tightening up the mainstays. Beefing the ribs. For a long
voyage, it needs even more work. Repairs. New paint job. Scrap the
bottom. Replace some old stuff. It's still a wonderful wooden boat,
though! They don't make sailboats like they used to, not like they've
made this one. It's over forty years old."

Kull eyes widened.

"That's okay, that's okay," Clive replied quickly in a comforting
voice upon seeing Kull's alarmed reaction. He gestured reassuringly
with his cigar. "In the case of a genuine wooden boat, at least, that's
actually a good sign. The boat's fit. A fine wooden boat is built to
last a long time. It has an excellent collection of nautical charts on
board, over a hundred of them. True, they're mildewed, but they
chart the south Atlantic, the mid-Atlantic Ocean, and parts of the
Caribbean. There's a sextant for navigation as well as other gear that
has to do with sailing the boat. There are binoculars, flashlights, a
handheld compass, a kerosene hurricane lamp with spare parts for
them, too. Whoever owned this boat, knew what he was doing. This

puppy's fit to roll. The boat's outfitted to hold one hundred and twenty-five gallons of water! Potable drinking water for a long voyage. The boat's been all around the South Atlantic and several times into the Caribbean."

"The Caribbean?" Kull asked.

"Oh, you'll, at least, want to go to the Caribbean."

"What?" Kull asked. "I will? That's over five thousand miles from here."

"I'm well aware of that," Clive chuckled.

Kull said in a cautionary voice, "Clive, I've told you. I loathe the sea. I will do whatever I have to do to obtain my freedom, whatever, but I'm no superman."

"No," Clive said, nodding his head. "Of course you're no superman. It'll be a place at least five thousand miles away. *But don't worry.*"

"Five thousand miles away? Beyond the Caribbean?" Kull asked.

"There are pirates there, real independent pirates," Clive explained, his voice rising with enthusiasm. "Not just the cutthroat kind you'd find round here. There are islands there too! Tons of them! Hundreds! That means there are many places to hide."

"So?" There was a look of unease on Kull's face.

Chapter Eight

BECAUSE OF SOME LIMITATIONS in supplies, it took six months to refit the boat. Clive broke out the charts. Clive rubbed his hands together. He had been excited about the adventure of Kull's impending voyage. It had been obvious to Kull that Clive had been living vicariously through the intricately worked out aspects of the journey. Kull knew how much the voyage meant to Clive.

"Now, this is exciting, Kull," Clive said. He chewed on the frayed end of a sandwich. He was so preoccupied with the charts he barely tasted the food he was chewing.

After listening to Clive talk nonstop for fifteen minutes, Kull interrupted him, managing to get a word in edgewise. Upon clearing his throat severely, he butted in by saying in a crisp, decisive voice, "Why don't I just sail straight for the nearest landfall, Clive? East. Not west. I've been studying these charts, too. There might be a more expeditious route to take than the one you're proposing."

Using the nautical chart, Kull showed Clive the course he had in mind. "This would be a voyage of 1200 miles. It's a much shorter route than you propose. I'd sail due east. In fact, aside from wrestling with the cross-currents, which it's true, will be a problem, it'll be a distance of just over 400 miles farther than sailing to the island of Ascension. Why don't I just sail east, and land on the west coast of Africa, somewhere, say, below the equator."

"*Say here?*" Clive asked. "Or say, here? Ah yes, I see, uh, I see." He nodded his head. "South of the island of Fernando Po? That's where you wish to land? Or perhaps further south? Depending on the cross-currents? Is that it? May I inquire as to what exactly you plan to do when you actually *land* there?"

Clive spoke in a voice that sounded at first mockingly gentle, but then his voice took on the tone of anger.

"What?" Kull asked. He was not prepared for the sub-magister's reaction. "I don't mean to presume anything that would jeopardize the...?"

"Jeopardize the journey?" Clive asked. "You're going to die there. That's what you're going to do. Uh, uh," he murmured, "that's right."

"First, you'll be sailing against a current—a strong, direct current. You'd be better off sailing a thousand miles *with* a current than sailing two hundred and fifty miles *against* one. Second, there's nothing on the coast of Africa. There's no life there. The only thing you'll find is death."

"What?" Kull asked. "What do you mean? Won't I encounter death anywhere I go?"

"Well, there's death, and then, there's death," Clive replied. "Before I became sub-magister, I worked there. I know all about that region. I've told you before...the horror stories. There are terror pictures that keep running in my mind."

"You worked there, then?" Kull asked.

"Why are you surprised hearing this?" Clive said in a peevish voice. "I wasn't a sub-magister all my life, you know."

Clive skirted discussions with Kull about his life before becoming a sub-magister, choosing not to go into the subject in depth.

"I managed the railroad shipments from the uranium mines in the interior to the plutonium factories on the coast, from 2042 to 2052," Clive replied slowly. "Oh God, that was a life. That's what I did during the war," he said in a low, uninflected voice. "The product was then shipped to the nuclear-powered wind machines, first here on St. Helena, then later, all around the world. Aside from the uranium mines and plutonium factories, there's nothing in the heart of Africa. The heart of Africa has been grievously damaged by the environmental destruction over the last forty-five years. The Eleven-Years-War destroyed the place. The environmental destruction prevented its recovery."

As the story went, Clive had been transporting uranium from the eastern provinces of Congo through the territory of Gabon to the west coast of Africa. There was a certain section of the Gabonian jungle that hadn't yet been devastated or even badly degraded by the ecological disaster due to the Eleven-Years-War.

Clive shook his head with a twinge of regret. He had to think again before he could find the right words to express himself. "God knows when and if it will ever make a recovery. You think your #12 rig was a living hell, you don't know what hell is until you've entered a plutonium factory. What was the life expectancy for a slave on a nuclear-powered floating rig, such as the one that you were born on, Kull?"

"Seven years," Kull replied.

"The average life expectancy for slaves in the plutonium plants on the African coast is nine months."

Clive's face went blank. "Nothing grows there. Nothing! The forests and jungles are gone. Actually they're still there. *They're rotting.*"

Kull grimaced.

"What about the next closest landfall after the continent of Africa?" Kull asked. "Brazil, for example? It's only 1800 miles away."

"And you call me an unrealistic hopeless dreamer," Clive exclaimed, his voice booming and his mouth tucked down to form a frown. He looked up from the charts. He grabbed the chart from the table and shoved it over, placing it immediately under Kull's nose. He traced the course with his finger, drawing it slowly over the surface of the chart.

"First," Clive said, "you sail north by northwest, Kull, following currents coming up from the south. When you've reached the South

Equatorial Current, at 5 degrees west longitude, exactly here." Clive
pointed to a spot on the chart. "South of the Equator. You sail due
west, following the prevailing current. You head straight for the
eastern bulge of Brazil. *There!* That's how you get the hell out of
here."

"Ahhh, now that makes sense," Kull said joyfully, rubbing his
hands together. He smiled and laughed. "Brazil. At last!"

"You'll land there!" Clive exclaimed, shaking his head. "But not
to stay. You'll land there only to draw fresh water, maybe take on
provisions."

"Why?" Kull asked. "I've never been any place else in the world
except St. Helena. If I am not to land there, or if I do, only to bring
on fresh water, what am I to do then?"

"I'll tell you what you do," Clive said. He circled the places on
the chart with a bold red marking pen. "Here, here, here," he said,
drawing large circles along Brazil's coastline. "The bulge of Brazil is
ringed with Gaia bases. It's dangerous. The Gaia military forces are
active. They are largely an unprofessional bunch of hooligans preoccupied with pillage, murder, looting. They'll sink their claws in you.
Also, the environmental devastation is terrible. Not as bad as in the
interior of Africa, true, but bad. The Amazon River still manages to
flow fairly clean and unspoiled, but the soil has been depleted around
most of that great river's tributaries, and the danger from sun death
due to ozone depletion is hazardous. Once you've entered the Gaia
world, away from places like St. Helena, you'll have to use their new
insane calendar! That'll be enough to kill you, too!" Clive choked as
he laughed, dawdling a little longer than necessary on the point.

"I thought the heavily Gaia controlled areas in North America
and Europe, with the aid of the nuclear wind machines, had stolen
most of the rain from the Southern Hemisphere," Kull said.

"Well, you thought wrong," Clive replied. "Most of it, it's true,
but by far, not by any stretch of the imagination, all of the water.
They've stolen most of the water from the surface of the oceans, but
they've only managed to steal about twenty-five percent of the rain

from the greater Amazon River basin. It's just too big a basin, and the formation of the mountains circling it makes stealing even more difficult. There is just too much rainfall in the Amazon basin, and the warming of the environment has caused more rain to fall in certain areas. Of course, they're always trying to figure out ways to take more and I'm sure they'll come up with some way, eventually."

Clive heaved a huge sigh and shot a protective glance in the direction of Kull. "Sun death is the other big problem. This voyage is filled with worries, isn't it? Unless you're lucky enough to live in the Domes, or at least have the protection of living in natural caves, practically no one is able to survive very long in the open, on the Brazilian coast, or in the interior. Then, when you are north of the Amazon River, you must stay clear of the land—of the coastal tide-land areas. You must be ever vigilant, Kull. Your problems will not be over."

"There are Gaia bases there, too?" Kull asked.

"No, not any Gaia bases to speak of," Clive said. "That's not the problem. Something worse."

"Worse than Gaia bases?" Kull asked. "What's that?"

"It's very important that you remember this," Clive said. "This is where you may end up facing the greatest danger. The coastal plain from about a hundred and fifty miles north of the Amazon River, nearly all the way to the border of Venezuela, to the Orinaco River, has been partially flooded because of the rising of the ocean levels. It is overrun with dead and dying mangrove forests. There are small groups of cannibals living in the tidal lands among the mangrove. These tribes live all along the coast. They have gone completely off the Richter Scale in terms of depravity. All the other people who lived there have all died of plague, war, sun death, cholera, malaria, whatever you have, long ago. Those remaining constitute less than ten percent of the original population. Some scientists even argue that they have regressed so far that they are no longer human, rather they have mutated to a sub-species due to the horrendous environmental devastation of the area. One group has no ears or noses and have hair that is completely white. I swear to God—I mean, *Gaia!*

They look almost like ear-less, nose-less trolls. They have acquired a special taste for human flesh. I hate to see you become a cutlet, Kull, but that's what you'll turn out to be if they should ever get their hands on you. I almost forgot to mention that ozone depletion is at its worse there, too. Most of the surface water is contaminated. Parts of the region were nuked several times during the Eleven-Year-War. During the war, it had become a testing ground, not only for tactical nuclear weapons but also for biological weapons."

Kull held his breath in anticipation of what he was going to hear next. The Caribbean now held no charm for him, more an air of horror.

"Oh, I forgot to mention one more thing," Clive added in an absent-minded voice. "All the crabs that live there walk backwards. Their biological and genetic programs and genes have been screwed up. Apparently, it's the result of the residues of the nuclear blasts which have gotten their instincts turned around backwards."

Kull nodded his head, as if he were visiting in his mind a place of inexhaustible toxic desolation, then he counted to ten, exhaled, and tried to feel better.

"You don't want to get stuck there, that's all I'm trying to say," Clive concluded. "You don't want to take *water* on there, either. But the ocean currents are with you. They are located a couple hundred miles off the coast. They flow in a north-westerly direction, following the contours of the continent—the direction you want to go. Stay on that path, follow the direction of the currents and winds and don't stray. You'll do okay. Then you've hit the opening of the Caribbean, between the isle of Trinidad and the coast of Venezuela. Then you'll know you've made it."

"Where do I go from there?" Kull asked.

"You have several choices," Clive replied, smiling. "You can go north-west, and find an island in the Greater Antilles; or you can go north, and find an island in the Lesser Antilles. Or you can keep going west, and land on the main continent, anywhere north of the Isthmus of Panama."

Clive suddenly fell into a trance. His eyes were shut firmly. There was a long pause.

"There was a man named Slocum," Clive said slowly. "He was the first to sail around the world single-handedly. He was the first to complete a voyage, circumnavigated the globe, you know—solo? Quite a feat. He wrote it down. When?" Clive scratched his head. "Damn."

Clive thought. "Can't remember." He shook his head. "No matter. However, I do remember he was fifty-one when he set sail from England and he did it in a thirty-six foot boat. The journey took him over three years to complete and when he finished he had ridden the winds over 46,000 miles." Clive laughed. "Of course, at age fifty-one, he was a little younger than I, but a lot older than you. Fourteen years later, Slocum sailed again. This time with the intent of exploring the Orinoco and Amazon Rivers. A place you'll be heading towards. Apparently he set out, but never returned. He was never seen again."

"Which do you suggest?" Kull asked. "Which should I prefer?"

"What?"

"Which direction to go? I get it, stay away from the Orinoco River area. Okay, got it. Stay focused, Clive. After I've passed the danger zone, which way should I go?"

"I suggest you go west," Clive answered. "If you have to choose between pirates and Indians, I'd choose Indians. Indians in the highlands north of Panama, Guatemala, Mexico, have done the best in adapting to the environmental destruction in their area. Believe it or not, some of these isolated groups have even survived with their traditional cultures intact. For two centuries, these hilly mountainous, terraced croplands have not been coveted by outsiders largely because of extreme land-overuse and also because the land is too difficult to cultivate except in a traditional, old-fashioned way. Because the mountainous terrain has constantly defied advanced technology, the inhabitants have been largely forgotten, especially during the terrible years of war. When the climate went haywire at the end of the Eleven-Years-War, the Indians reverted to primitive variants of corn, some of these variants were thousands of years old, which carried with them adaptations to the new variety of threats posed by the newly reconstituted environment. Some of these corn varieties had purple tassels that store heat, thus providing protection against hay-wire climate-induced frosts. Some have defenses against ultra-violet radiation, especially those growing in the high-altitude regions of southern Mexico, making them able to survive radiation due to ozone-depletion. These antiquated variants of corn are notoriously low-yield in nature. That's why they've been replaced by the more modern high-yield hybrid varieties during the last two hundred years. But guess what? They survive better than the new variants. That's what counts. So what if their yield is extremely low? At least, they grow. It isn't paradise, far from it, but it isn't hell either. At least they're not starving to death. There are worse places for you to land. The very far northern portion of the Mexican coast, for example. Keep away from there."

"But what about the Gaia armies?" Kull asked. "Haven't they attacked any of these Indian groups?"

"They've left these Indians alone, for the most part," Clive replied. "The Indians live in areas that are too isolated and too remote to be bothered with. That's why it's a good place to go. In terms of where a sailboat can land, the northwestern coast of Central America is the best place to go."

Chapter Nine

ON THE EVE of Kull's departure, the night before sailing, Clive and Kull held a bon voyage dinner. Kull was the guest of honor. It was to be their last meal together. Clive wanted to make it a special occasion.

Clive had Kull dress up in a formal tuxedo. Kull felt uncomfortable in it—what he mockingly called—*a monkey outfit*, but to please Clive he wore it all the same.

After dinner, Kull smoked a cigar. He also drank his first glass of liquor. He didn't like either of them. He didn't indulge for his own sake. He did it to please Clive.

Kull abhorred the practice of smoking and drinking, and he had spurned Clive's vices. Anything smacking of hedonism or ostentation was odious to him. Secretly, Kull always likened himself to being a "primitive," though he knew he could never be "a real primitive." Clive's teachings and books had robbed him of that possibility, but he was happy for the opportunity of education all the same, since it allowed him to understand why he had been a slave and why he was now alive, and in a sense, free.

Even after Clive took him in, Kull practiced the life of a true ascetic. He limited himself to scant rations of bread and water for days at a time, so he could remember his past slave life. Clive called these episodes Kull's fasting times. Kull typically slept on a hard floor. On a regular basis, he took freezing cold baths. He kept himself fit with daily exercise. He even whipped himself in secret, a rite of auto-mortification, not out of a sense of guilt or shame (as Clive had incorrectly assumed), but rather to remind himself of what he had left behind, so that he would never forget. Kull lived with bodily and physical denial. Kull decided early in life that it was necessary for him to be tougher on himself than he expected others to be on him. In spite of his relative freedom, the slave identity was still very much a part of him.

Kull's eye had always been on his preoccupation with finding and seeking survival. Kull decided not to offend Clive any longer with a lie. Since the arrival of the sailboat six months earlier, he decided that he'd tell Clive what he held to be the truth.

Kull was scheduled to sail right after dusk the next evening, under the protection of a moonless sky. The first seventy miles from St. Helena were going to be the most dangerous, because there was then the greatest possibility of detection and recapture. In any event, the voyage was going to be an extremely risky venture.

After dinner, Clive and Kull settled down in deep, comfortable easy chairs. Kull shed his tuxedo coat and loosened his tie. Clive continued to drink, as was his custom. But after his initial drink Kull refused to indulge. He hadn't even noticed what he had been drinking at the supper table, so ignorant he was of the nature of alcoholic beverages. He had surreptitiously tossed out some of the contents of the drink when Clive wasn't looking, diluting the contents of the little he did imbibe with water.

"I know you're ready to go, my son," Clive said, after they had seated themselves. "We've waited a long time for this."

"Yes," Kull replied. He appeared sleepy, although actually he was alert, wide awake, even edgy.

A chill of silence passed between them.

"The boat's ready," Clive remarked, trying to fill the silence with useless chatter.

"The boat's more than ready," Kull replied. "The boat's been more than ready for weeks," he added with a deep sigh. He remained distant, keeping his eyes closed.

"But what have you been thinking about these days?" Clive asked, having sensed Kull's remoteness.

"Pardon?" Kull asked. He, at last, opened his eyes, but only for a split second, then his eyelids returned to their position of droopiness. He kept his eyes shaded.

"What's on your mind?" Clive asked.

"Oh, nothing," Kull replied.

"Nothing? Don't you care to share your thoughts with me?" Clive asked.

"If sharing my thoughts with you brought you more unnecessary harm and discontent than was reasonable, would you still want to hear it?" Kull asked. The sheer formality of his voice sounded impertinent, verging on insulting.

"Ordinarily, I'd answer no to that," Clive replied, smiling in a way that he hoped would look like a smirk, but he didn't quite pull it off. He was slightly confused and baffled. "But on this occasion?"

"So this occasion is different?" Kull interjected in a cold voice.

"But on this occasion...," Clive continued, "since I'll probably never see you again, ever, I'll answer yes. In the affirmative." He blinked his eyes twice, self-consciously, as if to say, he really meant what he was saying. He was hurt that Kull thought it could have been otherwise.

"Very well," Kull replied. "So it shall be. But remember you asked for it."

"Yes," Clive said, pronouncing the word in a very delicate way: "Yes."

Kull jerked himself out of his repose, unfolding his arms. He suddenly stared at Clive with an intensity. He became animated. He blurted out: "*I hate your system. I hate your scam in it, too. It stinks. It's corrupt. It has turned the merits of the Gaia spirituality and replaced it with its diametrical opposite. In the name of Gaia, your government is destroying Gaia.*"

Clive was instantly, and as it turned out—prematurely, relieved.

He emitted a sigh. "Bravo, brother! You had me worried. Now after all these years, it comes as a surprise. 'You hate the system?' That clears up a mystery, doesn't it. Tell me something I don't know. How could I have guessed? If you hadn't hated the system with all your heart, with all your passion, with all your soul, you would have been a great disappointment to me! It's true. Enough! Explain what you're thinking."

"I hate you, too," Kull replied.

"Oh?" Clive replied. Now he laughed a little forcefully, as if Kull had been joking all along, or at least had not been truly serious, and was pulling his leg.

"Yes," Kull replied in an all too serious voice, so his meaning could not be misunderstood. "I hate you. *I hate...you. Do you want me to spell it out any more clearly than I already have?*"

"How long has it been?" Clive asked. There was a brooding silence. They did not move. They sat transfixed, immobilized. "Weeks? Months?" Clive asked. "How long? Years?"

Clive shifted his weight. "Surely, it hasn't been as long as that? Years?"

"I've hated you bitterly for a number of years."

"Oh really?" Clive said. "Bitterly? How many years?"

"About five."

"Five years?" Clive said. Clive's dismay turned into surprise. Then the surprise grew into wonder and fury. "AND WITHOUT, ALL THIS TIME, YOU EVER TELLING ME SO!" Clive shouted out in a burst of anger. He lowered his voice a little, but still spoke loudly. "Why have you waited till now to tell me this? I insist you answer me!"

"Yes, I do deserve that," Kull said. "Lower your voice, please, Clive. I understand your reaction. I owe you much in life. In fact, I owe you life itself. I'll give you my reasons. This is one of them— the most important one. Because you, too, are a part of this vicious system I so passionately hate. I cannot separate you from the system. And if I didn't hate you, I'd loathe myself—oh yes, hate myself. Ahhh yes, so bitterly. I'd have to detest myself, don't you see? Wouldn't you do the same if you were in my shoes? Don't you see I have no choice in the matter?"

"Wouldn't I do what?" Clive asked in a genuinely confused voice. "You have no choice in what? What the hell are you talking about? I've given you everything you have! And...and...you say you hate me!"

"Yes, of course, it's true," Kull replied in a strange-sounding voice. "I do hate you. The only way I can love you is to hate you, you see. But I love you enough to believe that—I, at least, am obligated to explain the reasons to you first. Does that make sense? You deserve that. You deserve that much. And so, I will do that. So trust me a little. And be patient with me, just a little longer. I'll try to explain."

"You're not pulling my leg?" Clive asked in a defensive voice. For an instant, Clive thought of striking Kull with his hand, quite instinctively, with a hard sharp blow, aimed at the temple. But the urge to commit the act died away. Clive was still muddled. He was hurt and confused.

"No," Kull said in a strange voice. It was the strongest voice he could muster. "I'm not pulling your leg. This is no joke. I'm perfectly serious. I've meant everything."

Clive tried to calm himself. He took a sip of his drink, then another, then another. "Oh my," he said ruefully, setting the glass down rudely. "I've always wanted you to have your freedom," he added. "Maybe the price I have to pay for that is more than I bargained for."

There was a noticeable calming and easing of tension. It was better to talk it out.

"Right then, out with it," Clive ordered curtly. Then what came next struck Kull as strange and took him off guard. "I know what you have to say will be good."

"I will be the last of the St. Helena slaves to experience freedom," Kull said. "The last one—the final one. I will perhaps also be the last of the nuclear-powered wind machine slaves anywhere in the world, who will be able to live a long and useful life, *a free life*. What I have now, I owe you a great deal. I'm referring to my emancipation now. However..."

When Kull continued, he changed his tack. "I am also a collaborator, a permanently corrupted part of an inherently evil machine, and, not to give myself such big britches, a common petty thief. If I were not these things also, I could not be the last of the slaves ever to obtain freedom."

Clive didn't reply. He nodded gently. With his eyes he begged Kull to continue. At least Clive was proud of the education he had provided Kull, the results amply illustrated by the high level of sophistication and articulation demonstrated in Kull's speech.

"The evilest and foulest part of the Universal Gaia State is not that all slaves are now bred to work and then simply die," Kull continued, "or that when it's all over, there'll be nothing to show for it, no one will remember they even existed. They will all be forgotten. I'm one hundred percent certain that your bosses' long-term plan and goal is that. Right? Am I right? Isn't it true?"

Clive nodded. "Yes, it is. You're right. Everything you say is true. Then what is the evilest part of the system, if not that?" Clive asked, without blinking his eyes.

"The evilest and foulest part of the Universal Gaia State is that in order to survive as a slave in the system, with a life longevity of more than a few years anyway, you must collaborate with it, you must be a part of it, you must make yourself a part of that evil," Kull exclaimed in a rush of words. "To survive in *that* system, you must erase the line of demarcation between good and evil. That is why I whip myself...to this day. Not for any so-called *aesthetic* reason."

"That has always been the case in all totalitarian systems," Clive replied in a cool, confident voice. "The Eleven-Years-War itself. But what makes the Universal Gaia State different from any previous forms, any imperfect predecessors of systems? For all its beautiful and noble ideals, there is nothing more deadly than the reality of the Universal Gaia State. The beautiful idea hiding the totalitarian method—the creativity of Gaia itself—is more beautiful, and the information technology used to push that initial beautiful idea—is more comprehensive and effective—but what else has changed? The near perfect technology of the Domes themselves? What else is new? I accept what you're saying...but not for the reasons you may suspect," Clive continued after a short pause and a little reflection.

"Before his death," Clive continued, "my eldest son had been a profligate, a drug-user, and a self-congratulating braggart of a nihilist. In contrast, there was my younger son. He was intelligent. Alexander was a perfect son. I have no idea what would have happened to my younger son had he lived. But I'm certain he would have turned out more like you, than like his older brother. I'll take you for what you are, Kull. I consider it to be the best that could ever happen in this world."

"I am neither of your sons. I am not your blood. I am a slave. Your slave!" Kull replied.

"Well, you may not be my son, and you may be a slave, as you say," Clive said, "but as my slave, I can make you be whatever I want you to be. And even if making you what I want you to be means you making yourself what you want to be."

"But what I want has nothing to do with it," Kull explained. "What I am has everything to do with it. I am a slave. If I can't live with that truth, I will always be living in an illusion, like this Dome we are under is an illusion, an illusion of freedom, when in fact it is nothing of the sort, it is its exact opposite: a cage for the weak...for those who bend their knee to the Universal Gaia State."

"I'd rather you be the way you are, a slave, and not my own son, more than anything else," Clive confessed at last, "...*if that is what you truly want*." Tears burst from his eyes. "Now, having said that," he continued, deeply moved, "and meaning it with all my heart, do you still hate me? Say you don't."

"I don't know what I think any more," Kull replied at last. He smiled. "You remember how much I loved to read *The Decline and Fall of the Roman Empire?*"

Clive nodded in the affirmative, with an expression of affection.

"I must have read it at least five times," Kull said. "I remember reading parts of the book aloud to you, maybe once or twice, well, at least once—even though you snored through most of the reading. When I was sixteen, it was my favorite book. I couldn't get enough of it. I know it inside out."

Kull's eyes lid up like the moon. "Gibbon said that the Latin word for 'son' was originally derived from the Latin word 'slave.' Why is that? Have you wondered? Strange, isn't it? Late at night, I've pondered that question. The Roman republic in its infancy and early years, while nothing more than a large city-state, had hardly any slaves, and the Roman army consisted mainly of free citizens—poor farmers true, but they were denizens, free-born. But by the end of the republican period, many of the people in the Roman-conquered world were either slaves or descendants of slaves, and the Roman army was no longer made up of free-born but instead, an assortment of mercenaries from conquered provinces. Sons of slaves. Or still slaves! How do you explain that?"

"So?" Clive asked. "That book was written almost 300 years ago by a fool who was writing about events that took place 1300 years before he was born. Who cares? Why are you quoting that stuff anyway? Even if Gibbon might have been the greatest historian of all time, what difference does it make? *History doesn't matter any more. What has it got to do with anything?*"

"Don't you see?" Kull asked. "Those Romans? They still thought they had a republic at a time when they had evolved into a totally corrupt empire! They thought they still had a republic! Even after they appointed emperors to rule them. They followed that practice for centuries! *In form,* it was still a republic, *but in content,* it was the exact opposite—an empire. That's why we call ourselves a Gaia state today. Protecting the world? We make the same false claims for the same puerile reasons. To hide the truth. But you don't hide anything. Not from slaves anyway. You hide the truth from yourselves! Just as you hide the existence of slaves from the common people in the Gaia-Domes. I bet you that the populace of the Gaia-Domes of North America have no idea that there are so many slaves all over the world slaving for them, so that they can live their lives in relative ease. I bet you it's a secret. If I said such things on the streets of a Gaia-Dome, I bet you I'd be ridiculed. A secret indeed!"

"You'd get off lucky if you were only ridiculed," Clive replied. "So what if I told you everything you've been saying was true. So is that the reason why you hate me?"

"I hate you because I hate myself," Kull continued. "And I hate myself because I hate the accursed world I was born into. I'm not too old to have forgotten the days when my father, my real slave father—I'm speaking of *him* now—got drunk. Yes! He got drunk. He got stinking, silly, disgustingly drunk. Just like you. Not on the finest spirits money could buy, as in your case, but on rotgut, on the cheapest brew, on the most dangerous home-made wine in the world. In the beginning, you could obtain alcohol on the nuclear *floats*—that's what we used to call them when they were being assembled, and on rare occasions, even slaves could steal a crate or two of illicit hootch. Anyway, my slave-father would get totally plastered with the stuff wherever he could lay his hands on it. In that state of booze-induced delirium he would scream at the top of his lungs that I must fight to the death to free all of the slaves of Gaia. His screeds weren't only directed at me. He screamed the same crazy stuff at my older brothers, too. He only spoke that way when he was drunk though. He never said such things, nor did anybody else I recall— talk that way, when they were sober. It was like letting steam blow off from a pressure cooker."

Kull stared at Clive with searching, plaintive eyes. "But later, things changed, didn't they? As conditions are known to alter from time to time. Even before the suppression of the South Pacific slave mutiny, nobody talked, either jokingly, or even when intoxicated, about any sort of slave rebellion. Not even demented fools dared do it, for it would have been madness—and suicide, to have rebelled. We would have been slaughtered like cattle. But, by then, anyway, it

didn't matter. My father was dead. My entire family was dead. Slaves'
lives were too short to become anything other than strangers to each
other. That was the perfection of the Slave system by the masters. We
died early and were replaced so quickly by fresh slaves. That's what
the last years were like, for me, before you rescued me."

"And so that's why you hate me?" Clive asked. "Because of my
complicity in the creation of this Slave system of Gaia?"

"*That* wasn't the perfection of the Slave system," Kull said in an
almost tearfully angry voice, shaking his head. "I beg your pardon. I
was wrong if I have given you that impression. The perfection of the
Slave system came later. That was just a little fine tuning, a nibbling
around the edges. The true perfection of the Slave system came later...
To survive, you had to side with your oppressors. Much later, however, in order to survive, you had to not only side with, you had to
identify with your oppressor. All fresh slaves were received and treated
with extreme hostility, if not subject to cruel tricks and outright bul-
lying by the veteran slaves, the remnants of the old slave groups who
were only still alive largely because they had collaborated."

"Now, wait a minute," Clive interrupted. "Just hold on. I distinctly remember when I found you that you were being punished
for stealing a loaf of bread? True or false?"

Kull nodded.

"And I distinctly remember also you having given it, or at least
having shared the lion's portion of it, with less fortunate slaves... I
remember that! No, no, you can't fool me!"

"True," Kull confessed. "That's true. I was different, I was still
a child. Not only that, I was a child whose growth was still stunted.
It's true, I didn't need much food then. But even so, my meager rations were nonetheless insufficient. From time to time, I still had to
steal to keep my strength up, to keep myself from descending into a
state of weakness and vulnerability that would have left me exposed
to the possibility of being the prey of brutes, the prey of sickness
and disease, the prey of death. From time to time, I still had to side
with the oppressors to make sure I secured work in the clean rooms

and the laboratories, where there was no fear of being exposed to nuclear contamination, the very thing that killed my family. That was as important for my survival...as was the illicit food...in the long run...perhaps, it was more important."

Kull paused for a moment. He wanted to make sure he had Clive's full attention. Only when he knew he had achieved that goal, did he continue.

"When I was assigned to the special technicians' lab, I enjoyed the luxury of a warm place. I was protected from exposure to dangerous radioactivity from the plutonium core. I was given an extra half-ration of food each day, though ironically, I was still very small for my age, that is—until I was eleven. During those years, I was not desperate, that's the main point. I happened to avoid serious illnesses even though there were epidemics raging all the time—typhus took my sister, cholera killed my brother, nuclear exposure killed my second brother, then my father, finally my mother. Why was I so lucky? The combination of my small size—natural thinness—gave me a nutritional advantage, and like I mentioned before, I received an extra half-ration of food every day while I worked in the lab. Half the time, while my mother was still alive, I gave that half-ration to her. The crucial point is that my mind remained sharp. That's why I've been blessed with such a good memory. Also I enjoyed a special privilege related to hygiene. And how I did! I received a new shirt and underpants once every two weeks, so as not to offend the lab staff by smelling too repulsive, a privilege denied to the other slaves."

"But if I recall correctly," Clive said, "you were in the lab only to the age of ten and a half."

"By that time, in fact, long before that time, I had learned how to organize," Kull replied. "That's how I survived."

"Organize?" Clive asked.

"You know—*organize?*" Kull said. He smiled, realizing he hadn't made himself clear. "You misunderstand me. *Organize?* It means to steal."

"Yes?" Clive asked.

"I stole," Kull said. "Organized. Stole. This is mind-splitting, a totally schizophrenic thing." He wondered if it wasn't so poignantly ghastly to try to explain a point that was, for him, so utterly important.

"I have your test reports," Clive interrupted, changing the subject.

"What?" Kull asked. He had worked himself up into such a fever, he didn't understand what Clive said. "Repeat that. What?"

"Remember when I asked you to give me one of your teeth?"

"Yeah..." Kull replied vaguely. "I almost forgot." Using his finger, he felt the spot where his incisor was missing. "Three months ago, right? You never told me why you wanted it."

"I wanted it," Clive replied, "so that I could take it to a lab where we could have it examined to see how much radiation your body had absorbed. We have a lab at the main plant that specializes in those sorts of medical examinations. From your tooth, they were able to determine the exact level of Sr-90, strontium-90, a nuclear fission product, in your bones, and therefore, in your entire body."

"So?" Kull asked.

"From that report," Clive continued, "you have some radiation, but compared to the high levels that slaves absorb, even just after two years, your levels are still fairly low. Way down the road, it may affect you, to be sure, but for the next several decades, you'll apparently be fine. You're very lucky. Sometimes, even free citizens have high radiation levels, higher than yours anyway. You're incredibly lucky."

"That's all very reassuring," Kull said. "It only goes to prove my point." He thought and reflected for a long time, before he took the time to respond.

"The true bearers of the truth—the witnesses of the truth—were only those slaves who died within a few short months, a year or two at most, from the time of their captivity. The rest of us, our memories too, have been tainted—by dint of our collaboration."

"After the first five years," Kull continued, "as you know, it was calculated that working slaves to their death was far more profitable than treating them humanely. *Even if I survive, the memories of the slave holocaust will be lost. All of it. The slaves who died. That represented 99 percent of all the slaves.* They could not stand to think, to articulate and crystallize anything into a form of abstract thought, because if they thought in any form, all they could think of was:

We are dying alone. It is hopeless.

We are dying alone. It is hopeless.

We are dying alone. It is hopeless.

Alone. So utterly alone. *We are dying.*"

Clive smiled warmly, almost chuckled, stopping short of that because he knew it would be inappropriate. "This is curious and more curious still," Clive said.

"When you consider the fact that without your unique education, which you have received under my generous care, you'd be back as an illiterate eleven-year-old, in a nineteen-year-old's body. An illiterate scamp, with great skills at stealing perhaps—a few other survival skills—but not much else. We all die alone. That's a biological fact. *You do not have to be a slave to die alone!*"

"Yes, I'm a real Frankenstein, aren't I?" Kull shot back.

Clive smiled again, but this time his smile was not warm. "Well, they say the Frankenstein creature was more human, far more human, than his creator ever was—who was, technically, the human one. It was Chekhov who said that a slave cannot be liberated by someone else. A slave can only liberate himself. The only way he can do that is to do it slowly, squeezing the slave out of himself, little by little, drop by drop, a little at a time."

"You've made me that Frankenstein, haven't you?" Kull added in a somber voice.

"Well," Clive replied, "as soon as you leave, that is to say, as soon as I have surmised that you are safely away, in other words, that you have not have been captured and brought back—say—under armed guard—say—in two weeks time... Then...I plan to commit suicide."

"What?" Kull asked. "You're kidding, aren't you?"

"I wasn't planning on telling you at first," Clive replied slowly, "but listening to what you've been saying, well, it changed my mind." Clive spoke in a mild, uninflected voice. "Before, I didn't think it necessary you should know my plans, but, I'm thinking differently now. I think you should know the reasons why."

"But why?" Kull asked. "Why kill yourself?"

"For the same reasons you feel the way you do," Clive replied. "Does it shock you to hear this? Do you know me so little that you find these words from my mouth so unbelievable and unthinkable? What do you think evil is, Kull? Something that heroes fight against? Something that is always destroyed—in the end—by bombs, by helioplanes, by armies? Evil is evil, because it is so bad that it contaminates everyone—every living thing. But, as bad as that is, that's not the half of it. Evil, true evil, is far worse than that. Most who are contaminated by it, don't even know that they are contaminated by it...that's the true mark of true evil...that's the cleverness of evil, the rest is....well just *misunderstanding and groping in the dark and listening to the angels sing, when in fact, the angels singing, are, in fact, just little devils in disguise carrying on a sweet tune.* No one is immune to it. No one. Evil is bad, not simply because it's bad, but because, in a sense, you can't prevail against it. It's undefeatable. It crushes everyone. It reigns supreme."

"I don't get it," Kull said.

"Why do you think I've planned your escape for this very time?" Clive asked. "Because there is no moon? Because there is going to be a fog? Good cloud cover? Because supposedly you're old enough to make a voyage on your own now? Because only now your boat will be in perfect condition? Because the gales are blowing moderately hard, but not too hard, to the north?"

"I don't know," replied Kull in a meek voice. "I admit the date has a certain arbitrariness about it."

Clive laughed aloud. "I was waiting for my uncle and aunt to die. You hardly noticed it at the time, not that you should have, you didn't even know them, but they died a little over a month ago. If they had not died, I would have delayed your trip. You see, after they died, I was the only one of my family left. My extended family was all gone too—who could they use against me? My uncle and aunt left no children and they were dead. My father had no other brothers or sisters. I've been waiting for *that*. Now there are no relatives that they could kill, in retaliation, if they captured you and implicated me in your escape. No brothers, sisters, parents, children, aunts, uncles, cousins, who were still living, see? Understand the logic of my actions now?"

Clive smiled as he noticed that Kull was straining to comprehend what he had been told.

"I have a great deal of power at my fingertips as a sub-magister," Clive said. "I can bend rules. I can cut corners. But I'm also subject to the same laws as everyone else is. So is my family. So is my extended family. How else do you think they control us so effectively? By filling our heads with the Gaia religion nonsense? By making us say such stupid things as we always end up saying—about the Universal Gaia State? That's not it. Well, they can't control me any longer. Because the only person they have left to kill in punishment for my acts, is me. For once, after all these years, I am untouchable. Suicide will be a great release. It will be an act of freedom. So all you have to do now, Kull, is do your part. Get away. Be a seafarer. Escape in your sailboat. Don't bungle it."

"So you will do this for me?" Kull asked.

"I will take that last pleasure away from them, yes," Clive replied with a deep note of satisfaction. "I prefer to see this act of suicide as an act of self-actualization."

"You saved my life. I am truly thankful for that," Kull said. "I don't know. I will never know. What I might have been had my life turned out differently...but..."

"But?"

"I don't know who I am."

"Don't be an idiot," Clive said. "You can be anyone you want to be."

"Is that so?" Kull asked. "Is there such a thing as that kind of freedom?"

Clive laughed whole-heartedly. "You will at least have the opportunity to find out. If there is such a thing as that kind of freedom in this world. Maybe there is. Maybe there isn't. But at least you'll have an opportunity to figure that out. The truth that the Eleven-Years-War demonstrated beyond any doubt was that human beings were a good deal more malleable and subject to manipulation than was hitherto thought possible. Given enough will-power, fanaticism, commitment, steady course of skillful determination, an incredibly unfavorable conjunction of circumstances, almost anything, at any rate, far more than was hitherto thought possible, could be altered in the behavior of humankind. Well? What of it? Aren't you a brand-new person, or are you what?"

Kull had no reply for that. He was stumped by Clive's clever display of brilliance, his out-and-out genius, his ironclad logic. He was also stumped by Clive's unexpected display of passion. If Kull had been in a boxing ring with Clive, what Clive said would have been more effective than a combination knock-out punch. Kull had no defense for it.

At last, Clive couldn't restrain himself. He gave in. He swiveled in his chair, reached across the space that was between him and Kull and took Kull's hands into his hands. No longer could he hold back the emotions that were welling inside him. In one final effort, he made a stab at displaying paternal affection. Clive sighed. Looking into Kull's eyes, he smiled and said, "Look, with all the palpable evil that exists in the world, it would cause any sane person to wonder if there could be a God—a *benevolent* God—who would allow such a mass of evil to exist. Don't you wonder about that? And if there is no God, and if there is all this evil residing in the world, who then is left to reside over and judge this evil? Without God, who is left to judge? Humans? A human being? That's why nihilism is such an attractive alternative in the world today, Kull, it's got an argument that can't be defeated—it's damn foolproof. We are in no position to judge all this evil. The world is evil. That's a job for a *God*...and for a *God* alone...to do. But there is no *God*. Perhaps the only thing left for humans to do is to survive—just the basic will and instinct for survival is all that remains. If that's the case, what makes us—the world of humans—any different from that of—say, the world of animals? Chimpanzees? Plants? A living cell? Even the substratum molecules of rocks and minerals? Are we not all then, just animals? Why do we deserve to breath any more than the next creature—the next living thing?"

"Is that truly the reason why you are going to commit suicide?" Kull asked.

"Yes," Clive said. "But...*however*...I don't know that answer for anyone else...*for you*, for example. That's why I emphasize the word *perhaps*...for you...*perhaps so, perhaps not*. Because it may be different for you. Who knows? And you need to go out and see for yourself. Make a complete and thorough investigation. Make sure first. Suicide is irreversible. You can't turn the deed back, Kull, once you've committed it. You have gone beyond the point of no return. You can't change your mind back on it...say...later. You can't say later, further on: 'Oops! I made a mistake. Oh no. A big mistake. I want to reverse that decision. May I?' No, you may not." Clive smiled an ironic, deeply satisfied, smile.

"Now, go and prepare your boat before I change my mind," Clive said when he realized that Kull had no response. He waited a little longer, just to see if Kull would say something, but Kull was silent. Kull did not know what to say.

"The important point," Clive said, "is that you get away and find some place where you can be free—away from the Universal Gaia State. Doesn't matter where the place is, anywhere, will do. Perhaps it is true that mankind harbors a secret wish to be politically, religiously and intellectually enslaved—a wish all the more perverse for being disguised as a search for freedom. There is nothing evil in the fundamental idea of Gaia, nothing at all. All the evil resides in its peculiar application," Clive said at last, "its *human* application. That's the important point. That's the only thing that matters. My death will mean nothing. Like all the slaves' deaths have meant nothing, alas...in the end..." Clive nodded his head. "Now, do you understand? Go away. Be free. Go. Before it's too late."

Chapter Ten

PILOTING, MANNING AND STEERING a thirty-six-foot-long sailboat, alone, across thousands of miles of seas, seas that on occasion could be hazardous and/or perilous, was no small feat.

Without access to the Gaia Global satellite navigation system or an antiquated CB radio (*Kull needed no means of communication, primitive or otherwise, because he had not a single soul in the entire world to communicate with*), the sea-voyage involved a level of risk-taking and a scope of commitment that went well beyond normal boundaries of caution and sensitivity.

On the other hand, Kull had at his disposal a compass, a top-notch sextant, a state-of-the-art chronometer, two excellent barometers, accurate sea charts, loads of goods, fresh water, and he had the added advantage of knowing more or less where he was going.

But he had one crucial handicap. No matter what, for fear of being detected, he wasn't going to be able to sleep for long, uninterrupted intervals of time. If he had, it would leave him vulnerable to capture, thus defeating his purpose.

Therefore, prior to initiating such an incredibly long and arduous voyage, and in preparation for the journey, Kull knew he needed to get as much sleep and rest as possible. Prior to the voyage, he slept without interruption through the night and the following day: nearly twenty hours. He knew that he would have to stay awake, and more importantly, remain relatively alert with the benefit of only thirty minute catnaps, every three or four hours, over the course of four to five weeks—and perhaps this catnapping regime would suffice till first landfall at Brazil.

He, and he alone, would be the "watch" twenty-four hours a day. Without peering out and scanning the entire horizon once every forty-five minutes—the event of an unexpected arrival of a ship could prove to be fatal. (In 40 minutes, a ship making 23 knots could travel from the horizon 12 miles away to Kull's sailboat. A battleship cruiser or hydrofoil or a V-20, traveling at top speed, 57 knots, could arrive in just over 20 minutes.) On the other hand, most ships were guided electronically, so they didn't require lookouts or watchmen and they could sail right by the tiny sailboat, less than a hundred yards away, and no one on board would bother to notice. But Kull had to operate on the side of caution. The only exception would be when there was a storm brewing. When the weather was becoming fierce, Kull didn't have any reason to fear detection by his enemies, but he had plenty of other concerns to keep himself occupied. In the case of inclement weather, his hands (and his head) would have been kept thoroughly busy: lashing the tiller to keep the boat on course, bailing out the bilge-water, manning the pumps, taking in sail or letting it out, as the weather changed, to keep the boat from capsizing.

In addition, to ready himself for the voyage, over the course of the last six weeks before embarking, Kull ate fifty enormously large meals. In each case, the main course consisted of potatoes. The preparation varied: baked potatoes, mashed potatoes, curried potatoes, potatoes in coconut milk, crouton potatoes, boiled potatoes, roasted potatoes, au gratin potatoes, hash-browned potatoes, souffle potatoes, potato soup, potatoes in tomato paste with green peppers and peas, French fried potatoes, et cetera—potatoes prepared in every imaginable way—giving his body ballast, a stability to aid in his adapting to a regimen of three or four months of constant shifting, rolling and pitching, caused by the motions of the sea. Kull ate mush porridge every day for six weeks too. He reckoned there was nothing better than a diet of potatoes and mush porridge to help him secure his sea legs. (Kull had to believe in *something* and he reckoned potatoes and mush porridge were the things he was going to believe in. The nineteen pounds he gained at his waistline was proof of that.)

Kull knew in advance that the initial part of the trip would be the most hazardous. Kull would have to make sure that he was not detected by any intruder on the ocean's surface or by any aircraft overhead. Since he would be traveling alone, he had to constantly be on the look-out for seagoing vessels or aircraft that might happen in his vicinity. This was specially true during his passage through major shipping lanes, as well as within 70 miles of St. Helena, where security patrolling was more frequent.

Waiting until thirty minutes after sunset, the complete onset of darkness, he manned his sailboat. Without ceremony, he slipped into an enveloping fog and didn't look back.

As if Clive's world was already dead and gone (and in it, Clive was buried), from the lapping edge of the island's shore, Clive waved forlornly to his "adopted" son. He waved without vigor or enthusiasm, as if Kull's world was the only one that mattered. When Clive couldn't see Kull, or the outline of his sailboat beyond the fog line, he brought himself to attention. Clive briskly clicked his heels. He snapped a salute. He held that sharp, razor-edge salute for a full three minutes. Beads of sweat formed on his upper-lip and jowls.

After Clive completed the salute, he couldn't explain even to himself why he had extended such a fancy courtesy to Kull. *Why did he do it?* Had he saluted on an instinctual whim? Or was it done on impulse? Clive didn't know the reason why he did it. Perhaps because he was at a loss as to what to do. He felt that he had to do something. Saluting was as good as anything.

Then a tear came to his eye.

The real reason dawned on him. Hitherto, the reason had escaped him, up until that moment. Then he discovered it. It came to him in a sudden burst of illumination. A secreted portion of his sub-conscious rose to the level of his conscious memory—and almost

instantaneously—a full-blown memory flooded into his mind. He recalled the first time he set his eyes on Kull. The young waif, a clever
eleven-year-old whippersnapper, was about to receive fifty lashes as a
penalty for being caught in the act of pilfering a loaf of bread. Clive
recalled that Kull, still a mere boy, did not struggle while his punishment was meted out. He remembered that Kull took every blow in
a manly manner, without flinching. He remembered Kull conducted
himself with a robust and spirited stoicism. It was that almost forgotten memory of that image of the then apparently doomed boy that
Clive was saluting. Clive was honoring the boy's courage, a tribute
also to his youth, to his heroic display of theatrical verve, finally, to his
calm and patience. There was no point in Clive attempting to deny it,
since he had first laid his eyes on him, Kull had been a class act.

For Kull's part, this was the part of the departure that made
him sad and glum. It wasn't just disillusionment that was forcing
itself upon him. Again, he was not acting out of choice—he had to
choose—if he wanted to survive, he *had* to depart.

Kull knew that he dared not look back at Clive, because once he
had pushed a hundred yards from the shore, he knew that if he did,
he might turn into a pillar of salt, or if something not that fantastical,
it would, at least, put a hex or a curse, on his journey. This concept
of a providential retribution, potentially to be meted out to him, was
something he believed in with a fervor.

Kull figured that if he was going to be alone on the ocean, he
might as well be superstitious, and think superstitiously. He might
as well welcome the honorable and time-honored tradition of the
superstitious way of BEING, of relying on right instincts rather than
learning, of relying on immediate and intuitive feeling rather than
analytical and abstract thought, using his heart rather than his head,
embracing the unknown with open arms. Perhaps the whole of life
could be gleaned from a moment's glance at nature. Perhaps one

impulse of nature could teach Kull more about humankind, and about the nature of good and evil, than could all the learning of all the ages, and all the wisdom of the sages. He might as well start at the beginning and be superstitious straight away, just as all the great mariners, seafarers, and seamen had been before him.

Staring out at the dark, impenetrable sky, Kull hummed fragments of an almost forgotten lullaby that morphed into a tune. The loose bits came together and became coherent. Proud of himself, Kull improvised a doggerel that went with the hastily re-constituted tune.

It was as if it had been summoned from nowhere. It was as if it had come from his sleep:

> I may not be a tar...
> I may not be a gob
> I may not be a swabbie...
> ...But I am a salty dog!
> *Haah-aah! Hee-hee!*
> *Yes'sir-ee indeed! I am a salt-y dog!*

Upon bellowing out each line in a false basso voice (at the same time fantasizing he was a crusty graybeard), maniacally, his eyes screwed up, Kull glared out at the ocean. The ocean harkened back with an uneasy shifting underneath the bow of the boat. The unexpected movement caused Kull to sway. The motion altered his vision. He could feel tension build in his spine, as he groped to capture his sea legs. He flashed a toothy smile. He attempted a laugh.

Upon his completion of a crude attempt at creating "rhyming verse," Kull then did, at last, as an afterthought, burst into an uncontrollable fit of laughter. He almost split his sides with mirth. He lowered his face and scrunched his eyes, unable to suppress his laughter. He beat his legs with his fists. He opened his eyes and proceeded to open his fists and beat his forearms and chest with his open hands—slapping himself all over. Ironically the gesture created a peculiar, clapping sound. The sound resounded, reached out into the open air, then moments later, came back in the form of an echo. It sounded like dogs barking. The echo made Kull feel that the ocean had grown larger—*incredibly larger.*

The more Kull tried to refrain from laughing, the more he choked. He was overwrought. A manic glee overwhelmed him. He fell on his side (yet, the very next second, he rebounded to his feet agilely) but at the same time, he almost caused injury to his foot as he awkwardly hopped from one foot to the other. His right foot became entangled in loosely coiled rope and rusting tackle.

Wiping tears from his eyes and at the same time disentangling his foot from the coiled rope, while gaining control of his laughter, Kull mercurially shifted his mood from one of gaiety to one of dread. A change of magnitude occurred in his attitude. He became despondent. He was overtaken by a powerful urge to reflect, and in that flickering moment of reflection, darkness occurred. Kull had been summoned deeper into the consequences of his own thoughts, deep into himself. The thoughts produced there were immense. These thoughts ambushed him. He could not escape from them, nor could he voluntarily shut them off. The immensity of the implications of these thoughts seemed to overwhelm him. They forced him into the strange confines of a feeling of awe:

It was this. To place himself at the mercy of the towering elemental force of the ocean was to surrender control. It meant he accepted the opposite of control: total submission. Upon reflection, he realized this was the fate, since time immortal, of illiterate, "stupid" sailors as they embraced "simplistic," "superstitious" beliefs. They didn't do it because they were incapable of or counter-intuitive to the whole lexicon of "reason," "analysis," "control," but rather because they were motivated by higher visions and deeper wisdom that taught them that there were far larger forces at play in the world and in the process of life than those contained within the narrow confines of a shallow, idiosyncratic, petty world of ego, selfish urge and vanity-driven will.

Therefore Kull didn't look back, not so much as a glance. He was touched, yet strangely disconcerted. He said to himself: "For all intents and purposes, for good or bad, for good or ill fortune, the ocean is my friend. The ocean will always be my friend. The ocean is alive. I must mightily respect it. With all my heart. The ocean is everything. I am nothing."

Saying that was the nearest thing akin to a prayer that the atheistically-inclined Kull could think of. And it was quite a dramatic turnaround from hating the sea.

Acting alone as his own coxswain and first mate, Kull's first night at sea was dark and dreary. He hunkered down. He shivered as he tightly gripped the tiller. (Especially during his first hours at sea, the tiller was not just an instrument of navigation but also an icon of reassurance.) However, as night wore on, Kull loosened up. He grew increasingly confident. The wind picked up. Kull experienced relaxation and moments of joy. He traversed the furrows of the deep Atlantic swells. Each steep wave tipped the boat into a deep trough, then shot it to the crest of the next roller. Kull was now well away from the island of St. Helena, and well out into the open ocean.

Ouh-weeee! Heady stuff.

Eventually, he was able to sail with all the sails set and the sound of them ruffling loudly in his ears. He had to tack unevenly toward the north in order to ride the current running directly north, but, on occasion, he zigzagged east and west, cresting and plunging—up and down—over the uneven swells, using his piloting finesse to the maximum.

To Kull's relief, he found that he had taken well to sailing skills. The sails flapped briskly in the wind. He found that the bilge pump worked well. What more in the nature of the agreeable could he ask for? He remembered Clive's inspiring words: "Kites rise against, not with the wind. No man has ever worked his passage anywhere in a dead calm."

Two hours before dawn, the sky grew clear, exploding with a profusion of stars.

The Milky Way streaked across the sky. It was an elongated stretch of star-matter, swathed across the sky.

"Wow!" Kull exclaimed. He had been drifting. He woke up. His head was reeling. His head throbbed. He groaned.

He jolted upright with a start. He slapped his face, using his right hand, then for good measure, his left hand—a double whammy. He cupped his hands and scooped a cup of seawater from the sea. He doused his face with the liquid. He rubbed his hands over his face.

Kull decided that it was better to expect *ANYTHING*, that could possibly happen, than to presume that only the best would happen. He convinced himself that he had to stay alert, using whatever means necessary.

Dreaming wasn't going to get Kull into his new state of freedom, or into a new brave world, or, more modestly, even to his next landfall.

Three hours later, Kull took his first catnap. He drew a light cover over his shoulders and fell asleep on the wooden open deck, not bothering to go to his bunk below. He set the timer for forty-five minutes, placing the small, mechanical, wind-up, timepiece gadget twelve inches from his head to make sure he would wake up on time. In the beginning, it took just under ten minutes to fall asleep. Until he learned how to fall asleep faster, he could only allow himself a thirty-five minute catnap. When he heard the alarm on the timer ring loudly in his ears, he forced his eyes open.

Chapter Eleven

SHORTLY AFTER KULL AWOKE, the sun rose, providing a profusion of light that afforded him a vista. What a relatively calm seascape there was to gaze upon too. There were gentle whitecaps peeling peacefully in the distance, in an otherwise calm sea.

As time went on, Kull discovered, to his delight, that now and then there were flying fish, manta rays, porpoises and small whales following the boat, always at a safe distance. When the algae naturally started forming on the bottom of the wooden boat after a few days at sea, a small and growing school of trigger fish would also follow the sailboat.

That first morning, Kull breakfasted on the contents of a can of sardines, four bananas and a pint of water. Kull was a prodigious water drinker. He began the voyage with an ironclad principle of habitually drinking at least a half-gallon of water daily. He had no intention of scrimping on his intake of drinking water, as long as his provisions held out. He thought that that was the only way to remain healthy and alert.

Seeing no land for the first time during daylight hours didn't disturb Kull because it reminded him of being a child on top of rig #12. In any case, visibility extended approximately three or four miles at normal times, up to seven or eight miles maximum, during clear-sky times. There was a murky, vague wall of mist and haze beyond a certain distance. With the aid of his high-powered binoculars, Kull could add another eight miles for a total of at least twelve miles. It took him a full seven or eight minutes to search the entire horizon. Once he completed the sweep and saw nothing, he was confident there were no ships in the vicinity.

An hour after sunrise, Kull put on his daytime solar protection gear, which vaguely resembled the upper torso section of a beekeeper's suit. UV-B radiation due to ozone depletion was least dangerous in or near the equatorial zones and was most dangerous in the far northern and southern zones of the planet, especially in the polar regions, but it remained hazardous everywhere on the surface of the planet. Protection was mandatory. Clive had personally designed the gear for Kull himself.

The outfit not only protected Kull's sensitive eyes from the dangerous rays of the sun, it also protected him from the cancer-causing UV-B radiation on the upper portions of his body. Filtered by the shades hanging down over his face from the wide brim of his large sombrero hat, Kull kept his eyes wide open through the day, the following night, day following night, night following day, taking only brief catnaps as he sailed. Of course he took it off at sundown, and although there was still UV-B radiation, he was less vigilant during foggy daylight hours or when there were rainy overcast skies. He was lucky he was making good traveling time, averaging thirty to thirty-five miles a day. On one outstandingly brisk and windy day, he traveled an amazing seventy miles. Usually, the wind was neither weak nor strong, just constant, temperate, moderate, the best, Kull could hope for to succeed. As long as the weather held, it looked like he could make good speed.

So he rode the wind as he rode the waves, swells, and occasional deep wells and walls of sea whenever the sea became choppy. Fortunately he didn't encounter heavy weather more than once during the first week out. By the vigilant use of compass, sextant, and chronometer, Kull remained on course. Once or twice the wind did die, but the doldrums lasted only eight or nine hours. Then, Kull was unable to make much progress beyond the natural drift of the current. Even then, he managed eight or nine miles per day. The wind picked up, after a certain hiatus, and was steady for the greater part of the journey across the mid-Atlantic. He set a course north-north-west, then north-west, then west-north-west, finally due west, sailing an arc right across the mid-Atlantic to the South American coast.

There was one exception to the generally favorable weather pattern. On day twenty, a low pressure system moved in. There was a huge storm, but fortunately it was far away. The surge from the high-velocity winds had a potential to capsize Kull's boat. The storm was centered to the east. The barometer began to drop rapidly. These winds could eventually endanger him. But by the time the outer edge of the storm reached Kull's boat, later on day twenty-one, the storm lost its punch. The winds dropped. The storm was no longer a storm, only a gale, as it arrived in Kull's vicinity.

Kull remembered the mantra he had memorized about the ocean on the first night at sea. "For all intents and purposes, whether for good or bad fortune, the ocean is my friend. The ocean will always be my friend. The ocean is alive. That's all I need to know. And I must mightily respect her. With all my heart. The ocean is everything. I am nothing."

Reciting the mantra calmed him.

Virtually no boat, helioplane, fighter plane, cargo plane, weather balloon did he see over the next fourteen days. Kull was all alone. Actually, using his binoculars, he did spot one fairly large ship, in the distance, a good ten miles away. By changing course, he was easily able to circumvent detection.

There wasn't much shipping active where Kull was sailing, but he still had to remain alert.

Kull's inability to sleep for sufficiently long periods of time left him, after four weeks, coming into the *early stages* of a psychotic breakdown. Even with catnaps becoming ever more recurrent, after two weeks alone at sea he was now taking them once every three hours, then, three weeks out, he switched to every two and a half hours, finally, four weeks out, he took a nap every two hours, but was still suffering from sleep deprivation.

Now that he was sleeping a fourth of the time, but only for forty to forty-five minutes at a stretch, he had discovered a way to fall asleep quite quickly, often in less than three minutes, but because of the nature of the nap, Kull was unable to achieve a real state of true restfulness.

Once, absentmindedly, he forgot to set the timer (either that, or the timer malfunctioned) and he slept on his bunk through the entire day and into the beginning of the next night. He slept uninterrupted for eighteen hours. What a huge relief it gave him. So far, it was the only time during the voyage that he had allowed himself so long a period of uninterrupted sleep.

After having slept so soundly for so long, after having gone without adequate sleep, he felt better and was refreshed for a while. But, unfortunately, he had drifted off the course he had set.

"What the hell was that?" Kull shouted. There was a stab of pain. He rubbed his head. The impact had been so sharp and powerful that it threw Kull out of his bed. He landed on the deck, skidding across the bulkhead. It took over a minute for him to regain his senses. He could feel a large bump, rising slowly, egg-like, at the top of his forehead. He realized he might have suffered a concussion. He had been awakened by a powerful lurching movement of the boat, which had struck something so hard that the bulkhead almost cracked.

"Omphh!" Kull said as he gasped and explored the damaged spot on his cranium, tentatively exploring the point-of-impact with his fingers. Instinctively, he clutched his stomach with his hands, and bowed from the waist. He took in several gulping mouthfuls of breath to calm himself.

After he regained the deck, dazed, confused, wondering what had happened, under the light of a high-sky half-moon, he spotted a whale as it was surfacing. The whale was about thirty-five feet long. He could hear the whale blow. In an unhurried fashion, the whale swam around the boat, circling it, swimming on the surface all the time slowly, appearing harmless and even friendly, as if it were inspecting its hoped for *backscratcher*, the boat.

Underwater, the whale must have rubbed against the shell of the sailboat, Kull surmised, in an attempt to remove some of the annoying barnacles. Kull could not remember where he read about it, but it had stuck in his memory that it was not uncommon for young whale calves, especially in the warmer climes, to crave such an activity from time to time.

Kull was only too glad to come to the realization that it wasn't a big ship that had collided with him, which is what he, at first, had guessed happened initially.

After the whale departed, Kull sensed that the creature would not try the barnacle-removal tactic again on the small sailboat. The boat was too buoyant and lightweight. It just "bounced" off and away from the whale upon impact. The young calf would have to find a more suitable backscratcher to really break off barnacles.

The whole incident served as a warning for Kull never again to sleep any longer than his allotted time.

Fortunately, Kull was only eleven days from the South American coast, although, at the time, he wasn't quite sure he was that close to land-fall, in spite of the use of all his nautical instruments, star sightings, and careful measurements. His calculations indicated that he couldn't have been more than fourteen days away.

Six days later, Kull spotted his first flock of land birds. They were flying south. It was a large flock. The birds were smallish in size, about two hundred in number. The sight of the birds increased Kull's feeling of confidence.

Chapter Twelve

KULL TRIED HIS HAND AT FISHING. He discovered early on that he was no good at it. He snagged a tuna—by sheer chance, and was able to eat much of it before the carcass rotted. He also caught a few mackerel that were part of a large school that passed directly under the boat. Once in a while he was able to catch a trigger fish. They were easy to catch, since they followed the boat everywhere, but they were decidedly foul-tasting. But other than that, Kull had no luck at fishing. Either he had no knack for it or he was plain unlucky.

Kull ate bananas. One day, he ate ten. There was a reason why he ate so many. The bananas and the few fish were the *only* fresh food Kull had to eat.

Kull had taken three bunches of bananas on board. Of course Kull didn't want all the bananas to ripen simultaneously. The first bunch of bananas was yellow and light green. The second bunch was green. The third bunch was a hard, unripened green.

During his first five weeks at sea, Kull could never say he didn't have enough potassium in his diet.

Once he had completely exhausted his stores of bananas, he then switched to trying to eat banana skins. The smell of them lying on the deck had a strange, hypnotic effect on him. After the second week in the equatorial zone at sea, slowly rotting around his bunk; they reminded him of freshly baked banana bread, so, he hesitated to sweep them off the deck.

"H'mmmm!"—he would smile as he closed his eyes and imagined the fresh frothy aroma of baked banana bread coming piping hot from the oven!

The distinct smell and homey aroma of the banana skins, in a way comforted Kull, especially in his state of isolation. Eventually there were dozens of rotting banana peels lying about the boat, not just around the bed where they first appeared, but covering the length of the boat—evidence of a change in Kull's mental state.

With time—*too much time*—on his hands, Kull tried an experiment.

It involved ascertaining the edibility of the banana peels. Chewing them was exceedingly difficult, but once he managed to swallow, he would throw them back up. So after five or six attempts, he determined that banana peels were "inedible."

He first cleaned the cabin, then the entire boat. As part of a general cleaning, he threw all the old banana peels overboard. Turning over a new leaf, he made a clean sweep.

There were times when Kull lost his mental balance. There were also times when he was lucid, coherent, and in complete control of his faculties.

Kull was reluctant to dispose of anything that might later prove useful. But he had to admit: in the wake of the results of his failed experiment, banana peels were useless.

However, something more pressing occurred four days after Kull celebrated his eighteen hours of sleep. He drifted back into a state of ennui.

One day later, Kull began to daydream vividly. It took effort and concentration to pull himself out of mental torpor. The more he yielded to the unhealthy practice of excessive daydreaming, the greater the effort was to pull himself out of these states of impaired mental acuity.

Fortunately, intense hunger or thirst seemed to have a positive effect. It sharpened his wits. Getting hungry or thirsty or having to attend to his bodily functions momentarily jolted him out of lethargy. However, as time went on, these "wake-up calls" from his "persevering" body to his "weakening" mind began to have diminishing effects. Kull began to lose his sense of time.

Was it—in fact—hallucination? Or was it something else? WHAT WAS HALLUCINATION? That conundrum unsettled Kull. How could he step back from himself to know if he was hallucinating when he was...well...in fact...*hallucinating!*

Yet there were some prolonged moments of clarity, between apparent states of incoherence. Also, because of his recurring depressed mental state, he was rewarded with occasional bursts of euphoria and exhilaration. It was always on the occasions when he had achieved optimum mental clarity that Kull checked to make sure that he was still on course for the Brazilian coast.

Yet, as the catnaps continued, and as time and the unchanging horizon stretched on, moments of clarity grew shorter in length. His ability to think clearly became less achievable.

For a while, in the middle of the fifth week at sea, Kull sought a remedy. He put a plan in place. It seemed to work for a while. When he felt dull and lifeless, he stuck pins in his sides. When his sides became sore, he stuck pins in his legs. When his legs grew sore, he stuck pins in his arms. The infliction of pain "gave him a jolt." It was a stimulus to the brain through pain. Over a fairly long period of time, he pricked himself with a pin several hundred times.

Over time, however, to maintain the desired affect he had to stick the pin deeper until he was inserting the pin to a depth of one-half inch. He bled. The self-inflicted wound scabbed over. He had to repeat it until he was doing it twice an hour.

He was able to continue to steer the boat, staring out to sea with a bland, haggard and deranged expression.

By now, his beard had grown long and his hair was long, straggly and filthy. In his shorts and tattered tee-shirt, he took on more and more the resemblance of a scarecrow.

Slowly, Kull was coming to the dim realization that he was losing his critical faculties.

In this state, how much time did he have left?

He arrived off the coast of Brazil exactly thirty-seven days after setting sail from St. Helena. Mesmerized, he stared at the thin line of land on the horizon. He still had a third of his stock of fresh water and half of his food, but other than that, he was extremely tired, ironically, so tired he didn't know if he would be able to sleep again! He felt that he was the most exhausted man in the world.

Even during catnaps, he dreamed lustily and relentlessly of sleeping for unbroken periods of time—twelve hours!—sixteen gorgeous, beautiful hours of uninterrupted sleep! He craved an uninterrupted bout of prolonged sleep like a thirsty man crossing a desert on his hands and knees, craved water. But now he was afraid he would not be able to sleep. His luck had been great—*at least, up to that point.* It was as if he had been blessed. The progress had been incredible.

Kull sighted land three days earlier than had been planned, at least according to how the trip had been measured and calculated in Clive's study. Kull made better time than he had ever dreamed he could. Even in his mentally reduced state, whenever he was coherent, he was able to read his chronometer and make accurate position calculations. The weather had been good. He didn't even have to immediately land. Thank God for that, too, since he wasn't able to land.

Every time he got within a mile and a half of the Brazilian coast, small patrol boats were awaiting him. They came out from the narrow inlets for apparently no other purpose than to apprehend him. They would always remain close to shore. They were strictly coast-patrol boats; thus, whenever Kull sighted them, he'd reverse course to scurry back to the safety of the open sea.

Fortunately, with the use of his high-powered binoculars, he was able to spot patrol boats approaching from a safe distance. Soon after his arrival during the night, he realized that he had made a mistake. On day *forty-one* after departing St. Helena, Kull had been inching along the coast without being able to land. Eighteen days had lapsed since he experienced his glorious "eighteen hour" sleep. He was beyond tired.

Too late, Kull realized that he had inadvertently landed in the center of a miasmic, unhealthy-looking mangrove swamp. No wonder there were no patrol boats in the shallow water waiting to intercept him. He reasoned it was never patrolled because of the unsuitability of the place.

From the start, the place sent a shiver down his spine. There were unhealthy-looking, dangerous vapors, bubbling out of the water. In addition, there were unfamiliar sounds of nocturnal creatures in the distance, alternately shrieking, crackling and howling. Though the creatures sounded menacing, they lay tantalizingly beyond his view. They could be heard, but not seen. Pointing a flashlight in every direction didn't help matters. It only enabled Kull to see shadows which produced even more feelings of gloom.

As weary as Kull was—bone-crunchingly tired—he slept fitfully that night. In the air, there was a faint odor of ammonia and a dash of sulfur. It caused recurring headaches and nose bleeds.

Kull managed to tie the boat to a partially submerged tree without having to wade through the waist-deep brackish water. Then he slept for twelve hours straight. In his hugely sleep-deprived state this was clearly a beneficial development, but afterwards his sleep became fitful and intermittent. He was visited by a disturbing nightmare which woke him a second time. Then there was another nightmare. It was cruel, violent and disturbing. His body had grown damp. He coughed blood. His throat burned. After that, he could not fall back asleep. His nightmare was so vivid, he could not get it out of his mind. It seemed so powerful, even long after he regained consciousness, Kull *felt* it.

Kull had dreamt he was a child again. The dream began with a three-foot-tall, underfed Kull opening a tiny door to a ramshackle hut with a tin roof, to see his father—his natural father. Kull's slave father's face was radiant, soft, with an air of sweetness, kindness, benevolence, and he had a manner about him that was different from his usual dissipated self. He told Kull, "It was time." He directed Kull to a door. But Kull was puzzled.

Kull crawled through a tiny door, into a "clean chute." A tiny elevator transported him to the top of a platform at an amazingly rapid speed. But when Kull emerged from the elevator, instead of being on the platform of the nuclear rig #12, he was staring down at a huge desert.

Kull didn't know what to make of the desert. Then he grew less anxious. He rushed down a slight slope to the wasteland below. The whole horizon was visible. Under the darkening sky the lights of a distant Gaia-Domed City flashed on and off. The air was charged as if lightning were about to strike. Kull realized that a bomb was about to drop. He ran to the place where the bomb was about to fall, so that he might greet it fully. He was not scared. At the spot where the bomb was suppose to impact there was thunder without lightning. Kull listened to the anguish of a tearing sky and the boiling of an inflamed atmosphere. But instead of a bomb impacting, an odd frog-like creature dropped out of the sky, floating softly, using its web-like feet magically to slow his descent, as if they were parachutes. The frog pirouetted to the ground. At first the creature appeared to be large, but upon landing, Kull discovered it was small.

As soon as the frog landed, it was attacked by people from the Domes. They beat the creature mercilessly. Kull intervened just as they were about to douse the creature with a inflammable liquid and set it afire. Just as quickly as the people arrived, they vanished.

Kull sat with the creature, reading to it. The book was Edward Gibbin's The Decline and Fall of the Roman Empire. The creature was intelligent, but playful. And naughty. Strangely, that irritated Kull.

The head of the frog changed, morphed, into the head of Clive! Perched on the body of the frog, Clive's head beamed at Kull. His skin was shiny. Then, with a nod of his head, Clive batted an eye. Clive's

head said, "Love thyself." An enigmatic smile spread glowingly. "Re-
member, love yourself."

Then as quickly as Clive's head had appeared, before Kull had an
opportunity to ask it a question, the head turned back into a frog's
head.

The Dome inhabitants appeared. Kull understood they were dan-
gerous and threatening. They propped open Kull's mouth. They forced
him to eat the frog-like creature. Kull resisted with all his might, but
alas! he was unable to prevail. Finally, the one-foot-wide creature, slimy
and foul-tasting, was stuffed down Kull's gullet. Kull awoke at this
point, coughing horribly, spitting up blood.

Chapter Thirteen

THE RANCID-TASTING BLOOD and a burning in his throat told him something was badly amiss. With no instruments to measure the chemical composition of the swamp vapors, and unable to determine their toxicity, Kull *knew*, nevertheless, that there was something in the vapors from the brackish water that was affecting his thinking. For the sake of his health and safety, he had to get out of that swamp.

First, Kull checked for leaks to make sure the boat was shipshape. He even swam underwater to inspect the bottom of the boat where the young whale had bumped it, to detect if there had been any permanent damage. Swimming in a caustic cesspool of water was a dangerous thing to do, but Kull knew he had no choice. Fortunately, upon inspection, Kull realized the hull was sound. After nightfall Kull turned the boat around and headed out to sea, without accomplishing his goal of getting at least four uninterrupted periods of sleep. One and one-half periods of rest were going to have to do.

Soon enough, twenty-four hours later, he was running with a good, strong current again, twenty-eight miles out at sea, north-by-northwest. Fortunately for him, he still had plenty of supplies. He did not dare take water in the swamp for fear of contamination.

Kull needed to find a good, safe harbor where he could drop anchor, rest and sleep, but every time he headed for the coast in the hope of finding a secluded anchorage, he saw coast patrol boats.

There was no reason for him to assume that any of these vessels were friendly, so to stay on the safe side he made a judgment call. He headed seventy-five miles out at sea. There was no point in denying the inevitable, he was going to have to make it past the main portion of the Brazilian coast before he could land.

He sailed for several hundred miles when he couldn't keep from falling asleep for several hours. He slept through the timer *again*. Suddenly he noticed not one, but three ships simultaneously, one of them clearly not friendly. After awakening just in the nick of time Kull could see through his binoculars that it mounted a pair of large laser guns on its foredeck, a Gaian Navy coast cruiser.

Kull didn't need to venture closer to any of the three ships to find out any more than what he already knew. To avoid three ships moving fast in different directions, and remain undetected, required fancy maneuvering on Kull's part. After successfully evading them, Kull drifted out one hundred miles from the coastline and after sailing leisurely for three hundred miles following the strong north-by-northwest Caribbean current, he almost ran into another ship. Fortunately for him, he spotted it in time and he was able to take evasive action.

Kull plotted a course that was one hundred and twenty-five miles from the long, undulating Brazilian coastline. He set a course, north-by-northwest, following the prevailing Caribbean current. He settled on sailing the middle-to-the-outer-fringes of the north-by-northwesterly current. Everything was going fine after he found the right course.

Kull fell asleep again, sleeping right through his timer. This time he slept for twelve hours. After awakening and thoroughly castigating himself for his lack of discipline, Kull realized these involuntary sleep-arrest *accidents* took him way off course. Moreover, they were increasingly habit-forming and addictive. Most important of all, because he could not be on the look-out for potentially hostile ships, the extended sleeps were dangerous. As he did in the past when he had slept too long, he instinctively reached over the side of the boat to bring water up in his cupped hands to rinse his face and refresh himself.

He inadvertently stuck his tongue out in order to taste the salt on his lips. But, strangely, there was no salty taste. Kull was perplexed and mystified. Maybe he was just imaging that the water was fresh. He needed to repeat the process. He cupped his hands and dipped them in the water again. He brought the water to his lips. He took a swig. There was no taste of salt. He drank. No taste of salt. Grabbing a large cup hanging from a hook on the foremast, Kull dipped it deep into the ocean and brought the cup to his lips. There was no hint of salt.

For purposes of solving the riddle, Kull decided he had to take an approach that was more scientific. For one thing, somehow, he needed to test the depth of the freshwater. He knew that fresh water weighed 62.4#/cubic foot. To sink it before filling with water, buoyancy of a large bucket required a weight equal to the bucket. So pitching an empty bucket over the side wouldn't do the trick of testing the salinity of the water, at least at a lower-than-surface depth, it wouldn't.

Then a much better idea occurred to him. Using bottle, cork, weight, fishing line, string (fishing line attached to the bottle, string attached to the cork) and fashioning them together, Kull improvised a makeshift apparatus. He constructed the apparatus in a way that the cork could be removed from the top of the bottle, after the bottle was submerged and lowered to a certain depth, thus capturing the water at that depth. In this way, he was able to test the water at a depth of fifty feet, one hundred feet, even two hundred feet. Fresh water! Every time. All of it, all of the water, tasted like fresh water, even the water that had been drawn from the deepest depths.

Indeed it was fresh, *good-tasting* water at that!

(Separate from other considerations, this was a healthy sign: Kull's brain was not so far gone that he couldn't engage in some fairly tricky applications of problem-solving.)

But aside from that, Kull couldn't believe it. He was far out at sea, one hundred and twenty miles from shore, at least according to his latest navigational calculations. The existence of fresh water far out in the ocean didn't make sense. He grew perplexed. Was he where he should be?

Kull went below and rechecked the nautical charts carefully. Then he discovered what had happened.

He was at the mouth—at the actual mouth—of the Amazon River. It was at the place where the river continued, unbroken, undiluted, into the ocean. Fresh water came from the two-hundred-and-fifty-foot-deep and twenty-mile-wide main channel of the largest river in the world. Every once in a while, Kull saw a semi-submerged tree-trunk. The river apparently flowed continuously without breaking up or diluting with the surrounding salty sea water until the huge volume of water had traveled farther than one hundred and twenty miles out to sea. It was an intact river, flowing in the ocean. That was it! Far out in the ocean, it was still a river. Kull had been drinking from it.

Kull filled all his twenty-four kegs with Amazon River water (one hundred and twenty-five gallons), 90 percent of which had been empty. So, although Kull had only 30 percent of his food stocks left, he now had 100 percent of his water restocked!

Even though Kull looked gaunt and hapless, resembling a straggled scarecrow, up to that point, his voyage had been miraculously, even stupendously, successful.

Chapter Fourteen

AT FIRST KULL DIDN'T NOTICE the bullets or arrows. As a child living on nuclear rig #12, he had been accustomed to labeling the aircraft flying overhead, calling the faster ones "flying bullets," and the slower ones "flying arrows." He didn't see them at first because he was too busy below. At the startling sound of a massive sonic boom, however—a huge popping sound similar to the report of a massive battery gun—Kull rushed out on deck, knocking a pot of boiling beans over. He caught a glimpse of the first helioplanes.

One minute later, Kull saw the rest of the formation fly by, thousands of feet higher. There was a squadron of helioplanes, followed by hundreds of more aircraft, then followed by an even larger group of cargo planes. This formation was flying slower than the first two groups and much higher. It was an impressive sight.

"I wonder where they're headed?" Kull whispered to himself, straining his eyes. "Rio de Janeiro? Buenos Aires?"

Another twelve days went by and Kull had sailed four hundred miles closer to the entrance of the Caribbean Sea.

Then Kull recalled Clive's severe admonition. Approaching the Caribbean meant Kull had to be on guard for hurricanes. But he had to be especially aware of a new phenomenon, only recent in the world, "the super-hurricane."

Sure enough, the barometer suddenly fell as Kull, one hundred

and twenty miles from the South American coast, approached the
common border regions of the former countries of Guyana and Venezuela. He moved with haste. Kull had to adjust his course not once,
but four times, as the seas grew rougher and choppier, until he realized that to achieve even a modicum of safety he needed to make for
the nearest landfall.

The rain came pouring down. Kull took in some sail, then reefed
some more. The wind began to gust up to sixty miles-per-hour. By
then, Kull had taken in all sail. The bilge flooded. The bilge pump
jammed. Kull quickly cleared the suction valve and resumed pumping. He was expelling water at the same rate that it was coming over
the gunwale. Within minutes, however, the pump quit again. And
then the full fury of the storm hit Kull's sailboat.

Kull realized that after a one-hell-of-a-long-run, forty-seven
days of more or less reasonably good weather, he had apparently run
out of luck. At least this storm wasn't a super-cane or even in a class
of a large hurricane, but rather a gale-force storm that was not yet
hurricane size.

Within sight of land, huge waves began spilling over the gun-
wales. Rain was pouring down in buckets. Kull went below to get a
bucket and frantically started bailing water. He worked fast and furi-
ously. Within fifteen minutes, his arm ached so intensely he thought it
would fall off. He worked faster. He was like a powerful engine. Kull's
breathing had grown labored and more pronounced. His heart was
pounding fiercely. His head was whirling, making him feel dizzy.

Miraculously, he managed somehow to bail water almost as fast
as it was filling the hull, an accomplishment he only half-believed he
was achieving even as he was doing it.

A huge wave came over the side, rocking him back and over-
powering him. The foaming sea water splashed on Kull as he fell.
The blow was so hard it almost rendered him unconscious. He was
swept off his feet and left floating overboard.

Nothing was visible in the distance. The clouds seemed to be
lower on the horizons. During the intermittent cracks of light, Kull

could see he was drawing closer to land. He somehow managed to swim directly back to the boat and climb on board.

He instantly returned to the task of bailing water. A wild, violent wind whistled. The whistle was shrill and predatory, blowing under the clouds right over Kull's head. A few times the winds jostled the boat so fiercely that Kull had to hold on to a rope, or the side of the boat, lest he be swept overboard again. Kull worked hard and fast bailing water. The water had risen above the calves of his legs. Soon the water was above his knees.

Kull grew aware of a heavy pounding sound. The sound grew louder and more ominous. But he couldn't see what was causing it; it was too dark. Then Kull realized it was too late, there was a cracking, wrenching sound, and the boat suddenly lurched forward, as if it were freed, as if it were shot forward like an arrow discharged from a bow. It must have been a huge wave that was picking up speed as it rolled into the beach. The boat gained speed with the roller, and was thrown violently on the beach as the wave broke.

Several minutes later, an even larger roller drove the boat farther up on the strand, depositing it on a slightly tilting sand pile. The boat was now high and dry.

Kull went below in his soaking wet clothes. With his declining strength, filled with an bone-crushing weariness, Kull threw himself down on his bunk and immediately fell into a deep sleep.

Kull slept for an uninterrupted glorious eighteen hours.

When he awoke later, all signs of the storm were gone. There was no wind. The sky was cloudless. There was an unbroken sheen of green on the landward side of the boat. On the other side, there were sounds of waves gently lapping, not more than thirty feet from the edge of the boat.

Kull was experiencing something strange and unique: a rich tableaux of hauntingly perfect weather.

Ominously, he thought, though, there wasn't something right.

Chapter Fifteen

V ERY QUICKLY, just after Kull had enough time to arise, come out on deck, before he had a chance to have a good look around, scratch himself, stretch his limbs, he discovered he was not alone.

Ten spears were suddenly pressing up against or near his flesh. Before he had time to bellow out "hey," he discovered he was hemmed in by threatening weapons.

Brandishing spears were nine 4' 2" miniature persons and one 4' 10 3/4" person. They were the most despicable, foul-smelling creatures, yet also vaguely human-looking. They possessed wild blue or whitish squinting eyes, with crinkling tuffs of hair and bald spots on the sides of head, chest and upper-thighs.

Many were cruelly deformed with mammoth hunchbacks; several had no legs and "walked" crab-like by means of an extra appendage. Some were equipped with extra fingers and toes. A few had a withered, non-functioning arm jutting out of their side. One had a withered, non-functioning leg protruding from his thigh. Some had goiters the size of tennis-balls. In one case, purple-colored and pink-colored brain-matter was exposed—showing through a partially-cracked skull. Kull suppressed an urge to vomit. But with the weapons so close and threatening, he remained upright.

Especially menacing to Kull was the look of intense hostility shining in the creatures' eyes.

Among the pygmy-size figures was one tall one who moved forward. Was he their leader?

He didn't have the bearing of a leader. Kull surmised he had been the victim of an earlier capture. He stepped to the front. He had been moving painfully slowly—as if he were walking barefoot on broken glass.

He was somewhat taller than the rest, 5' 6" tall. He was lame. In order to walk, he used a pathetic-looking handmade crutch.

He had typical ears and a regular nose and normal hair. Only part of his face was deformed. He had a huge raspberry-color blemish on the right side of his face. His gentle eyes were non-threatening, lending him a sympathetic appearance.

As he drew closer, Kull noticed that more than half of his fingers and toes were missing. The digits looked like they had been removed, one by one, not surgically, rather by a blunt instrument. They were not bound with cloth. Kull could see that the stubs had not completely healed.

He was walking barefoot, nearly naked, with only a ragged loincloth, no larger than a kite-tail, concealing his privates.

The man hobbled forth on his crutch. He wore a smile, or rather the mask of a smile. The smile made him appear maniacal. Although the man wasn't trembling, he was a little frightened. His facial expression was that of a professional clown—*and also that of a slave.*

The spears were still threatening Kull. Not a sound came from their mouths, not a grunt, or a murmur.

As the man drew closer, Kull recognized him for what he was: a slave. He may have been a messenger—maybe a herald of some importance—for these sad, pathetic, dangerous-looking, apparently mute troll-like figures, but Kull knew from his smile, make no mistake about it, the man was their slave, perhaps a distrusted captive whom they had brought along to be an interpreter.

There was a curious mixture of followers and leaders in the group too. The troop had a pecking order. Kull deduced this simply by looking at them. The dominant ones held their spears with powerfully gripped hands, knuckles clinched. Their eyes were rust-colored and aggressive. They were near to pushing the points of their spears into Kull's skin. In contrast, the submissive ones held back. The points of their inferior sticks did not come close to touching Kull's body. The few with totally deformed legs—that is, "legs" that looked like extra arms and hands—hung even farther back.

Kull could also tell that the *top* leadership was not present in this particular raiding party. Kull had digested this information, all of it, while they were threatening him with their spears and pointy sticks. At last, the man's mouth opened and the words came pouring forth in a profusion.

Chapter Sixteen

A S IF THE "TROLL-PEOPLE" KNEW exactly what the spokesperson was uttering, and confirming the message, they chimed in with a provocative display of body language. They thrust spears at Kull's face and upper torso, repeatedly pricking his skin. Droplets of blood began to bead up around Kull's neck and collarbone. Eventually there were ringlets of blood circling his neck and a little pool of blood formed in his cartilage notch above his sternum, running down like a stream to his abdomen.

One spear came close to penetrating Kull's eye, but he dodged the blow, just before the lance could find its mark.

As if referring to the most mundane, everyday matter, the lame man said: "Drop to your knees. Easy. Slowly. Place your hands in front of you, as if you were praying, better yet, as if you were begging for mercy."

"Then raise your hands slowly, above your head," he continued, "wait a few seconds, then lower your hands behind your back, so they can bind your hands. Easy does it. No sudden movements. I can't save your life if you don't do exactly as I say. I know you're scared. Okay to be scared. They're scared of you too! *A real man!*"

"What about my boat?" Kull whispered.

"What?" the spokesperson asked.

"What's going to happen to my boat?" Kull said in a measured tone. Moving his hands slowly towards his back, he couldn't stop them from trembling slightly.

"Don't worry about that," the spokesperson said. Then he shouted, "Away, you beast-man!"

He glanced over his shoulder to confirm the troll-men were duly impressed by his performance.

Next, the lame man winked. The wink was so quick, Kull almost missed it.

"Your boat isn't going anywhere," the lame man added.

The man's smile was nonetheless phony. If his jaw had dropped it would have shattered like a piece of porcelain. He held the unnatural smile for an unusually long time. All the same, Kull thought the man smiled a genuine smile, through the manifestly false one.

Kull thought: 'Stupid I am! To land here! Of all places! And Clive warned me too!'

Only when all of the spears were pulled back, did Kull crane his neck to get a better look. But unless he completely turned his body around, all he saw was a view of the ocean. They aimed their spears in such a way that he believed they clearly wanted him to look in that direction.

They bound his hands behind his back, using a make-shift rope constructed out of bark, resin, and creeper-crawler roots. They grabbed Kull, lifting him as he himself directed his own legs over the side of the boat (the boat was pointed downward, listing), thus without difficulty obtaining the ground. They then placed a similar make-shift rope noose around his neck to provide a halter so they could pull him along. They tied a frayed-at-the-end rag around his head as a blindfold.

They marched him frog-leg through a dense tidewater mangrove swamp. In some places the brackish water was only a foot or two deep, but in other places the water came up nearly to Kull's waist (thus approaching the lower level of the troll men's chests). The captors never loosened Kull's blindfold, nor did they let Kull drink water to slake his thirst, nor did they allow him even a moment to relieve himself. Arriving at a slightly higher plateau farther inland, they entered the troll men's camp—the journey taking about two hours.

In a clearing in a large fresh-water swamp, surrounded by tentacle-shaped, majestic-looking trees, they removed Kull's blindfold. The rope fell from his neck. They forced him to kneel. But he was too exhausted, and he collapsed, toppling over on his side.

Kull decided to catch his breath before trying to remove the half dozen or so inch-long leeches that had attached themselves to his skin.

The leaders lived high in tree-forts while the followers dwelled on the ground. Kull surmised that much, as he managed to brush some of the leeches with his legs, moving them back and forth.

The lame man arrived at the camp prior to Kull, having traveled by an alternative means of conveyance. Perhaps by means of a boat? He could not have walked directly through the swamp in his condition.

"They won't kill you if you totally supplicate yourself to them," he told Kull. "Don't cross them. They'll mutilate you. They'll do it if for no other reason then for pleasure's sake. They are dangerous."

"Look," Kull said, coughing. "I've seen some strange things...in my time...weird things. But I've never seen anything like this. Is this real? Is this what I'm seeing?"

The lame man gave Kull a curious smile. "They might eat you later on—for supper. That's only because they haven't yet determined if you're worth more than meat to them. I'll wager they've decided that, or they would have had you hanging upside down, gutted and dressed, hot from the knife already. Such strong shoulders and large biceps, you have, man!" The lame man pretended to kiss an imaginary partner, putting his arms in the air where there would have been a person's back, and fondling that imaginary back. "And just let me feel one of your muscles one time, with my itty-bitty, helpless little fingers. Oh! I am so weak. And you're so strong!"

The lame man, thin as a reed and weakened by stress and fatigue from months of continuous and prolonged ill-treatment, couldn't stop quaking with laughter. In the camp, having been the object of

so much derision and having been the butt of so many jokes, the
lame man teased Kull about something that went beyond Kull's understanding.

Kull could not make out the lame man's antics or the meaning
of his ludicrous gestures.

Having imaginarily kissed the air, the lame man winked, then in
an exaggerated way, smirked, as he ended his strange tirade.

Kull had to suck his own spittle just to get his mouth lubricated
enough to speak. Every time he tried to swallow, it hurt his inflamed
throat where he had a rope tightly tied around his neck. On several occasions, during the march, the rope had nearly choked him.
He had powerful rope-burns on his neck and on either side of his
Adam's apple were reddened hash-marks.

"I'm terribly thirsty," Kull said. "I was afraid to ask for water.
I was afraid they'd jab me, for making an impertinent request. Can
you help me?"

"I'll see what I can do," the lame man replied good-naturedly.
"Be patient."

Then the lame man grew angry. "No matter how long you suffer them, you can never get enough of their stench. Sewer rats are
higher evolutionary muck. Where they smell human flesh, is where
they find their quarry. That's how they found you. Their eyesight is
not too keen, particularly at night, because of all that damage caused
by the sun I suppose, but they can smell a human being at a distance
of a mile. It is their olfactory ability that makes them deadly hunters. They have great zeal in running to earth their prey. I've seen it.
Make no mistake about it, they're powerful hunters, poor eyesight
and all. And that's why you'll not escape. Not easily, anyway. Take
my word for it."

"Come to think of it...," the lame man began, but abruptly
stopped. He wanted to share his innermost thoughts, but he also
wanted to keep something in reserve. He was dying for company
and for conversation, but he wasn't sure if he could trust the new-
comer with everything he had on his mind. He felt compelled to

exercise some caution and restraint, at least for the time being.

Then the lame man looked up, as if taking stock. "In many ways, this place is a cross between an orphanage and an abattoir. It's hell. It's a cauldron seething with resentment and rage."

The lame man got up from the ground. He fetched Kull a large gourd of water. Returning, Kull thanked him profusely.

"I never had a chance to thank you properly for helping me," Kull then replied, drinking deeply from the gourd as the lame man held it for him, tilting it back slowly, as he drank. "Thank you for saving my life. My name's Kull."

Kull wanted to offer his hand to the lame man, but his wrists were tied behind his back, so he wiggled his shoulders playfully.

"I don't often save a life," the lame man replied, happily enough, (he actually flicked a leech off Kull's stomach, a friendly gesture, awkwardly using one of his remaining fingers). "I am pleased to make your acquaintance, Kull. I was just doing my job. My name's Stoolie. Or, at least, that's what the chief-king calls me."

"How did you end up in a place like this," Kull asked.

Stoolie smiled. "I was employed as a groom and body-servant for a Gaian High Command Brigadier General. I had worked for him for many years. He operated from a base in central Brazil. The helioplane we were traveling in crashed in the jungle. The General, the pilot, and I were the only survivors. This band of—*whatever you want to call them*—found us. For some reason, they decided not to kill me. At the time, I wasn't sure why that was. They had my General for dinner—and I don't mean as a guest. They ate the pilot for breakfast, the very next day. The rest of what remained of the dead crew were turned into hors d'oeuvres a few days later. Smack your lips."

Hearing this, Kull grew restless. He surmised that the lame man could not have been much his senior—maybe ten years older—perhaps close to thirty. Kull could tell Stoolie had suffered from sun exposure too, but fortunately not too severely. His skin was mottled and dry, parchment-like, but there were only a few places showing tell-tale signs of sun death. Equally important, Stoolie's eyesight apparently was still intact. Kull realized that the group must have spent most of their time in the shade under the canopy of trees, giving them protection from the ultra-violet rays.

"Oh, you'll prove that you're worth more than a meal to them, I'm sure!" Stoolie twitted Kull reassuringly, speaking almost in a friendly, comradely way. "Not like the others," he added. He glanced around as if he were in possession of vital information. He continued to appear cagey and teasing. Stoolie smiled with a counterfeit sweetness. "Look at you! You are so young an' so strong an' so virile. So big and strong you are. Your muscles!!!" he exclaimed in a taunting parody.

"*Why are you talking to me like that?*" Kull asked. He couldn't understand why Stoolie was speaking in such a strange manner. "You sound like you're mimicking a little girl or something. What gives?"

"Aren't you getting touchy these days?" Stoolie replied. "Go easy. You'll be glad I am talking to you like that," he added sarcastically, "soon enough, you'll see."

"So big you are, you big buster, ah, so big you are, you...," Stoolie continued, not wanting to let up. "I can just imagine her pumping her legs...barely able to damn up her drool when she gets an eye-load of you," he added. There was a look of both contempt and genuine male camaraderie in Stoolie's eyes.

"Knock it off!" Kull hissed. He tore maddeningly at his bonds. In the struggle to free himself, Kull managed to only draw the ropes tighter on his wrists. Finally resigning himself to the futility of freeing his hands, Kull abandoned hope, not wanting the welts and bruises to fester worse.

"Why don't you strike your head—*really hard*—I mean *hard*—against a large rock," Stoolie exclaimed. "What good it will do you. You're trapped. You know it. That's it. You've got to learn to relax."

A few minutes later, the grand chief of the troll-clan descended from his tree-house throne. He was shorter than the rest—fatter and squatter as well. He was about 3' 10" tall. He sported a six-inch-long splinter of a bone in his nose, the object piercing both nostrils.

His crinkly white hair was wilder and with larger tuffs than the rest of the mutants (no bald spots though, at least not on the crown or sides of the head) and he had white squinting eyes. He was old. There was no one anywhere near his age in the group, or at least that's how it appeared to Kull. Kull noticed that the chief-king had surprisingly small, delicate hands and smallish feet.

The chief-king carefully examined Kull. He walked around him, circling counter-clockwise, delicately moving in an exquisitely regal and courtly way. He squinted his glinting white eyes at Kull. Out of the corner of his eye, Kull noticed a troll-warrior pulling a large piece of moss from a low-lying tree branch and enthusiastically munching on it.

The chief-king grunted and belched. Kull's face was pressed so close to the chief-king that he could hear the chief-king's stomach rumbling. The chief-king methodically opened Kull's mouth. He examined the cavity of Kull's mouth and throat. He held Kull's mouth open with his fingers, stuck his nose inside and inhaled deeply. Then the chief-king shut Kull's mouth with disdain. In a regal and exacting manner, he announced in a loud voice, "He smells of bananas. Sweet, gorgeous bananas. He's a banana eater!" Then he added, "Such a mouth—it is utterly impermissible!"

The chief-king laughed. He ran his hands down the full length of Kull's arms, caressing—slowly—all the time staring unflinchingly into Kull's eyes. Kull was baffled. Was the "touching" gesture meant to be sexual, or gastronomical, *or both at the same time?*

The chief-king belched again. "Your skin smells...of bananas. What have you been eating so much of lately, my boy?"

This caused an uproar. The troll-warriors stomped their feet and clapped their hands. They brandished their spears victoriously. Kull noticed that hardly a sound emerged from the mouths of the celebrants. There were some who managed to gnash their teeth while a few others emitted a strange "zizzzz" sound. It was a full minute before the commotion died down.

Through the corner of his eye Kull noticed that the troll-man had finished his bark-and-moss snack and was digesting it content-edly. The chief-king was clearly proud of the celebratory reaction he had caused. He took a bow. Kull had to admit that though the chief-king was fat and smelly, nevertheless he possessed intelligence and an eccentric form of charisma. Many in the group respected him. The rest who did not respect him, stood in awe of him.

Kull realized that of all the troll-like creatures, at least the chief-king had the power of speech.

"Are all your men deaf-mutes?" Kull asked matter-of-factly, without a trace of fear. Kull could see the chief-king liked it when he referred to his tribes-people as "men." He was unhappy with the fact that, though all his followers were mute, they weren't deaf. Then, nodding in the direction of the lame man, Kull added laconi-cally, "with the exception of your alternate spokesperson, of course, Stoolie, you speak."

"*You* speak!" the chief-king exclaimed, clasping his hands to-gether. "You've made an observation. Although it is not one that is entirely accurate." He laughed aloud. He waved his hands in the air, as if to seek attention. He pondered carefully what Kull had said. Then he regarded Kull with disapproving eyes. Chillingly, he stared right through Kull, as if he didn't exist.

"We have a spokesperson *already*, do we not? Do you think we need another? Don't speak unless you're spoken to." The chief-king looked ferocious, but Kull could tell the hostility was mostly bluff. The chief-king was intrigued by Kull's boldness.

In response, Kull nodded apologetically, but he did not show fear.

"Good!" the chief-king smiled good-naturedly, seemingly ap-peased. "I think we understand each other."

Quickly, the chief-king turned to face all the troll-men. He shouted in a bellowing voice, "Open your mouths! So our guest can see. Open your mouths. Do it now! I order you. All together now."

The troll-men obeyed. They opened their mouths *wide*. As if having their tonsils removed, they collectively mouthed a silent, baleful, mysterious: "Aaaaaaaaa," combined with a few "Zizzzzz's." Some put fingers to their lips as if trying to pry their mouths even wider—so as to better obey the command. They showed Kull what was obvious: each had his tongue ripped out. The withered nubs of hacked-off tongues retreated to the back of their throats. What a ghoulish and gruesome sight it was. It made Kull's stomach queasy. They all looked like ignorant and dependent children, seeking a form of parental approval.

"Why?" Kull mouthed boldly, addressing no one in particular.

"We need few tongues for this operation to work," the chief-king replied with a majestic nod. "Eyes believe themselves. Ears believe others. Too many tongues makes for too many opinions—and that gets in the way of the functioning of things. Such a mess. Such a danger, too. They all accepted the excision. That's the law. They know the rules. By God, they'll follow them, too. Before, I told you to be silent. What would it have taken to get your attention on this point?"

Kull realized he may have been a simpleton and a fool, but he thought that no one so powerful as the chief-king would address him with such simplicity and respect if he was destined merely to be "food" garnishing a table for a bunch of foul-smelling cannibals. Nevertheless, he was anxious. He hadn't, for a moment, forgotten his status. He was a captive.

Chapter Seventeen

K ULL DIDN'T SLEEP AT ALL that night. Despite being tired, he tossed and turned. At the cleanliness of the hut, he was surprised. The earthen floor was swept clean. His hands were still tied but the rope around his neck was gone. The rope binding his wrists was tied using a complicated knot that Kull couldn't break, or untie, even using one hand and his teeth. Although his wrists were tied well, and in front of him, he could separate them up to eight inches apart, and waved them in front of him. He thought this was a strange way to detain and restrain him, but it worked. Kull realized that these trolls knew their sailor's knots better than if they had been professional seamen themselves.

When he crawled to the door and peeked between the slats he saw not one, but five guards, standing at attention outside. He could have overpowered one or two easily, maybe even three, but not all five. Escape was not an option.

Not long after dark and after a troll-guard had fed Kull a gourd of manioc mush with an extra large gourd of fresh water to wash it down, they brought in a maiden. She didn't look at all like the others. She had normal human body features. In Kull's eyes, she could have been Kull's younger sister, though she didn't resemble her. The girl was fair. She was wearing a cloth brassiere and a wicker skirt, otherwise she wore nothing except silver bangles on her ankles. Kull guessed she was sixteen-years-old, maybe seventeen.

The girl wasn't beautiful by any stretch of the imagination. She was plain. But she was mobile and seemed surprisingly healthy.

Upon a second look, compared to the rest of the creatures, she was, in a sense, *subtly* beautiful. Her eyes radiated an innocence. She was large with bountiful hips: Rubensque in shape. *Upon reflection, Kull realized she might have been older than he first thought. She was clean, handsome, and surprisingly comely.*

Within a short time, Kull's heart was pounding. He was afraid. Within reach was a strange and primitive generosity that he absolutely wanted no part of. After the girl had delicately disrobed in a highly suggestive and provocative manner, as if she were performing a dance or a striptease, Kull changed from being mildly perturbed and chagrined to being deeply embarrassed. By the time she had completely disrobed, leaving only the bangles, Kull was shaking like a leaf. Tsunami storms in the dead of night, fifty lashes for stealing a loaf of bread, a whale rubbing up against the bottom of his boat, spear-chucking troll-men frightened Kull, but this was different: This strange woman-child frightened him even more.

To say that Kull had never experienced anything remotely like this—would have been a gross understatement. He had never been introduced to sex. *And he was enormously proud that he had not.* He saw sex as a cheap thrill, a freakish trick of nature, a strange compulsion, a kind of moral and physical degeneracy.

Kull had been raised in an environment where sex was only deemed necessary to produce future slaves, or used as a bargaining chip in exchange for food and other privileges. He looked on his body as something to control, to master, to serve as a *slave* to his rational mind.

Kull took pride in what he considered to be a highly principled form of asceticism. He thought of the words the lame man had kidded him with: making fun *of his strength, of his virility,* and he now knew what the lame man had meant by the joke. He clearly was expected to service the girl. The present stock of "people" were pretty inferior, genetically-speaking, that went without saying. Had he had been chosen by the chief-king to act as a sort of stud?

Like a runaway train racing out of control, the thought kept racing back through Kull's skull: after he had performed, after he had successfully impregnated the girl, what would happen then? Would they murder him. Ritualistically devour him? After he had rendered his service, what next? Would his fate be the same as Stoolie's brigadier general and the pilot of the downed helioplane?

The maiden lay on the mat, in an overtly sexually supine position. Kull stood stock-still. If she made the slightest move toward him, he backed further away.

The girl stared face up at him, but Kull could not return the gaze. He stared dumbly at the ground. She lay opposite him. He stood stock-still. They maintained this stand-off position until sunrise.

During the night the girl never made a move to cover her nakedness. She did not speak but only cooed passively, and when that didn't work, she clacked her teeth aggressively. Kull was certain it wasn't because she was mute like the rest of the tribe but that she was taciturn. (*She still had a tongue.*) She appeared to have been a captive, a healthy girl, perhaps captured at a very young age. She probably had been held captive by the group—perhaps cuddled by them, even pampered. She had been shielded from the sun, apparently for her own protection. She had unblemished, milky-white skin. Perhaps she remained silent out of a sense of obligation or duty, in accordance with a tribal taboo. Kull felt sorry for her. But he felt even greater pity for himself.

Kull spent the night standing apart from her, filled with a growing contempt for himself. If he had been religious or spiritual, instead of a doubter and an atheist, he would have prayed to every saint imaginable.

In the morning, several troll-men walked in and removed the girl. The chief-king apparently was not offended by Kull's strange behavior during the night, rather he thought that Kull, in order to behave in such a manner, though obviously not imbued with a special mystique or supernatural status, may have represented some sort of inexplicable omen or, at least, a cause for superstition.

In the late morning, the chief-king ordered that Kull be given plantains to eat, the closest thing he had resembling bananas. The chief-king knew that Kull liked bananas. *Did he, in some way, favor Kull, Kull wondered?*

Chapter Eighteen

ONE WEEK PASSED, and Stoolie entered Kull's hut. "Would you help me out, please, by explaining to me what is going on?" Kull asked. In place of the usual meal-deliverer, Stoolie brought Kull's midday meal himself.

The lame man smiled expansively as he set Kull's tray on the dirt-floor. Placed in gourds, Kull's meal consisted of plantain, grubs, manioc mush, and a large gourd of fresh water. Stoolie then sat himself on the mat on the floor next to Kull.

"I've managed to piece together bits of information—no Kull, no, go ahead, eat," Stoolie said. "I know how hungry you are. They don't mind if we converse. They've grown completely accustomed to your presence. You're not a novelty to the troll-men anymore."

Since Kull was famished with hunger, he nodded his head and dug into his food.

As Stoolie talked Kull ate. Kull dipped his fingers into the different gourds of food. The room was bare except for the well-swept mat.

"The only reason why I have a mat, and a fastidiously clean one at that, is because they expect me to copulate with that girl," Kull said, between bites of food. "Otherwise, this room would be completely bare. I'd be wearing worse than these tattered rags, I'm sure."

"You got that right," Stoolie said.

"Do they worship the Gaia religion?" Kull asked. "By that, I mean, are they adherents to Gaia?"

"No," Stoolie said. "Originally, they were refugees from the persecutions of the Universal Gaia State. They chose to settle in this cesspool. It's a former nuclear and chemical battlefield, filled with dangerous wastes. When they arrived, it was uninhabited. Five of the wives in the cult were pregnant before they got here—but most of the rest, about forty in total, became pregnant after they arrived. The chief-king was twelve years old and was the very first of the lost children to wander into the camp from the outside world. He wasn't one of their own. He had been marooned on the coast by a band of pirates. His father, a pirate, had died. The chief-king grew up as a mutant. He was the first really chewed-up mutant, but apparently the more distinguishing and noticeable aspects of his deformity didn't become fully evident until much later. With the exception of the four or five normal children that had already been conceived, those here were almost all mutants, with several variations. There were, also, about a dozen severely deformed children who wandered in from the jungle. Later, the normal children were killed, one by one, by the mutant children as they slowly took control."

"Their parents weren't mutants also?" Kull asked.

"Yes, most of them. An extra toe here, an extra finger there. Some had facial disfigurements. However, none of them were as far gone as their children, or the children who descended from the native population. The descendents from both backgrounds, took things to a whole new level of mutation. Remember when you first came here? The smell of death? The putrefaction of the vegetative matter in the swamp? Well, believe it or not, that condition has improved, not getting worse."

"I see," Kull said.

"The leaders of the cult eventually acquired an unconventional set of beliefs based on visions they professed to have received from God. After that, members were forbidden to speak to one another, except in prayer or during religious instruction, 'because conversations lead many to tell lies about their neighbors,' according to the cult's self-declared golden rule. As a result, cultists developed a primitive sign language. That's where all their 'mute-fetishism' business began. They believed they had been chosen by their God but others didn't fare as well. In their Doomsday book, the rest of South America would be invaded by insects, Europe, Africa and Asia would suffer from massive fires and huge famines, and the Universal Gaia State would be destroyed 'by its own technology.'"

Kull nodded. "After things started going wrong what caused things to *really* unravel?"

"Most of the older ones and practically all of their wives died due to disease and sun-death within the first five years of the covenant. The chief-king, still young, but growing prematurely old—quickly killed off all of the older generation in the group who were already weakened and dying from diseases and unhealthy sanitation. Very early on, he also saw to it that five healthy children were butchered. Some of the children with only mild or minor defects were also eliminated. The rest of the children ate them. Once the chief-king's power and authority had been solidified, he began to cut the tongues out of the heads of the younger children who had been born with severe mutations. He had a small coterie of higher-tiered followers, about four or five individuals, whom he placed at the top of his kingdom's hierarchy. They kept their tongues and enjoyed special privileges, but in the end, they too were eliminated, once they were of no use to the chief-king and he had decided he could easily survive without their support. Now only the chief-king had full powers of speech. A whittled down piece of femur the chief wears in his nose came from the leg of the last of them. The chief-king ate his last victim's right arm, ritually—since he had been, until then, his 'right-arm man.' You can criticize the chief-king for being a lot of things, but he's sneaky and diabolical. And make no mistake about it, he's capable of being quite clever. He may look like he's sixty-five years old, but he's actually in his late twenties. He suffers from rapid-aging acceleration disease. The goddess—I'm speaking of the girl they wanted you to mate with—was captured in a raid on a big paddle boat steaming down the Orinoco River ten years ago.

They slaughtered all the others on board but they kept her alive."

"How did you come by this information?" Kull asked.

"I learned some of it from the girl, of course," Stoolie said. "Who else? She's got a tongue. I had another source. The great storyteller himself."

"The chief?"

Stoolie nodded. "He likes to gab a lot when he drinks. The chief-king kept the girl alive in the beginning because he thought she could grow into being his soul-mate. Apparently, along the way, she tricked him into making her a goddess. It must have been one neat trick on the girl's part. She's smarter than she looks."

"Why weren't you killed?" Kull asked. "You're not a mutant like the rest of them."

"I think at first they thought I might be able to impregnate the girl myself. None of them could get the girl pregnant. They are too diseased, too unhealthy, practically all were totally impotent. The chief-king's impotent, I am sure. But, like half the people who are left in this accursed world, I'm impotent too. Who cares?"

"Why didn't they cut your tongue out?"

"Search me?" Stoolie asked.

"You're much smarter than I thought you were, as compared to my first impression of you when I first met you," Kull said. "Much smarter. I have a confession to make. I've totally misjudged you."

"And I you. At first, I thought you were nothing more than a willful, vengeful ex-slave."

"You can tell? I was a slave?"

"Of course," Stoolie smiled. "It's obvious."

"What's so special about the girl?" Kull then asked.

"She has the vocabulary of a seventeen-year-old. If it wasn't for me, she'd have the vocabulary of a nine-year-old. It took me a long time to get to know her. It took me even longer to learn anything from her. Maybe that's why they've kept me around, after all. To give her some companionship! So that she wouldn't become despondent and lonely. Maybe that's why they didn't cut my tongue out. I don't know, but at least it's a theory. A possibility?"

Kull finished off the last of his boiled grubs and drank the last drops from his water gourd. He wiped his mouth with the back of his hand and let out a contented sigh.

"Would they go to great lengths," Kull asked, "to make sure that the girl gets pregnant?"

"Of course they would," Stoolie said. "They want her to become pregnant, that's for sure." He shrugged his shoulders. "Eating, sleeping, scratching an itch, filling what's empty, emptying what's full, what else is there for them? Worshipping the girl is their only religion. Believe me, they do *worship* her. Yes, the chief-king occasionally yearns for intelligent conversation, especially when he's in his cups. In the beginning, he was accustomed to talking with me. But not now. I've run out of things to say that would amuse him. Look, I want to escape from this place. But we don't have much time. Your boat on the beach has improved our odds greatly, but we have only a small time-window left in which to act, if we are to act. Are we going to act?"

"Yes," Kull said.

"Yes?" Stoolie asked. "Well then, you can count on me."

"When's the best time to make a break for the boat?" Kull asked.

"After dark," Stoolie said. "More specifically, a few hours before dawn. It must be a moonless night, of course. In the dark, we are better able to see more effectively. But we'll have to be far away before we're missed. They'll be able to follow our scent, even over the water."

"With your mashed toes," Kull said, "Stoolie, you won't be able to make it through the swamp. As strong as I am, I won't be able to carry you the entire distance. Besides, shouldn't we try to save the girl, too? Wouldn't that be the virtuous thing to do?"

"Save the girl?" Stoolie said. "Frankly, I don't see the point."

"What did they use to smash your toes?" Kull asked, changing the subject.

"The weirdest contraption you've ever seen in your life," Stoolie said, scratching his head. "Damnedest thing. It was a mallet. Head of it is less than an inch wide, but it was twenty inches long. It was tapered to a three inch girth at the rear of the head, made of solid iron. When they apply it, they swing it over their shoulders and come down with it—as if using a short-handled pick. Like everything else here, of course, they consider it a weapon. As you see, they've spent a long time practicing on me. I've no idea where they found it."

"A mining tool," Kull said, "left somewhere, maybe in the mountains. They know how to tie knots, too—just like a professional sailor or a young pirate would teach them. In spite of their filthy habits, they do know something about foraging. They're capable of learning more."

Stoolie pointed to the stumps of his seven amputated toes, then displayed his hands with his five missing fingers. He smiled a hurt-filled smile, yet it was a proud smile too.

"I don't know what you have in mind, but I want this escape to be successful," Stoolie said. "I have only eight of my twenty digits left." He sighed. "As you can see, I can't afford to lose another finger or toe."

"You're not going to lose any more toes or fingers," Kull said. "I swear to it. We're going to get you out of here."

Chapter Nineteen

EARLY THE NEXT MORNING the chief-king was in a sullen, melancholic mood. He stared out into the world with eyes that radiated hostility. Stoolie stood next to him as he sat on his throne. Stoolie whispered something into the chief-king's ear. Then he whispered more. After an initial expression of doubt, the chief-king seemed to warm a little to the words he was hearing.

"You say he wants to impregnate the girl?" the chief-king asked. "And he wants to do it as a public ceremony?" There was a look of paranoia in the chief-king's eyes, but the look was softening.

"With everyone present?" the chief-king asked. "With all watching? He wants to do this—in front of me? In front of the troll-men, too? Why?"

The chief-king knitted his brows, suggesting an inner conflict, but he listened intently, suggesting he was nonetheless well disposed to what he was hearing.

Stoolie whispered nonstop into the chief-king's ear for a full five minutes, explaining the matter, then going through it a second time. Stoolie finished his presentation with a salute.

"Is that so?" the chief-king asked with an expression of deep fascination. "You swear? This time the ceremony will work? And it's the *only* way it will work?" The chief-king licked his lips. His eyes narrowed. "This business of...conception?"

"Yes, your lordship," Stoolie whispered. He nodded.

"Well, no one's done it successfully before. We've failed. So I guess there's a point to it," the chief-king said. He nervously drummed his fingers on the armrest of his throne, following the upscale beat of an ole pirate's horn-whistler's tune. "So, let me get this right, when the sun, the moon, the tides, are realigned, this morning, the girl's ready to conceive? That's it? That's why there's this urgency? This timing!"

Stoolie whispered again the words that Kull had instructed him to say.

"And explain to me again why it has to be done in public?" Stoolie whispered.

"And they used to do this—where? Bali?"

"No, your grace. Babylonia."

"Well," the chief-king chuckled, "I've never heard of Babylonia, but I've heard of Bali plenty. If nothing else, it will serve as a good form of entertainment."

The troll-men gathered and formed on the two sides of the aisle in front of the elevated dais where the chief-king held court. Kull marched the girl down the aisle. He had one arm elegantly draped around the girl's shoulder and his right hand clasped to the girl's left hand. It was as if Kull were taking his bride up a church's aisle.

The girl conducted herself with pliancy and cooperation. Together, Kull and she marched proudly, adding just a little bit of pomp and circumstance to their performance.

At the foot of the dais, six feet from the elevated chair, Kull laid the fully clothed girl on a mat. With special effort he made doubly sure she was comfortable. He took care to fluff her pillows. She was going along with the proceedings—by nodding, indicating she was a willing participant. (Earlier that morning, Stoolie had carefully coached her.)

Kull wondered to himself how the sexual proceedings could

have been more nightmarish considering the context in which it was taking place. It was surreal: the powerful stench-exuding presence of the mutated troll-men, the short, rotund chief-king perched on his throne, the splinter of femur bone lodged in his nasal cavities glinting in the sun, the surrounding circle of majestic trees which gave the place a spectral aureole of awe—as if the ritual was being conducted in a Druid temple or in a forest cathedral.

Kull stood up. He ceremoniously bowed to the chief-king. Seated on the throne-chair, the chief-king was presiding from a commanding height. He eagerly nodded. As Kull began to slowly pull his shirt over his head, he stopped short, as if he had forgotten something. "My goodness. I almost forgot. *Ahem.* May I approach the chair, sire?"

The chief-king nodded.

Kull took a step forward, then stopped. He turned to the troll-men and shouted in a barking voice, so that all could hear: "First, I need the chief-king's blessing—in order for the magical powers to work. Shall I approach the dais to address his majesty?"

To demonstrate their support, in unison, the troll-men nodded their assent with a genuine burst of enthusiasm. Some clapped their hands together, others pounded the butts of their spears on the ground.

In a loud voice, Kull said, "And if the chief-king refuses his blessing, what steps shall we take to insure the protection of our Goddess so that no harm will come to her?"

The troll-men eyed each other anxiously. They exchanged looks of confusion.

Kull didn't wait a second longer. He rushed forward, bounding up the steps, climbing at top speed to the top of the dais. With all his might, Kull slapped the chief-king's face, knocking him back in his throne.

Before the chief-king could reach for the saber he kept next to him, Kull grabbed it with his left hand, and with his right hand (Kull was *both* double-jointed *and* ambidextrous), kept the chief-king from falling by grasping a full handful of his hair. Then, lifting the chief by the hair, with one swift blow, Kull decapitated him.

Before the troll-men realized what had happened, Kull dropped the saber. He faced them. With his arms extended, he shouted: "Hurrah! The girl's saved! Long live our Goddess! May our Goddess-Queen reign forever!"

Kull still held the head by the hair. But the spotty patch of hair on the crown suddenly slipped from Kull's grasp. With a thwacking sound, the head fell to the ground.

It plopped down the dais, bouncing on each step. It came to rest near the girl, who was now sitting bolt upright, facing the dais, tresses of her long hair falling to her sides. The chief-king's head came to rest, precisely, facing her.

THIS WAS UNPLANNED.

Attempting to fall asleep during the previous night, teasing out every nuance in the next day's itinerary, Kull had played it out in his mind every conceivable potential scenario of "things going wrong." But he hadn't figured on this.

But the girl was surprisingly calm. She even gazed up at Kull with a slight trace of a smile on her lips.

Kull didn't waste time waiting for the favorable mood to swing against him. He rushed to the foot of the dais, gathered the girl in his arms, and embraced her. The girl smiled back at him.

The troll-men seemed to hesitate. They were not accustomed to acting without receiving orders first, and that's exactly what Kull had planned on.

The longer they hesitated, the longer they did not move, the safer he would be.

But in all Kull's shrewd machinations and careful planning, he had overlooked one thing. Stoolie. Before Kull had struck the chief-king across the face, Stoolie had descended from the dais, and so as to not arouse suspicion, he was mingling with the troll-men.

At the first sign of violence, acting on instinct, a troll-man grabbed Stoolie from behind and ran his spear through his side.

Blindsided, Stoolie never had a chance to see his perpetrator. He didn't even have time to raise his arms in protest. Seconds later, Stoolie was laying on the ground in a pool of blood.

As quickly as Kull had realized what had happened he ran to where the crowd had formed around Stoolie's body. Kull rushed down and bound up Stoolie's wounds as well as he could. In spite of the massive amount of blood that had poured out of Stoolie's wound, Kull managed to stop the bleeding. Severely weakened, dazed and slipping into a state of shock, Stoolie managed to give Kull a faint smile. Otherwise they didn't exchange words. At that moment, Kull knew that the mood of the mob was fickle and it could move in a different direction.

As soon as possible, Kull returned to the side of the girl. He shouted in a voice that all could hear: "She's our leader."

Kull tried to whisper a word into the girl's ear, but she placed her index finger to his lips.

The girl turned to the troll-men. She intoned in a powerful voice, "You're my people. I'll stay with you. I'll guide you." And then she curtsied.

The girl's words had ten times the effect of Kull's words. The troll-men moved forward, showing their willingness to follow her. When the girl gently commanded them to back away, they all seated themselves on their haunches, hugging their knees, weeping and sniffling on one another's shoulders, huddled together in one sobbing mass.

Kull turned to the troll-men: "You've heard your queen speak. I ask you this. Will you take care of her?"

The troll-men nodded enthusiastically. A couple of them stood up, standing upright with a bold, newfound dignity, but the rest remained sitting on the ground, cowering.

"I have two pieces of advice," Kull shouted. "First, when you work, always pull together, especially when you're in an emergency situation. Second, please learn how to groom each other."

The troll-men stared.

"Understand your chief-king is no more!" Kull proclaimed. "The cause for your fear is no more. You don't have to obey the dictator anymore."

Kull could see that whether the troll-men listened or not, they were inclined to hear what he had to say only so long as their Goddess was at his side, smiling approvingly. In fact, it was only for that reason that they bothered to listen to Kull at all. The Goddess had effectively saved his life and here he was mouthing off as if he were now their new boss-man.

The girl turned to Kull and said: "Would you please shut up, already. You don't know when to stop, do you? You're on the verge of ruining everything!"

There was a long pause. Kull was flabbergasted. He didn't know how to reply. He just stared at the girl.

"Well, don't look at me like I've announced my pregnancy. We'll give you your boat, so you can leave this place," the girl said. "You can take Stoolie with you. I doubt you'll be able to, though. He looks like a goner."

Kull said, "Are you sure?"

The girl whispered into Kull's ear, "Stoolie would have risked everything to escape. *Everything*. He stored great faith in you. You did the right thing."

"They know," the girl continued, "that they can only grow up to be mutated monsters—*and that's the best thing they can ever hope for in this life!* In this, they reflect the natural order of things. Their world is one of barbarism and horror. They will be forever lost souls, half-men, condemned. I'll be the girl who kept them from wading into a worse sinkhole of filth—kept them from sliding into a worse state of depravity. At least, I hope so. LOOK AT YOU! Your mouth's agape. Cat got your tongue? Shocked to discover I am not slow in speech? What is that? That I can act? You bet I can act. I can give a performance of a lifetime. Watch me! You haven't seen anything. For someone who could have been devoured several times over, I concocted a pretty good set-up for myself, haven't I? How did I do that? By acting stupid—far more stupider than I am. I acted like a drooling idiot. Does that make me one? When I first arrived, I was a half foot shorter than I should have been. That's how I fooled them. I'm at least six years older than these dullards thought I could have been. I'm at least four years older than Stoolie thought, and you thought too. Right? I didn't always have to clack my teeth to get your attention, now did I?" she added.

"And I came along?" Kull asked.

"Yes, and you came along." the girl nodded.

"Come with us," Kull said, speaking with animation.

"Go be captured by the Universal Gaia State and be sent to a slave colony, thank you, no. That's where I'd end up. *That's where you'll probably end up too.*"

"But there's also the pirates," Kull said.

"I'll have no part of that."

"But..." Kull began.

"Look at the outside world!" the girl interrupted. "Is there even a quarter of humanity left from before the Eleven-Year-War? The Gaia-Domes control everything, everything."

"But...?" Kull said.

"I know this place," the girl interrupted. "It's my home. Where else am I going to be treated like this. *Treated as someone special? Treated like a goddess?* Think about it."

Chapter Twenty

IN SPITE OF the Goddess's prediction, Stoolie wasn't a goner after all. Kull stitched Stoolie's wound back together. To do it, he rendered Stoolie unconscious by applying a sharp rap to his temple. Sixty stitches later, Kull managed to patch him up.

It took Stoolie two days to regain consciousness. Afterwards he suffered from dizzy spells, black-outs, and nose-bleeds. Stoolie remained permanently weakened by his near-fatal mishap, in fact, he never regained his previous strength. Kull was able to keep part of his bargain however: Stoolie did manage to survive.

So thirty-two days after the slaying of the old chief-king, the two of them pushed off from the beach in Kull's newly provisioned sailboat. There was little fanfare, only a low-key send-off from the troll-men and their new queen. Kull and Stoolie took as many plantains and other fruits as they could load, along with yams, two sacks of dried fish, grubs, two large sacks of manioc mash, tree bark and tree moss. They took the tree bark and the tree moss not because they had any intention of eating the indigestible stuff, but because it was offered with the other food. Singling out and rejecting particular offerings would have been impolite. It was Stoolie's idea. Stoolie still had a knack for thoughtfulness and diplomacy, even when he was extending it to his former abusers and tormentors.

On three occasions Kull offered to take the girl on the boat and drop her off anywhere she wished along the route of their voyage, but she pooh-poohed the idea.

"As far as I'm concerned," she said, "the mangrove forest is my home. This is where I belong. I am Goddess to the lost boys. And you wonder if there's progress? Already I've tried to persuade them to desist from indulging in cannibalism. Progress is slow, but already I've seen some positive changes. If that isn't progress, what is?"

The one thing Kull regretted was that the tribe could not see them off with a proper cheer. Kull would have loved to have heard the sound of their voices had they been able to speak. Kull was more than ready to set sail, in any event. So he was at least contented to have departed without a showy send-off.

Right from the start, Stoolie enjoyed sailing the open sea in an open boat. He liked the feel of salt spray on his face. Even though he suffered from abdominal cramps, retching sickness and fainting spells, he took to the sea. Moreover, unlike Kull, he was an able fisherman. He could fish even though he was handicapped by his amputated fingers.

Stoolie's secret was simple: He knew he was dying but he carried on as if he would live forever. He knew that he would never completely recover from his wounds—there was constant internal bleeding—it was just a matter of time before he would succumb.

Kull was happy and pleased to have Stoolie accompany him aboard his sailboat. An extra hand was helpful. Aside from Stoolie's constantly replenished catch of fresh fish, they could take turns at watch, and that was an even more important advantage, allowing them the luxury of eight hours of uninterrupted sleep each night. They were able to enjoy the company of each other during the re-maining eight hours of the day when one or the other wasn't sleeping. They took their meals together. Their partnership was convivial. But Kull knew that Stoolie was dying.

Stoolie shared with Kull all the news, gossip, and information he had absorbed about the greater world—right up to the time of his abduction by the troll-men. He told Kull everything he knew about the Universal Gaia State, filling in gaps that Clive had left unfilled. Stoolie had served many years as a man-servant to a Gaian Brigadier General and had traveled extensively. He knew a lot about the geography of the Gaian Empire, including that which pertained to the region of Central America and Mexico.

Stoolie told Kull that the best place for him to hide was in the region south of the Forbidden Zone, the isolated mountainous region of Central Mexico. It was his own pet theory. "*If I wanted to be free, that's where I'd go,*" Stoolie offered.

Kull thought that the plan was a good one. It appealed to his inner strivings. The idea of living alone a few hundred miles south of the Forbidden Zone appealed to Kull's instincts for ascetic beauty and bare-bones simplicity. It also fit in nicely with his yearning for solitude.

Before reaching the Yucatan Peninsula, near the line where the western boundary of the Caribbean Sea meets the eastern boundary of the Gulf of Mexico, Stoolie came down with a fever. A day and a half later, Stoolie's temperature rose. The burning grew worse and worse.

The fever's intensity increased. Near the end, there was a blood-curdling scream. Without warning, Stoolie jerked his head. His face was taut. Blood gushed from his mouth, not from the side—a wound which had *externally* healed. Apparently suffering from long-term damage to his internal organs, it all imploded inside as his fever shot up even higher and he died shortly afterward.

Chapter Twenty-One

AFTER BURYING STOOLIE AT SEA, weighing his body down with ballast rocks, Kull sailed his little craft around the peninsula of Yucatan into the calm waters of the Gulf of Mexico. The last leg of the voyage took less than a week to complete. Kull decided that he would pull out all the stops and risk detection in the little traveled coastal waters of the Gulf of Mexico. He put the boat on auto-pilot by immobilizing the tiller. Now that he was alone, he slept in three or four hour stints every twelve hours, instead of the forty-five minute catnaps to which he had restricted himself on the voyage across the Atlantic. It was a riskier mode of travel, because it made him vulnerable to patrol boats while sleeping, but it made him more alert when he was awake. Kull decided not to go into that murky, twilight mental-clime that had afflicted him during the earlier leg of his voyage.

As soon as Stoolie had come on board, Kull had secretly thrown his anti-UV-B radiation gear overboard so that there would be no confrontation over its use. Nevertheless, Kull didn't take any unnecessary risks. For example, when the sun was out and strong, Kull always wore a large, floppy hat. But Kull realized that he couldn't completely protect himself from all the deadly rays of the sun, so he tried to stay below deck as much as possible.

Kull landed on a long thin island. He knew he was close to the southern border of the Forbidden Zone. He decided to explore ashore before traveling any farther north.

After landing, Kull abandoned his boat. He crossed the sandy spit of the hump of the island to the sheltered shallow bay on the other side. There he swam two miles over the becalmed waters, towing an inflatable sack carrying his water-tight provisions.

After arriving on the farther shore, he headed inland with nothing more than the contents of his sack: a small, efficient, light-weight laser gun, several knives, several gallon-size gourds of potable water, a ten-pound package of dried manioc, and a single extra set of clothing.

He traveled inland, walking mostly during the night, in order to beat the heat and also to avoid unnecessary exposure to the sun.

He crossed two rivers, one small, the other large. The climate temperature was steady—staying around 90 degrees Fahrenheit.

Several months passed. Kull worked his way farther into the interior, crossing several valleys and bridging a broad plateau. It was at this point that he ran into a ragtag band. It was by-all-evidence an armed-to-the-teeth guerrilla band. The group was located along the southern flank of a river.

The group of approximately one hundred were bivouacked at the end of a hair-pin bend of the river. Thin threads of smoke curled up from their campfires as they were just in the process of extinguishing them.

They were just starting to break camp. The scene was most remarkable because the troopers were accompanied by about one hundred sturdy-looking horses. The horses had tattered Universal Gaia State emblems and Universal Gaia State blankets under their saddles, so Kull surmised they had been recently captured.

Kull could tell they had picked a perfect campsite—from the point of view of defense. The group's position could easily be defended from assaults coming from any direction, from upstream or downstream where the river narrowed into a gorge at either end, and also from attacks coming cross-country from north or south, as long as they kept sentries posted on the cliffs overhanging both sides of the river.

A lone individual, without mount and traveling light, just as Kull was doing, for example, might have been able to come within sight of the camp—but several individuals, or a small group of hostile army scouts, would have been detected.

Kull could tell by examining how these men had laid out their camp that they were experienced, battle-hardened troops, accustomed to being on the move, striking fast, breaking away, dissolving, then reconstituting themselves later.

Although Kull wasn't sure, his intuition told him that they were remnants of what had once been a larger army, an army that had seen better days, an army that had fought successful campaigns and could lay claim to having won a number of battles, an army that had, alas, been decimated, slowly—so slowly, whittled down, over years. They, and perhaps other groups like them, were all that was left of what had once been a full-fledged and, perhaps at one time, a fairly formidable army.

Drawing on a hasty and simple visual observation of the dismantling of an irregular army camp, how did Kull *know this?* He had had no experience in military affairs in his personal past, yet all the same, Kull knew instinctively that his judgment of the guerrilla band had been sound. He had read much about the art and nature of warfare *in books*. Clive had taught him some practical things on the subject as well.

Kull decided that if the group was willing to accept him, he'd join it. He decided that he could learn more about the climate and the terrain of this new land—but more importantly, the dangers and potential hazards, by joining. By acquiring knowledge from the group's experience, he could get his bearings and solid footing before he struck out on his own. The band welcomed him.

In the bargain, Kull learned to be an efficient warrior. To be fair, he never actually learned how to beat the numerically superior, technically more proficient adversarial Universal Gaia State military machine, but he learned how to outfox it, get around it, thus denying the enemy the fruits of their own operations. (From beginning to end, evasion and tactical retreat were the principle tools in his survival kit.)

Kull could have made himself a leader of the guerilla group, he was that good (he was talented, charismatic and capable). Others in the group looked up to him as a leader. But he had no overriding ambition in the direction of leadership. Besides, for the guerilla band's successes—and there were successes, Kull instinctively knew that it was only a matter of time before the guerilla band would be annihilated, even if with luck they managed to survive for another few years.

All Kull's passion and willingness to believe in a good cause could not prevent him from seeing the reality with complete clarity. The Universal Gaia State military machine hadn't finished them off yet only because they represented merely a sporadic nuisance rather than a genuine security threat.

Potentially, a brilliant and great guerilla warfare chieftain Kull could have been, but only if the goals of the guerilla warfare were of a more lofty and elevated nature. When desperate and hard-pressed, the group, albeit only on rare occasions, stole from others, even when the "others," i.e., peasants—were in greater need than themselves. (To their greater distinction and credit, however, the guerilla band defended the peasants against the predations of the Universal State Gaian army on occasions, too.)

If he had pursued his true calling of striking out on his own, Kull might have left the group at an earlier date. But instead, he perfected his skills at hunting, foraging, and "hiding out," while he bid his time.

But where was he going to escape to? The answer came in the form of a visit from an outsider who was nevertheless familiar with his group—a woman doctor. Because of the affiliations with previous Anti-Universal Gaia State activities, the woman doctor made her rounds to the group—to provide needed and highly-valued medical assistance. She visited the group about once every three years.

▶▶▶▶

The doctor, middle-aged, was experienced. She clearly had an understanding of the world that went well beyond the confines of the group. Her knowledge of conditions that were local was impeccable, but what was more striking to Kull was her grasp and understanding of events that occurred much farther away, even planet-wide.

She stayed with the guerilla band for a couple of months, rendering medical treatment. During that time, she had some extensive conversations with Kull. After the doctor got to know Kull better, she revealed to him, in the strictest of confidences, there was a place that would fit the existence of a loner, such as Kull. All he had to do, she said, was find a cave in a mountain.

When the doctor explained to Kull in only vague terms where the mountain was located, she insisted that the adventure upon entering the region would be filled with risk. But if a person was able to find the cave, then that person would be set for life, being able to live a life in a state of autonomy and freedom. When Kull pressed the good doctor to explain why others had described the region as dangerous, especially from the point of view of finding water, the woman confided, "Don't worry. Mind you, trying to find water in that region and establishing a habitable cave are both goals that would be difficult to achieve. Even for the courageous, the odds are tough. One-in-three? One-in-four? But if you were able to succeed, *what a life...* For one thing, you would be able to stay clear of the company of this bunch forever, and believe me, this group is living on borrowed time. I've had twenty-five years experience of what the Gaia-Domes military machine can do when they get their dander up, and believe me, they will, in the fullness of time, swat this troublesome fly that is an itch on their back."

Kull began to speak, but the doctor shushed him.

"I implore you to hold a counsel of secrecy on this. If you were to tell others what I've told you, you'll only encourage them to do the same. That would only diminish your own chances for success."

Strangely, Kull noted that through the course of their conversations, the woman had never revealed her name.

When Kull said to her, "Oh well," he was leaning toward following the proposition of heading out toward the cave in the mountain, she smiled deeply.

When two weeks later he told her that his convictions were waxing ever more firmly, she then decided to take Kull into even greater confidence.

The doctor told Kull the story about September Snow and Regis Snow. She told Kull everything she knew about the Anti-Gaia rebellion, its origins, antecedents, history, successes and failures. She told him about the attack on the nuclear-powered wind machines that occurred at the island of St. Helena. She told him about how successful the rebel forces had been in disrupting and eventually destroying the nuclear-powered wind machine structures on a global scale, but also how the attack had been a suicide attack, and how all those who had participated had died, thus rendering the future prospects for the rebellion thereafter a moot point. The success of the attacks had rendered the movement of the Earth's climate warping back toward a more positive generation and amelioration, even if the entire culmination of the process would take decades, perhaps even centuries, to occur.

Kull said to the doctor, "I'm from St. Helena."

"I know," the doctor replied. "I've known all along. You were a slave there once too. Yes, you have the mark of a slave, but *in other ways*...you're not *quite*...a slave. You're strange. You have a certain way of talking, an accent, that's a giveaway for the South Atlantic. I guess it to be more precisely a St. Helena sub-patois. Where did you come from? At one time, there were many platform rigs off the island of St. Helena."

In an uncertain tone, Kull asked, "In what way, well, as you said, am I strange?"

"You're a hybrid," the woman doctor said. "That's what I meant by you being strange."

"A hybrid?"

"Yes," the woman doctor said. Kull detected an indication of marvel in the lilt of the woman's voice, as if she had made an important discovery. "You're a hybrid. Hybrids are extremely rare. You have a certain education. No slave, not even a personal body servant slave for the highest grandmagister would have acquired an education such as you have. Even when you hide your education, it shows through. You were placed under the wing of somebody high up in the system, high up in the Universal State Gaia system, maybe a magister, or, at least, a sub-magister. This person taught you things that were forbidden by the official Universal Gaia State faith. You were exposed to dangerous ideas...*forbidden tomes...censored books...subversive writings that could have resulted in your execution*. My guess it that you were given a thorough grounding in the classics. Your case is not the only one in the world where this has occurred but, to be frank, there are few instances. In your case, in order for that to have happened, even though you had been a slave, this Gaia official must have cared for you, been fond of you, perhaps even *loved* you. This part of my theory is the part that is inexplicable to me."

The doctor's speculation brought out the confessional in Kull. He confessed to her details of his background. He told her about St. Helena and the sub-magister Clive. He talked about his early childhood. He spoke about all the things he did to survive, not excluding the more disagreeable details. He spoke about being raised by Clive. He spoke about the forbidden books in Clive's secret library and how he devoured them. He spoke about how Clive had taken him in, as if he were his own son, eventually treating him as if he were a substitute for his lost son. He spoke about the boat and the solo journey across the ocean.

"You must have departed just before all the installations on the island of St. Helena were destroyed by September Snow," the doctor said. "You must be marked for something special in this world. How else do you explain the timing of your salvation? You realize that IF the Gaia-Domes were looking for you, all they had to do was use their radar. The fact that the wind machines on St. Helena had been destroyed—a week or two after your departure—everyone perished in the attack, of course—the Gaia-Domes would have had no reason to be searching for you. They would have concluded that you must have died at the time of the attack with all the others. On the high seas, all you had to do was keep away from them. You're a lucky man."

"It also explains why there has been some subtle, but vital, changes in the weather—*already*," Kull said, grasping a further point. "You know, we've noticed some of these changes."

The woman doctor's expression was noncommittal. "The destruction of the climate-changing wind machines on St. Helena was a success, the biggest success of the Anti-Gaia rebellion. September Snow and Regis Snow were not originally anti-Gaia. More exactly, they were *anti*-Universal Gaia State. They were followers of Gaia... strange...it was only after the true spirituality of Gaia had been hijacked and corrupted by the Universal Gaia State that the Snows became known as 'Anti-Gaia' rebels. It seems so long ago, but it wasn't. September and Regis were the true followers of Gaia—the Gaia that existed long before the Universal Gaia State had a chance to consolidate its power. Confused? I bet you are. It's still going to take a long time before all the beneficial changes occur—weather-wise."

Kull spoke about his adventures during his journey on the boat. He spoke about the radiated zone along the swampy part of the South American coast. He spoke about the mutant boys and the mutant chief-king and the Goddess. In the end, he tore open his shirt and exposed the horrible scars on his back. "You're right, I'm a slave," Kull said.

After regarding the scars, the doctor tried to comfort Kull. In a soothing voice, she said, "By the time you were under the protection of Clive, and in his care, Regis Snow, had already been executed for treason by the Universal Gaia State, right?"

"Yes, before I came under Clive's care," Kull said. "Let me see if I can put together the sequence of events. So I learned about it under Clive's care. Clive told me what happened to Regis Snow, and how he tragically met his fate. Just before that time, the harbormaster got into trouble for allowing the daughter of Regis Snow to escape. The girl was only three-and-a-half years old. She apparently made her escape through the aid of pirates. I don't know how he did it, but Clive somehow managed to protect the harbormaster from his accusers. That's how Clive was able to get a sailboat for me. I used the vessel to escape from St. Helena. That's how it happened."

"So Regis was still alive when you were young and a slave. On the platform rig."

"Yes," Kull said.

"I see everything clearly now," the woman doctor whispered. "Go seek out the cave in the mountain. You'll find something there that'll surprise you. *You'll find it there.* A hybrid fauna."

"A *what?*"

"A hybrid fauna...that is a rarity...like you are," she said. "Don't be hasty. Your journey must be carefully prepared and well planned. Wait at least eight weeks before you depart." Her lips were pursed. Then her face broke into a broad grin.

Chapter Twenty-Two

HAVING TAKEN the woman doctor's advice Kull waited eight weeks. Then, when no one in the guerilla camp was looking, in the middle of the night, Kull slipped away.

In search of the mountains (where there were reputed to have been caves, but no water), on the edge of the desert, thirty-five miles south of the Forbidden Zone, Kull traveled west.

The region was different from anything he had experienced before. Several mountains loomed before him. As he came to the foothills of these mountains, there was no evidence of water!

During the last fifty miles of Kull's journey, his movements were monitored and tracked even though he had no idea he was being shadowed.

Kull was alive only because Iona and not another had been following him.

He was the first person she had ever allowed to stay alive, within twenty-five miles of her cave.

Iona had been in her place for five years, guarding the cave as its only occupant from the age of thirteen-and-one-half, when she arrived.

Kull was not the first to intrude upon Iona's territorial space. There had been other incidents of intrusion. Of those cases, most attempts had been made by groups of ten individuals or more, and most of the time, they packed up and turned back when they couldn't find enough water to live on. The individual intruders who obviously weren't going to leave of their own had to be scared off. When that failed, as it did in one case, Iona finally had to kill the intruder. She terminated him through the use of her bow and arrows. But Kull was the first intruder who was within six years of her age, who by her perception she did not deem as being an enemy, who obviously was not a cannibal, and more importantly, was not a military spy or assassin sent out by the Universal Gaia State. (The woman doctor had warned her about those types and to be on her guard, many years before.)

The reason Iona knew these things was that only two weeks earlier, she had received a strange communication from the woman doctor. It had been the first communication Iona had ever received from her, ever since she had been deposited at the foot of the mountain, five years before. The gist of the message contained a brief description of Kull and said he might be coming. If he came, Iona was ordered not to kill him but the message was more than clear on one point: Iona was to make doubly certain it was him and not someone else, before she welcomed him.

After two days of following Kull, and observing him carefully, Iona decided she would allow him to live because she had become convinced he might have been the one the woman doctor had described. She decided she would give him a chance to prove himself.

Although Kull may have fought with the guerillas (Iona was such a loner that she was even suspicious of them), Iona could tell that Kull had not been bred to be of their breed. He didn't have the demeanor—nor the attitude—of a guerilla warrior.

On a day of her stealth-like shadowing of Kull, Iona dressed herself up in animal skins and applied war-paint to her face, arms and legs, utilizing the provocative color of bright cobalt blue. By doing this, she deliberately wanted to stand out and acquire the intruder's attention.

Hitherto, Iona had blended into the scenery so successfully Kull had not noticed her.

Descending from a ridge, Iona suddenly darted out in front of Kull, blocking his path.

Kull stood still in his tracks.

Iona had her blonde-brown hair pulled back tight. With her bow pulled back tautly, Iona had an arrow aimed at Kull's heart. He took a deep breath, allowing himself just enough time for his fear not to turn into panic.

"If you had traveled by night," Iona said, "you might have eluded me. At least for a night or two. But no, you traveled by day. I've been shadowing you for three days. Are you not afraid of contracting sun death? LOOK AT WHAT YOU'RE WEARING! ARE YOU CRAZY!"

"You speak," Kull said in a calm voice. To Kull, the young woman looked like a savage if not an outright cannibal, which made the words coming out of her mouth seem all the more incongruous.

"I wear a hat when necessary," Kull said. "Not today. I ordinarily wear face protection. But again, not today. Why are you so interested, anyway?"

Getting over his initial shock, Kull didn't give any evidence of being perturbed.

"Even a hat and face mask won't save you in the long run," Iona said. She had not relaxed her grip on her bowstring. Her bowstring was still pulled back. If released, the arrow would have instantly pierced Kull's heart.

Kull whistled. "This is my plan. I'll travel a few days in the sun... then...with an enormous amount of luck...I'd stumble upon a hidden cave. *Voila! Salvation!*"

"You think you'd find a cave? What extraordinary chances you're willing to take."

"Well," Kull said, "this much I know. You're not going to kill me. Or at least, something has stopped you."

With showy display and without prompting, Kull voluntarily disarmed himself. Carefully holding the gun upside down by the butt, he threw the weapon—a standard Gaia military issue laser gun—fifteen paces away. Kull decided to place his fate in the young woman's hands. "There. You see. You've disarmed me."

Iona dropped her bow, simultaneously releasing the spring of her bowstring. But she kept the arrow in place. "Step farther away from your weapon," she ordered.

Kull complied by taking several steps further from his discarded weapon.

"Boy, you distrust me," Kull said. "And come to think about it, what are you? Of course you are made up to look like a savage, but only to fool me. You'd *frighten* a cannibal, upon my word! You look like you'd frighten a Gaia-Dome assassin. Do you have any idea what you look like?"

"Why do you think I'm not a cannibal?"

"Because you're too elegant in your speech," Kull said. "You can express yourself. Cannibals tend to be a taciturn bunch."

"What should I have done to convince you I was a cannibal?" The color of bright blue on Iona's face, arms and legs glinted in the sun. She raised and drew the bow back again—so that the arrow was primed and was once again aimed at Kull's heart.

"I DON'T KNOW!" Kull screamed. "Grimace. Emit a guttural sound. Gnash your teeth."

"What would I do to convince you I was a Gaia-Dome assassin?"

"Kill me."

"What?"

"Blind side me. Death out of nowhere."

"Are you not afraid of death, intruder?"

"Death will come," Kull said, "whenever it chooses to. Fear has nothing to do with it."

Iona was intrigued but she remained uncertain if courage lurked behind the facade of bravado. She slung the bow over her shoulder, snapping the string and then strapping it to her back. Iona walked around to stand behind Kull. She tied his hands behind his back and blindfolded him.

*This seemed odd, Kull thought, to be blindfolded and bound, but he
accepted the treatment voluntarily.*

Iona ordered Kull to march, but as she did he continued his
one-sided conversation.

"It's no mystery, you know," Kull said smiling. "A bit of knowledge can go a long way. Caves. All of them are inadequate for human
habitation. But there's water. In crannies. Bits. But only hill-lets of
barren rock and earth? Nonsense! Without any apparent appearance
of surface water? That's a mystery! You live in a cave. This place has
caves...that's my best guess."

"Be *still*, will you?" Iona asked.

"Small caves, not big enough for a man, but big enough for a
mouse," Kull said. "But you found one that was big enough for you.
You know how to conserve water. But even then, you had to have another trick up your sleeve. There's still not enough water! That's what
has kept others out. You have devised a special scheme. What is it?"

"Oh, please, be still," Iona said.

"Even if you hadn't stopped me, I wouldn't have found a cave.
I would have searched, but to no effect. Then you would have been
done with me. All you'd have to do, was wait it out. You only needed
patience. Eventually, I'd give up. I'd depart. You'd have won."

"You talk too much."

"I talk too much?" Kull asked laughing. "If it wasn't for me
making conversation, I'd be dead!"

"Be still. Are you even capable of being quiet?"

"You say you've been following me for what?" Kull said. "Three
days? Then you ask me if I was concerned about me getting sun
death because of too much exposure to the sun?"

"Yeah? So?"

"You don't ask questions like that and then kill a person. Unless
you plan to kill them by asking questions."

Iona grimaced at Kull's sarcastic remark. "It wasn't your conversation that stopped me."

"Then what did?"

"I didn't think you were—how do I explain it—bad."

"Not *bad*," Tom asked, not believing what his ears were hearing. "While observing me, you've drawn a conclusion about my character? By observing me? By observing my movements? Is that how it works?"

"Because you want to be alone," Iona said. "It's written all over you. You also value living things."

"Because I want to be alone? And I value living things. What the hell are you talking about? By watching me, you've come to a certain conclusion? I'm not bad. Oh, I forgot, I also want solitude."

"I'm perfectly capable of thinking any way I choose," Iona said.

"If I'm not a bad person," Kull said, "why am I blindfolded then. Answer me that?"

Iona had to think for a moment before she was able to reply. "Because I need to be cautious. There's still one more test I must give you."

"She needs to be cautious so I have to be blindfolded," Kull said, stumbling for a moment as he stepped on an uneven rock on the path. "Now I see perfectly."

Resting now and then, during the course of a long day's journey, they managed to walk eight miles. As they traversed, with his eyes bound, Kull could see nothing but dim shades, or when he looked up, a vaguely growing blot of redness where the arcing sun would be. However, he could sense they were walking uphill. They walked in sunlight but also in shade. But that could only have meant that they were traveling under a canopy of towering walls of blasted rocks. He could feel the coolness of the shade yet even while blindfolded. They climbed to a higher elevation where overhanging rocks provided even more coolness. Kull could only guess what kind of terrain they were passing through—but he knew that they—in a roundabout way, were scaling a fairly steep mountainside, though at times the path seemed to wind between uprights and pinnacles.

"How high up is this mountain that we're climbing?" Kull then asked.

"High."

"How high are we going?"

"A ways up."

"Is it much farther?"

"Shut up," Iona said. To acquire some simple peace of mind, the thought of killing Kull momentarily crossed Iona's mind. Instead she untied Kull's hands, but she left the blindfold on.

After another twenty minutes, and during that time traveling in complete sunlight—without benefit of shade, Kull felt a sudden coolness. Then they had to crawl on their hands and knees for two minutes, a difficult crawl, at two points there were portals that were only four or five inches larger than the width of Kull's midsection—he could only squeeze through. Eventually Kull realized—even with the blindfold on—he was now in an apparent state of total darkness.

Still on hands and knees, but no longer slivering like snakes on their bellies, the two stopped all movement. Iona ordered Kull to stand upright. He complied. He discovered there was plenty of space for him to stand upright.

The air felt cool.

Iona untied the blindfold from the back of Kull's head. At first, there was total darkness. Iona lit a candle. Then she walked about in a large circle in what seemed to be an ideally shaped cavernous space, using one lit candle to light other candles that were located in little notches in the walls, at sixteen—more or less—equally distant, different points. After lighting the last candle, the enclosed space took on the look of a flat-bottomed sphere.

Having completed the task of lighting the candles, and the candles coming to full strength, Kull was able to see the room in its totality with a shimmering magnificence. Most of the floor was rough-stoned, as if lined by flagstones, and the ceiling was twenty-feet high, although in one place, nearly sixty-feet high. This part of the orifice seemed to form a tapered, narrowing flume that reached to the very top of the cave.

Iona showed him other adjacent smaller rooms, some rooms

holding simple clothes, primitive footwear, handmade tunics, tiny sacks of corn, squash and beans, peppers drying (though not very effectively, as peppers needed to dry in the sun), tufts of cotton and unfinished pieces of homespun. In one room was an assortment of wild plants. The plants were divided evenly. One group constituted wild plants that were edible, another group constituted plants that were medicinal in nature. Kull could see that Iona had gathered these plants with great care, some from the desert floor, some from the mountains, a few gathered from a distance away, including one or two from as far away as the sea, perhaps.

"In order for us to survive into the future," Iona said, "we must be as proficient at foraging as our ancestors were ten thousand years ago. Perhaps we need to get more proficient at foraging than our ancient ancestors were. It can feed us. It can cure us from what ails us. But if we manage to do the foraging at night! Consider that! That may be the way we beat the Gaia-Domes. You know, something to be thinking about."

Kull took this unusual direction of conversation as a further encouraging sign that Iona had no intention of killing him.

The sub-rooms took on the shape more of alcoves—altogether forming one large cavern. So that Kull could get the total effect, Iona provided even more light by lighting even more candles.

Though Kull had seen caves on the island of St. Helena before, they had been nothing like this. This was the most beautiful cave he had ever seen.

Fed by a spring located higher up in the mountain, there was a tiny rivelet, not more than three inches wide, that trickled through a tiny funnel-like indenture in the curvature of the rocks, running through the bottom of the cave.

Kull turned to Iona. "This must be the safest place around. If I had searched for a hundred years, I'd never find it! Not in a million years."

Kull looked at the cave with amazement. "You realize that with the damage done to the ozone layer, with the exception of the Gaia-Domes, this is as perfect a place as one could find to keep oneself safe. This cave is in fact safer than being inside the Domes *because here, for goodness sakes, you're free!* On top of that, the cave has the greatest defense against any possible intrusion!"

Kull stood before Iona in a state of astonishment. "How did you find it?"

"I didn't," Iona replied.

"You didn't?"

"I didn't find it," Iona said. "It was found for me."

"Found for you?" Kull asked. "How so? I don't get it. Explain."

"It was found for me by my parents."

"Found for you by your parents?" Kull asked. "Quit talking in riddles."

"True, it was found for me," Iona said. "It's a natural cave. But parts were added on, fashioned by human hand, enhancing what was already there, to make it more inhabitable. This happened back in the olden days. *Back at the time of the end of the Eleven-Years-War, and at the time of the beginning of the rebellion against the Gaia-Domes, before I was born.* If you're wondering why I have so many candles, when I first arrived, I found them stored away in some old rusty crates, protected inside by water-proof packs."

Iona stopped for a moment. "Would you please remove your shirt, please."

"What?" Kull asked.

"Take your shirt off," Iona said. "Please."

"What?"

"Don't object," Iona ordered. "Do as I say."

At first Kull was reluctant to comply. Iona grabbed her bow. She grabbed an arrow and placed it on her bowstring and drew it back and pointed it at him. It was all done in one smooth movement, all done with incredible speed. "Do it or I'll kill you," Iona yelled.

Kull flinched. He chuckled to himself but it was a chuckle reeking of false courage. He slowly removed his shirt. Iona asked him to turn around so he could display his back. Self-consciously, Kull did as he was bid.

Holding a candle next to Kull's skin, Iona observed the crisscross of scars that was the result of healed-over wounds that were clearly caused by the application of lash-strokes. The scars ran from the top of Kull's back to the bottom. Some of the scars were fairly straight, others were crooked, but all of them were fairly deep. Iona ran her fingers over the ridged edges of the deepest scars. When Iona counted over a dozen, she stopped counting them.

"I'm sorry," Kull said. He tried not to show his humiliation. "I am an ex-slave from the island of St. Helena. I have traveled thousands of miles to get here. I've worked hard, taught myself, prepared myself... You should have *killed* me. By logic, by the dictates of common sense, you should have finished me off. If I were you—in your shoes—I'd have killed instantly. I wouldn't have hesitated. Why am I being allowed to live? You shouldn't have to compromise your safety, by showing me this special place." Kull looked down, feeling low. He was in a state of abject wretchedness. "Receiving those lashes, that was a terrible thing, it took me a long time to get over it. But there are deeper cuts—invisible cuts that are deeper inside me— and those have not healed."

Iona withdrew her bow and arrow. Iona's face broke out into a broad display of hilarity and smiles. She stepped up to Kull and placed her index finger to his lips, making a sideways, wiggling gesture with her finger, as if to suggest he should remain silent for a change.

"It's time we sort things out," Iona said. Then she went into some detail discussing her background. She covered a lot of ground. At the end, she added, "You should not be ashamed of your wounds, Kull—the ones on your back, or the ones invisible inside you—rather, you should be proud of them. *I know who you are. In fact, I've been half-expecting you!*"

"The woman doctor!" Kull exclaimed, shaking his head. "I get it. How grand! There was no talk of the cave being occupied by a young girl. Oh no. 'OCCUPIED BY NO ONE!' I remember the woman doctor's words. When I think of it. Steering me in this direction. So clever. A mysterious cave, located in a mountain, where I could find myself. A place where I'd be alone. I'd be in solitude. I'd be able to experience peace and autonomy and freedom. All lies."

"What did that woman say to you?" Iona asked. "What were her exact words? Try to remember. What did she say that you would find here?" Iona laughed. "A fauna, right? A rare one? A special hybrid?"

Iona could see that there was no point in threatening Kull with her bow and arrow any more.

The awkward shyness of their first meeting, each more enchanted with each other than they dared to reveal, flowed more naturally after they surmounted the worst barriers of their fears.

Chapter Twenty-Three

I ONA MADE KULL FEEL AT HOME. She gave him a grand tour of her cave, acquainted Kull with her defense systems that radiated out from the cave itself and then radiated out from the mountain. The defense systems, reaching out as far as eight miles in the least accessible direction, twenty-five miles in the secondarily accessible direction, and up to one hundred miles in the one direction that people most likely would try to approach the mountain—*the sensible approach,* were simple but of a peculiar kind. To the untrained eye, they were undetectable. (The defense was not a barrier, a reef, a wall, humanly constructed to keep others out, but foliage, rocks, leaves, loose dirt, sand—natural things—placed in such a way that no one could pass over an area without disturbing the ground, thereby making their presence known.)

Iona explained her strategy. "Blend into the environment so you are invisible. Your farming implements? Invisible. Your produce? Invisible. All your possessions? Invisible. Your water? Invisible. Your home? Invisible. You? Invisible. You blend into the environment so you don't exist. If everything that you have does not exist, what is there to defend? *You don't exist.*"

Iona also showed Kull her elaborate system of food procurement, production, and storage, and the ways in which she so effectively hid them. Tiny patches of corn planted only in box canyons. Other plants, namely manioc, squash, tomato, sorghum, onions, planted in hiding places. All of the food and the simple tools were always stored in the cave. *Always the water, always the water, stored in the cave...*

Iona showed him her elaborate system of gathering water—and her even more elaborate system for storing the water after it had been gathered. This was of vital importance for long-term survival.

"Here in the desert," Iona said, "we get a very heavy downpour, but only once a year, or even only once every two years. Even then, it's a very sudden downpour only at the highest elevation of the mountain."

Iona then took Kull to see the cistern. Inside the cave where the seepage ran into a tiny spring at the bottom of which was a large cistern, carved into the rock by the force of human hands.

"It's very dodgy, you see," Iona said. "The cave floods, or at least semi-floods, soon after a big storm. So I have to get myself and my possessions out just before the storm hits. That's one reason why I live such a Spartan existence here. I can only keep those things that are essential. The cave was prepared twenty-five years ago by people sent out by my father. I was told he set up a few safe spots at remote and isolated places in the world. This is the last one that is still hidden and also functional. They hewed the cistern out of the rock, so that when the rain falls, the run-off fills it—up to fifteen feet deep. It provides me with enough water for up to twenty months. This is why I am able to survive, no matter what happens to the weather. Because the climate is changing for the better, it is not as necessary now, and it will continue to become less necessary, but for the first three and a half years of my life here, it saved my life. Without this cistern, life would be impossible."

"That was a lot of work, carving a large cistern out of stone," Kull said.

"They had also widened the aperture of the cave opening in two places where the passage was too narrow," Iona said, "so that I could crawl through. Before they had done so, there were places where the cave opening was too small even for an adolescent child. All of this had been prepared for me in advance, of course, and it had all been done with extreme care and secrecy. They used penetrating radar, sensory detectors—sophisticated instruments—along with a lot of muscle."

Only after Iona had given Kull an opportunity to thoroughly understand the practical and operational aspects of her cave system did she allow him to ask the more obvious question: Why had she accepted him into her home?

"You had been described to me in brief. I only had to check your back—to see the scars. Then I knew for sure that you were the one I was expecting."

"If the woman doctor gave you the message of my arrival," Kull said. "why didn't she take the time to explain everything so that there wouldn't have had to be this useless game of charades. Answer me that. She put me up to this, didn't she? Oh, the mountain is the best place to be. The cave in the mountain is the best place to be autonomous. Freedom! Solitude! You'll love it! Now that I have a chance to look back, they were a pack of lies. Look at you! A rare and special hybrid fauna indeed!"

"Why are you so angry?" Iona asked. "Because you were deceived? You were deceived for your own good. You were deceived for my protection as well. The woman doctor has never set foot on the mountain herself. She had no idea where the cave was, just that it existed. If she was caught by the forces of Dome-Gaia army, she could have never given away my hiding place, even if she was tortured. When she communicated with me, it was only through smoke signals that were from twenty-five miles. *She couldn't explain everything clearly, unfortunately.*"

"Well, why didn't she tell me you were here?"

"No one is supposed to know I'm alive. As I explained earlier, when I was five and a half, my mother went to great lengths to fake my death. If the official Gaian authorities knew about me, they would have stopped at nothing to seek me out and kill me."

"Do you at least know what her name is?"

"Whose name?"

"The doctor's name!"

"No," Iona said. "No name. She's just the woman doctor."

"The bizarre extremes you people go to just to keep things secret," Kull said, shaking his head. "You guys are so secret you don't even know who you are—in relations with each other!"

"Who are we?" Iona said. "We are no longer a group. The woman doctor and I are the only ones, at least the only ones on the southern side of the Forbidden Zone, who survived after the collapse and destruction of September Snow's rebellion. There may be—or there may not be—remnants of the old rebellion on the northern side of the Forbidden Zone, but we don't know for sure."

"You mean to tell me the woman doctor communicated all this information and instructions to you with smoke signals?" Kull asked.

"Of course not," Iona said. "The smoke signals gave me instructions—and directions—on where to find a written note. That piece of paper was located in the exact spot where we had last seen each other five years before, twenty-five miles from here. What was written down in simple and crude code was information about your scarred back and the business about the metaphor of my being a rare and special hybrid fauna."

"So you can read and write?" Kull asked.

"Yes," Iona said. "Of course."

"Aside from Clive and the woman doctor, you're the first person I've met through all my travels who knows how to read and write. Have you read many books?"

"None," Iona said.

"None?" Kull asked. "How did you learn to read and write then?"

"As a child, I studied with a man. His named was Tom. He was good. He was also knowledgeable. It was as if—through him—or rather, through his *talking, that is*—I was supposed to acquire the wisdom of the ages. *Ideas of the recent times, books of the past.*"

"But without the paper of books, or paper and pen, how did you learn to read and write?"

"Tom scratched letters in the sand with a stick. After I learned to master the alphabet, he scratched words. After I mastered the words, we went on to higher levels of composition. Eventually, we were writing treatises back and forth to each other. In the sand, of course."

Iona handed Kull a piece of animal skin that Tom had given her just before she had left him to attempt to cross the Forbidden Zone.

On the animal skin, a message was written in a small hand: "All history is philosophy, and all philosophy is religion, all religion is literature, and all literature is art, all art is music, painting, dancing, and all music, painting, dancing are the heart, brain, hand of man and woman, through all of time."

Very quickly, and in a hasty, cursory fashion, Kull examined the skin, but spent a long time examining the lettering.

"This small scrap of animal skin, this is the only thing Tom wrote for you to keep?" Kull asked.

"Yes," Iona said.

"Interesting," Kull said. As he held the animal skin, he appeared lost in thought.

"In your travels, you must have visited some dark places," Iona said.

"Yes," Kull said. "But the truth is my childhood was the darkest place of all. There were horrible occurrences. People would do anything, sell their mother, slit the throat of their father, to save their own skin. The message—the philosophy—on Tom's skin says something that is the complete opposite of all that. It's a great message. It's truly wonderful. I wish I could meet and get to know the man who composed these words. What did you say his name was?"

"Tom," Iona replied.

"Just *Tom?*" Kull asked. "A man with a single name? Was he, by chance, a slave?"

"No," Iona said. "His name was Tom—Thomas—Novak. He wasn't a slave."

"So he raised you from a child—to be—to become, a woman?"

"Yes, he was like a father to me," Iona said. "After my own father had died, of course."

"He educated you?"

"Yes," Iona said. "After my mother September left, the two of us were alone in the desert for eight years. When otherwise not procuring food, I spent almost all of my time being taught by Tom Novak."

"Is Tom still alive?" Kull asked.

"Good question," Iona said. "If he is, he's extremely old. In his eighties. If they are not higher authorities in the Gaia-Domes—in the areas they administer—they don't allow anyone to live past the age of sixty. No one escapes. The Gaia-Dome magisters are ruthless in imposing their policy of euthanasia. They're strict. If Tom has fallen into their hands, under the Gaia-Dome's control, he'd be dead."

Kull closed his eyes and thought deeply.

"Are you willing to fight against the Gaia-Domes?" Iona asked.

"Why do you ask me that?" Kull said. "I hate the Gaia-Domes, that's for sure. They have enslaved the world. The message on the animal skin reminds me of something that I haven't thought about in a long time. Your Tom must have been an extraordinary person. It's only when I think of the slaves, not just the ones I left behind on St. Helena, but all the slaves—the slaves everywhere in the world— do I think of the need to fight the Gaia-Domes. But I just don't know for now."

"Hating the Gaia-Domes," Iona said, "that's a start." She smiled knowingly. "I think the rest will come."

Chapter Twenty Four

IONA AND KULL LIVED TOGETHER in their idyllic hide-away for five years. The outside world did not exist for them; in fact, there was no outside intrusion whatsoever.

The couple lived in a state of simplicity. Instead of rain just once a year and then in only a short burst, during those five years it rained three times a year, harder and for longer duration than in the previous years. The weather was changing, ever so slowly—but at least it was changing for the better. Just barely, but crops did grow. Over time the occasional crop failures were of shorter duration and occurred less frequently. In those hard times Iona and Kull were able to forage.

With boldness and imagination, they were also able to vary their crop rotations when there was precious water for use. They managed to include cotton along with their staples of corn, squash, and beans, and from this fiber production they were able to make new clothes. Over time, the terrain became slightly more verdant although, relatively speaking, it was still a harsh desert.

Iona and Kull knew that it would be far too risky to contemplate leaving their bubble of confinement. There were still threats from sun death. Dangerous and unhealthy cancer-causing UV-B radiation continued unabated. For even the toughest survivalist, with all the environmental damage that had been wreaked the outside world was still a grim and cruel place to live in. In addition, the Gaia-Domes ruled in other parts of the world with an iron fist.

For Iona and Kull, although life was not an Eden-like paradise, it was good. There could not have been a happier couple living in the world in the year 2081 (YEAR GAIA THIRTY). They could not imagine anyone living a life as *safe, isolated, and vigorous* as theirs. Their cave was more protected than any castle could have been (or any uber-modern Gaia-Dome in New York City). They had the limited range of land to roam without fear of molestation or detection— although they generally chose the nights, moon or no, to do their roaming. In light of the need to be protected from the baleful effects of UV-B radiation, Iona converted Kull into a nocturnal creature. But their greatest asset was that they had each other. For both of them, solitude became less a precious state of being. Little by little, Iona and Kull not only grew fond of each other, they fell in love.

Then, just as everything was going so well, the outside world intervened. In the third month of the sixth year of their existence together, when Kull was (only by estimation) twenty-nine-years-old and Iona was turning twenty-four, they were visited by the only visitor that there could have been, the only person who knew vaguely where they were located—and how they had been all those years so effectively hiding from the outside world.

The woman doctor had promised that she would never see Iona and Kull again. But she broke her promise. When she bumbled into their lives once more, she brought some urgent and significant news.

She sat cross-legged on the floor of Iona and Kull's cave and in spite of some misgivings about her visit, there were smiles all around.

"I thought you said you didn't know where the cave was located," Kull said. "Remember? Back at the guerilla camp? Remember what you told me then? How in the world did you find us?"

"I didn't," the woman doctor replied. "But I knew if I managed to get close enough to where you lived, one of you *might* find me. To facilitate that, I moved around in circles. Egad, you can get lost in these hills. To an outsider, one of these slopes looks like any other. I didn't know where the cave was, or the mountain it was in, but I had a vague idea so I just kept moving. By accident, I came close, apparently, within twenty-five miles, and while Iona was out on a hunting expedition, she saw my campfire."

Even with the breach of security, Iona and Kull were happy for the company.

"So you were lonesome, is that why you came to visit?" Kull asked, laughing.

"I wish it were true," the woman doctor replied. "You have responsibilities—great and grave responsibilities—that go far beyond achieving your own happiness. You thought you were going to live your lives in a state of splendid isolation? For how long? Forever?"

"What's this? What are you talking about?" Kull asked angrily. His eyes narrowed. "Oh, watch out, I see something coming now. Look out!"

"There have been plans for you since before you were born, young man," the woman doctor said in a scolding fashion. "You dislike false thinking, Kull, and you loathe deceit, Iona. It's time you both learned the truth. The cave was placed at your disposal because there was something bigger—a higher design—that involved the hopes for the future of the Earth. There is a dream. It is a dream that binds together all humanity, the dead to the living, the living to the unborn. Frankly, I don't care whether you call this dream the one true Gaia cause or you call it something else."

"Why now?" Kull said, raising his voice in anger. "Why didn't you tell us before? Why spring it on us now?"

"Maybe it was deceitful of me," the woman doctor said, "but it wasn't intended to trick you. I wanted you to be able to enjoy what you had—during the time you had it. To be honest, I didn't know when your idyllic moment was going to end. I just knew that it was going to end—at some point. I didn't even know back then what your mission was going to be."

Kull was on the verge of objecting but Iona hushed him with a look of mild rebuke.

"Easy now, dear," Iona said. "*Calm yourself.* This person knows what she is about. She knows what her business is."

Then addressing the doctor, Iona leaped and pounced. "This makes perfect sense to me," she said. "With my background, thinking of my father Regis, my mother, my teacher Tom Novak, all this makes sense. I'm not surprised by this turn of events. I'm not surprised that I was destined for a higher calling. And there's more. I know that ever since Regis was executed for treason and my mother became a leader of the rebellion, the Universal Gaia State has feared what might become of me when I came of age. Ever since the pirates took me from St. Helena, ever since my death was faked in South America, strangers have been making decisions for me. *But they were making them to protect me.* And part of that is not being told what was going to happen next—until I was finally given a new set of marching orders. All my life I've been accustomed to serving these directions. But what about Kull? He's an accident here. How does he fit into this scheme?"

"He's no accident," the woman doctor said, "and he fits into the scheme very well."

She opened a satchel and pulled out some hand-drawn maps. Opening them up, she arranged them on the floor in front of the couple. As both Iona and Kull pored over the maps, Kull could see immediately that they were going to be heading south. They were so entranced by the maps that they almost did not catch the first part of the woman doctor's narrative.

"Twelve years ago," she was saying, "a high-born grandmagister went renegade against the Gaia-Domes. From time to time a magister might change sides, that happens on occasion, but it was a one-time rarity for a high-grade grandmagister from the inner circle of power to come over to our side. He was a huge catch. When he found out how horrible the Gaia-Dome government had become he decided to risk everything and switch sides. It was when they decided to initiate their sixty-years-and-older forced euthanasia program. He paid a high price. As a result of betraying the Gaia-Domes, practically all of his immediate family was executed in reprisal. Most of his extended family members were shipped off to slave colonies. The authorities decided to make an example of him. But the grandmagister managed to escape with one of his sons. The heirs of Regis had found a special hiding place for them in a super-secret hideaway in the high Alps. The son—who would be a young man today had he lived—was being groomed to become a companion for you, Iona. A companion with a special mission. Five years ago, he was meant to join you here in Mexico. Well, he was captured by the Gaia-Dome army while en route and after being tortured, he was summarily executed. He didn't disclose anything about you during the torture sessions, Iona, only because he didn't know anything about you—and he didn't know much about where he was headed. The point is, without you even knowing it, Kull, you became his stand-in."

Something about the woman doctor's voice, its tone and rhythms, had made the cave seem to darken, so that everyone seemed less animated, more reflective, thinking about the boy's death.

"A stand-in?" Kull asked. "For a grandmagister's son who met a sad fate? Come on! I'm just a slave. I was born the son of slaves. I don't have a fancy pedigree. I sure as hell don't have an earth-shaking, earth-transforming destiny."

"Once you were a slave, true" the woman doctor corrected. "That was before. Now you've become something more. *Much, much more.*"

"Let me get this straight," Iona interjected. "You selected Kull after the one who had been chosen for me had been executed?"

"Kull selected himself," the woman doctor said. "No one selected him. I just happened to spend four years looking for him before I could find him, that's all."

"That explains so much," Iona said after a moment of reflection. "My father was supposed to escape from St. Helena and join me in the hiding place in the high desert below the Sierra Madre in northern Mexico. That had been the original plan. But something went wrong. Regis didn't escape; instead, he was executed. I got away. Tom became my father's stand-in. My God, Kull, you've come to me in the same way Tom did. It all happened by accident."

"Nothing is accident," the woman doctor said. "Planning happens in good times. Scheduling happens in good times. But these are not good times. Improvisation happens in austere times. These are both austere and hard times. Because it wasn't meant to be, I don't want to get a little too weird here, it was meant to be."

Kull shook his head. He wanted to say something that was dissenting and contradictory, but instead, he chose to keep his own counsel. Iona also kept her thoughts to herself. They all fell silent. Then, as if on automatic pilot, Iona and Kull again resumed their study of the maps.

The woman doctor gave them time to examine the maps on their own. Then, after a brief interlude, she came back and rejoined them.

"Iona?" the woman doctor said, wanting to turn things toward a lighter subject. "Those many years back, remember our talk? Tell me. Did you ever learn to hunt large animals?"

Iona smiled. She remembered the doctor looking at Iona's bow and arrows and asking her about the small creatures; the mice, the squirrels and the prairie dogs, that she hunted.

"Yes," Iona replied. She came over to the doctor, leaving Kull alone to pore over the maps. "I now hunt jackrabbits, too. Sometimes they come up from the south, from the opposite direction of the Forbidden Zone. I have to travel more than eighty miles to hunt deer. Once I had the good fortune to follow the path of a coyote. Where there's a predator there are bound to be prey animals. I had to travel more than a hundred miles to do that."

"Did you break the rules to do that?" the woman doctor asked.

"Yes," Iona said. "Of course I did! When I was young, when I first arrived here, you ordered me to stay within a one hundred and seventy-five mile radius of the cave. Do you remember why? It was for my own protection! That was one of the first rules I broke. I've made many excursions since then, over a dozen of them. Three times I went as far away as the sea. On two occasions, I visited parts of the Forbidden Zone, going all the way to the other side. The second crossing wasn't as horrible as my first crossing was. I know exactly what I'm doing now."

"*Good!*" the woman doctor exclaimed. "Improvise! Good. When do you hunt?"

"I only hunt at nighttime, of course. The only game we have are usually mice and squirrels."

"And Kull?"

"I taught him how to hunt at night, too," Iona said. "He's pretty good. I know if we were to find the coyote, the bobcat, and the mountain lion in the same place, it'd be a sure sign we'd be on the mend, environment-wise! On the road to recovery! But that may be years away." Iona stopped short. She faced the woman doctor and riveted her with a severe expression. "In a steep ravine recently, I once cornered a live coyote!"

"No! No way! Did you kill it?" the woman doctor asked in an excited voice.

"Are you kidding!" Iona said, looking horrified. "Absolutely not. He was probably the only coyote within a radius of two hundred miles. He had mange. He was scrawny. I pitied the poor thing. I hope there'll be a return of bobcats, and even better yet, mountain lions! By the way, when do we leave?"

"Don't worry," the woman doctor laughed light-heartedly. "You have two weeks before we need to depart. You'll have plenty of time to pack your things. You'll have time to figure out how to solve the...*availability of water issue*. The first one hundred miles is going to be a problem."

"Availability of water?" Iona asked. "Water will never be an issue. We leave in three days time, if we leave at all," she concluded. "We have practically nothing to gather up because we'll decide right here and now to own practically nothing from here on out, right, Kull?"

Kull nodded in assent. "As long as we bring Tom's skin with

us, with his little piece of philosophy written on it, I'll agree to the rest."

"There, you see!" Iona said. "If necessary, we'll travel with only the clothes on our backs. If necessary, we'll carry water only."

"Spoken like a true blood!" the doctor beamed with pride. "Spoken like your mother!"

"But September died in the end," Iona said. "No, this will be different. Kull and I will see through this, past all difficulties. No, I'm certain of that. We know how to forage."

"We've seen all the maps," Kull concluded. "We're headed many, many miles south of here. It is a journey that will take not days, but weeks. Many weeks. We are going into the jungle. It's going to be a long journey. It is a place where Clive had told me to go when I asked him the best place to go in America. But where exactly are we going? And why?"

"A place where there are caves," the woman doctor said. "Large ones. The countryside is honeycombed with them. But here's the interesting part. The people are all children—younger children, plus a smattering of older teenagers. The oldest ones act as guardians for the younger ones. The parents have all been killed off or transported to the slave colonies across the sea by the armies of the Gaia-Domes."

"How many children are there?" Kull asked.

"Hundreds. But later on, there'll be more. Oh yes, there'll be more."

"Why were we chosen to be leaders of this group?" Iona asked.

"The parents were hopelessly tied to their old ways," the woman doctor said. "They tried to appease the Gaia-Domes and ended up being destroyed. The land adjacent to the caves where the children have moved is fertile. There is ample rain. There are places to forage in the jungle as well. The caves provide the children with protection. But they need something more. They need to be taught that there is a future."

"But the children are free?" Kull asked.

"What does *that* mean?" the doctor asked. "Free? What does that mean?" She chuckled. "If by that, Kull, you mean free from the clutches of the Gaia-Domes, well yes, they're free. But beyond that, freedom can mean vastly different things."

Chapter Twenty-Five

THE THREE OF THEM SET OUT on their journey. Half-way to their destination they passed through Mexico City. Or what was left of it. The remnant was once a metropolis of twenty-five million people in 2040 A.D. But after the Eleven-Years-War in 2051 A.D. the population had dwindled to just over three million. Thirty years later, barely 25,000 souls lived there.

"It really consists of eight villages now," the woman doctor said. "The Gaia-Domes resurrected New York City and London and other cities. They did the same for Rio De Janeiro and Buenos Aires. But they left Mexico City to its own devices. All the skyscrapers have been leveled to the ground. The roads have weeds sprouting between the cracks, and vines snaking over them. Wild boars roam freely and domesticated pigs root through the husks of derelict buildings. Everything is encrusted with plants. Even young trees have been seen sprouting up through the cracks of foundations. The only thing left still standing is the central cathedral that was built on the site of the old Aztec temple and was re-commemorated as a Cathedral of Gaia. But vestiges of old superstitions are undying and unending. Now, temporarily, the eight villages are a neutral zone. Sometimes, I am able to trade medical supplies there in exchange for food or clothing."

"You say it's a neutral zone?" Kull asked. "Why didn't the children flee here?"

"It's a neutral zone, all right, but only for the time being," the woman doctor warned. "Every six months or so, the Gaia-Dome army sweeps back in to occupy the villages and turn everything topsy-turvy. People are rounded up and executed in the square in front of the Cathedral of Gaia. We mustn't linger long, it's dangerous to stay even for more than a day or two. We need to get what we need and get back into the countryside."

So they journeyed on. The farther south they traveled the more plentiful the rain became. They saw farmers eking out a living by raising crops in the fields, but they didn't even have a donkey or an ox to pull a plow. Instead, they did everything by hand. They dug long rows of holes in the ground, using a stick, and after dropping the seeds into the holes they covered them up with their feet.

When they reemerged into the area patrolled by the Gaia-Dome army, the party of three returned to the safety of traveling at night. Almost exactly one month after they had set out, from new moon to new moon, they arrived at a dense, remote, mountainous region.

Semi-rotten roads regressed into boggy byways that in turn turned into narrow but serviceable walking trails that turned into narrow (and much less serviceable) pathways that turned into animal tracks that disappeared into the jungle. The last thirty miles of their journey involved traipsing into the high ups and downs of narrow-ridged mountains.

Through the last part of the journey, the party literally hacked through thick jungle growth. All they had for that purpose were machetes and compasses. When they arrived at the partially hidden old Mayan ruins, they knew that they had arrived. They found themselves deep in the densest part of the jungle, hemmed in not just by dense plant foliage but by land that was almost entirely vertical, steep-ridged mountains crisscrossed by deep river gullies. If it hadn't been for the guidance of the woman doctor, Iona and Kull knew that they could never have found the old Mayan ruins, much less the nearby cluster of seven caves—so well hidden they were.

But after resting in a clearing all day long, they soon discovered that the place was busy and active with occupants.

Iona and Kull found something promising in the children. They found the first stirrings of order and organization. The rudiments of teamwork and purpose had been provided by the older ones—who, at the age of 15, 16, or 17, were only a few years away from becoming adults themselves. They were the only ones who had been guiding the younger children. Except for them, all of the children, and there were hundreds of them, seemed dejected. Most of them were frightened. All were baffled as to the reason why they were stuck in the jungle—*living in caves and forced to endure such serious bouts of hunger.*

To get there, the vast majority had traveled long distances, walking through danger to get there, along the way crouching in holes in the ground as their sole protection against nature and human predators, shivering in the dark, burning up in the heat, often possessing nothing but a rag or a scanty piece of animal skin to cover themselves, all illiterate farmer's children who had been ruthlessly and abruptly orphaned.

The doctor greeted the children and introduced Iona and Kull to them. Most of the children fell on their knees, some even prostrated themselves. Iona and Kull were not just ill at ease, they were embarrassed. But they took heart when they saw wiser ones—a smaller band of older children—there were exactly twelve in number, arranging themselves in a semi-circle around Iona and Kull, acting as aides-de-camp to the couple.

Iona and Kull could see that the older children—were many years older than they appeared. They had already formed the group into sections based on the organization of the seven caves.

Setting up their residence in a central cave, which they aptly named the Eagle's Nest, Iona and Kull took their first opportunity to share a moment of intimacy. Iona said to Kull, "These children are like clean slates. They have nothing written on them. It's as if they were waiting for someone to come along and have something written on them. As human beings, it's as if they are utterly unformed."

"That's partially true," Kull said, holding Iona tightly in his arms and kissing her. "But there's other good news. When the parents were alive they must have protected these children from the worst ravages of sun death. They must have loved these children dearly! The woman doctor hasn't detected any signs of mutation-forming disease in the camp. None! It means the caves will continue to keep them healthy. We have that much to build on. It's as if we have our own natural Dome world here."

"*What are we going to do then,*" Iona asked, "besides feed them?"

"We don't have to decide that immediately," Kull replied. "We'll work it out."

Iona was not satisfied with Kull's response. "What are we going to do then?" she asked in a firm voice. She stabbed Kull with a mean, menacing look.

Kull sighed. "All right. You win. You're a hard taskmaster. It's obvious we must do more than just be caretakers. Because of the jungle and the caves, no one would come to this place unless they absolutely had to anyway, we have protection and security. The next step? I don't know. We must set up a food system that will continue to sustain itself. Foraging. Farming. Even hunting. Then we can begin to do the central thing: teach the children at least what we know."

"That's not good enough," Iona said in a stern voice. She kissed Kull fully on the lips. Seductively, she played with Kull's ear. Then she abruptly and tantalizingly withdrew. She regarded Kull in a semi-threatening way.

"Woman!" Kull shouted. "Enough already! Will you quit your seduction!" He looked exasperated but he laughed good-naturedly at the same time. "All right, we'll try to help them become self-reliant and successful human beings. Easier said than done! Now, does that please you? Are you happy?"

Iona was relieved by Kull's words, but she was not completely satisfied and Kull knew it.

It was Kull's turn to smile. "All right, I get it. The important thing—the big thing. The thing that matters more than anything else. The thing that will liberate these children. The marvelous trick—the one that nobody knows—certainly the Gaia-Domes don't. The big one. We'll teach them how to forage *during the nighttime!*"

In one gesture, Iona threw her arms around Kull. She hugged him. She squeezed him for dear life.

"So we are going to take the seven caves and the Eagle's Nest and we are going to build a city?" Iona whispered into Kull's ear. She had a sly and cunning look on her face, but it was also a determined and forceful look. "Right?" she asked. She seductively played with Kull's ear again.

"Yes," Kull grumbled. "Build a city. An underground city. Built on the principles of the true Gaia. No executions. Not like what the Gaia-Dome does in the square of the Cathedral of Gaia in Mexico City. No. We will never have slaves either. Everywhere the Gaia-Domes impose their order, they impose repression. Everywhere we scratch out a living space that is protected, we will create a breathing space for regeneration, for future human liberation." Kull nodded his head with enthusiasm. "Oh Iona, I believe it can be done."

"To build a city, an underground city," Iona sang, "built on the solid principles of the one and only true Gaia." Her voice resounded with lyricism. It had a lilt about it that made it sound as if Iona were rejoicing "The kind that would make September Snow and Regis Snow proud."

"Yes," Kull said. "But first, we must build an army."

"What?" Iona asked. Iona felt a tugging inside, a moment of resistance. "We must be tough, I'll grant you that. But you yourself said, I was getting ahead of myself. Are we not moving too quickly?"

Kull could not be diverted. "No. I'm standing my ground on this. An army. From the stuff of these children. One way or another. If it takes ten years—twenty years—doesn't matter. Reality is staring us in the face. But it'll be an army such as the world has never seen before. An army that will be for a good cause. We just need to come up with a name for it."

"The Gaia-Domes will not allow us to do that," Iona said. "You're perfectly aware of that."

"Give them half a chance, they'll crush it," Kull said. "Of course. But I see it clearly now. I know exactly what the woman doctor had been thinking all along. I see what the long-term planning has been. September Snow and Regis Snow were brilliant. They weren't looking at the day after tomorrow, they were looking fifty years...one hundred years...into the future. And since the rebellion has completely collapsed in almost all places all around the planet, nobody will suspect us, nobody will be looking for us. In fact, eventually, we'll catch the Gaia-Domes by surprise. But we will not be able to stay here forever. Down the line, at some point, we'll have to move. It will be necessary. To do that, we will have to be an army. Yes, I see it so clearly! Strap yourself in Iona, we're headed for a whirlwind."

"We'll call it: *The Unseeing Watchfulness of Gaia*," Iona said in an excited voice.

"What?"

Iona smiled. "Gaia is something beyond human comprehension, Kull. It's a dark and impenetrable truth. It's to be pondered and cherished and not heedlessly exposed and explained away. It is to be held in the bosom of one's heart with the highest regard and value, not diminished by puerile intellectualizing or simplified by one-dimensional word games. It is a fact and a value combined. In other words, it's a mystery. And by virtue of the fact that it's a mystery, it's intrinsically inexplicable. Being a mystery, it means more than just being strange or foreign, it means it is 'unseeable,' also 'unseeing.' I partially borrowed the core concept from what Tom taught me years ago, but I dreamt up the larger context myself. Gaia is, to humankind, an 'unseeing watchfulness.' It is a paradox that one 'senses' only in the darkness of the cave—when and where all of one's consciousness of senses has been stripped. Living in the cave for a long time without the benefit of sunlight, indirect sunlight, or fire, my first time alone—utterly alone—that's when I came to understand Gaia. In the worst of times of eco-devastation, the cave is everything. The cave is life. The cave is truth. The coldness and darkness of the cave is where life has a chance to be incubated. That is the cave. And that is where one comes to know what the true Gaia is. Just a hint here. Just a clue there. Fact and value combined. That is the true Gaia. That is the real Gaia. That is life. It is the message of the cave. *The Unseeing Watchfulness of Gaia*. That's the mystery."

"I'll leave the philosophical and spiritual stuff to you," Kull said, "it's beyond me. I may think in an analytically sound way, and I hope for once I might be strategically correct about this army business, but when I speak, well, my words come out as if weighed down like leaden bullets. However, when you speak, your words are beautiful, Iona. You're the poet. The Unseeing Watchfulness of Gaia. It has a marvelous ring to it, doesn't it?"

Before the woman doctor departed, Kull asked her to take a walk with him alone in the jungle. Kull felt that he had so much he had to talk to her about.

During the walk, Kull turned to the woman doctor and said, "I know you're going to see us again. Don't lie to us. Some time in the future, when we least expect it, you will stop by to determine how far we've progressed."

"Yes," the woman doctor said, "but at some point you will be on your own. We'll give you a shove in a certain direction, true, and we'll provide you with some guidelines, but other than that, you will be on your own."

"What's your name?" Kull asked. "You can tell us now. Things have evolved too far along for us to continue to call you something as stupid as 'the woman doctor.'"

"What about security?" the woman doctor asked, as if she hadn't heard his question.

"You'll never be subject to torture because should you ever be captured, you'll never reveal anything about us," Kull observed. "I know this is true. You're too savvy. And you're a doctor. I'm sure you're carrying a suicide pill with you."

"How did you know?" the woman doctor replied. She pulled a small container holding a single cyanide pill from her front pocket and showed it to him. "After the grandmagister's son was killed, I thought, I must get more sophisticated about security. The pill was extremely hard to come by. If I had any extras, I'd give them to you. But I have only this one. I may need it myself. You're safe here in the jungle now. We can make a further minor alteration in the security precautions, I suppose. My name is Marjoram."

"Marjoram?" Kull smiled.

"My mother named me after the herb," the woman doctor laughed. "She feared life during my time would be boring and lacking in flavor. She got half of it right. Aromatic and mint-like. She looked at me as one who would provide seasoning in an otherwise bland and tasteless world. Where did you get your name, Kull?"

"The Gaia-Domes gave it to me. My family didn't choose it for me."

"If you don't like it, you can change it, you know."

"I know. No. I keep it as a reminder."

"A reminder of what?"

"That I am a slave. Let me ask you a serious question, Marjoram. How do I free myself from being a slave...having a slave mentality."

"Don't be stupid. It's plain that you are no longer a slave. Why pose such a silly question?"

"But, *psychologically speaking*, I'm still a slave."

"Free others and perhaps you will free yourself in the bargain,"

Marjoram offered.

Kull mulled this. "The way to free yourself is to free others? I'm intrigued by this. What do you mean?"

"More specifically, it's a Buddhist thing," Marjoram said. "As a girl, I was introduced to Buddhism. But I changed the Buddhist saying to fit you. The original saying was: *If you are suffering, find someone else who is suffering and help them and thus by doing so, you will help alleviate your own suffering.* I changed the saying to: *Free others and perhaps you will free yourself.* Gaia isn't really different from the older religions, Kull. They all have their truths, falsities, fanaticisms, gestures, practices, procedures, rituals... After all, are there any virtuous religions? Remember, all religions can be used for many purposes, including bad ones. Obviously, Gaia, at long last, has been used for *terribly* wrong purposes—by the Gaia-Domes."

"Does humanity ever get it right?" Kull asked.

"Yes. But when it does get it right, it doesn't last forever. That has always been the human tragedy."

"I think I get it," Kull said. Kull looked at Marjoram in a new way. "You're a free spirit, aren't you?"

"No," Marjoram said gloomily. But then her frown relaxed into a smile. "Well, I try. Every once in a while, every once in a blue moon, I manage to succeed. *But only for short bouts of time,*" she added with a quirky, robust snort of laughter. "But you will free yourself, Kull. I know you will."

Kull smiled.

"Yes, well, while we're talking about everything under the sun," Marjoram said in an absent-minded way, "that old guerilla band you used to hang out with years ago was completely wiped out. I warned you that it would eventually happen. Well, it finally did. They fell on hard times. They had succumbed to outright banditry. They ended up stealing, especially from the poor. They got shut down. Gaia-Domes did them in in the end. We face a new world. In this new world, above all, Iona must be seen as the leader. For the group itself, it doesn't much matter, but in the larger scheme of things, it's important that Iona be seen as the person at the top. If you are ever able to make yourselves strong enough to bargain with the Gaia-Domes, even if this should occur many years from now, they must see the daughter of Regis Snow and September Snow as the arbiter and negotiator of the force for good. You understand that, Kull. Do you understand that?"

"I'm many steps ahead of you," Kull said in agreement, nodding his head. "I've already thought of that. You're absolutely right. That's why I wanted to talk with you separately, without the presence of Iona. The only way I can get myself out of this predicament is to attach myself to a cause that is much larger than myself. Iona is our strength. Besides, I love her. This much I know. Iona will always be the fountainhead of this new thing that we will bring into this world."

"I've been meaning to ask you," Marjoram said. "I don't mean to pry into your private life, but, in a sense, you are not going to have much of a private life from here on out. Have you decided if you are going to have children?"

"Iona and I have thought long and hard on this...we've decided not to," Kull replied. "Five years ago, we decided on this. The world is too horrifying. Ever since we've come here and seen these children, we've come to realize that they are our true mission. We have other reasons not to have children now."

"How is that?" Marjoram asked intrigued.

"For the longer term," Kull said, "we don't want to set anything up that smacks of dynasty. We don't want to create something that could be turned into permanent hierarchy. In the nearer term it doesn't matter, but in the longer term it could turn into something unhealthy. We don't want to set too firm a print on these children, these adopted orphans of ours. Even though in effect we will be mother and father to them, we prefer to look at ourselves as, well, as aunt and uncle. Besides, we have our work cut out for us. We don't want to take on any additional burdens that we may not be able to handle. And we know that more children are likely to come and join us. Each birth will be a rebirth of the human race. It's going to get harder to handle as time goes on. But the dynasty will end with Iona. Eventually, when the children have become full adults, they will have to take on a larger share of the burden of managing their lives. We must prepare them for that, too. But we don't want to go too far. Iona will be the foundation and the fountainhead. We owe them that much. After all, nothing can be added, nothing created, without a foundation."

"You're a wise man," Marjoram said. "The wise one is he who knows when he must lead, but also knows when he must be led. Have you a name for this new thing that you are bringing into this world?"

"Oh, yes. It's going to be called: *The Unseeing Watchfulness of Gaia*."

"The Unseeing Watchfulness of Gaia," Marjoram pondered. "Has a ring to it. I like it. But you didn't coin it. No way. That would be impossible. I bet you Iona dreamt it up."

"Yes," Kull laughed. "How did you know?"

"Of course," Marjoram said. "It goes without saying. It's beautiful. If there's anything I know, it's that Iona shall be the poet in the organization. Iona is the one with the vision."

Chapter Twenty-Six

 IT WAS THE FIRST YEAR OF Iona and Kull's arrival in the jungle. Iona had already set up a regimen so that every female and male received an initiating experience similar to the training she received under the guidance of an old blind Indian. This training took place when she had been ten years old. The regimen of training was not as severe as Iona's training had been, nor did it last the same prolonged period of time, but it did accomplish a vital and important goal.

The focus of the ordeal was to acclimate the initiate to live in complete darkness for two weeks. During this time the initiate was blindfolded and limited in his or her food intake so he or she would be forced to learn how to survive both inside and outside the cave—inside the cave in order to learn to live in total darkness, outside the cave to learn to forage for food, and also seek out water, without use of eyesight.

As long as the experience lasted no longer than two weeks, Kull approved of it. But he didn't see the point of it going on for 31 days, as occurred in Iona's case. Iona had been blindfolded, with ears and nostrils plugged to prevent her from smelling or hearing. In the darkness, she banged her head once, causing a concussion. She experienced recurring bouts of hallucination caused by a dangerous combination of sensory deprivation and dehydration. At one point, toward the end of her ordeal, she came close to actually dying of thirst.

In the past, according to Tom Novak's *assessment,* the blind old Indian, in setting up this peculiar training formula, was either a brute and a demented sadomasochist, or a one-of-a-kind, brilliant visionary who knew exactly what Iona needed to learn to become a leader of a post-apocalyptic generation of younger people who had no idea what life had been like before the wrenching changes occurred to both the world environment's natural order and the world community's social order, but who would be able to learn to survive in the debris of the totally collapsed world.

Though the initiation was less severe than Iona's had been, it taught the initiates how to be strong, self-reliant, and independent, and it gave them a strong impression of how dangerous the world could be. It also gave them a taste of what could happen if they did not prepare themselves thoroughly for extreme conditions.

Children were now growing up to look forward to the initiation. They saw the surviving-of-the-ordeal as a badge of honor. In many ways it had become their coming-of-age initiation, a first and vital step in their quest for achieving full adulthood.

Over time, it became known as The Cult. Iona had tried to insist on calling the ordeal The Gaia Initiation, but her title for the process did not catch on. The Cult was what it was called. (Children have a way of naming a thing—using their own argot—and by doing so, making the thing entirely their own.)

Iona gave up trying to label many things Gaia-inspired. The children were vehement about this. Except for the older children, who had a broader perspective and a wider understanding of the true merits of the true Gaia, Gaia meant nothing to the youngest children except Gaia-Domes, and Gaia-Domes meant oppression and the deaths of their parents. The youngest of these children were one and a half generations removed from Iona's mother September Snow, and almost three generations removed from Tom Novak.

At the conclusion of the initiation, each child was made to memorize the words that Tom Novak had written on the piece of skin. Over a period of years, "All history is philosophy, and all philosophy is religion, all religion is literature, and all literature is art, all art is music, painting, dancing, and all music, painting, dancing are the heart, brain, hand of man and woman, through all of time," was memorized by thousands and thousands of children. That was the essence of The Cult. They may have not known what many of the words meant, but they knew they had to memorize them!

Aside from the original twelve wise ones and a growing number of assistants, Iona and Kull were unable to make the time to teach the huge majority of children any literacy skills. So what they recited were words they learned by rote. The children often didn't know what they were reciting. The words on the skin did not have *actual meaning*. Rather, they were almost synonymous with a prayer that had been written in an obscure, or only partially understood, language.

Calling it a cult or not calling it a cult, one thing was certain: The children were to be known as THE UNSEEING WATCHFULNESS OF GAIA! Iona made certain that no challenge would ever be broached, much less allowed, over that one key issue.

The art of foraging, especially *nighttime foraging,* hunting, small-scale, scratch farming, a survivalist school of home economics, self-defense—those were the things that they were taught. Later in life, many of them were taught some martial arts as well, but again these arts were mainly defensive in nature.

Kull was also worried that The Cult could turn itself into an ominous form of indoctrination, or even worse, an out-and-out form of brain-washing. But Iona felt no qualms on that score.

As Iona was tireless to explain: "We grow stronger and bigger. But it will be the miracle of the ages if we survive as a group. Next year, drought could take us out. Later on, the armies of the Gaia-Domes could destroy us. We need to be able to disperse our children, in tiny groups, in carefully targeted groups, some sent not too far, others sent very far away, in the event of a catastrophe. We need to be able to do this at the drop of a hat. The Cult is tied to learning the essential skills of being able to forage everywhere: in the jungle, in the desert, in the mountains, by the sea, but most importantly at night! The way to survive is for our children to be able to live off the land, no matter what happens. But more importantly, they must be able to do this in a way where they can't be seen. In that way the army can be built, brick by brick. In five years time, some of the children will be adults. In ten years time, most of them will be. In twenty years time, all of them will be. By then it will have become a decentralized army, an army that can disperse, reunite, disperse again—at a moment's notice. It will be an army that is *powerful, extremely flexible, and can successfully hide from any forces the Gaia-Domes may throw up against us!* "

Over time, Kull came to marvel at Iona's vision and brilliance.

Also, Kull learned within the first nine months of their occupation of the caves that if the children stayed inside the caves without experiencing time outside—to see the light of day—they experienced a strange form of sensory deprivation, and even more critically, found themselves succumbing to a maladjusted sleep regimen whereby they stayed awake for thirty-six hours nonstop and then typically slept for eighteen hours.

To prevent this maladjustment from becoming permanent, Kull required every child to spend at least three hours outside the cave every day, either during the early morning hours, just after dawn, or during the late afternoon hours, just before dusk. They weren't going to live in the caves forever.

Years later, as the children grew older, they had to learn how to protect themselves against the dangerous effects of sun death. They were allowed to spend longer periods of time outside during the daylight hours. They were also taught additional skills in foraging and hunting, in order to increase their chances of survival, and were instructed in how to travel without risking detection by the forces of the Gaia-Domes.

As Kull had explained to the twelve wise ones: "teach the children to forage, teach them to live on next to nothing, teach them to live off the land—that will make them stronger for the future, their future."

When they turned seventeen, Dominic and Elsie, two teenagers and part of the original group of wise ones, became the principal trainers. They subsequently trained dozens of younger trainers. Over a period of six years, the training program grew. No one called it an army, but that's what it was becoming.

But it was an army that was the opposite of a rank-and-file organization. The foragers were composed of highly-skilled individuals who traveled alone, in pairs, in groups of three or four, or in groups of ten or twenty, but never in groups larger than that. A group of one hundred could not travel two hundred miles without being spotted. A group of one thousand could not travel ten miles without being spotted. But a group numbering less than twenty could go anywhere without being spotted. Any group larger than the size of a platoon was dangerously vulnerable. In the final two years, the children were taught to travel hundreds of miles, and they learned how to use and maintain small boats and navigate bodies of water. Eighty percent of them traveled almost exclusively by night, but a smaller group were taught how to travel undetected during the daylight hours as well. These became a special elite.

In eight years, this "Unseeing Watchfulness of Gaia," this hidden band of frightened children, had grown from a group of 339 disoriented youngsters living under makeshift conditions, to an army of five thousand. From village to village, news traveled by word of mouth. Farmers and peasants sent their children to the caves, knowing they might have a better chance at survival if they joined. They now lived in the original seven adjacent caves, plus twelve major cave complexes, and fourteen minor ones, spread over an area of several hundred square miles of mountainous jungle. They traveled like ghosts—as if their feet were gliding over the ground—never leaving a trace behind. They moved like body-less spirits, like gusts of wind, like vapor. Their greatest gift was their ability to spend their entire lives living like primitive survivalists.

The oldest of the children were now at least twenty-three-years-old, the very oldest twenty-five. The leadership eventually had to make a rule that a child had to be at least fourteen years old, or be in fear of imminent death, to join. Then, those selected were sent through a secret underground passage where they could be whisked away to the caves. In Medieval times, they might have been the chosen few, sent to a monastery, or a university. But in these times, it was to the caves, so they could become a part of the "unseeing watchfulness."

Once having gone away, the children almost never returned to see their parents. Outside the Gaia-Domes, there was nothing, no alternatives but death, destruction, slavery, or the lowest form of debasing submission. True, sometimes the Domes did pick up a child from among the outsiders and come to treat the child with fairness, but that was rare. Yes, the child was then given a chance to live under the protection of the Domes, where he or she experienced security and perhaps even love. But the level of forced indoctrination that the child was subjected to was severe. For an outsider to give their child away to the Domes in that fashion was like giving their child away to the devil. Or at least, that's how the majority of the outsiders, being exploited peasant farmers themselves, saw it.

Iona and Kull were brilliant at keeping the entire group in hiding. As the group grew larger, they expanded by making their organization increasingly decentralized. In spite of their smaller groupings, and their distance and isolation, they still managed to form a solid group. But as their numbers grew over the years, they began to feel hemmed in. Ten years from the time they had formed, the group's growth and space limitations caused increasing difficulties.

And ten years from the time they had formed into the community that Iona had named *The Unseeing Watchfulness of Gaia*, Marjoram, the woman doctor, returned to visit.

▶▶▶▶

Kull noticed that Marjoram had aged considerably. Her shining black hair had turned dullish gray with large streaks of white. Marjoram's eyes appeared sadder and more care-worn and the lines on her face had deepened and become more angular. Kull had noticed in Marjoram's right hand a particularly acute aging process. The woman doctor's right hand was twisted and withered.

But the most noticeable thing of all was that she was missing her left arm. Also, there was a long, horizontal, jagged scar running high above her right breast that had not properly healed. This was more than aging.

"What happened?" Kull asked.

"I was in a scrape."

"Oh?" Kull asked. "The Gaia-Domes?"

"No," Marjoram said. "I was woken in the night by four mangy cannibal-scavengers. I lost an arm and received a wound along my right clavicle, but the price they paid for disturbing me in my beauty sleep is that they won't have the opportunity to eat again."

"You're too old for this," Kull said in a blunt voice. "You shouldn't be traveling solo anymore. *More importantly, you shouldn't be alone at all.* If I were you I'd, I'd..."

"I'll travel any way I please," Marjoram shot back. "What are you going to tell me? And what's new? It's rough and nasty out there? You plan on naming yourself my protector?"

"We never know when—or even IF—you're coming," Kull said, changing the subject. He relaxed a bit. "In any event, you're always welcome here. However, it has been such a long time since we last saw you and we didn't know if you were still among the living."

Marjoram laughed so loud her voice came out in a hacking, crackling way. "With the forced euthanasia plan in place for almost twenty years, the Gaia-Domes have been killing the elderly off right and left even before they reach 60. With really good street smarts you can elude them for a while, but for how long? I'm 67. It's been only in the last fifteen months that I've aged so much. That's when my hair started turning white. I've got cancer. I'm living on borrowed time. I know that if they were able to take a good look at me now, they'd shoot me on the spot. I'm not here to address that subject, however."

Marjoram breathed heavily. There was an urgent quaver in her voice. "You might have issued an incredibly large calling card to the Gaia-Domes, you've grown so large and so fast. But no. Do you know how fortunate you are? There are several reasons why your secret hasn't been blown before now. First, you've managed to remain so cleverly hidden in your caves. You get big points for that. Second, when you travel, you travel at night and in small groups. Your group is still largely composed of children and young people, although that is changing, they are growing older. There has been so much pillaging, death and destruction going on outside the Gaia-Domes the disappearance of the children has gone largely unnoticed. That, too, by the way, is going to change. The poor and ragged people who still manage to eke out an existence outside the Gaia-Domes hate the Gaia-Domes so profoundly and with such a bitter resentfulness, they've managed to keep your secret too—*at least up until now they have.* Don't expect them to keep the secret much longer. Recently, spies have been placed among them. But here is the most important reason why you aren't all dead. Over the past ten years, the rebels who fight against the Gaia-Domes have been decimated, almost annihilated, everywhere, on every continent, so much so that the new generation of Gaia-Domes leaders has grown complacent and flabby. They can't imagine that a group like yours could ever have formed and flourished in the first place. So what do I attribute your continued success to? Well, by my reckoning, luck."

"Where is this heading?" Kull asked.

Marjoram sighed. "What am I trying to say? The rebellion is dead. There is nothing happening in Europe. The rebellion in Asia is, well, moribund. For all we know, you are the only group left that is still active, *but you've never once shown yourself in public or come out of hiding.* It's been over twenty years since September Snow led her rebellion against the wind machines. When September Snow did that, the environment got a reprieve and a chance to heal itself. But otherwise, everything's been going downhill since. You're *it.*"

"We're *it?*" Kull asked in a slightly bewildered voice. "What do you mean, we're it?"

"The Gaia-Domes will soon be on to you. And sooner or later, they are going to come after you. That's why I'm here, to warn you. Where's Iona?"

"She's out in the desert."

"Has she traveled far?" Marjoram asked.

"Of course she traveled far," Kull said. "She's training new recruits. And that's not all she does. When she goes on one of these expeditions she ends up climbing some mountain on her own, so she can experience one of her visions. She fasts for days. Then she tries to communicate with the spirits of the likes of a Tom Novak, or some such nonsense. How old would Tom be now? Ninety? Maybe he's avoided the forced euthanasia plan somehow. But how? Unless he's shape-shifted into an animal. Maybe he changed into a coyote! Or, better yet, a mountain lion! Let's stop fooling ourselves. He's dead. I'll wager he's been dead for years. Years and years ago, when Iona had an encounter with an injured coyote, she thought it was the spirit of Tom Novak—*in the animal*—trying to communicate with her. I don't trust the *true* Gaia religion, Marjoram, even when it's being administered by the so-called *good and safe* people like our wise ones. And I don't trust all the mysterious hocus-pocus that Iona has fallen into. She bathes in this mystery stuff like it's the point of all existence."

"But the young people in your group love it, don't they?" Marjoram asked.

Kull nodded. It went against the grain of his thinking, but he admitted it. "Some of them," Kull said. "They love the Gaia religion stuff, especially the wise ones. Many of the children, however, are indifferent, or even hostile, to the Gaia philosophy. But the mystery stuff? That's different. Wherever they are, whether they are wise ones, or recent recruits, whether they are children, a nine-year-old, for example, or someone who's been with us since the beginning, and is hitting 30, they love the mystery stuff. That's where Iona is most effective. And now Iona is blending the two—the mystery stuff —and the authentic Gaia philosophy and science— together. Frankly, I find it totally disturbing."

"They're almost all illiterates Kull, what do you expect?" Marjoram said. "They're scared! If you don't have a myth to live up to, you must create one. That's the job of Iona. That's the job of all visionaries. *Trust her.*"

"Well," Kull said, shaking his head, "in my opinion, by doing these things these children are getting farther and farther away from the truth."

Marjoram smiled. "It has nothing to do with the truth, Kull, it has to do with survival. Do you really expect to succeed and defeat the Gaia-Domes if you don't have a commanding myth—a myth that's more powerful than the Domes' own countervailing myth? We know that their myth is a false one. We can reason it out. But almost all of your followers are illiterates! Do you want to tell them the truth? Do you want to tell them about the sad state of the rebellion. All over the world, the rebellion has fallen into defeat. *Everywhere!* Better to tell them a comforting myth!"

"This is untrue," Kull said in a low voice. "That is deliberately leaving a false impression."

"Or, maybe," Marjoram said, "eventually, the myth will turn into the truth? Have you ever considered that possibility? Maybe that's the deeper reasoning behind Iona's thinking. Why do you think you've gotten so many recruits in the last few years? Admit it to yourself, you told me yourself. Your recruits have tripled—even QUADRUPLED—in number, during the last three or four years. More than anything else, I bet you it's the mystery stuff, that's turned the trick. They're searching for something."

"What you say is true, but I didn't expect this from you, Marjoram," Kull protested.

"I've been lying to you," Marjoram said in a calm, business-like voice, "from the very beginning. It's true that I met September Snow, and that there was a real rebellion. It's also true that I was sent on the mission to find Iona on the edge of the Forbidden Zone and escort her to her new home. But that's where it all ended. It all ended there. It's like seeing the light of a star that burned up a million years ago. We're still seeing the light, but it's light from a dead star, from the past. A lot of what I've told you, I made up. There was no rebellion waiting in the wings. It was almost completely destroyed twenty years ago. There was no grandmagister, no son of the grandmagister, hiding in the Alps, no mission for you. I made it up. September and Regis Snow had no idea what was going to happen to Iona, they just wanted to give her a chance to survive. Tom Novak was improvised, you were improvised, *The Unseeing Watchfulness of Gaia* was improvised. You people are alive today only because the Gaia-Domes have not been fighting against a serious rebellion of any consequence for over two decades. Why are you alive? The Gaia-Domes are rusty. They've been slipping."

"Does Iona know all this that you are telling me?"

"She's known it from the beginning, Kull. Ever since she was alone in the cave when I found her, she's known it. She has seen through everything from the beginning. She knew the star had died a long time ago. If the light in the sky is still there, even if the star that emitted the light had long since ceased, did that make the twinkle an untruth, a *myth*? The star's dead. Fine. But it once was there."

"Why didn't she say anything to me?" Kull asked in an angry voice.

"She didn't have to," Marjoram replied. "She just played along. She just let me play my role too."

"All along, the two of you have been making plans and winking at each other behind my back," Kull said. "In this life, ever since she left Tom Novak, I've been the closest person to Iona. Why didn't she say anything to me?"

"She thought you would function better if you didn't know."

"Well, that's great. Well, thanks. That's fine. I'm glad she trusts me so much."

"You must attack."

"Iona will not attack," Kull said. "I know. She won't attack unless we are attacked first."

"Well, in this she will be wrong. But you are on your own. You must attack. You are the one who is going to be making the military decisions, Kull. You must decide."

"Stay with us," Kull said. He thought of mentioning Marjoram's missing arm and her twisted, claw-like hand. But he didn't. Instead, he imagined the scene of Marjoram in her old age; grappling and scuffling with a group of cannibal-scavengers as they threw her to the ground and she fought back with all her might, subduing them within an inch of her life. He looked carefully at the wound above Marjoram's right breast, blistery, *unhealed*, then he noticed the indentations, the cannibal's claw-like scratches and teeth marks, faint, but still a part of the wound. No wonder the wound hadn't healed properly. Not a straight and narrow surgical scar—instead it was gaping and jagged—caused by the actions of clawing and chewing. How ghastly the incident must have been.

"Ah Jesus, Marjoram, have you had a chance to look at yourself?" Kull asked. "You've grown so long in the tooth..."

Marjoram laughed at the unseemly, bad joke. But she was grateful for it. Nonetheless she covered her right shoulder, clavicle and wound with the tattered ends of a shawl. "I'm coming to resemble Iona's old, dying coyote more and more these days, aren't I? I must look a fright!"

"Geez," Kull said. He felt a wave of mortification and embarrassment flood over him. "How stupid of me! How clumsy! I didn't know what I was saying. Forgive my stupidity."

"It's funny," Marjoram said. "Now don't worry about it, it doesn't matter. Now I disappear. And this time I am not lying to you. You will not see me again."

"Where will you go?" Kull asked.

"To a dreary, outlying, out-of-the-way sort of place," Marjoram said. "To some obscure mountaintop, high above a surrounding desert, a desert that is as dry as a bone. Such a place will always be the best place to go when you're old, all used up, dying. In the old days, two thousand miles north of here, that's what the elderly Indian Apache chiefs used to do. That's what I want to do. I want to die of thirst. Alone. That's where I want to go. Kull?"

"Yes?"

"Hate the Gaia-Domes. Remember not to hate me."

"I won't hate you, Marjoram. I promise I'll always hate the Gaia-Domes. That's easy to do."

"Good. And attack the Gaia-Domes. Do it. And forgive Iona too. At times, compassion can be more important than wisdom."

Chapter Twenty-Seven

BEFORE IONA EVEN HAD TIME to return to the Eagle's Nest, Marjoram's prediction about the Gaia-Domes came true. Kull received the terrible news. A group that was larger than their usual limit—a long distance foraging group—had been attacked and nearly annihilated by a small detachment of the Gaia-Dome army 390 miles north of the outlying cave-center-complex. Only two of the party of thirty managed to survive the attack. Traveling at night, one of these two survivors broke his arm and fractured his ankle in a rock slide and had to be left behind. The other survivor, fully ambulatory and fiercely strong, knew how important it was that he report back as soon as possible. He managed to make it back to the caves and the Eagle's Nest in less than fourteen days. Running twenty-eight to thirty-four miles after the sun went down each evening, crawling into the shade and sleeping and napping during the day-time hours, he emerged from the incident miraculously unscathed.

Kull maintained a long-standing rule that bad news be reported to him as quickly as possible.

"What happened?" Kull asked.

"We were ambushed," the survivor replied.

"You were trained not to take chances," Kull said sternly. "It's in the code. What happened?"

"As required, we traveled only at night," the survivor said with a faint look of guilt on his face. "We did not light a fire. In daylight sleep hours we dispersed into small groups as prescribed. We did worse."

"Worse?" Kull asked. "Go on."

When there had been an incident, returning patrol leaders were required to respond to questions posed by the Eagle's Nest with "yes's" and "no's," and where appropriate, with "worse's" and "better's." Since the patrol leaders were dead, the survivor of course spoke for them.

"It happened during the day," the survivor continued. "We found a swimming hole. Fifty miles from the edge of the Forbidden Zone. Imagine that! Fifty miles! Never could have found something like that five years ago."

"Go on."

In spite of his bone-weary fatigue and haggardness, the survivor could not hide the fact that he was filled with guilt. His eyes shifted nervously. "A swimming hole. Large enough to accommodate us all. It was splendid! There wasn't a soul around. Everything was perfect. How could it be dangerous? Just an hour or two of bliss—dipping into the coolness of the water. We were surrounded by rock formations. A gorgeous azure blue sky above us. And plenty hot!"

"In the middle of the day?" Kull asked. "The whole group exposed?"

"Worse. No overgrowth of bows of plant matter growing and flowing and rotting and constantly covering the sky—as in the jungle—or darkness of the cave. For once, we could stretch out in the sun. It was as if we were alive."

What's there to complain about, Kull mulled silently to himself. They were children. All they wanted to do was live. They were as blind and stupid as plants struggling toward light. Kull was shaken from his reverie by the survivor's peevish comment: "Was it all that foolish? Was *it* all that wrong?"

"We won't be living in caves forever, you know" Kull said in what he hoped would be taken as friendly, kindly, consoling advice. "We'll move on—*eventually. You need to exercise patience.*"

"Some of us have been living in caves nearly all our lives!" the survivor barked back in an angry voice. "I was marched here when I was five. I'll be seventeen next year. I don't want to spend the rest of my life in a cave! I'd rather die of sun death, or be enslaved by the Gaia-Domes, or be eaten by mindless, crazed cannibal-scavengers than live a long life but ending up dying in a cave. In the cave I live in, there are cavefishes down in the pools. They're completely blind. The only thing they eat are tiny cave-dwelling invertebrates that the cavefishes detect with sensors on their head and body. Take away all the Gaia bullshit, is that what we mean by the 'UNSEEING' part of the 'WATCHFULNESS'? Huh? Mimic blind fish living in dank, dark caves? *That isn't living!*"

"Agreed," Kull replied. "It isn't living. By the way, if you're caught, you won't be *enslaved* by the Gaia-Domes, you'll be butchered. Your little sisters, some of whom haven't been born yet, some of whom won't be born yet for another hundred years, they'll be the ones who will be *enslaved* by the Gaia-Domes. *Worse than enslaved.* Now, did you make any divisions?"

Kull spoke his words in rapid succession, bringing the subject right back to the attack.

The survivor snapped back to attention. "Worse. No divisions."

"Did you post guards or sentries?"

"None."

"How did you manage to escape?"

"Nature called. For me it was blind chance. When the attack occurred, I was relieving myself."

"Anyone captured?"

"Better. Commander, sir, none."

"Are you sure of that? That's the important thing. Remember well."

"Better. None were captured. Absolutely. I saw the whole thing."

The survivor described the incident. "I was completely hidden from view by a low-lying overhang, in the rocks. When the attack began I crawled in deeper. Everyone was shot. It happened so fast. The firing was so fast that they practically cut all of my comrades in half. The bodies collapsed. It looked like the guns weren't shooting bullets either, it was like laser beams. A helioplane flew over and dropped a jelly-like substance over the bodies. They burned for a few minutes and only ashes were left—there was no odor of burning flesh, no funny chemical smell. No odor at all, nothing in the air, just the smell of ashes as if in a fire ring. The operation was accomplished with surgical precision. With one body part they almost missed, they actually came back and attacked this lone torso floating in the water, incinerating it. Five minutes later the Gaian army was gone. The helioplane departed."

Kull gazed long and hard at the survivor, using his most intimidating and abrasive-looking scowl. "Did you employ a safe route? You know what I mean, along the western slope of the continental divide? At least when you were in the vicinity of places that had a history of known enemy activities?"

"Yes," the survivor replied eagerly. "Except once. Except for that one night before we arrived at the water hole."

"But for the night before?" Kull said. "Go on."

"It was a gorgeous night. There was a full moon. By moonlight, we could see everything—and so clearly—in front of us. Our lead took the eastern slope of the divide for a journey of twenty miles that night."

"Why in the name of Gaia did you do that!" Kull exclaimed.

"Thirty-five miles away, there was snow on a mountain top. Beautiful snow. All along a lone mountain ridge too. *Deep snow.* Has such a thing occurred in nature before? Perhaps so. But none of us had seen that before. By walking the eastern slope we could gaze at the snow in the glint of the full moon for the whole night journey. If we had taken the western slope, we would have had no view, or a lousy view."

"A lousy view?" Kull asked musingly. "No view? The joy of aesthetics, enjoying nature for what it once was and what it will eventually become again, and the simple joy of living—*for once in your life,* splashing in cool water, and it all ends in death." Kull's voice softened. For a moment, he stopped speaking in his role as commander. "Those were the things—the good things—that Tom talked about in his philosophy on the skin. Those were supposed to be the things that we were to prepare ourselves for."

Kull resumed his interrogation with a renewed intensity. "You made it out alone, then?"

"No, there was one other," the survivor said. "At the time of the incident, he was miles away. He had been sent out to reconnoiter an alternative route down from the swimming hole. I teamed up with him that very night. We ran fast and hard, but he fell in a rock slide. I left him at a rock-crop overhang to recover from his injuries on his own. *But he wasn't at the waterhole when the attack occurred.* He may make it back. Or, he may not."

"If he is captured, he will be tortured—horribly tortured," Kull said, "you understand?"

"I know," the survivor said.

"He would have plenty to offer in the way of telling them—*showing them*— how to find our caves in the jungle."

"Doesn't matter," the survivor said. "He knows how to prevent himself from being taken alive. Better." Taking a deep breath, he paused. He swallowed hard. "May I speak plainly, sir, *and freely?*"

"Yes," Kull said.

"With a leader like Iona, fighting against oppression—as the primary commandment given by the commander—is a whole lot easier to do than simply seeking our own freedom."

"No, you're wrong there, fighting against oppression IS freedom," Kull said. "I'm sure you've heard this over and over. I'm sure it's been drilled into you many times. Iona would argue that that is the ultimate point of your following the true creed of the true Gaia."

"Fighting against oppression being the equivalent of freedom is a debatable point," the survivor shrugged. "But if I were to argue the point with Iona—in the end, ultimately—she would silence me."

For a moment, Kull had to internally debate this point with himself. "I can't speak for Iona. Although I would prevent you from destroying our chances of survival, I would not stop you from thinking, and I would not stop you from talking. *Even if we were at war. And we are.*"

"Is that a promise?" the lone straggler asked.

"You're dismissed," Kull ordered.

Kull did not let on, but he was secretly grateful and gladdened in his heart that the young man was not afraid to say what he was thinking. Iona had always said that the day a subordinate can't speak his mind or complain is the day we've lost all right to command. Kull never mentioned it to anyone, not even in the strictest confidence, but he was sick of constantly dwelling in caves too. But what was the point in bringing the subject up?

That night Iona returned. Before they even had a chance to greet each other, Kull told her what happened. Kull also related to Iona all the information Marjoram conveyed to him.

"They have attacked us first," Iona said. "Now we shall attack them."

"Where?" Kull asked. "When? And how?"

"We won't go near where the army operates. That's just what they want. That would be a suicide mission. We'll attack a garrison. Not the nearest garrison to the jungle, nor the next nearest garrison, either. No, we'll attack a garrison that is many miles away, at least 800 miles away. We'll make sure the farmers and country people know all about our accomplishments after we've completed our mission. Then we'll make another feint. We'll threaten a Gaia-Dome, *faraway and in a diametrically-opposed direction,* but we won't take the Gaia-Dome. We'll just shake things up."

"What will we do then?" Kull asked. "They'll be expecting us to attack again. We'll lose all element of surprise. More importantly, they'll be looking for us. Surely, they'll take the offensive."

"They'll know we exist," Iona nodded, "we won't be able to change that. Once our animal is skinned, the fur won't grow back. Marjoram was right to warn us. But they don't know just yet where to find us. Day or night, the jungle is dark. And we are now better spread out. If they did know where to find us, we would have been attacked at our home base, and in a large force. They'll know we exist, but they won't know *where*."

"We attack again?"

"No."

Kull felt compelled to speak his mind. "If we don't attack them again, and they find us, they'll attack us, and they'll annihilate us. They'll destroy us outright. WE WILL BE THE ONE'S THAT WILL BE EXPOSED! They'll have the air power. They'll have the eyes. You know that."

"Yes, you're right," Iona said. "I agree. There's no question they will. They'll have strong motivation, too. High-technology robotics, unlimited firepower, they have it all. That's why we have to be careful in keeping a distance from them. No, after we destroy the garrison, and after we threaten one of the Gaia-Domes, we'll surprise them. We'll disappear. We'll spread out into even smaller groups into thousands of square miles, and like water evaporating in the sun, we'll disappear. But we won't disappear. We'll only seem to disappear. We'll seep underground. We'll become inactive, like underground water. Then, wait. Wait. Wait forever. It will seem to them as if it were waiting forever."

"Wait?" Kull said. "I don't get it. Just wait? Wait for what?"

"Wait for as long as it takes," Iona said, shrugging her shoulders. "Ten years? Perhaps even longer. All of our children, at least the ones who are growing up now, will have by that time matured. All of our leaders, the wise ones, and their growing number of assistants, will be in their prime. When the magisters of the Gaia-Domes have forgotten about us, and everything has seemed to return to normal, we'll regroup. Then we'll move. And our movement will be swift and bloody and deadly and sure."

Iona paused.

"An unflinching awareness of the difficulties to be overcome is more important than action taken without such awareness. We'll break into small cells. None of the cells will have contact with each other, except for those immediately adjacent to one another. The Gaia-Domes may penetrate a cell. They may destroy it. They may make their way to a neighboring cell. But that cell will know that it's time to commit to suicidal death before they allow themselves to be penetrated, thus breaking the chain. If we manage to do that, the Gaia-Domes won't be able to infiltrate our group as a whole. Total isolation through complete decentralization. No hierarchy. Everything horizontal. All communication horizontal. *The Unseeing Watchfulness of Gaia* will become invisible. It will give us time to figure out a way to survive so we can fight another day."

"The Gaia-Domes have formidable advantages," Kull said. "They have ruthlessness, brute force, the latest and greatest in military technology, and all the resources the world has to offer. Imagine that. Allayed against us. We will be the flea and they will be the elephant. By the way, I thought I was the military commander."

"You are the military commander," Iona nodded, "no question about it, but this is where my vision intervenes with your strategy. Relax Kull, we have some advantages too. We have patience, time, the willingness to die rather than be taken prisoner, and invisibility. We will have sleeper cells that will enter the Gaia-Domes' domestic service as slaves and servants and gather information. Our young girls will be strong. They will be devoted. When they escape, and they will escape, they will return with intelligence about the Gaia-Domes' vulnerability. The Gaia-Domes' growing dependence on slaves and servants shall be their weakness. Even in the most powerful of organizations, that can't be a healthy development. *They're changing. Their adaptation shall be to their disadvantage. We're changing too, but our adaptation shall be to our advantage.*"

Chapter Twenty-Eight

THE OVERLYING STRATEGIC DECISION to attack the far-flung garrison was made by Iona, but the tactical details were left to Kull. Straightaway, he figured out a plan. The plan was daring and extreme on the one hand, but also paradoxically conservative in key aspects of its implementation.

One group of older children (in their early teens) deliberately allowed themselves to be taken prisoner by the garrison's guards. This was a dangerous ploy and extreme discipline was required on the part of the participants. Another group, led by one of the wise ones and three assistants, attacked the garrison from the outside. This group posed as humble, harmless farmers bringing food to market. An interior spy—a favored servant girl of the garrison's assistant commander—acted as a go-between to the interior group of recently-captured prisoners and the external group of warriors posing as farmers. The servant girl's younger brother was one of the recently-captured prisoners and it was through him that the special mission was communicated to her.

The success of the endeavor hinged on two things: surprise and timing. The external group carried underneath their clothing a few laser guns (standard Gaia military issue), but what was critical for their success was gaining access to the garrison's arms cache, and also, simultaneously, being able to liberate the newly-captured prisoners.

The ability of the servant girl to leave the premises of the garrison at will and to provide intelligence, copies of keys and code-words both to the arms cache and to the holding pen that housed the newly captured prisoners, was critical to the mission.

The attack on, and the complete annihilation of, the garrison of three hundred troops 900 miles north of the edge of the jungle turned out to be a brilliant tactic. No one was expecting it, least of all the garrison's commander. More importantly, no one in the Gaia-Domes high command military structure was expecting the attack to occur so far from what they had defined as potential areas of activities of forces calling themselves The Unseeing Watchfulness of Gaia.

Within four weeks of the attack, and the immediate propagandizing of the event to the population outside the Domes, the Gaia-Domes army sent out patrols. They sent fifty detachments within a 350-mile radius of where they had attacked The Unseeing Watchfulness of Gaia foragers at the large water hole, and these detachments were massively armed. But all they could turn up were farmers who even under torture would not speak about the whereabouts of Iona's jungle stronghold. They had no idea where it was.

And from the Gaia-Dome army, no one wanted to patrol the jungle. Those who had been sent out made only ineffective passes into the region. And the unexpected attack at the garrison 900 miles away to the north drew nearly half of the Gaia-Dome patrols into a wild goose chase in the wrong direction. The troops themselves preferred to do their search and destroy missions in the deserts, in the farming areas, in the mountains, but not in the jungle, because they feared the dangers that lurked in the jungle the most.

Then a Gaia-Dome was attacked, in the opposite direction, 1000 miles to the south, in Central America. But no substantial violence occurred. The water system was attacked and sabotaged. Some of the glass in the Dome was cracked. Some of the slaves who had been held inside were set free. But it was more a symbolic gesture than a major military operation. And that was it. Then the attack was suddenly broken off. Like ghosts in the night the attackers came, and like ghosts in the night, they disappeared. They did make a great deal of noise about one thing: To all the farmers they ran into, they celebrated themselves as The Unseeing Watchfulness of Gaia. Slowly, a legend began to grow.

And the ultimate mission had been accomplished. The armies of the Gaia-Domes were stretched ridiculously thin, from north of the Isthmus of Panama to the region 300 miles north of the Forbidden Zone, a distance measuring almost 2000 miles. And into this huge mass of territory, the Eagles' Nest send out small parties—cum—underground cells, where, like moles, they burrowed into the sand, and they seemingly disappeared.

And then, SILENCE.

Absolute silence.

Chapter Twenty-Nine

KULL HAD A CHANCE to conduct a brief interview with the one person who was the key to the success of the attack on the garrison, the twenty-one-year-old servant and slave-girl, Conchita.

Within months of the garrison's attack, the news of Conchita's accomplishment had spread throughout the region. It had spread throughout the caves of the jungle naturally, even before she herself had a chance to make a visit on her own, but her fame was resounding also in the world of farmers and peasants everywhere. Driven by despair, suffering from hopelessness, eking out a near-subsistence existence outside the protection of the Gaia-Domes, and constantly preyed upon by the Gaia-Domes, the farmers and peasants were thrilled to have a popular heroine, someone to believe in.

When Iona heard news of Conchita's exploits, she was overjoyed. "Excellent. Well done. We'll make Conchita the figurehead for our cause. Her exploits will be highlighted and dramatized. We need to keep my name out of it. The Unseeing Watchfulness of Gaia needs to be seen for what it is, a deeply philosophical revolt against the Gaia-Domes, but also a proper slave revolt. The longer the Gaia-Domes don't know that I am alive and involved in this revolt, the better. It will keep the leaders of the Gaia-Domes guessing and perplexed about our overall purposes and goals."

Kull was taken aback by Conchita's appearance, he was expect-

ing someone strong, heroic, and larger-than-life. She was barely five
feet tall, thin-boned and petite. Although she possessed an inner
pool of grace and natural beauty, there was something hard-bitten
and threatening about her exterior. Life certainly had been cruel
to her. Her eyes had a strange combination of "faraway-look" and
edginess: like she was constantly assessing things, never at ease. She
seemed incapable of living a life of idleness, boredom, or passivity. If
ever there was a person who had been born to seek revenge for the
death of others, it was she.

"You wanted to see me?" Conchita asked Kull, coming straight
to the point.

Kull greeted her with a friendly smile. "It's not that I have a lot
of questions to ask. I just want to know how you managed to defeat
the enemy."

Conchita was nonplussed. Kull felt that she was perhaps a little
resentful of all the commotion that she had caused. It was clear that
it was not by her choosing that she had been made the poster-child
of the slave revolt. But she took to her new task as a matter of duty.

"I dreamt of doing it every day I was in captivity," Conchita
said. "It was easy. All that was required was that I—at the right moment —slit my master's throat. I had plenty of opportunities. His
wife was there to bear his children and be the mother of his legiti-
mate offspring, but I was there for everything else that pleased him.
It was often that he drank from the cup that I bore for him."

"But how did his death bring down an entire garrison?" Kull
asked.

Conchita's eyes narrowed. "There was always one impediment.
Always one. I could have walked away a free woman at any time. I
had access to escape. There was no one within the garrison's reach
who was trusted more than I. The problem was what would happen
to everybody else left behind. I had the power to save myself, but
I didn't have the power to save others. They would have been torn
apart, brutally raped, tortured, murdered *in payment for* my escape.
There would have been the taking of hostages. What the authori-

ties are willing to do to *others*, not to *you*, but to *others*, is how they command obedience and allegiance. I couldn't do it on my own. My mother, my sisters, and when he had allowed himself to be recaptured, my little brother, too, they would have all perished. More than that. The village that we came from would have been razed to the ground."

"But you did walk away a free woman," Kull said. "And your mother and your sisters and your little brother walked away too. And more importantly, you freed other slaves that had been suffering under the yoke of the garrison commander. *For thousands of miles, they are now singing songs of praise about you! You are called Conchita the Great!*"

"Only because we were able to disarm and destroy the entire garrison. Only because there was a plan and a way to take on the whole group. That was because of *The Unseeing Watchfulness of Gaia*. Once accomplished, we all walked out of there. It required a comprehensive, worked-out, strategic plan."

"Once again, was it hard killing your master?" Kull asked, repeating himself. "I mean, after all, you were his slave. Whatever gift of life you had, he held it in his hands."

Conchita became angry. She wanted to spit in Kull's face, but she suppressed the urge. "I was never his slave. I never allowed him to hold that power over me. I was always free. He was just...in the way. And that's why when I killed him, it was no different than slitting the throat of a chicken. If you are willing to risk death, you are never a slave. You can't wait for freedom to be given to you. You must take it. Even if it means with your own bleeding hands. To do otherwise is to collude in your own defilement and enslavement. It is to be a collaborator."

Kull thanked Conchita for her time. He told her he knew that she was tired of telling the tale and that she was a very brave person.

"There are slaves all over the world but not all of them are in the service of the Gaia-Domes," Conchita murmured. "There are slaves who are enslaved to many things. Slaves who are enslaved to material things. Slaves who are enslaved to an indolent life. The leaders of the Gaia-Domes are slaves like that. Because I never was a slave I never had to be freed. *In my heart I never was a slave. If you suffer from that problem, sir, then you are at war with your own heart.*"

As Conchita began to depart, as she started to walk away, Kull called her back. He had felt relief in her answer but he decided to change the subject. He had one more question. "As the former companion of the garrison's assistant commander, you must have had access to information. To the north of your garrison, was there any talk of the existence of a very old man?"

"What?" Conchita asked. "A very old man? You mean a magister?"

"No, no," Kull objected. "I mean a civilian. Someone who escaped the death directives of thirty years ago."

"They're all dead," Conchita replied. "You must know that. My parents told me how the elderly were placed in so-called 'work-camps.' They were never put to work. They were snuffed out. My grandmother lived with us—we hid her—beneath the floorboards in our hut. She taught me a lot during that time. Taught me a lot? *Goodness me, how much she taught me!*"

Kull did not give up. "I know what happened. But I'm talking about somebody who lived alone, who was a hermit, living in a region where nobody was supposed to be able to survive. I'm talking about somebody who managed to dodge the death order not just for five years, or even ten years. I'm talking about close to thirty years. Someone who would be in his mid-nineties by now."

"Let's see," Conchita said, thinking. "At the military base in Nogales. Yes, he survived on his own in the desert for many years— how he did it is a mystery. He wandered into the military compound and the military commander took a shine to him."

"Was he," Kull asked, "by any chance, in his younger years, before the Eleven-Years-War, a novelist and a poet?"

"A what? How should I know about those things?" Conchita sniggered. "Why are you asking me that? If he ever had existed, which I doubt, his writings and his books would have been destroyed eons ago. Poet? Writer? Pah! The stuff of legend. Just as there isn't a single dog left in the *Sierra Espinazo del Diablo*."

"Hah, just thought I'd ask," Kull said. "Only a thought. You're dismissed."

Conchita thought for a minute. "Wait a second," she said. Something held her up, and suddenly, her eyes brightened up. "Come to think of it, it had been said there was a very old man who was a master of storytelling. He was—how do you say?—*a conversationalist,* or more accurately, an amateur entertainer. That would have been the reason why—the only reason why—the military commander kept him around. He kept him around so to relieve him of his boredom. Now that I think about it, I guess our garrison commander five or six years earlier saw the gray-haired old man do a speechifying event once when he was up there on an official visit. He had been struck by him enough to have commented on his speaking abilities. That's what I remember being told."

Kull's face lit up. "What was the old man's name? Was it...Tom Novak?"

"Who? The garrison commander? No. He's dead. I shot him in the head. He actually wasn't that old. Why are you asking me so many questions?"

"No, no, no, I mean, the *very, very* old man," Kull begged. "Please get back on point. The civilian, you know, the *conversationalist.* The entertainer of the military commander in Nogales."

"Oh, *him*," Conchita replied. "I don't know. I don't even know if he had a name. The military commander at Nogales died of a heart attack eighteen months ago. With him gone there would be no reason to keep a contraband old man around, in standing contradiction of the law. You can get into trouble for that."

Kull did not relate to Iona the story Conchita had told him

about the illegal existence of the old man under the protection of a military commander in Nogales. With the death of the military commander in Nogales, his protector, the old man was probably dead too. Kull did not want to create any false hopes along those lines.

Besides, the last thing Kull wanted to do was give Iona motivation to send out another attack unit to try and take over the military base at Nogales. That would have been pushing their luck. The military base at Nogales was twice as large as and more firmly fortified than the garrison they had successfully attacked and destroyed. It was 1800 miles away. There was no powerful slave like Conchita safely hidden away in the barracks of Nogales to aid them.

Kull was now firmly in charge of all tactical military questions. He knew that they needed to decommission all military operations, once and for all. For all intents and purposes, THE UNSEEING WATCHFULNESS OF GAIA must seem to have completely disappeared.

Chapter Thirty

THE SPECIAL MAGISTER, Lloyd Thompson the fourth, was seated at his desk. He got up, walked over, and with the wave of his hand, removed a heavy metal curtain grate and looked out through a long, oblong-shaped window. What could he see? Nothing. There was practically nothing but thin air. He was one thousand feet high in a tall, slender cylinder. He was at the top of a high control tower, like a space needle, high above New York City, looking at what had been left after all the destruction of what once was—a massive sea of humanity below.

Like his father before him, and in the final fifty-one years of his life, his grandfather before his father—the special magister had spent his life inside the Domes. From birth, for thirty-six years, he had spent his life in a state of opulence, nurtured in caste privilege, safe in the protective shell of the cozy Dome universe.

The previous year, at age thirty-five, this gentleman had acquired the sobriquet: special magister. With his special education in Hominid and Post-Hominid Studies, there were only four like him in the entire Gaia-Dome system.

He returned to his desk. He read a bulletin. The first items were nothing special. There had been a couple of coups in the Domes in Europe. The rulers of the European Domes were a fussy, erratic lot, typically more volatile than the more stable rulers of the American Domes. And there was some growing evidence of climate change in Greenland and North Africa. This was the boring and predictable news. It was followed by more of the usual: the business climate between America and Europe had improved, while business had declined somewhat between America and Asia. Then, at the bottom of the bulletin, there was one bit of news that was different. In particular, it caught his eye. *"Group of rebels destroy garrison in Mexico. For one month, threatened Dome. When subsequent interception was attempted, unable to locate group. All scouting expeditions unsuccessful. Cannot be spotted. Origins of rebels: completely unknown. Route of retreat of rebels, also completely unknown. Course of action undetermined."*

The more the special magister thought about it, the more troubling this last bit of information became.

His intuition told him to make a special note of it.

Then he remembered what he was required to do the next day. His presence was required at a trade show in Chicago.

The special magister murmured to himself: "I hate going to these shows."

From New York he left for Chicago the next day.

In Chicago, after spending the day at the trade show featuring New Farming Implements and New Weapons Technology, he was wheedled by some magisters into attending an after-hours, illicit event.

The special magister tried to beg off. "I'm tired. I beg you. It's been a long day. No thank you."

But his colleagues insisted. Many of those present were younger than he. Their insistence was adamant. The ringleader, a blond-haired, blue-eyed fellow, who couldn't have been more than thirty years old, spoke on behalf of all. "You've got to see this show. I'm sure they don't have anything like it in New York. It's a must-see."

"Sickies, aboriginals, and circus freaks, no thank you," the special magister said in a tired voice. "I've been to these dungeons and mental institution pits before."

"You're too set in your ways! Just like your father was. Ah, this show is different!"

That night, they picked him up at one of the central Domes.

Most of the displays at these shows nauseated the special magister. What disturbed him the most were the mental retardation cases. Men and women, with shaved heads, bound hand and foot, were forced to conduct themselves in multiple positions of humiliation and knavery. When their tongues—spouting forth gibberish, began to grow silent—they were doused with buckets of water, and their tongues wagged and the flow of nonsense started up again. Some of them engaged in the most frightful form of calisthenics. They all smelled bad. These shows had always left the special magister demoralized. To his chagrin, upon viewing these proceedings, the other young magisters hooted and jeered, gawped wide-eyed, enjoying themselves, as if they were children.

When the special magister insisted he'd seen enough, his hosts said there was one more exhibit he had to see before closing time.

The last exhibit was a cell holding a single individual.

There was a sign attached to this individual's chest that read, "Thomas Novak."

He was seated in a chair. His hair and beard were long and flowing. He wore on top of his head a crown of green laurels. In his hand he held a staff, burnished the color of gold flake. Bunched around his shoulders was a robe. His naked thin knees stuck out in front of him.

In front of the cell was a sign that read: "Ninety-seven-year-old man. Miraculously preserved! Miraculously still alive!"

The special magister looked carefully into Thomas Novak's eyes.

Thomas looked back, staring straight back at him. The two of them stared at each other for a minute. Tom reminded the special magister of his grandfather, one of the most eminent and important grandmagisters of the world-wide Dome system, who had died three years before, at the age of eighty-two. As the special magister stared into Tom's face carefully, he realized Tom and his deceased grandfather bore a certain resemblance. The special magister shivered as a memory from his childhood struck him.

The special magister demanded to see the owner of the show, without delay. When he found him, he insisted on seeing him privately. The owner took him to his office in a back room.

"How did you come to acquire this man?" the special magister asked the owner, referring to Tom.

The owner's eyes shone with greed as he smelled the potential for a profitable transaction. His eyebrows shot up. "You have a professional interest in this piece of property?"

"I could have you put away for this, for trafficking in this serious contraband," the special magister shouted in an angry voice. "Just answer the question. Don't play games with me. I am in no mood to be humored."

"I bought my share of him from a certain businessman who had a partnership with me a while back, a year ago. He had picked him up in the Western Quadrant, in Nogales, near Mexico."

"Mexico?"

"Yes. Near the old border."

"How did he get *there?*"

"I don't know," the owner said. "My understanding is he was from the south. How he eluded the mass euthanasia of the elderly—so many years ago—now that's a mystery beyond my comprehension."

"He can talk?" the special magister asked.

"Oh, yes, he can talk, all right," the owner said. "He doesn't talk much, though. Very rarely, anyway."

"I noticed he has a cough. Is he sick?"

"Yes."

"If he dies between now and the coming of the morning, I'll

have you killed, understand? Have him cleaned up, properly clothed and decently fed. Then have him brought to my hotel room tomorrow afternoon, 3 o'clock sharp, understand?"

"Yes."

"You're to mention nothing about this to anyone, understand? You'll be given a small token of reimbursement for your trouble. From now on, you are to act as if you have never known anything about this man, understood?"

The special magister confiscated the contraband from the owner and sent him packing with a warning.

He secretly transported Tom Novak back with him to New York. He placed him in an unused room, in a retirement home, set up specifically for the use of old retired magisters.

He gave explicit written instructions to the caretakers that Tom was to be well taken care of and he was even allowed books to be read, if he asked for them.

When the caretaker asked him why he was keeping him alive, in spite of the rules, the special magister replied, "I have this strong suspicion that some day this man's memory will be of some value. I am banking on a hunch. Only a slight hunch. Time will tell. We shall see."

"A hunch?"

"This man once knew my grandfather. Actually, he didn't know my grandfather—rather he impersonated him, stood in for him, as an actor, in a 'History of the Cosmos Show,' or a 'History of the Universe Show,' it was one or the other, I don't remember the exact name of the show. Anyway, Thomas looked exactly like my grandfather. *Spittin' image.* They could have been identical twins. The show occurred in New York City. I believe it was in YEAR GAIA ELEVEN. I was six years old at the time. It was a long time ago, but I can't get the memory of this man out of my head."

"How could you be sure it was him?" the caretaker asked. "After all, you're referring to something that happened thirty years ago. You were just a little boy."

"I know," the special magister said. "I checked the secret archives. There is only one mention of a Thomas Novak. He was specifically defined as an 'ex-writer,' *an exotica flora.* Back then, there was this tiny group of graybeard ex-writers who were holdovers from the pre-Gaia days. They had been active writers in the pre-Eleven-Years-War days, that's how far back these dinosaurs went. Thomas Novak had been famous for writing a book called *Expressions Without Illusions.* The book came out in 2034 A.D., old calendar. Today, of course, nobody knows about it. There were archives back then, International Archives, Big Boy also, but they don't exist anymore. Well, the only reason why the archives mention him at all is because he served in a minor capacity in our Propaganda and Information Department for five years, between YEAR GAIA SIX and YEAR GAIA ELEVEN."

"He should be dead," the caretaker said. "He would have been sixty-eight years old or thereabouts in the YEAR GAIA ELEVEN," the caretaker added. "He would have been subject to the citizens' euthanasia. In the retirement homes, *inside* the Gaia-Domes, the authorities didn't even bother killing the elderly. They turned off the heat. They quit bringing food in. They starved them to death. Or in the height of cold snaps, they froze them to death. The authorities could control things so much better inside our own protected biospheres. It was much more complicated outside the Domes, where they had to round the elderly up and put them into camps. Took longer to accomplish the task."

The caretaker stopped going on when he realized by the look of dissatisfaction on the special magister's face that he clearly wasn't interested in hearing more sad stories from the bad old days.

"Is there anything else in the secret archives that is interesting?" the caretaker asked.

"Only this," the special magister said. "In YEAR GAIA ELEVEN, Thomas Novak simply disappeared. Vanished into thin air. Not a trace. Gone. Eradicated from the record too. And then this old 'smiley-face' pops up out of nowhere, like a corpse that won't die, and he has the potential for opening up a whole new can of worms."

"I'm confused," the caretaker said. "From where you were standing when you were six years old, how could you swear that this Tom Novak was the same man who impersonated your grandfather? So long ago? So much has happened over the years."

"I know, I know," the special magister said in a testy voice. "Makes you think though. Does the name, Regis Snow, or the name, September Snow, mean anything to you?"

"No," the caretaker said. "Should their names mean anything?"

"How about the name Iona? Regis and September Snow's daughter. Does that name ring a bell?"

"No."

"Odd, isn't it?" the special magister said. "It's as if they've been scraped clean from our collective memory banks by the official historians of the Gaia State, but they all existed. It's true. Not a product of myth but for real. The parents, September Snow and Regis Snow, were once leaders of a great rebellion. Their names were purged from the archives. Even the secret archives doesn't mention them. *And the young daughter, Iona?*"

The caretaker stared straight ahead. He compressed his lips. He looked at the special magister with a blank expression on his face. Over the years, he had seen so much.

"Maybe I'm wrong," the special magister said. "Maybe it's just something I want to believe. It's all speculative on my part. But I think there's something here. And if there isn't something here today, maybe, just maybe, there will be something here tomorrow. Or the day after tomorrow. After all I've seen in life, I'm a patient man."

Chapter Thirty-One

BEGINNING IN YEAR GAIA THIRTY NINE (2090 A.D.), four years of struggle went by. Iona and Kull continued to soldier on with their mission. They believed with every fiber and muscle of their bodies that they had to march forward. They carried on their shoulders the burden of a seemingly hopeless mission, but they never allowed thoughts of failure to enter their minds. They never displayed anything but endless fervor and a never-diminishing hope. To all their followers they were a family portrait of ever-growing confidence, radiating with a spirit of galvanizing trust. The words "despair" and "hopelessness" were forever banished from the collectives' vocabulary.

Iona was a born natural at the task of fostering unbridled hope. Not a single setback ever fazed her. She was almost fanatical in her belief that anything could be accomplished through the use of indomitable will—*her indomitable will, the collective's indomitable will, Gaia's will.*

Kull was less visionary, more realistic, and more calculating. But he maintained a high level of steadfastness. He was driven by a profound sense of duty. He was methodical, practical, but always in a pinch, highly resolute and never lacking in follow-through.

Although Iona was regarded as the titular head of the group, in their own inner-workings, Kull and Iona worked as a team, more or less as equals. In a profound way, in a good natured way, they critiqued each other. They also supported each other.

Iona was different from Kull (and different from the wise ones) in that she was driven by one thing and one thing only: a super-sensitive, hyper-charged fire given to her through the poetic mani-festation of a prophetic foresight. Her fire was there for everyone to experience. But the insights that fed this fire were drawn from powerful visions. She had visions of THE UNSEEING WATCH-FULNESS OF GAIA defeating large Gaia-Dome armies. She had visions of liberating hundreds of thousands of slaves. She had visions of the group being able to seek out and find a homeland, a place that was safe and secure from the reach of the Gaia-Domes, where THE UNSEEING WATCHFULNESS OF GAIA could thrive and prosper and provide permanent hope for the future of humankind.

To Kull's consternation, Iona continued to have visions of Tom Novak being alive. She thought if they tried hard enough, they could find him—and in finding him, reap the benefits of his knowledge, his wisdom, and his experience.

Kull judiciously kept his thoughts to himself, but if Iona's vi-sions were true, why didn't they tell her where Tom *was located*. Sure he was hard to find, it was almost certain he was dead!

Iona was upbeat. She was also disciplined in her displays of lead-ership. She was revered by all. She appeared to her followers as if she were a celestial creature, in the role of an all-conquering, aveng-ing angel. To her followers, she was more than human, seemingly hovering over them, watching over them, and guiding them. Iona's followers not only felt safe in her hands, they drew deep pools of comfort from her steady leadership. It was increasingly clear that Iona was only one or two steps away from making herself a goddess, with all the good and bad that that transformation might entail.

In his private thoughts, Kull had become more somber and concerned about these disturbing aspects of Iona's leadership. He kept these thoughts to himself, but he wondered about them with a growing unease and fear. *Were Iona's followers becoming overzeal-ous in their devotion? Were they becoming overwhelmed by powerful*

emotions that could drive things spinning out of control? Iona's follow-
ers sought from Iona judicial balance and wise council, but they also
wanted more. From his readings of the forbidden books in sub-magister
Clive's library, Kull had studied how the dispossessed peasants of me-
dieval Europe were driven by irresponsible leaders to go on murderous
crusades and seek out false messiahs. When they were drunk on messi-
anic promises, Iona's followers showed similar signs of fanaticism. Were
they also on the brink of following irresponsible leaders? To Kull, the
step from ecstatic vision to fanatical frenzy was short. If they did not
tread carefully, Kull could see everything they were building collapsing,
degenerating into self-delusional excess and mass hysteria.

Sometimes, in the case of Iona's followers, especially in the case of
the younger ones, THE UNSEEING WATCHFULNESS OF GAIA
was becoming eschatological in scope and exaggerated in its "height-
ened sense" of spirituality. But then Kull balanced his worries with
counterbalancing thoughts. Considering the nature of the crisis they
faced, extreme measures were required. Drawing on the wellsprings of
a fundamentalist religious impulse may have been the only thing that
was keeping the group from disintegrating. Kull had to face some hard
facts. Being divided up into small, isolated cells, all of the followers
were now required to fend for themselves, becoming isolated risk-takers,
without the comfort of nearby leadership. Considering the enormities of
the dangers they faced, maybe the motivation deriving from extreme vi-
sions was necessary. Maybe fanatical religious passion wasn't conducive
to somber rational thought, but at least it was necessary for those facing
impending disaster. Deep faith eliminated fear. Maybe Iona's last secret
weapon, extreme radical religious piety, was the last and final arrow
she kept in her quiver. To shift the metaphor, puritanical religious piety
was like that last measure of gruel you kept in the bottom of your sack to
sustain yourself when all the other foodstuffs had run out, and that thin
measure of gruel kept you from going over the brink.

And indeed, as they came to realize too abruptly, the four-year-
long ordeal became a brutally harsh crisis that almost destroyed them.

One hundred and seventy-six cells were destroyed by the armed forces of the Gaia-Domes in the first three years alone.

In the end, a total of 287 cells were lost out of 850 cells, a loss ratio of one in three. Iona never expected that the loss to the organization could have been so great or so widespread.

Among the dead was Conchita, who met her end in fierce hand-to-hand combat. Dominic and Elsie, the two highest leaders of the wise ones slid to their deaths in a loose rock avalanche. Of the other twelve wise ones, seven also perished: four dying slowly from starvation in the middle of the Sonoran Desert and three from an attack by units of a Gaia-Dome army. The loss of so many wise ones was keenly felt, for they were the most educated and experienced of all the adherents.

Yet, throughout the four-year-long ordeal, the organizational integrity of THE UNSEEING WATCHFULNESS OF GAIA remained intact. Throughout the onslaught there was never a hint that the armed forces of the Gaia-Domes ever dreamt they were facing an organized group. In their reconnaissance missions, the Gaia-Domes failed disastrously. In the individual cells, iron discipline had been maintained to a fantastical degree.

It was as if the Gaia-Domes swatted and killed small groups of bees, but they never found the main beehive, much less discovered the queen mother.

By the beginning of the fifth year of "the ordeal," the attacks on the rebel cells, at least under the supervision of the armed forces of the Gaia-Domes, all but ceased. By the end of the sixth year, the Gaia-Domes conducted no more attacks on the cells at all.

The Gaia-Domes apparently had completely given up trying to locate THE UNSEEING WATCHFULNESS OF GAIA. The high command of the Gaia-Dome armies had even begun to wonder if any such underground guerilla organization had ever existed. Some of the cells had been able to reform themselves into larger groups, gaining greater protection against the natural elements and against the small attacks of the cannibal-scavengers.

Under the leadership of Iona and Kull, a central group was also formed, although most of the time they kept on the move, constantly dividing and re-uniting. Most of the time this moving organized force spent their time in the isolated mountains on the western slopes at the southern end of the Sierra Madre Occidental Mountains in Mexico, where any kind of movement was extremely hard to monitor on the part of the Gaia-Domes. As they so successfully had done before, they always traveled at night, and always in small groups.

What was left of the group were the most battle-hardened and toughest survivalists that ever existed in the world.

Any one individual component of this UNSEEING WATCHFULNESS OF GAIA army was more forceful and stronger (and far more motivated) than twenty conscripts in the Gaia-Domes army could ever be. THE UNSEEING WATCHFULNESS OF GAIA had become a magnificent machine.

By the end of the fifth year of "the ordeal," Iona and Kull knew that the time had come.

In the YEAR GAIA FORTY-FOUR (2095 A.D.), Iona and Kull sent out explorers to see if there was anywhere—anyplace—where the entire group, *en mass,* could migrate. It seemed like an impossible dream but Iona knew it could be done. A total of ten groups, consisting of twenty-five members in each group, were created by the newly-formed central command. They were sent out to explore, reconnoiter, and return with a report.

Two groups traveled a mere five hundred miles. With the same purpose, three groups traveled one thousand miles away. Of these five groups, all of them were completely unsuccessful in finding a safe base-camp large enough to accommodate even a group that was one-quarter the size of the larger group.

Five groups traveled a farther distance, 2,500 miles to 4,000 miles away. Two of these groups traveled to South America, deep into the Amazon River region, and even deeper still, into the central and southern valleys of the Andes Mountains.

Simultaneously, three groups traveled to the north, to the heart of North America. The first group went to the western coastal strip. The second group went to what had been formerly named the "Midwestern" section. Third group went to the "Western Quadrant," an area that included the northern part of the Sonoran Desert and the area north of that, the entire Colorado River plateau, including the western drainage of the Rocky Mountains and the western deserts reaching all the way to the eastern slopes of the Sierra Nevada Mountains, the largest single unpopulated area.

Of these five groups, two did not return, not even a single straggler came back. They were destroyed when they got there, met their fate along the way, or were waylaid on the journey back. These two groups had been sent to the "Midwestern" section, and to the western coastal strip, places where the forces of the Gaia-Domes were especially strong.

Only one search party found a place where the entire group could settle and survive. The safe area was in the northern half of the "Western Quadrant," north of the Colorado and the Little Colorado Rivers, the area of the Rocky Mountain western drainage, and the area of the high deserts east of the Sierra Nevada, an area that had been left empty, where there was plenty of space to expand.

They found that the region had been a difficult place to live in even before there had been any climate change or sun death. Some of the fiercest fighting in the early years of the Eleven-Years-War occurred in the region, which devastated the fragile natural membrane that allowed human life to exist in the first place. Even before the environment had gone into a huge attack mode, it had already been practically uninhabited. The subsequent climate change and sun death *kept* it uninhabited.

But the area was perfect for THE UNSEEING WATCHFULNESS OF GAIA. They had adapted to live in small, isolated, self-sustaining groups during the worst and most trying times of "the ordeal." There were overhang areas, almost cave-like, which offered protection from sun death and predators. In the high desert regions, there were unoccupied expanses of land perfect for development, for those who could live as survivalists. It was an area that the Gaia-Domes had apparently given their lowest priority.

It was a place that would accommodate everyone in the group, where they could all live in peace, harmony, safety, but above all, with plenty of space to grow. They could become hunters and gatherers, or primitive farmers, *or both*, perfectly suited to survive outside of the Gaia-Domes. And unlike the ruling elite of the Gaia-Domes, with its increasing reliance on slave labor and repression to maintain its privileged existence, the cruelty of the environment would never allow THE UNSEEING WATCHFULNESS OF GAIA to grow flabby, bloated, or complacent, thereby allowing them never to succumb to a debilitating degeneration into decadence, or hamstrung by a calcifying institutional inertia, very unlike the seeming future fate of the Gaia-Domes with their undiminished imperial ambitions.

The problem was, how could they survive if the Gaia-Domes decided to invest all their remarkable resources and splendid technology in a project to wipe them out. After all, the Gaia-Domes had done that before. They had done it with extreme prejudice during the time of Regis Snow and September Snow's rebellion, when they responded with pinpoint focus and ferocity.

In the mean time, the leadership of Iona and Kull had other things to work out. Seemingly, the only thing they had going for them, besides their resourcefulness and training, was the fire of Iona's visions. Relying on Iona's visions kept Kull's mind rife with anxiety and disquiet. He knew what the Gaia-Domes were capable of doing once their interest had been directed and focused.

Chapter Thirty-Two

Iona and Kull began preparations for their move to the Western Quadrant in earnest. From their base in the Sierra Madre Occidental Mountains in south-central Mexico, it was a journey of 1800 miles. All of the individual cells had been contacted. They all had to be given their long-term instructions. The more decentralized the group had become, the more crucial the long-term planning had to be.

They had to form an army for purposes of protection and to facilitate possession of territory. They had to travel like an army, but the army had to be broken up into much smaller groupings. They could only strike as a combined force when it was strategically necessary.

The first thing Kull did was send a group up the Gulf of California in small boats. They would then travel up the Colorado River to form a base at the northern end of the Sonoran Desert. They were sent out in three different waves.

Then he sent two other groups up the two chains of mountains of the Sierra Madre Occidental and the Sierra Madre Oriental, to provide forward base camps for the army to follow when they made their move to the Sonoran Desert.

Then came the army itself. Forming the army just meant calling in all the cells. Whenever possible, the army would bypass all settlements, not just formal Gaia-Domes, but even smaller establishments. More importantly, the army would do whatever it could to circumvent and go around the Gaia-Dome armies. If necessary they would go underground for six months to prevent a direct assault or hazard an open battle. The best way to engage the enemy was to keep away from it as far as possible, by dispersing and regrouping, then dispersing and regrouping again. Constant movement and flexibility were the two great advantages they had. They used both of these tactics to the utmost.

But they knew that along the way they might have to face the enemy in the form of a Gaia-Dome army and they would have to fight a battle. An actual battle: that would be something new and dangerous, something they hadn't experienced before.

But they would *travel* differently—like no army had ever traveled before. Kull divided THE UNSEEING WATCHFULNESS OF GAIA into fifteen parts. Always hiding during the daylight hours, they marched at night. During the entire 1800-mile-long journey, they had only three rendezvous points, where they reunited. Their reunification points lasted only for a few weeks and they tried to place them at intervals that were as far away from permanent Gaia-Dome establishments as they could manage. All went well for the first 1200 miles. At one point the Gaia-Domes tried to set up lines to trap them, but they simply penetrated through the weak points in the line. The Gaia-Domes had not faced an enemy like this before. Even in the context of traditional engagements they had had little experience. The new troops and their leaders were not battle-prepared and not battle-proven. Peace-time had lasted too long for them to come up against a "nighttime-traveling-only" army that never stayed in one place and was spread out over a five-hundred-mile-wide front. THE UNSEEING WATCHFULNESS OF GAIA enjoyed the benign neutrality, if not the active support, of literally every single civilian they met along the way. That was indicative of how much the Gaia-Domes were loathed and feared by everyone who lived outside the Gaia-Domes. It was easier to find a rat in the desert—during the daylight hours—than it was to find a member of Iona's phantom army.

But then at one point in their movement everything changed. THE UNSEEING WATCHFULNESS OF GAIA came up against something that was totally unexpected. They realized that for them to continue forward they'd have to act as a regular army, if only for a few weeks. At one place less than one hundred miles from the old border between old Mexico and the former United States, in the middle of the Sonoran Desert, they were going to meet a Gaia-Dome army of 50,000. There was no going around this force. And there was no turning back. The Gaia-Domes had placed this army in their path because it was the only way they could think of to stop their progress.

At this point, because of the slaves and peasants they had picked up along the way, Iona and Kull's army now numbered 8,500. But even with this buttressed force, they were outnumbered by the Gaia-Dome army by a ratio of six to one. It seemed like an impossible equation. But Iona came up with a novel idea. Since they had control of the "nighttime," they could stay undercover until the last minute. If they could force the Gaia-Dome to fight on their terms *at night,* it would minimize the Gaia-Dome's greatest advantage, air power. But that in itself could not undermine the Gaia-Dome's numerical advantage. They needed something more.

If they could control the access of water to the Gaia-Dome troops—*if only for three or four days before the attack was to occur*—they could change the odds.

Sabotaging the Gaia-Dome's rations and munitions was a next to impossible task. But in the middle of the desert, sabotaging the water source, that had a better chance. An army, whose morale could not be particularly high if it could not rely heavily on its air force to tilt the balance, could not fight effectively if it had run out of water.

It required twenty-five suicide squads to perform the task. Iona, always the supreme optimist, placed the odds of success at one in three. Kull, the realist, had placed the odds at one in ten.

"We are all going to die here, you must know that," Kull said to Iona. "I'm not worried—you understand, we must do what we must do, I'm fully committed, but I'm trying to be objective."

Iona thought this through. "Probably, you're right," she replied. "But have you ever heard of a Gaia-Dome army being defeated through the destruction of their water sources, fifty miles behind their lines? They won't expect it. If I were them, I wouldn't expect it. They think the air power of their helioplanes will destroy us, but they can't attack what they can't see. They're setting up their attack lines right here in the middle of the desert, not out of choice but out of necessity. They can't do it in the mountains because it won't work, we would go around them, that's what they've learned from our progress over the last 1450 miles. They can't do it on the coast either, because we aren't on the coast. Their over-reliance on air power is going to be their biggest mistake. Their army will *fry* out there in the desert. And unlike the professional battle-hardened soldiers they used to rely on twenty-five years ago, or even as recently as five or ten years ago, their land forces consist of press-ganged conscripts. If we can convince them that water won't come in time—and they can't depend on air power to back them up—their troops will surrender in droves."

"A great plan," Kull repeated, "but we're going to die out there, all the same."

"Why do you insist on being so negative and defeatist?" Iona asked in a calm voice.

Kull was insistent. "A guerilla force, regardless of its size, has never defeated a standing army of the Gaia-Domes—*ever*. I don't know why I need to remind you of that stubborn fact. The only thing we have going for us is that the Gaia-Domes army may turn out to be extremely incompetent and suffer from extremely low morale. That's my hope."

"We'll surprise them," Iona said. "We'll even surprise ourselves by our valor! You'll see."

Kull was unconvinced. "Your overconfidence amazes me," he said. "Understand, I'll do anything you ask. I'll go to the gates of hell if you demand it. But consider. Because even if we surprise them by creeping up unbeknownst in the dead of night, the Gaia-Dome air force will not hesitate to attack us even if it means killing their own troops. I'm talking about helioplanes. They'll attack their own, indiscriminately, along with us. Their army is just bait anyway. *That's what they do! That's their strategy!*"

"We have no choice," Iona said. "All we can do is roll the dice. We shall succeed."

The suicide squads were dispatched and placed on a forced march of one hundred miles on the first night, in order to go around the Gaia-Dome army. At the farthest extension, the Tarahumara Indians—the Raramuri—the greatest long-distance runners in the world (able to run 130 miles at a stretch), were dispatched to the farthest outreaches. They destroyed the water sources at every location behind the lines, within a radius of one hundred miles. Water could be brought in from greater distances away within four or five days, but not sooner. And the Gaia-Domes helioplanes waited for the army to appear, but it didn't. It traveled undercover, even in the desert.

Kull led the first assault wave that hit the front line of the Gaia-Dome army exactly four days after the water sources in the rear had been sabotaged. Timing was everything.

Iona waited for the first groups to come back.

Kull came back on his own. He was limping. As he drew near, his limp grew more severe and pronounced. When he got close to Iona, standing right next to her, she looked down and saw a gaping wound on Kull's leg. It was nine inches long, running down the back of Kull's upper thigh. Blood was flowing freely down Kull's leg. Kull's eyes looked ghostly and unfocused. Was Kull in pain? Iona was able to deduce by the intermittent and occasional shaking of Kull's hands that he was.

"You were repulsed?" Iona asked, ignoring his wound. "We kept waiting to hear the sound of the helioplanes. You never made it to their lines? They attacked you? They came forward and attacked you? You never made it half-way there? What happened?"

Kull collapsed into a chair. He sprawled out—with his legs sticking out in front of him. Grasping a towel from the back of a nearby chair, using both his hands and his teeth, he tore the towel into pieces. He placed two broad pieces of cloth, methodically, oblong, on his wound. Then he grabbed another towel from the back of another chair and started tearing it into strips.

Quickly, Kull tied the strips around the two pieces of cloth that he had placed on his wound. He applied the strips of cloth with precision and swiftness. What made this activity so bizarre was Kull was able to apply all of these makeshift bandages on the *backside* of his thigh—utilizing a dexterity that would have impressed the most nimble of gymnasts. Kull was *both* double-jointed *and* ambidextrous.

Kull twisted the strips around the pieces of cloth, cinching the strips down with firmness. He then tied the knots so quickly, with such dexterity, Iona couldn't believe it. Miraculously, the broader pieces of cloth stayed in place, secured by the strips of cloth. He turned to face Iona.

"How did you do that!" Iona exclaimed. "I'm amazed. Could you do that again?"

Kull had worked so fast, he was like a speed-demon, like a man possessed.

Acting as his own physician, Kull had formed a perfect tourniquet. His breathing became less haphazard and less pronounced. Kull sighed.

"During all those five years I fought with that hopelessly ragtag guerilla band, my greatest fear was having a survivable wound—but only myself to treat it. During one intensely-fought battle, I had to lie alone in a ditch under enemy fire and pull a quarter-inch piece of shrapnel out of my scrotum. The only thing I had to bind my wound up with was a dirty sock. *Now that was difficult.*"

For a quick moment, Kull gasped. Then he demanded water. "I've never been thirstier in my life."

Iona quickly handed Kull a large gourd that was filled with water. Taking large gulps, yet pacing himself carefully, Kull drank down almost all of the water. He was silent for a minute.

"As you predicted, the Gaia-Dome front-line troops ran out of water," Kull said. He drank down the last dregs of the water in the gourd. "Happened day and a half ago. Most of them didn't even bother to pick up their weapons. Man alive, were they frightened. As you also predicted, their officers panicked. Most of the troops ran toward us before they could even sound the alarm. They surrendered in droves. A few stragglers ran to the rear, but they didn't do so in an orderly way. It was a miserable disorderly rout. With us crawling on our bellies for six hours, they didn't see us coming—not until we were right on top of them. When we jumped up, they panicked. They *wouldn't or couldn't* call in their own air force *in time.* That's a miracle. Apparently, by the time they saw us, it was too late. That's why I got back here before everybody else. Our 7,500 troops are out there right now trying to corral 20,000 dazed and confused prisoners. That's the good news. The bad news is that they divided their army into two groups, with a distance of five miles between the two lines. What we've defeated is only *half* the Gaia-Dome army. We have neutralized 25,000 troops, better yet, many of them may even defect to our side, but there is a second line of 25,000 troops five miles to the rear. Although their water is being rationed, the second group hasn't completely run out of water, yet, apparently. We've learned that by interrogating prisoners. Do you have another miracle to pull out of your bag? With the second half of the army, there will be no surprise *this* time. And their helioplanes, their mighty air power, will be ready. They won't make *that* mistake a second time. They will attack us by air." When Kull realized that the tourniquet was having a positive effect he emitted a massive sigh of relief. A look of joy briefly flickered over his face. "This is going to be a tough act to follow."

"How did you get hurt, Kull?" Iona asked.

"One of their officers insisted on playing hero."

"What?"

"He was lying on the ground, pretending to be dead. When I stepped over him, he reached up with a knife and tore up the back of my upper thigh. The wound is quite long. It tore laterally into deep muscle tissue. The back side of my upper thigh is a hopeless mess."

Kull cried out in extreme pain. "My! Gaia! I think that for more than an hour or so, I was pumped up on adrenalin. Amazing! I crossed all that ground. I must have been a mad man. *On this! On this!*" He pointed to his leg.

Iona smiled. "Lie down. You've lost a great deal of blood. That's a nasty wound. You need to rest."

Kull smiled. "On our side, we couldn't have lost more than fifty people outright. And of the wounded, there are only a few hundred, but I'm one of them. It's a great victory. The most important thing is we managed to get them to surrender without their helioplanes bearing down on us. *You were right about that.*"

"It's the water," Iona said, "or rather, the lack of it. For the uninitiated the desert is a frightening place. Their troops were green. The suicide squads did their job. Except they weren't suicide squads, after all."

"What?" Kull asked. "What do you mean?"

Iona gave a huge smile. "Eighty percent of them returned unscathed. Their plan of sabotage was a complete success. The enemy never thought they could go around such long lines of a dug-in army, but they did. They were successful in blowing up most of the water depots between here and Nogales, Cananea, Agua Prieta, and Janos. They are our true heroes. They blew up most of the water depots going back as far as one hundred miles, twice as far as we had planned. Come tomorrow night, the Gaia-Dome troops that remain in their trenches will be without water. Sure, they will be able to fly the water in from farther away. But it will take them several days, perhaps even as long as four or five days, to do it. Of all the contingencies they planned for they never had planned for this one, water in the desert. It's too simple. It's elementary. Water in the desert."

"Maybe with a crutch I can lead the next attack," Kull said. "We won't have this opportunity again. This is a marvelous opportunity."

"With that wound, you're going nowhere," Iona insisted. "It's amazing you haven't passed out already. It must have been—as you said—all that adrenalin. It's only because you're so strong you haven't gone into shock. You need rest. It's going to take many weeks for you to recover. The answer is simple. I'll lead the next attack."

"That's impossible," Kull said. His eyes were clouded with fatigue and pain but he spoke with clarity and resolution. "You mustn't do that. I insist. You mustn't do that."

"Why not?"

"Well, you're our leader, aren't you?" Kull said "It would be a dangerous risk. We can't afford to lose you."

"Well, that's the whole point, isn't it?" Iona said laughing. She clapped her hands together. "I'll be in the front line of the second attack. That's settled. A woman leading an attack. If nothing else, it'll shake the magisters up, hiding in their Gaia-Domes. They'll be afraid to sleep. Frightened a woman slave will steal in the night and stab them as they lie in bed. Kull, that *also* is where the battle lies. In the hearts of our enemies. We'll play on their worst fears. To defeat a Gaia-Dome army of 50,000 strong. Amazing! Unheard of! Word will travel. At least, for a while, the upper echelons of the Gaia-Domes' hierarchy will experience *real* fear. Our actions will result in the liberation of thousands of slaves. You mark my words. There'll be nothing to bar our way. The way to the central and northern area of the Western Quadrant will be open to us."

"You're going to get 25,000 *more* troops of the Gaia-Dome army to surrender, *just like that?*" Kull asked. He snapped his fingers.

"Are you going to shoot down the Gaia-Dome Air Squads with your bow and arrows? Are you going to get the rest of the Gaia-Dome army to surrender by a timely intervention? Perhaps through the timely intervention of a miracle?"

"Maybe I just will," Iona said. "Maybe I have another miracle up my sleeve. You'll see."

Kull stayed quiet. He closed his eyes. He started to slump over. He roused himself.

"What's the matter?" Iona said. "Goodness, Kull, you're starting to turn green. You need to rest. I heard your story about your scrotum, but how did you do it?"

"Do what?"

"Dress your own wound. Make that tourniquet so effectively."

Kull closed his eyes. Then he reopened them. "I once had an opportunity to bind up a person's wound. To save a life. The life to save—his name was Stoolie. But I didn't succeed. I wasn't quick enough. I was all thumbs. For many a year, night after night, I dreamt of saving him. But I didn't. Over and over, night after night, more frantically, more desperately, I tried to save him, but I couldn't. I did manage to keep him alive for a while, but later, he succumbed. Over and over, I tried. Ironically, I saved my life. But I couldn't save his. I can tie knots now, even in my sleep."

Kull began to nod off. Like a glutton for punishment, he managed to rouse himself again. What was driving him? Iona wondered. Why didn't he desist? Why didn't he allow himself to rest?

"One thing, I didn't expect...occurred...in the battle," Kull said. His voice was slurred. With stupendous effort he managed to rouse himself yet again.

"What's that?" Iona asked. Iona could see that she couldn't stop Kull if she tried. It was as if he were possessed by a demonic force.

"Even when the outcome was certain," Kull said. "Even when victory was preordained... There was so much...so much..." He paused. He couldn't find the words. He looked grief-stricken and awkward for a moment.

"So much *what?*" Iona asked. Iona was intrigued yet baffled by Kull's unreal, out-of-character diffidence. His story about Stoolie—his obsession, it all seemed so surreal.

"Go on?" Iona asked. "Speak."

"Confusion," Kull said. He looked as if he were on the verge of collapsing again. He slumped over. Then he raised his head again. "That's it. There was so much horrible, bloody disarray. Confusion everywhere. That's what the battlefield was...confusion, confusion, confusion. When I saw my first death, so many years ago, I thought, I couldn't have been more than three or four years old at the time, I thought I was going to throw up. But I didn't."

A field commander from the battle appeared out of nowhere. He saluted both Kull and Iona. Addressing both of them, he reported that everything on the battlefield had been stabilized, everything was under control. A smile beamed across his face. He looked thrilled and happy. It was obvious that this had been his first battle.

Kull smiled. Iona thought, what a brilliant commander Kull was. All this time, all this talk, some of it idle, some of it otherwise, that's what had kept Kull awake. It was necessary for him. He needed the report. All this time, he had been waiting for *that*. Now he could allow himself to sleep.

In his chair, Kull slumped into a state of unconsciousness.

Chapter Thirty-Three

KULL WAS TAKEN TO A CAVE in a mountainside sixty miles removed from the edge of the battlefield. Requiring ninety stitches, his wound was bound up. But a minor infection set in. Because of the infection the wound had to be continually drained, redressed, and looked after. During his convalescence, Kull fell into and out of a mild fever. The doctor, a young woman of eighteen, who was watching over him, had informed Iona that Kull's life was out of danger, but he needed rest, and above all, he could not be moved for four weeks.

Upon hearing this, Iona put Kull out of her mind. She did not think of him for the next two weeks. All of Iona's energies and focus were concentrated on the plan to capture the remaining Gaia-Dome army and do it without helioplanes inflicting severe damage on the army.

Iona decided to double-down. The suicide squads could not attack the water sources again. *That* element of surprise had been lost. Besides, during the time it took to take control of the many thousands of prisoners, twenty thousand altogether, there was no longer a crisis in the enemy's water supply. Most of the suicide squads were ready to make another attack. The water could be replenished even if it had to be brought in from farther away (although that would have tied up some of the enemy Air Squads and prevented some of the helioplanes from assuming combat assignments, which was also a net plus) but the element of surprise was lost.

Yet all of the remaining suicide squads were ready and eager for another fight.

In an intimate setting, Iona drew all of the team members around her. She asked them point blank whether they'd be willing to risk a suicide mission a second time. They all replied in the affirmative.

"But this time the danger will be greater," Iona cautioned. "Most of you may never come back."

One person was chosen by the group to speak on behalf of all. "Some of us have been waiting all our lives to do this. Besides, we think we've figured out what it is that we've been doing that is keeping us from being captured."

"And what is that?" Iona asked.

The woman who spoke was a seventeen-year-old girl with a dark complexion and closely cropped raven hair. She brought out a tattered (but once laminated and therefore fairly well preserved) seventy-five-year-old petroleum map that showed the exact location of all the gas stations that had existed in the greater region of the Sonoran Desert in the year 2022 A.D.

"The map shows the exact places of each gas station from Ciudad Obregon and Alamos in the south, to Tucson and Phoenix in the north, showing both sides of the old borderline markers between Mexico and the United States, back when they were independent nation-states. We already know now that the map is accurate."

Iona studied the map carefully. She shrugged her shoulders. "So what?" she asked. "Practically all of those gas stations were completely obliterated during the Eleven-Years-War. In most places, you can't find a single cinderblock left. And the old derelict gas pumps, scavengers tore them apart decades ago. I know, I've traveled through this region before. In most cases, not only is there no physical presence, but the ground has been swept clean."

"Yes," the young woman said. "What you say is true. But the cavities where the underground holding tanks where the gasoline was stored are still there. And most of these cavities still have the empty gasoline tanks themselves, hidden under the ground."

"Empty storage tanks? Hidden under the ground?" Iona's asked. Her eyes lit up. "As you cross the most exposed parts of the Sonoran Desert, you're hiding in the empty underground gas tanks. How ingenious."

"Exactly," the young woman said. "By day, they won't see us when we're hiding in the tanks. And in between bouts of hiding, we can travel by both day and night and not be detected. Traveling during the daytime hours and nighttime hours gives up more time. That's why we were so unexpectedly successful at sabotaging their water systems and then were able to report back to you. We used the map the first time. It will work again the second time."

"Those water systems were at most one hundred miles out," Iona said. "This is a mission that will require you to push farther afield. Three hundred miles out. Even farther. And the depots where the helioplanes are parked will be much better guarded."

"Sabotaging the water systems was a practice run. This will be the real test."

"You can hit every helioplane port within four hundred miles north of here?" Iona asked.

"We can hit each one of them. I believe so."

"They can still scramble helioplanes from far away. Even a thousand miles away," Iona warned. "Even a thousand miles is just a few hours trip."

"But it will take them longer to release those helioplanes," the young woman replied. "Sabotaging and crippling helioplanes will be a lot harder than sabotaging water supplies and we'll have to travel farther distances. We can't do anything about helioplanes stationed a thousand miles away. You'll have to disable the enemy army extremely quickly, before they can be scrambled."

"Even if three or four helioplanes get through they can do horrible damage," Iona said. "Just three or four helioplanes attacking when our troops are at their most exposed could take out half of

our army. The water sources were a numbers game. All you had to
do was knock out most of the water sources and you caused a two-
day-long water shortage in the enemy's front lines. But you have to
get practically all of the helioplanes." Iona smiled. "You don't have
to destroy them, just cripple them. Cut their fuel lines, lock down
their landing gears, pour water in their fuel tanks, break the windows
in the pilot's cockpit, I don't know." Iona remembered when her
mother September Snow had flown Tom and her in a helioplane
from Bolivia to Juarez. She remembered that her mother was a brilliant aviator and an unparalleled flyer. Iona had only been six at the
time but she remembered the incident very well. From this experience alone Iona knew the extraordinary things helioplanes were
capable of doing. They were profoundly lethal weapons.

"Slice their tires," the young woman said. "It's the simplest
and easiest way to cripple helioplanes. We've agreed it's the quickest
way."

"Which means we have to take out every single one of them,"
Iona said.

It immediately became clear to Iona that the young woman had
been sorting out these problems days in advance. Sabotaging aircraft
was the easy part. Getting to them was the trick.

"We've already set up a system of interrogating prisoners to
glean information about where the helioplanes are located," the
young woman replied enthusiastically. "They freely give information. They feel no ties of loyalty toward their former masters—in fact
they now see their former masters as monsters and criminals. They
seek revenge on the hated Gaia-Domes and when we're able to show
how vengeance can be theirs, they cooperate with eagerness. Some
of these individuals are even willing to act as guides for us, as unbelievable as that sounds."

"As suicide squads, how did you know I was going to be asking
you to go after the enemy's helioplanes?" Iona asked.

"It's logical," the young woman smiled. "Besides, the enemy
won't be expecting it. Your mother, September Snow, sent out sui-

cide squads almost thirty years ago to destroy the nuclear-powered wind machines that were destroying the climate that your father set up for the Gaia-Domes. If it wasn't for that sacrifice, we wouldn't have a glimmer of a chance of succeeding at what we are going to try to accomplish over the next few weeks. It's as much for them as it is for us."

"So you knew I was going to ask you to go after the helioplanes?" Iona asked. "You've demonstrated significant strategic vision of your own. I wish Kull had been here to see this, and to hear you speak. He would have been thrilled. But consider. It means almost certain death for many of you, you know."

"We have no choice," the young woman said. "If necessary we will blow ourselves up to get at the helioplanes. It's only an Air Force. It's only technology. Death is not bad when it's for the right cause. Death must come at the right time. If we can achieve access to the helioplanes, all we have to do is disable them. Slice their tires. It's the simplest way."

If the suicide squads did their job, Iona knew they would succeed. The second half of the Gaia-Dome army, a mere twenty-five thousand troops, was just ripe for the taking.

Chapter Thirty-Four

THE ARMY, NOW DOWN TO 6,500 combatants (they needed 700 personnel to guard and oversee the 20,000 prisoners they had accumulated) were ready to go. Once the battle was over, they decided they would free the prisoners. There was nothing they could do to hold them. *They had barely enough provisions to feed half of them, and even providing them with water, even in just the short term, was daunting.* It would have been a logistical nightmare to try to bring more than two-thirds of them to the Western Quadrant. Only the ones who could prove they had a genuine yearning for joining THE UNSEEING WATCHFULNESS OF GAIA would be given a chance to join their ranks. A week after the last battle, the rest would simply be let loose to fend for themselves, and if they wanted to return to the Gaia-Domes, then they would be allowed to do so.

Iona had told the suicide squads that they had five days to complete their mission. On the sixth day—without waiting for word of success—the attack on the second half of the Gaia-Dome army would commence. If the suicide squads had done their job, all would be well. If not, most of Iona's followers would die and those that were left would be blocked from continuing north.

Beginning in the middle of the night, the army crawled out on their stomachs—but this time, to be extra cautious, they crawled for eight hours—before they arrived at the front lines of the Gaia-Dome army. Then they jumped up, and attacked, using a blood-curdling scream. By the time they got to the front lines, they discovered that most of the Gaia-Dome army had already melted away. The rest of the army fled in the direction of Iona, waving their arms in the air to surrender. Some were screaming, "The helioplanes are coming. They'll destroy us all. You and us combined. We must get away from here." Iona thought she would never see the day when enemy combat troops would be sent out with such incompetent leadership, poor discipline, and lack of morale. *Practical and consistently dour in his thinking and prognosticating, Kull had been right about that all along.*

Iona told the potential prisoners that they needed to run for their lives, that they would not be taken as prisoners. She ordered her own troops not to take any prisoners. She ordered her own troops to pick up any laser guns, if there was enough time, and take them back with them. Then she ordered her troops to run back to their hiding places, and lay low, until they received further orders.

Within weeks, word had gotten back to the magisters in the Gaia-Domes from the last remnants of the army that they had suffered a huge defeat, and a woman who was fearless and heroic was the leader of the group that had attacked them.

The myths and legends of THE UNSEEING WATCHFUL-NESS OF GAIA grew beyond all reason. Level-headed magisters were skeptical of most of these claims. But there were four things the magisters could not deny. A Gaia-Dome army of 50,000 had been utterly destroyed by an unknown guerilla force. The Gaia-Dome helioplanes, so critical for tactical success in any major combat situation, had been kept from being deployed in time to turn the tide of the battle. More than 14,000 prisoners of the Gaia-Dome army had not returned and most of them were presumed to have defected to this mysterious guerilla army. Throughout the Western Hemisphere, a certain number of slaves, first a small trickle, then a larger group, were reported to have "gone missing," having escaped from the hold of their masters in the Gaia-Domes. Even though they had no way of knowing how to survive from sun death in the real world, which meant many of them would certainly die of exposure, these slaves risked escaping anyway.

Without warning, for two months, there was mass disorder in central and northern Mexico, ranging all the way up into the heart of the Western Quadrant.

But then the magisters realized that the worst was over. The battle was lost but there weren't going to be any more battles in the near future. The routes between the Gaia-Domes stabilized. Things simmered down. Some of the escaped slaves came crawling back to their masters, begging for mercy and to be let back into the Gaia-Domes, freely allowing themselves to be re-enslaved. The outside world was still a dangerous place to live in. But others threw themselves into the waiting arms of the followers of Iona, and gladly joined the growing ranks of THE UNSEEING WATCHFULNESS OF GAIA, as it prepared itself for its march north into the empty quarter of the central and northern sections of the Western Quadrant, just north of the Colorado River.

While all this was happening, Kull lay in his cave recovering from his wound. He drifted in and out of a fever-induced sleep. Running up the backside of his upper leg and thigh, the wound kept him from resting in a sitting position. To sit upright, even for a few minutes, caused extreme pain, placing the wound in a "bent" position. To get from a lying-down position to a standing-up position was awkward, painful and difficult, and now Kull didn't dare try to walk even a few feet without the aid of a cane. He had to take all his meals standing up. Since he was unable to exercise his legs, in order to build up his upper body strength, he lifted hand weights.

For the first time in many years, having so much free time on his hands, Kull reflected on his past. He thought back to all the events that had occurred since he had left on that fateful night in the small boat given to him by Clive, departing from the island of St. Helena. At that time he could not have dreamt of what was going to happen to him.

When the doctor was not in his presence, Kull spent much of his time staring at his wound. In a detached way Kull held a certain fascination for the affected area of his leg. There was no morbidity in this experience, rather he regarded his wound with a detached air of objectivity, almost a clinical-like curiosity. During these intervals, what Kull was fixated on was less on the wound itself and more on the thick blue veins that ran in large curves on the side of the leg—on the leg directly beneath the wound. The blue of his veins reminded him of the Colorado River canyon, at places a mile deep (albeit a brown, silt-leaden river, a mighty river though, all the same), and crossing that river would bring THE UNSEEING WATCHFUL-NESS OF GAIA to their new home. It was a real river located a mere 375 miles to their north. It was to be Kull's river, Iona's river, THE UNSEEING WATCHFULNESS OF GAIA'S river, the river for the future. Kull knew that if Iona won the battle, the river was where the group was headed.

After fourteen days of convalescing, a transformation came over Kull. The fever caused by the minor infection in his leg abated. He learned that Iona had not only won the battle, but had achieved a smashing victory. Hearing this news, Kull felt a sense of relief. He had not made his journey for nothing.

Kull had known since talking to the woman doctor, Marjoram, many years before, that the most arduous form of emancipation was self-emancipation. This had been Kull's greatest personal battle. Miraculously, Kull now realized he was no longer a slave—or, to be more exact, he no longer was held down by the slave mentality. A change had occurred for Kull; he had gained a sense of his inner freedom. The healing process helped Kull by freeing him from the dark incubus of seeing himself in the old way. But what was it exactly that freed him from being—psychologically—a slave? An inexplicable epiphany? No, it was just the humble realization that Kull could not keep blaming the crippling events of his past for the attitudes and positions he held in the present. He had to unchain himself from the moorings that had shaped him when he was a boy and a young man, so that he could be reborn as a new man. *In essence, he had grown up*. Events having happened a little differently, the knife could have killed him. Or, in the aftermath, the fever from the knife wound could have killed him. Or not having the cave to hide in, under the protection and supervision of an altruistic and caring doctor, the knife could have killed him. He could have met the same fate that his old friend, Stoolie, had met.

Recovering from his physical wound meant that Kull could recover from the psychological wounds to his feelings as well. Just letting nature take its course and letting his body rid itself of the impurities and waste from his healing wound meant that he could do the same for his mind and his soul. Wash it away. Dry his tears. He was alive. That's all that mattered. Why not cut himself away from his past, so that he could free himself for the future? Cross the river. Cross the Colorado River and, in the process, cut himself away forever from his past. Do it for Conchita, or for Stoolie, or for Clive, or for Iona, or do it for himself. Cross the river. And he would no longer be a slave.

It took Iona twenty-one days before she could find the time to visit Kull in his hideaway cave.

"I'm sorry it took me so long," Iona said. "As you can well imagine, I've been terribly busy."

"Doesn't matter," Kull smiled. "I know you're busy. I needed time to recover anyway."

The doctor smiled and left the cave to give the couple their privacy.

Iona embraced Kull at his cot. By now, Kull was able to sit upright for short periods of time. He was also able to walk longer distances with the aid of his cane. He was only a few weeks away from becoming completely ambulatory again.

"Only now have I been able to find the time to break away," Iona said. "Dispersing the prisoners took more time than it took to capture them. And vetting the ones who want to stay with us took even more time. We've dispersed into five hundred smaller groups. The Gaia-Domes won't find us now. We're safe. We're ready to go."

Kull smiled at Iona.

"Are you comfortable?" Iona asked.

"I am," Kull said. "But comfort means nothing to me now. It's not my concern."

"Well then, is your wound healing well?" Iona asked.

"My wound is nothing. It's no concern of mine." Kull gave Iona a short kiss. Then Kull gave Iona a long, lingering kiss. To Iona, it did not go unnoticed by her that the second kiss was most uncharacteristic of the otherwise ascetic, puritanical Kull, a man who had a near-obsession with his own sense of propriety and purity. With all of his upper-body strength Kull embraced Iona for a long time. At last they broke off.

To Iona, Kull looked changed. There was something clearly different about his appearance.

"I am a new man," Kull said at last.

"I'm glad to hear it," Iona said. "But I'm baffled. I don't know what you mean."

Kull took Iona's hands in his own. He interlaced his fingers with hers. Gallantly, he kissed Iona's hand.

"I shall not be the last slave to figure out ways he can set himself free. I won't be the last. I also won't be the last who can find his way back home."

Chapter Thirty-Five

HAVING BEEN VICTORIOUS beyond their wildest dreams, having defeated a Gaia-Dome army of 50,000, having increased their ranks to 24,000, THE UNSEE-ING WATCHFULNESS OF GAIA dispersed into five hundred groups. Their mission was to rendezvous with connectors, *leaders* of the dispersed groups, two to three years in the future, on the north side of the Colorado River, in the tractless dry lands of the high desert, high plateaus and low mountains of the western side of the Rocky Mountains. In their trek, they scrupulously bypassed the larger Gaia-Dome cities. They also avoided all the smaller communities along the way. Some groups fanned out to be on a trajectory as far west as the eastern slopes of the Sierra Nevada Mountains. Others fanned out to be on a trajectory as far east as the low reaches of the western slopes of the Rocky Mountains. Still others, the principal body of rebels, trekked north, into the heart of the region. From end to end, over a broad expanse of more than 700 miles, in very small groups, they traveled north.

It was planned that Iona and Kull would set up a temporary base camp in four years eighty miles north of the Colorado River, in a deep and mostly dry fold of a lower reach of the Escalante Plateau, one of the most isolated, desolate, and hard-to-get-to places in the world. Their plan was to find a place so remote that no one from the Gaia-Domes would ever venture forth to try to find them. But before they could do that, they planned to cross the one mile deep Colorado River canyon to the relative safety of the north and for three or four years, explore on foot the whole length and breadth of this otherwise forgotten land.

Three or four years would also give the small groups of THE UNSEEING WATCHFULNESS OF GAIA an opportunity to establish their tiny, isolated communities, spread out over the broad expanse of land.

Chapter Thirty-Six

SIX WEEKS AFTER THE VICTORY over the Gaia-Dome army of 50,000, Lloyd, the special magister in New York, entered the 103-year-old Tom Novak's cell. His purpose was to try to get Tom to talk about the identity of Iona, and to confirm his suspicions about who the leader of THE UNSEEING WATCHFULNESS OF GAIA really was.

But he failed. In spite of his extreme old age, Tom's mind was still nimble and functioned well. All Lloyd managed to do was get Tom to predict a heavy rain and lightning storm nine days in the future. (Tom had an uncanny ability to predict the weather and his forecast turned out to be accurate.) Tom, four weeks shy of his 104th birthday, died a few days before the storm actually hit.

Lloyd said, "Well, do you have anything more to say for yourself?"

"No," Tom said with a brave grin, "I have nothing more to say."

With Tom's death, Lloyd's one slender connection to Iona, the daughter of September Snow and Regis Snow, was gone. But Lloyd still held on to his suspicions that Iona was the leader of the new rebel group and he spent the next year studying everything he could find in the official archives and in the secret archives about the suppressed history of the accomplishments of Regis Snow when he was chief czar of the nuclear-powered wind machine project, as well as the subsequent September Snow rebellion. Now he was confronted with a new heretical alternative to mainstream Gaia theocracy and religion: the spirituality of the rebel group called THE UNSEEING WATCHFULNESS OF GAIA. These rebels preached against the rigid establishmentarianism of empire in favor of humility, simplicity, chastity, and a survivalist credo untainted by dependency on hateful technology and corruption-ridden armies.

After four years Lloyd had become a kind of expert on the subject of Iona (if it was indeed she) and her followers. He was able to interview two prisoners who had been captured combatants taken from Iona's army. He also came to know some things about Kull, Iona's cohort: both of them originally came from the island of St. Helena, one the daughter of the highest and most prestigious scientist in the then Gaia-Dome world, the other, a son of slaves.

Lloyd learned a few things about the group known as the wise ones. Over time Lloyd had become quite knowledgeable about Iona's group that was characterized by the magisters as "a sect of outsider fundamentalists," or as "primitive barbarians."

In contradiction to the official party line, Lloyd's opinion was that THE UNSEEING WATCHFULNESS OF GAIA represented a hope for the future of humanity; and a hope for the regeneration of the planet. Of course he kept these subversive thoughts to himself.

In the interest of his own survival, Lloyd maintained silence on the subject. In any public pronouncements he carefully toed the party line. Even though they were considered illegals, out-of-bounds; or simply the enemy, Lloyd longed to visit them. He wanted desperately to see how they lived so effectively in the safe retreats of the fastness of the wild, in the otherwise empty Western Quadrant. He was curious about their nomadic, shifting-and-moving life styles. (Lloyd had to admit, enclosed as he was in the Gaia-Domes and protected from the ill effects of normal weather, that he probably sentimentalized and even romanticized Iona's followers.)

Lloyd had been partially converted to the ancient wisdom celebrated by Tom, a wisdom he realized had been almost entirely lost to all of the inhabitants of the Gaia-Domes over time.

Lloyd was an exceedingly patient man. And with his long-suffering forbearance, he couldn't believe what turned out to be—eventually—his most profound turn of luck. Four years after the defeat of the Gaia-Dome army of 50,000, in the YEAR GAIA FIFTY, (2101 A.D., old calendar), Lloyd was ordered by the Domed-city Gaia Magistrate System to act in the capacity of ad-hoc ambassador to the leaders of THE UNSEEING WATCHFULNESS OF GAIA. He was to make the journey and visit them in their stronghold in the Western Quadrant. All of the grandmagisters on the council thought there was only a fifty-fifty chance that Lloyd would come back alive.

This was to be a feeling-out mission, its exact purpose deliberately kept vague and ambivalent. The real purpose was to determine whether the Gaia-Domes should conduct an out-and-out war of annihilation against THE UNSEEING WATCHFULNESS OF GAIA, or whether they should negotiate a tentative truce, or even a longer-term protocol for peaceful co-existence. All possibilities, at least officially, were still open.

Lloyd was to carry a sword in one hand, and an olive branch in the other, even if the Domed-city Gaia Magistrate System had it in their minds, ultimately, to finish the group off and use Lloyd's peace-seeking efforts as a stratagem.

Lloyd knew the mission was fraught with danger, and not only the danger of being the first emissary ever to be sent to the enemy camp. For one thing, he would not be traveling alone. He was to be accompanied by an aide.

The Domed-city Gaia Magistrate System trusted Lloyd Thompson the fourth for his knowledge but the magistrate council did not trust him entirely. Lloyd's educational strength was, paradoxically, his liability. *Lloyd was too deeply influenced by the ways of the pre-Gaia-Dome past to be completely trusted.*

Chapter Thirty-Seven

JAMES CLARE, AT AGE 63, was the second-ranked grandmagister, representing Zone C of North America. He met with his subordinate, Lloyd Thompson the fourth. Only one of twenty-four grandmagisters worldwide, ordinarily festooned in his august uniform of purple-on-greenish-purple multi-layered robe with a large bejeweled balloon hat, James Clare wore his unofficial clothing. He was dressed in a simple pair of trousers and an open-necked tunic, clearly indicating to Lloyd that this was an off-the-record meeting.

In his capacity as grandmagister, James Clare never left the safety of the Gaia-Domes. When traveling, he flew only in helioplanes, visiting only other Gaia-Domes. Like all grandmagisters, Clare was a slave to the insularity of the Domes. In fact, he was ignorant of what the world was like outside the Gaia-Domes, except for what he was able to glean from authorized reports, official briefs, and, perhaps most importantly, informed gossip.

In his handling of underlings and subordinates, James Clare typically conducted himself as any grandmagister would. So long as a subordinate treated him with respect, he could be courtly and polite. But when his authority was threatened, he acted like a cobra—striking back at the merest hint of insubordination.

James Clare had been Lloyd's boss for fourteen years. But atypical for a system that prided itself on imposing rigid adherence to the absolute dictates of hierarchy, the two of them rarely operated in the same orbit. Even though James Clare represented Lloyd's primary link to the magister organization's chain of command, they rarely met in person. When they did, it was usually at formal-dress affairs and quasi-official religious ceremonies. This was an arrangement that was to the benefit of Lloyd. Not a day went by that Lloyd did not appreciate the fact that he was privileged and protected. James Clare was a buffer for Lloyd, cushioning him from the other grandmagisters. In this regard, James Clare was Lloyd's cut out. It was an arrangement that afforded Lloyd an ability to operate with a degree of autonomy scarcely seen in the Gaia-Domes, functioning in isolation, remote from court intrigue, out of contact with the people manipulating the daily levers of power. Not one to be ungrateful, Lloyd was aware he owed this special arrangement entirely to James Clare's commanding patronage and influential presence on the world magistrate council.

Since being notified of James Clare's order, Lloyd wondered if he was crazy for secretly welcoming the charge?

Only seven years previously, the world magister system underwent one of its more severe power purges. Whether one's position was high or lower down, no one was safe. Seven years previously, one-fifth of the personnel in the magister system were declared "heretics of the official Gaia faith" and were allowed the mercy of a quick death by suicide, or a slower one, by execution.

Since that time, there hadn't been any purges, but people on the magister level and above had grown wary and cautious. But how could you toe the line while you were commanded to do something heretofore not attempted? That was James Clare's conundrum. That's why he selected Lloyd for the mission, a man on the inside, but who was insulated from the daily grind of politics.

"You know the man assigned to you will spy on you," James Clare said. "His *raison d'etre*, his sole purpose, will be to watch you. He will try to catch you doing something wrong."

"I wouldn't expect anything less," Lloyd said. "Who is it?"

James Clare smiled. "Celsius Vance. Security. He made his bones
in the security apparatus during the Delias Rebellion. He successfully
mixes candor and careerism, having risen through the hierarchy by
seeking out powerful patrons, impressing them with his can-do attitude, making no secret of his absolute devotion to the directives
of the Gaia-Domes. He has repeatedly risked his life in the name
of those directives. I don't want you to be too frightened by him
though. He doesn't have one-tenth the education you have, just
ambition. He will be jealous of you. Don't be flattered. Considering
the reputation of your grandfather, you're naturally a target. He will
perceive you as practically having royal blood. He will be charged
with watching your every move. I have no doubt you'll find a chink
in his armor. At first, you must convince him you are wholeheart-
edly committed to the brief. You must draw things out. His mind
will wander. If possible, try to set up under his radar a subterfuge
sub-language with your negotiating counterpart. I know that will be
difficult, but try. Now for the trickiest part."

James Clare sat up straight, smiling gently. Daintily, he fingered
Lloyd's shirt sleeve. Lloyd found James's behavior inexplicable, but
he had learned over the years not to make any comment. Using the
tapered ends of his fingers, James Clare gently pulled again on Lloyd's
shirt-sleeve. Suddenly, with a jerk, he pulled hard. Striking like lightning, James Clare clasped Lloyd by the forearm. Grasping Lloyd's
forearm tighter, in a vise-like grip, he pulled Lloyd up, holding him
by his bicep. Slowly rising from his own chair, James Clare practically
lifted Lloyd out of his chair. Lloyd was flabbergasted. For nearly fifteen seconds James Clare stared unblinkingly into Lloyd's eyes, holding Lloyd up by his bicep, straining over Lloyd's chair. Then he let go.
Lloyd sat back down. James Clare looked coy. Lloyd was unharmed,
but his arm ached. A mirthless smile traced James Clare's lips.

"When I was thirty years old, I once broke a man's arm by doing that. I never stopped working out with weights. Keeps me fit.
I'll get Celsius recalled. If I *can't* pull *that* off you'll have no alternative but to follow your brief. Sacrifice the rebels. Double-cross

them. Stab them in the back. Show no mercy. Hang them. Save your own skin. Do what you need to do. *If I can't get Celsius recalled, the rebels aren't worth it.* However, if I do get Celsius recalled, you must give him one-hundred-percent guarantees you are performing admirably—up until the very moment he departs. In that process, you undoubtedly will scare the rebels' representatives. Undoubtedly there will be parties on both sides who will want to kill you, but without Celsius's presence, his junior assistants will be neutralized. They're all unimaginative yes-men anyhow, easily intimidated. You'll need to earn the rebel's trust—but how? Then suddenly, you'll try to make them trust. But how? After all your saber-rattling about how the rebels will be obliterated if they don't toe the Gaia-Dome line as a submissive sub-state, will they then listen to you when you change your tune and offer them something good? That's the challenge. But back here we'll make the most of the mission's ambivalence."

Lloyd wanted to reply but instead he remained silent.

"Once Celsius is gone, you're on your own, of course. None of us will want to know what you did afterwards. *The need is for absolute secrecy on your part.* Celsius must never know—before and *after*—that you broke from your prepared script. He must be played from beginning to end."

Lloyd nodded. "Is this an attempt to lay the groundwork for the destruction of The Unseeing Watchfulness of Gaia or is this mission truly an attempt to save face by officially abandoning the Western Quadrant to the rebels without allowing it to appear to them a passive acceptance of a fait accompli?"

"Oh, you're good!" James Clare exclaimed. He clapped his hands. He loved it when Lloyd pretended to be a *real* diplomat. "Of course we're entering uncharted territory. We have no diplomatic corps to speak of. If we had, no reason to send you. We've never negotiated with rebels before, we've just eliminated them. In the past, we've had no reason to *talk* to them, just kill them. I, on the council, wanted you. You were chosen to go on this mission because of your talents. I pride myself on having done quite a selling job on your behalf."

"Am I to be thankful?" Lloyd asked.

"I was able to prove to the council that there is a close relationship between an inquiring mind and intellectual honesty. We have gotten away with viewing ourselves exactly the way we wanted to without being challenged from the outside—for far too long. We're too arrogant. We need to be brought back to reality. If we want to survive, if we want to be around 500 years from now, we have got to start dealing with the contradictions in the outside world more creatively, without destroying everything."

"But you still avoid the question," Lloyd said. "Are we going to kill the rebels, or are we going to allow them to co-exist with us? It's as simple as that."

"In the short term, it is the latter," James Clare said. "As I said before...ambivalence. Extol doubt! Embrace ambiguity! Have a little faith, my son!"

"Of course I don't have your word on this," Lloyd said in a strangely cheerful voice. "Why am I asking? You can't give me a straight answer. Who else besides me is taking all the risks?"

"Don't be cheeky now, I'm taking risks too," James Clare said. "Just by having this conversation with you, in the eyes of the hardliners, I've committed treason already. I know what happened to your father. It wasn't the reforms he enacted that killed him. They were inevitable, they would have happened anyway. It was just that his timing was bad. *Bad luck.* Allow me the opportunity to disprove the political nostrum that no good deed goes unpunished. The good do not always come to good ends, it's a universally understood principle, but if I have anything to do with it, you might."

Lloyd was reconciled to what was in store for him. "It may work out satisfactorily or it may not," Lloyd confided in a measured and understanding voice. "By the way, how am I supposed to get *there*? The Western Quadrant? Apart from a few forays in a bubble car, I've never ventured more than twenty-five miles from a Dome. It's a journey of over two thousand miles. I know you've never been there. The closest you've been is what you've been able to see on a satellite scan. Twenty-five miles from the protection of Domes in the Western Quadrant, I've heard you can be eaten alive by wolves or devoured by cannibals. And then there's the sun. It can kill you."

"I know more about that than you think," James Clare warned. "The first 1700 miles of the journey will be easy. A routine trip. You'll fly in a helioplane to the farthest reaches of our outpost Dome just to the west of the Rocky Mountains. A little place called Glenwood Springs. We can't send an army unit out to defend you because the rebels will smell a Gaia-Dome army unit from three hundred miles away. Therefore the rest of the journey will be tricky. You're going to be smuggled in by cross-country contraband movers. By the way, it takes many years of exposure to direct sunlight to be killed by sun death, so don't worry, your mission will last no more than four months. And these contraband movers know at least something about these rebels. Some of them lived with them. I don't think you have to worry too much about wolves, but cannibals can be a different story."

"Smugglers, you say?" Lloyd sniffed.

"Once in the Western Quadrant, they'll follow the route of the Colorado River, through the red rock and flinty sandstone all the way into the heart of rebel country."

"And these smugglers are trustworthy?"

"We're offering them gold. Also promises of lucrative trade deals in the future."

"But can they be depended upon?" Lloyd asked. "Once out of sight, what's to prevent these criminals from cutting me into little pieces. How can you prevent them from slitting my throat and dumping my remains in a ravine?"

"Upon your safe return, they'll be given ingots of gold. A large carrot. There's also a stick. We're holding their wives and daughters as hostages. We've promised to rape, torture and execute their wives and daughters, beginning with the youngest—the oldest white-haired hag being the only one we'll leave untouched—and a tongue in her head to tell them what she witnessed when we forced her to observe us violating their nearest and dearest, if you don't return safely. These men are scum. They're miserable. But they value their wives and daughters."

"Nonetheless..." Lloyd said. He unsuccessfully tried to interrupt.

James Clare was testy. "It took us twelve months to round up their wives and daughters, we're not taking any chances, *we want you to come back, quit thinking about it so much.*"

"Of course I'm willing to do it," Lloyd said in a mild voice. "I truly want to."

"I wonder," James Clare continued. "I've never seen you demonstrate physical courage before. You're forty pounds overweight. You've been pampered since the day you were born. Physically, you're not the ideal specimen for this mission. It could get rough out there. But you still want to do it?"

"Yes," Lloyd said. "For years now, I've dreamt of going to the Western Quadrant. *Seeing it with my own eyes. Touching it with my fingers.* Are conditions out in nature as bad as we're told? Official reports! How truthful are they? You must have wondered about this. I've dreamt of seeing Iona. In all my studies, I've never seen anything that was more interesting than this group of energetic primitives. Also, the history of Regis and September Snow intrigues me. And Iona, their daughter. *Is she different? How so?* They don't just pay lip service to the religion of Gaia, as far as I can tell, they actually believe in it! Isn't that wildly bizarre? But you've got to give me the details about what really happened when that rag-tag army of theirs defeated our army of 50,000 in the Sonoran Desert. You must reveal to me the *whole* truth."

"You've had access to the official reports. I'm sure you read them too."

Lloyd guffawed. "Official reports? Half-truths at best. There's something out there that has frightened you or you would have destroyed this group a long time ago. And I have another question. Is Iona really their leader? Has there been any independent confirmation? Why are we all being so secretive about Iona's identity?"

"Iona was supposed to have died at the age of five years, ten months, in Orura province, in Bolivia. It's in the official report. It's still the official truth. Study it."

"I did study it—I don't believe it," Lloyd said in an irritable voice. "When it came to their daughter, I really believe we were fooled by September and Regis Snow back then. They really pulled a fast one on us, didn't they?"

James Clare sighed. "Of course they pulled a fast one on us, and of course Iona didn't die. Your suspicions are correct. You are beginning to understand why it wasn't *that* hard to get you selected to be the leader of this mission. You're going to go see Iona in person, right? Some of the other half-truths corrected? At the conclusion of that famous battle in the Sonoran Desert you mentioned, a large number of our troops, defected to the other side. They have *permanently* defected. They are our enemies."

"How many?" Lloyd asked. "Five hundred?"

"Guess again."

"A thousand?"

"Guess again."

"Two thou..." Lloyd began. He looked doubtful and perplexed. "Four thousand?"

"Fifteen thousand."

Lloyd whistled. "No wonder we're keeping this under wraps." He shook his head. "Years ago this never could have happened. The Gaia-Domes have never seen anything like this. Iona is the real thing, isn't she?"

"Can you imagine what would happen to the morale of the army if we disseminated this information?" James Clare replied. "Number two half-truth debunked: Ever since that battle, everywhere The Unseeing Watchfulness of Gaia has established itself, we've lost control of the surrounding countryside. We have no way of monitoring their comings and goings. Or their size. Or their intentions."

"Don't you offer monetary inducements and other rewards to

those who denunciate our foes?"

"Standard procedure, of course," James Clare declared. "We make threats *and* we offer rewards. No one will finger them. They have built up such an ironclad loyalty. Number three half-truth debunked: We couldn't use our helioplanes to defeat them. The reason is because just before that famous battle you mentioned, they sabotaged our helioplanes. We haven't figured out yet how they traveled across the desert undetected, or how they breached our security, but they did. Suicide squads sent out to commit suicide, who don't have to commit suicide, now that's success. Air mobility and firepower have usually been all it takes to defeat our enemy, but not in this case. By the way, you watch your talk about the religion of Gaia when you're out there. Any questions about our doctrines or beliefs is off-limits. Gaia, *our* Gaia, is the one and true faith. The inner council, both hardliners and reformers alike, see The Unseeing Watchfulness of Gaia not as an alternative religion but as a superstition, a hoax, a fraud. If it were a counter-religion, it would be judged heretical. Don't misunderstand me, Lloyd, there is only one Gaia. *Our* Gaia. All else is heresy."

Lloyd remained silent, not daring to say something ironic or sarcastic.

"Number four half-truth debunked: We keep thinking we're zeroing in on their headquarters? Really? Either they don't have one or it moves around. Can't pinpoint it. There are thousands of little groups, scattered all over the Western Quadrant—but they are constantly moving. Living like ants underground. The Western Quadrant is so desolate. How do they grow crops? Unsuitable soil? Not enough water? Doesn't matter. They're like wizards They're miracle workers. The rebels are still functioning like a military organization. Their discipline is, well, unique."

"And Iona?"

"How many times do I have to tell you, Iona is the leader of the group. The smugglers have confirmed it! The few rebels we've managed to capture have pleaded the same case. Iona is their sole leader.

At first, the council chose not to believe it. It played on their vanity that the leader of this rebel group could not have been connected to the Snows by blood. They take this woman, Iona, to be a sorceress, a she-devil, a witch. Iona seems to rely heavily on her oratorical and theatrical gifts to sway people, and in this, she's profoundly gifted. In war, she's courageous, decisive, tough. In peace, she's calming, wise, brilliant. In negotiations, you'd better hope she's receptive to you. I suppose you know she's *educated!* Someone taught her. Not her mother. Her mother would have been too busy trying to organize her own rebellion to have had the time to educate Iona when she was a child. But who then? Her father was dead. Out in the desert, living like a hermit, functioning like a primitive, struggling against all the elements no differently than an animal would, how did she get educated? Answer me that!" James Clare shook his head.

"After the defeat of our army of 50,000, what about the slaves that liberated themselves from the Gaia-Domes?" Lloyd asked. He murmured beneath his breath, "I know the answer. I know who educated Iona. *Tom Novak...*"

James Clare was so distracted by the first question he chose to ignore Lloyd's whispered words. "Okay, another half-truth. There's one bright spot here. After word of our defeat, true, some slaves escaped. Before being recaptured, some of them even made it to the rebel-occupied area in the Western Quadrant. In their eyes perhaps Iona had the power to achieve something worth risking one's life for. But of *those* who made it to the Western Quadrant, *by their own choice,* some of them slinked back with their tails tucked between their legs. I guess they didn't realize how hard it was going to be scratching a living out there, living miserable lives in the Western Quadrant. Most slaves would take life in the Gaia-Domes, bearing up to the certainties of whips, chains, and shackles, and the constant threats of punishment, than face sun death and subject themselves to a lifetime of foraging and living on roots and bug larva. By the way, Iona's rebels won't need runaway slaves to augment their population any longer. They're breeding again."

"What?" Lloyd interrupted, as if waking up from a reverie.

James Clare smiled. "The Unseeing Watchfulness of Gaia is regenerating their population the old-fashioned way. Apparently, six months ago, Iona lifted their ban on breeding."

"The key to the success of their rebellion was to keep their women of child-bearing age from becoming pregnant," Lloyd declared. "I know this. I learned it from interrogating those two rebel prisoners. That's why they were able to stay as long as they did in the caves. That's why they were victorious in battle."

"Well, not anymore. Up until six months ago, under strict enforcement, no breeding was allowed. When they lived in caves, in the south, a male faced death if he got a girl pregnant. Moving from cave to cave, they were living in such harsh and primitive conditions, they couldn't regenerate their population that way, they couldn't afford to have babies and also manage to survive. The potential mother was left off the hook, but a man caught in the act, look out! Apparently it was their second-in-command, someone by the name of Kull, who was the strict enforcer. It was only the intercession of the wise ones, acting as an independent judiciary, who exercised clemency in many cases of infractions. Severe threat. Followed by clemency. That's their pattern. After all, they were in the process of turning everyone, male and female, into fierce warriors. They wanted to create an army that we could not defeat. I guess they feel that they are secure enough now to make babies. If my math is correct, Iona is about forty-four years old. Perhaps no more than a year or two younger than you yourself, Lloyd. She's past—or nearly past—childbearing age. We hope we will not see the creation of a dynasty. But their lifting the ban on reproduction is further proof that the move to the Western Quadrant is permanent. They're affirming life by creating more of it. A headlong dive into the clutches of optimism in so bleak a time... amazing, isn't it? Takes your breath away."

Lloyd took a moment to digest all of this information.

"By the way," James Clare continued, "*Your* minder, the one assigned to you, Celsius, was born outside the Domes. He lived in the land of the sun. Like a feral animal. For eight years. Then, as an orphan, he was brought in to the safety of the Domes. He suffers from mild sun damage. He's not as ugly or deformed as some of your previous assistants, but nevertheless, a little scary. The one big difference, he hasn't aged *abnormally,* an extra thirty or forty years, like some of the others who have suffered from severe sun poisoning. He's a lean wolf, true, but not so aged."

Lloyd looked down in disgust. "They always turn them into such diabolically fanatical true-believers, these orphans our army rounds up. Why does security insist on arranging assistants for me who suffer from sun poisoning, or some other ghastly affliction of environmental damage? They're always orphans swept up like trash, taken from the bowels of the earth."

"Maybe it's the security force's way of reminding you how lucky you are that you live under the protection of the army and the Gaia-Domes," James Clare said.

"Once this mission is accomplished," Lloyd said, "all I ask for, is to be set free. I want to be let go. I want to go back to my studies."

"What?" James Clare exclaimed. "We may want you to set up a new diplomatic corps, just in case we need it, in the future. We have those crazy rebels in the Himalayas Mountains to contend with. And then there are those bizarre religious cults that are springing up in Europe. There are those penitents in Oceania that won't go away. We're entering a new age."

"None of those groups pose a threat to our security," Lloyd said, shaking his head. "Once I get back, I want my old job back. I want to return to being a residential scholar in Hominid and Post-Hominid Studies. I want to be above the fray, above allurements, above distractions. In a word, I want my old privileges back."

"One of the final acts of your grandfather, on his deathbed, was to make me swear an oath that I would protect you upon his death," James Clare declared. "Your grandfather was a great man. You'll get your old job back. I promise. I took a solemn oath that I would protect you. Just manage to get back here alive."

Chapter Thirty-Eight

THE FLIGHT FROM one of the major Gaia-Domes in New York to the main Gaia-Dome in Denver was uneventful. The party of Gaia-Dome diplomats was propelled swiftly by a fast-moving helioplane. Zooming across the well-protected sky-lanes, they were moving at speeds in excess of 1200 miles per hour. The trip by helioplane took only two and one half hours to complete.

Lloyd Thompson the fourth, Celsius, and a party of ten junior assistants changed helioplanes in Denver after a quick two-night stay-over, so they could make the quick jump across the Rocky Mountains to the outpost Gaia-Dome located at Glenwood Springs.

By the standards of typical Gaia-Domes, the one in Glenwood Springs appeared a bit outlandish to Lloyd. The main Gaia-Dome structure was strong, built to last, and the Dome covering had an expansive cover, protecting a colony of 3500 people. But the surrounding out-buildings were made of flimsy materials and had no proper covering. The unlucky ones inhabiting these out-buildings, a population of 1000 people, called themselves the inhabitants of proltown. They looked demoralized, feckless, and forlorn.

Needing to stretch his legs, Lloyd took a walk to the outside of the protective cover of the Domes—guarded at all times by a trained and armed enforcer. Lloyd saw legions of proltown children crowding each other, jostling each other, clutching sharp sticks, foraging for rats. They looked impoverished and malnourished.

The enforcer assigned to Lloyd appeared at first sight to be atypical for his kind. He did not have the usual stern expression on his face that Lloyd had come to expect. Instead, he looked mild-mannered. But that look was deceptive.

It was when he smiled that everything changed. His smile was crooked in the extreme, his teeth filed down to form truncated, skinny nibs. With the addition of a fierce, impenetrable stare, when the enforcer smiled he looked like the Grim Reaper, scaring the daylights out of Lloyd. But the smile and the nasty gaze were useful. It could scare away any potential attacker—for the enforcer smiled only when the potential for violence was imminent.

Lloyd and the enforcer walked along the street together. In contrast to the squalor, they heard sweet-sounding music broadcasted over loudspeakers. They found themselves bathing in the music. Lloyd found the musical experience incongruous, surreal and inexplicable. Posted on poles, at distances of fifty yards apart, the loudspeakers blasted in every direction soothing pieces of music.

Upon being questioned on this point of the music, the enforcer gave Lloyd an explanation.

"At first, the authorities piped in Gaia religious sermons," the enforcer said. "People didn't like it. They considered it nauseating stuff. These inhabitants are not Suits, Middle-middles or Upper-minds mind you, people who live under the protection of the Gaia-Domes, people who are fairly well treated but are not free to come and go. Instead, these are drudges living *adjacent* to the Gaia-Domes, surviving on their wits and picking up whatever jobs they can find. When these people heard the Gaia sermons being broadcasted, they came out of their hovels in protest. Some of them tore down the poles. Others dismantled the loudspeakers. The Gaia-Dome authorities could have taken reprisals against them, but instead they decided to take a different tack. They put the poles back up, remounted the loudspeakers, but this time, instead of sermons, platitudes and rants of the official Gaia religion, they piped in music—lovely music—Beethoven, Bach, Mozart, and some other composers. It calms them."

Having given an explanation for the music Lloyd expected the
enforcer to smile, but he didn't smile. Lloyd remembered how fierce
he looked and how dangerous he could become when he did smile.
It was the enforcer's trademark.

Even though the Glenwood Springs Dome system itself was comfortable and had many amenities, the crew operating the Gaia-Dome
looked like rough characters. Lloyd remembered that Glenwood
Springs was considered to be a frontier posting. In Lloyd's imagination, the Dome protectors reminded him of trappers and mountain
men he used to read about in adventure yarns when he was a boy.
This was the farthest outpost of the Gaia-Dome system on the eastern
edge of the Western Quadrant. The place had been built to serve one
purpose and one purpose only: a barrier protection for other Gaia-
Domes. It protected the other Domes located hundreds of miles to
the east, mainly on the eastern side of the Rocky Mountains.

Along the Western Quadrant periphery the next major Gaia-
Dome rim-protecting centers were miles apart. The principal ones
to the south were located at Pueblo, Albuquerque, and Flagstaff.
The ones to the north were located at Jackson Hole, Cody, and Bill-
ings. The next major Gaia-Dome system was located due west on the
western rim of the Pacific Ocean.

The Pacific West Coast Domes were rich, luxurious, and brilliant, similar to the ones in Chicago, Philadelphia, and New York. It
was in the interiors of the Gaia-Dome system of city-states—that the
power was weakest. On the West Coast, in San Francisco, Los An-
geles, Seattle, and a number of points in between, there were richly
developed Dome cultures. But twenty years after the Eleven-Year-
War, thirty years earlier in the year 2071 A.D., the western interior
of the North American continent had been effectively turned into an
uninhabited empty quarter.

After taking four weeks to be outfitted, they joined the party of twenty smugglers of precious gems and metals, who were armed to the teeth and looked as rough as they could get. The smugglers escorted Lloyd's party of twelve down the Colorado River.

Following the snaking course of the upper reaches of the Colorado River, they traveled first by land, using horses for transport and pack animals to carry the baggage train. Most of the way, they hugged the sides of the river. Lloyd had never traveled by horseback before. To everyone's surprise, he took well to it. They pampered Lloyd. He was exempt from all camp work—no setting-up camp duties, no breaking-down camp duties, no lifting, no water carrying, no tending to the cook fires, no cooking, no hunting. For the first one hundred and fifty miles they traveled this way.

From the beginning, Celsius repeatedly took Lloyd by surprise. Celsius gave the appearance of being a bit of a wild man. Strangely, at least from Lloyd's perspective, Celsius fit in well with the smugglers. He was a true chameleon, and after a few days Lloyd couldn't tell him apart from any of the smugglers. Celsius appeared to have had some rough experiences in life, having lived outside of the Domes over extended periods of time. During these times he had fought in the service of the Gaia-Domes, putting down rebellions, more military man than bookman, indeed, more adventurer than military man. Celsius had repeatedly risked his life in the cause of the Gaia-Domes. Lloyd didn't feel friendly toward Celsius; the man was too mean, ruthless, and uncouth, but Lloyd envied his elan.

Even though Celsius's scarred face made him look scary, he had a robust regard for life. And even though he could have obtained amusement at Lloyd's expense, Celsius always treated Lloyd with at least an outward demonstration of deference and respect.

Just as Lloyd was getting the knack of horseback riding, after eleven days, the party reached the confluence of the Green River and the Colorado River. At this point some of the smugglers erupted into a heated argument. It took death threats from Celsius to put an end to something that could have turned into a potential mutiny. Finally, the leadership of the head smuggler, prevailed.

It was at this point that the waters of the Green River mixed with waters of the Colorado River, forming a new river, a major system. Past the confluence point where the two bodies of water converged, there was enough water flowing downriver, for it now to constitute a major waterway.

Here the party of smugglers rested several days. Then they were met by another group of smugglers, who specialized in smuggling people. They had floated down the Green River from the north on four rafts. Having pulled to the banks, they loaded up the provisions on their rafts. Now there were fifty in the group total, twelve Gaia-Dome members and thirty-eight smugglers. From here, they propelled themselves down the lower reaches of the Colorado River, heading into the heart of the Western Quadrant.

Having held back, Lloyd decided he would speak directly to the leader of the human smugglers. Up until now, he had delegated all communication with the smugglers to Celsius. Now Lloyd wasn't so sure that had been such a good idea. It had become clear to Lloyd that whatever authority Celsius exercised over the smugglers, it was because he threatened death.

They meandered down a stretch of river where the current was strong but the surface looked placid. Intermittently, the river could turn turbulent, dangerous, and treacherous. Lloyd said to the lead smuggler, "Where's Iona? Do you know where the headquarters of THE UNSEEING WATCHFULNESS OF GAIA is located?"

"No," the raft smuggling leader grunted. "And I'm glad I don't. No one knows where Iona is at any given time. And the organization you mentioned doesn't have any headquarters."

"How are we going to find them then?" Lloyd asked.

The smuggler leader laughed. "There's no 'there.' They're a moving target. Nine months ago, the rebels were located between the Paria River and Last Chance Creek. Six months ago, they were in the Henry Mountains. A year ago, they were six hundred miles away in the Ruby Mountains. Two years ago, they were occupying the mountains near the Gunnison River. Four years ago, I have no idea where they were located. Where are they now? Your guess is as good as mine. They're nomadic. Up until three months ago, Iona had a huge price on her head, but now it's been rescinded. Doesn't matter."

"You said you've met Iona in person?"

"Yes, indeed. A piece of work. Someone you don't want to mess with, I'll assure you."

"So how are we going to find her?" Lloyd asked.

"That's impossible." The leader of the smugglers sniggered. "We won't find her. She'll find us."

"We've floated on this river a good distance," Lloyd said, looking around. "How much longer are we going to be traveling like this?"

"Not much longer. Farther down stream, the river can be sullen. There will be places where it will be nearly impossible to navigate. We may lose some rafts. We may lose *all* of our rafts—on the rocks. This is dangerous. If the river meanders, you should be happy."

"You don't sound too optimistic about this trip," Lloyd said with a note of anxiety.

"Let's hope Iona's scouts find us soon. Guides us up a creek to safety. You realize these rafts can go in only one direction. They drift downstream, but they don't travel back up. This is a one-way trip. The Colorado-Green River system flows south, then west, then southwest, finally south again, slowly picking up more water from its tributaries, cutting deeper and deeper, until it cuts a half mile deep into the Grand Canyon. Then it enters the high mesa desert, and finally the low desert. We'll probably die trying, but after we drop you off, we're going to shoot the rapids in the Grand Canyon, then head all the way down river to the Gulf of California, or bust."

"Why are you willing to take so many chances?"

The leader of the smugglers smiled. "Our three sins. Greed. Avarice. Money."

"Without rafts, how can we get back home?" Lloyd asked.

"That's up to Iona and the other smugglers to figure out. Gird yourself, you're entering a new world here."

Chapter Thirty-Nine

THE RAFTS HAD BEEN TIED UP along a sandbank, adjacent to the main flow of the river. In the middle of the night, after everyone but two lookouts had retired, there was a crashing sound that echoed throughout the camp. Then shots were fired. In the midst of this mayhem, one of Iona's troops entered Lloyd's tent, raised him up by his arms from his sleeping mat, stood him up, and casually tossed a cloth hood with a breathing hole over his head. Marching him frog-legged at the point of a sharp instrument, the trooper bound Lloyd's hands behind his back and took him away.

He was placed on a horse with someone walking beside him, guiding the horse, and someone leading the horse, the two walking in tandem. The horse never ran, much less galloped. Directed from the front, the horse clip-clopped at a constantly uniform walking speed.

They traveled like this for about six hours, until the break of dawn. With the hood over his head, all Lloyd knew was that they were always traveling uphill, and usually the ascent was gradual. He guessed they were traveling north, away from the river. Eventually, Lloyd began to feel the warmth of the sun hit his back. That was the only way he knew morning had come. They trudged on like this for the rest of the day. Every three or four hours, they took a break. Lloyd was given plenty of water to drink during these breaks, but he was offered no food. When they gave him something to drink they took his hood off. It was then Lloyd realized he was the only one in the group traveling by horseback. Everyone else was walking. They were a fit and nimble crew, thin and sinewy, perhaps even unnaturally skinny, but not emaciated. When night arrived they did not stop to take a meal break. They kept going until morning. When darkness descended on the second night, they untied Lloyd's hands, and he was free from having to wear the hood. This allowed Lloyd to sleep while he was riding in the saddle. He was surprised to find that sleep came easily to him, the rhythmic movement of the horse—clippity-clop—lulled him. He also discovered that even though he had not taken nourishment in the past twenty-four hours, he experienced no hunger pangs. Whenever he was offered water, he drank large drafts of it, taking more than his fill. Someone in the group started to sneeringly refer to him as "the water-guzzler."

The next morning they arrived at what appeared to be a temporary camp. A tiny stream ran through the severe cut of the steep valley, at an elevation of 7,500 feet. It was a high, steep canyon, with walls towering high above the valley. In the background, at an elevation of about fifteen hundred feet higher up, there was the top of a seemingly impenetrable box canyon.

In the distance, Lloyd could make out the top of this oval-shaped canyon, rimmed at the crest by a crust of verdant conifers. Directly above, there was a cloudless sky, starkly blue in color. The cliffs of the canyon walls themselves were pink, purplish, and mauve. Closer at hand, Lloyd could see some green—fragile plants and a few scrawny trees growing along the narrow slit of the stream. With such a huge array of colors, it was a strikingly beautiful and peaceful place. It also seemed totally inaccessible.

Iona came out to greet him. She was dressed in a white cotton robe, homespun. She had just turned 45 years old.

"Where are my companions?" Lloyd asked.

"There were no horses for them. They must travel on foot—like the others. They will be traveling by different routes, for security. They must travel with hoods covering their faces and it will take an extra two days for them to arrive. We know we must bring the smugglers in with your people. Our scouts can travel 175 miles non-stop—without taking a meal or resting for sleep. But your people can not move with such ardor and discipline."

"And you are *the* Iona, I presume?" Lloyd said in a magisterial voice.

"I am," Iona replied. "And you are Lloyd Thompson the fourth, special magister, counselor-in-general, ambassador, plenipotentiary, for the Universal Gaia-Dome State, I presume."

"At your service," Lloyd said, bowing deeply. "But how did you know my name?"

Iona took a step closer. She placed her feet squarely in front of Lloyd. "Nine months ago, we planted scouts and agents in your Gaia-Domes. We know everything that happens in these Gaia-Domes, especially the one at Glenwood Springs. We receive reports on a regular basis. The Gaia-Domes have no reach here, but we know what happens there."

"Why was I given a horse to ride?" Lloyd asked.

At first the question struck Iona as inane and foolish. "Because you're the leader of your group," she said, laughing. "Besides, you're fat. No one would ever expect you to actually walk here on those wobbly legs of yours."

Lloyd bowed deeply, offering an ingratiating smile. "But I am here, as you see."

"You seem pleased," Iona said. She paused for emphasis. "...by the change in your circumstance?"

"I don't..."

"Allow me to clarify," Iona interrupted. "The fact you are free of those rafts," she added, smiling.

"Why, yes!" Lloyd exclaimed. He beamed with delight. "Nothing has made me happier. The arrangement we made for transportation was unorthodox. Those raft-traveling second-group-of-smugglers we temporarily teamed up with were going to kill us, that's for sure. Those rafts are deathtraps. They're dangerous. I hope you've sent them merrily on their way."

"We did." Iona spoke in a voice that was gravelly and humorless. "The rafters were doubly happy. Happy for the gold the Gaia-Domes gave them, but more luxuriously happy for the larger amounts of gold we gave them to bribe them to do things the way we wanted them to. You think these smugglers rafted down that river on a whim? It's no accident you camped two nights ago at that particular sandbank. We don't like leaving things to chance. We also permanently broke-off five members of your diplomatic party, plus two guards, that were posted that night at the sandbank. It was part of our experiment to see if a very large bribe, timely placed, could somehow overcome substantial fear in the lexicon of the human soul. *It can.*"

Lloyd almost giggled out loud. In Iona's voice, Lloyd detected something that sounded so familiar. In Iona's speech, Lloyd heard the verbal tics and nuances that characterized Tom Novak's speaking style. If Lloyd closed his eyes, he could imagine the ghost of Tom Novak's voice residing in Iona.

"Shall we dine?" Iona asked.

"Where are the other members of my group?" Lloyd asked again. "Actually, who I mean more specifically—Celsius. He will be mightily upset that he was separated from me."

"You're ALL guests," Iona said in a friendly tone. "And you're far away from home... Celsius," she muttered beneath her breath, looking down, "is not our prisoner. But we are not his prisoner, either." She smiled. "You are all our guests. He will join us in two days time. Let's dine."

Lloyd knew Iona was going to make a formidable opponent and a firm advocate for her cause, so educated, so refined, yet paradoxically, in this strange environment, so seemingly in her element. Lloyd was amazed to have finally met this mysterious person.

The dinner fare was sparse. To Lloyd's taste, the food was horrible. It consisted of pieces of enigmatic twigs swimming in a mysterious soup. The food left Lloyd's stomach queasy, and he was hungrier at the end of the meal than when he started.

A group of thirteen young men and women dressed in matching white cotton robes were brought in to entertain Lloyd. They were thin and lean. At first Lloyd thought they were a dance troupe, but when they began to perform he realized they were going to take turns reciting, or rather singing, lines of poetry. Each one sang, describing different segments of the ordeals that the larger group had endured. The first and second individuals, a man and a woman in their mid-thirties, traded off and on the singing lines, about the crushing slavery of their peasant-parents. The third and fourth singers, roughly the same age, chronicled the ten years of scarcity in the caves. The fifth and sixth singers, a younger team, narrated the four harsh, bitter years of hiding in small groups. This poetry-song lasted longer than the others. They mentioned the death of nine of the twelve wise ones, and how some of them died through starvation. The seventh and eighth singers, younger than the previous team, sang about the battles, the large ones, the small ones, and even the inconsequential ones. The ninth and tenth singers, younger still, sang about the journey traveling north over 1800 miles through tracks of jungle, mountains, valleys, and deserts. And finally the youngest, the eleventh and twelfth singers, who looked no more than sixteen years old, talked about the ongoing struggle of scratching out a living, surviving in their new environment, in the Western Quadrant. They also sang about how they had, at last, found their home.

At the end of each lilting, rhyming, beautiful piece of poetry-song, they addressed the crowd, singing in unison, repeating the words over and over again, like a full-throated mantra: "Give sorrow its words."

"Give sorrow its words," the crowd responded back in kind.

Finally, the thirteenth individual came forward, a young woman, in her mid-twenties. She was showing, indeed flaunting, six months of pregnancy. She came forward displaying prominently a handful of clay. With her hands extended, she held the lump of clay on high, so that everyone could not only observe, but also ponder, adore, and venerate.

Beholding it, as if it were a gift, everyone in the crowd gasped at the lump of clay in awe and wonder. Lloyd looked around himself in bafflement. What was happening, he wondered. What did this ceremony mean? Were they worshiping a lump of clay? Were they trying to propitiate or appease a potentially wrathful god, with this strange and unique offering. Lloyd thought he had some sort of understanding of this group, but now he wasn't so sure. *What was going on?*

Lloyd leaned over and asked Iona for clarification. "I do not mean to pry, but...what does the performance mean?"

"What do you mean—*what does it mean?*" Iona repeated in an annoyed voice.

"This lump of clay?" Lloyd asked. "Is it supposed to symbolize something?"

Iona whispered back into Lloyd's ear, "Doesn't mean anything. Certainly doesn't *symbolize* anything. It's only clay. Consumed, for short periods of time, it can tear your insides apart and give you a bloody stool but it will keep you from starving. It is what some of us were forced to eat, when we had nothing left to eat, in the harshest of places, in the desert, when we were forced to travel through the wastelands of what had once been known as the Forbidden Zone. In a different time, thirty-one years ago, it was a place I knew only too intimately. I never ate clay then, but nonetheless, it was a miracle I did not die. Clay means, for us, the edge of death."

The performance and the poetry-reciting were over. Not a word had been spoken about Gaia, nor had there been any mention of the future, nor a peep about the leadership of Iona and Kull. There was only the expression of sacrifice, ordeal, and love.

Despite all his well-ingrained dispositions, Lloyd was nevertheless touched by the performance of the young men and young women.

After the dinner, Lloyd was assigned a small hovel to reside in. By

Lloyd's standards, it was a hovel, but it was actually the largest single-
dweller dwelling in the camp. What Lloyd did there was fall asleep and
sleep quite soundly. Afterwards, he was given his fill to eat.

At Iona's command, her assistants had supplied Lloyd with a
private larder of their own native food. Except for pieces of dried
squash and corn, and a paste extracted from pinto beans, Lloyd
didn't recognize the food. He couldn't stomach nettle soup, dried
locust, or grease root. Although the taste was agreeable, he had difficulty chewing green root—the twigs in the soup he ate at the initiation dinner. At least he understood the "symbolism" of the clay, he
understood he wasn't *expected* to eat it, it was garnish.

But Lloyd came to relish the pinyon nuts which were served to
him in his domicile. When he ran out of them, he asked his hosts to
supply him with more. He wolfed down a pound and a half of the
tasty little nuts at his first meal, leaving the shucks gathered in a pile
beside the back door.

From that day on, upon Lloyd's request, Iona ordered that
Lloyd not be delivered dried locust, grease root, green root, nettle
soup, or clay—*ever again.* He was to be offered only the best. He
was to be served dried corn, dried squash, paste from pinto beans,
and lots of pinyon nuts. Even if he exhausted the entire supply of
pinyon nuts in the camp, he was to be given a pound or two of pinyon nuts, day in and day out.

(A small contingency was then sent out to gather more pinyon
nuts from as far away as twenty-five miles. Iona understood negotiations could not proceed if Lloyd did not have plenty of pinyon nuts
to eat. She said to the leader of the retrieval group, "In any given
day, Lloyd eats more in one meal than you eat in a day and a half. We
better keep him supplied with plenty of pinyon nuts, or we'll have to
kill a horse just to keep the man's appetite satiated.")

When Celsius arrived two days later he was in a foul and irritable
mood. From his perspective, everything had gone wrong. He was
angry about having to wear a hood covering his face and head during the entire journey. He had been under direct orders to never let

Lloyd out of his sight and already he had been separated from him—against his will.

There were other areas of concern that had Celsius fuming as well.

When the rebels had surreptitiously entered the camp, he had been taken completely by surprise. The two lookouts he had posted not only failed to give any signal of warning, but shortly after the attack began, they just disappeared. And they never re-appeared.

Celsius did not like being showed up in front of his subordinates. These rebels were different from the types he had been used to dealing with. They were clever, disciplined, trained to use their wits, utterly fearless. They were the best shock troops he'd ever seen. (They handled themselves far better than any Gaia-Dome shook troops he had seen in action.)

Worse, five of Celsius's ten junior assistants disappeared at the time of the attack. Either they had gone absent without leave, apparently electing to continue down the river, taking their chances with the raft smugglers, in effect abandoning their posts, or they had been abducted by the raft smugglers in a way Celsius could not figure out. He could only imagine that they had been bribed, either directly or indirectly. Either way, it was a bad omen. Upon entering the Western Quadrant, the changed atmosphere was having a strange effect on his junior assistants. Now he wasn't so sure he could depend entirely on their loyalty. They were in enemy country, where the old rules they were accustomed to no longer applied.

On top of all that, he learned that of the twenty smugglers they had began their trip with, five proved to have been plants, assigned to surreptitiously come to the aid of the rebels when they came to make their assault.

Celsius asked the chief smuggler to give him an explanation for this, since the chief smuggler was the one who had recruited them in the first place.

Grabbing the chief smuggler by the scruff of his neck, Celsius spit in the man's face and shouted in his ear, "You're responsible. It's your fault. I should have you executed on the spot."

"Well, we got here, didn't we?" the chief smuggler offered lamely.

Celsius let go of the man's neck. The chief smuggler then said, "The ones who were apparently disloyal had been recent arrivals. I'm sorry for what happened. It won't happen again."

"Next time you make a mistake like that I'll carve you into little pieces," Celsius said. "Don't even think about what will happen to your wife and daughters being held hostage in Glenwood Springs. Watch your step from here on out."

Iona asked Lloyd if he needed more time to rest before negotiations started. Lloyd said no, he was ready to go.

Therefore, beginning at sunrise the very next day, the negotiations began.

To protect them from the sun, a makeshift shed had been hastily constructed. A long table was placed in the center of the shed. On The Unseeing Watchfulness of Gaia's side of the table there were Iona, Kull, a military adjutant named Fiona, and two of the three remaining wise ones, Aglaia and Armando.

On the Gaia-Domes side of the table there were seven: Lloyd, Celsius, and the five junior assistants under the command of Celsius.

Iona began by thanking the Gaia-Dome team for having made such an arduous journey in such a short time.

"Let us listen to each other with renewed faith in the glory of a possible favorable outcome," Iona said. "For whatever is reached through the articulation of words is far better than what can be reached through the infliction of pain, suffering, and death."

"Hear! Hear!" Fiona shouted out, seconding Iona's words on their side of the table.

Lloyd began by thanking everyone for participating in the discussion.

The first four-hour-long morning session was taken up with the establishment of credentials and in the formation of an agreement over agenda and format. Once these had been established, Lloyd went into a two-hour-long discourse on what he called the history of Gaia. He spent an enormous time, with details in statistics and numbers, discussing the range of ecological and environmental damage that was inflicted on the Earth during the destructive mayhem of the Eleven-Years-War. At the end of the war Lloyd showed how the creation of the Gaia-Domes was the only thing that had kept world civilization from falling apart. His presentation was elaborate and ponderous. Lloyd spoke in a dry, monotonous voice.

As Kull surveyed the room he could see that Iona hung on every word Lloyd spoke, but several people, including Celsius, appeared at times listless and bored by the proceedings. At times, Kull caught Celsius staring off into space, and a few times he even saw him close his eyes.

Lloyd concluded his remarks by saying, "A brief recounting of the history of what happened to the planet Earth, between 2040 and 2051 A.D., before the development of the Gaia-Domes is necessary if we are to understand the gravity of the predicament we face today. I'll try to be brief. The environmental damage caused by man-made climate change and global warming was rapidly speeded up by the eruption of the Eleven-Years-War between 2040 and 2051 A.D. The detonation of multiple nuclear devices by rogue states, the outbreak of pandemic diseases, some of them caused by germ warfare waged by the major powers when the outcome of the war became increasingly dubious, the sheer tonnage of conventional bombs exploded over eleven long years, were only three of the major developments that pushed us more quickly into an ecologically-damaged world. One and one half billion people perished, either directly or indirectly, due to the conflict."

Celsius yawned. Again, he closed his eyes.

Lloyd continued. "The Gaia-Domes were created as humankind's last chance to survive in a horribly devastated world. Without the tenacity of the Gaia-Domes, civilization would have perished from the Earth. The Universal Gaia-Dome State made horrible decisions, true, I won't pretend that it was otherwise, but it was all done to keep the flame of hope for humanity still flickering—for future generations. I will not downplay these decisions' devastating impact. Triage inflicted on humanity, draconian colonization, dreadful experiments, these were only a few, but all of these were necessary, fruitful, and inevitable if we were to survive as a species and continue to have at least a fighting chance of surviving. I remember pieces of legislation my grandfather enacted: *Euthanasia of Reluctant Colonists, Elimination of Outside Aboriginals,* and his crowning glory, *Uniformity of Religious Belief.* Without the wisdom, foresight and leadership of the Universal Gaia-Dome State, the only thing that would have been left in the world would have been scavengers, cannibals, and the chaos, mayhem, and violence they perpetrated. The existence of the Gaia-Domes was the only thing that pulled us away from the abyss. Five hundred years from now, when humanity looks back at the dark ages we have gone through, humankind will be thankful to the Gaia-Domes for having provided a beacon of light for the future. That was its number one directive if we were to survive as a group, as human beings."

Celsius frowned, looked at first disconcerted, then angry, but he chose to remain silent.

Lloyd coughed hard and cleared his throat.

"I do not have to make an apology for the existence of the Gaia-Domes, the Universal Gaia-Dome State IS because it MUST BE. We are alive now because the Gaia-Domes did what they did—providing while others dithered. But the environment, if even at a snail's pace, if even too slowly for the hopes of our great-great-great-great-grandchildren, will eventually improve. This we can bank on."

Celsius became increasingly angry, but he did not intercede.

Kull observed that Lloyd kept referring to their joint discussion, but the preceding two and a half hours had been one long uninterrupted monologue.

Lloyd concluded his remarks with an anecdote about traveling on the rafts on the Colorado River. The anecdote fell flat. Trying to recover from his *faux pas*, he followed up with a joke about pinyon nuts, but that joke also missed its mark. Then trying to smooth over the resulting awkwardness, Lloyd said, "They say the inhabitants of the Gaia-Domes have no sense of humor, well, maybe that's true."

Iona responded to Lloyd's more general comments with the utmost of decorum, discretion, and tactfulness, *at first*. "Thank you for your kind and thoughtful remarks, Lord Negotiator, Lloyd Thompson the fourth, special magister, counselor-in-general, ambassador, plenipotentiary," she began. "What we discuss here is of weighty importance. But we insist on looking at things differently from the way our most august representative from the Universal Gaia-Dome State does. Perhaps we can agree to disagree on this matter."

Then Iona grew bolder in her words. "The Unseeing Watchfulness of Gaia is a force to be reckoned with. We have our own points of view. We do not share all of your views on the modus operandi of the Gaia-Domes, or on the history of the Gaia-Domes. For we believe that we represent another strand of hope for humanity. From the point of view of the world, is it safe and prudent to put all our eggs in one basket, to wit, in the basket of the Gaia-Domes? The future hope of the planet Earth is not to be manifested through unity but through diversity. Do not ask us to talk about your rendering of the history of the Earth, for not so much as in your admirable presentation, my lord Ambassador, but rather in the stated official ideology of the Gaia-Domes, have you falsified and betrayed a great deal of that historical record. I offer an example. Before the complete consolidation of power in the Gaia-Domes, between YEAR GAIA ONE and YEAR GAIA TEN, there were many different views of Gaia in the world. In fact, Gaia began as a safe haven and an intellectual clearinghouse for divergent views held by a vast array of spiritualists and philosophers who were opposed to the economic, political, and religious establishments of their day. Do I need remind you that the original followers of Gaia began as an *underground* religious sect, functioning at times as a *clandestine* movement? The very earliest pioneers of Gaia, one hundred and twenty years ago, would surely have been seen as rebels and heretics in the eyes of the Gaia-Domes today. Yet they were the ones who created the first notions of Gaia. It was only your totalitarian impulse and police-state tactics that effectively destroyed the memory and legacy of those people. The past may be lost, perhaps never to be regained, but we do not accept the logic or the premises of your Official History, in fact, your Official History is a lie. And worse than that. You have no historical memory. It's as if you have embraced amnesia. The original rationale for the mass euthanasia program of the elderly which occurred between YEAR GAIA ELEVEN and YEAR GAIA FOURTEEN was that the elderly were seen as superfluous and redundant to the necessities of the system, but a secondary reason for the program's implementation was to destroy the collective memory of the past so that the system could start from scratch by robotizing the minds of the young. What did that have to do with the original principles of Gaia? Nothing. The original Gaia theory was that life on Earth—the totality of living organisms—created a favorable atmosphere for itself, which it maintained at an optimal global temperature. This was accomplished through complicated feedback loops that included the release and storage of carbon dioxide, the weathering of rock, tiny marine algae, clouds, volcanoes, and trees. Although these systems of regulation were never seen as purposeful or sentient, they mimicked the coherency of a living organism. They provided us with an image of the planet which we now call Gaia. Three or four generations ago, Gaia's ability to self-regulate itself was disturbed by the human production of excess carbon dioxide and other changes. If there still is a remnant of independent people left alive five hundred years from now, in trying to understand what happened in our present time they will look back not to the false claims of a moribund Gaia religion that had long since quit living up to its ideals, but rather to a humanity that failed itself, and failed the world's environment. GAIA, IN YOUR HANDS, HAS BECOME THE OPPOSITE OF WHAT IT ONCE WAS, IT HAS BECOME THE IDEOLOGICAL COVER FOR THAT FAILURE."

Iona waited a moment, then she continued, "The alternative to the Gaia-Domes is not just anarchy, chaos, nihilism, mayhem, violence—cannibals, scavengers, biological mutants, pirates, mercenaries, smugglers, there is also us. We are not perfect. Far from it. Give us enough time and we'll make mistakes. Fifty years ago, the Gaia-Domes faced horrible choices. But we do not kill billions, and call it necessity. We do not use military force to destroy anyone we please, and call it peace. We do not systematically propagate lies about ourselves and others, and call it the truth."

Celsius slowly rose from his chair. Standing, he seemed to be smoothing away imaginary wrinkles in his pants. At first, Iona thought he was going to ask to be excused. But instead, Celsius gently bent over, grabbed his chair by its hind legs and held it high over his head. He then forcefully threw it down. The impact of the blow shattered the chair into pieces. Celsius then picked up from the kindling the seat of the chair. Grabbing it with his bare hands, he smashed his foot through it, smiling triumphantly as he did. He then declared the day's proceedings were over, concluding that all that had been said was null and void. "This won't do," he said.

He stormed out of the room.

Following Celsius, as if pulled by an invisible string, the five junior assistants dutifully exited behind him. Before his own departure, Lloyd lingered a moment. He smiled briefly at Iona. "Shall we resume tomorrow?" he asked, shrugging his shoulders.

At the exit point, Lloyd turned back one last time. He bowed deeply (so deeply it was as if he were deliberately making fun of himself), and in a wheedling voice, added, "Please excuse my colleague's manners, he's new at this game. But there's no call for such intemperance. Your stated position on diversity, however, is unacceptable. We must define unity, and then face the truth. The Gaia-Domes shall predominate in this matter. Or else what? Or else you'll be destroyed. I bid you good day." Lloyd then bowed (this time, more curtly and discreetly).

After the negotiating team representing the Gaia-Domes and

Lloyd had left the shed and all was silent, Kull turned to Iona and said, "You think they're being serious, but it's all a charade, a walking through of the motions, and it's only going to get worse with time."

"No, I don't think so," Iona said. "I think the ambassador is trying to tell us something, although I don't know what that something is. I think he just can't find the right words to say it."

Kull disagreed. He sighed with a note of pessimism. "In the end, what difference does it make? They'll kill us all. All right, at best they're playing for time, but soon enough, they'll sweep down and destroy us. *After that monster Celsius has had enough time to snoop everything out.* We should never have allowed this diplomatic mission to come here in the first place. *They're spies.*"

"Of course, you're right in principle," Iona said. "We can never trust the Gaia-Domes, in the short run, or the long run. At the end of this session, we must quit this camp. We must never return here again. Nonetheless, I think there's something different about this strange fellow Lloyd."

"Understand, this is a dangerous game," Kull rebutted. "You enjoy the diplomatic give and take, I can see that, and for some reason, you are growing fond of this Gaia-Domes' ambassador. Why this is so, I do not know."

Celsius returned with Lloyd to his quarters. "What do you call that display of foolhardiness? You call it leadership? You call it showing strength?" As Lloyd trudged along in the dirt, trying to keep his distance from Celsius's clutches, Celsius sneeringly hissed into Lloyd's ear, dogging him at every step, "What do you call that! A performance?"

After they entered Lloyd's hovel, Celsius planted himself squarely in front of Lloyd. Lloyd looked up at Celsius with a startled expression. Celsius blocked Lloyd from reaching his table, which was waiting for him with kernels of corn, sacks of nuts, beans, and squash. "No, you're not going to stuff your face and fill your gut to the brim, not until I've finished with you."

Celsius put his hands up and threw Lloyd against the wall. The wall was so flimsy it caused the rafters to shake. Lloyd was shocked and surprised by Celsius's action. Celsius then pressed forward, pinning Lloyd's hands. With the eyes of a hawk between meals, Celsius stared into Lloyd's eyes. He continued to hold Lloyd's hands up against the wall. "You disgust me, you know," Celsius hissed, eyeballing Lloyd. "You have crossed the line."

"I was sent here to do difficult things," Lloyd said in his defense. "It's a difficult task." In an even lower voice, he murmured, "I beg you to let me go. Do unhand me, sir."

Celsius was on the verge of exploding again but he restrained himself. He let go of Lloyd's hands and stepped back. "I'll make something clear to you once more," Celsius said. "We don't make excuses for anything. We wipe people off the face of the Earth. We have the right to transfigure this planet. It's our right. Your speech started out with a purpose, but in the end, it took a wrong route. You think I wasn't listening? You think I didn't detect the way you changed the subject? One year ago, for saying less than what you implied, a person in the Gaia-Domes would have been put to death."

Awkwardly, Lloyd smiled. "It's a difficult job, Celsius. I understand the directive of the mission. The counsel wants to destroy these pesky rebels, true, but at this given moment they don't have the military means to do so. THAT'S WHY WE'VE BEEN SENT HERE IN THE FIRST PLACE! To find another way. If I can bring these rebels around through cajolery, foolery, flattery, analytic prowess, display of arcane knowledge, implied threat, teasing humor, fibs, lies-heaped-on-lies, I'll use any of those means. Okay, in my presentation, I drifted away from the parameters of the official history, I admit that. Do you realize that in the official history of the Gaia-Domes, Iona's mother and father don't exist! But they did exist. Regis Snow, Iona's father, was once as powerful—*actually more powerful*—than my grandfather. IN THE GAIA-DOMES! Before his execution, he had been the most prestigious and most powerful scientist in the world. He actually understood the relationship of the atmosphere to the ocean currents, and their joint interaction, in the formation of the world's climate. Not that that matters to you. Single-handedly, he created the theoretical basis for the development of the climate-changing machines. But we killed him. His name, along with that of September Snow's, were eliminated from the official record. Prior to her becoming a renegade, September Snow, in her own right, was a major spokesperson for the official Gaia philosophy and religion. Prior to her becoming a leader of that old rebel group, she was one of the highest placed leaders in our government. Official history! What does that mean? I was only trying to find a place where we could establish common ground."

"If you want to inject foolery—and what did you call it, flattery?—into the proceedings, go ahead," Celsius said. "If you want to tell a joke about wolfing down pinyon nuts until you're ready to burst, do that too, so long as it concludes in the rebel's capitulation."

"Yes, in their capitulation," Lloyd concluded. "But not in their total humiliation. I'm sure it was deliberate the rest of you were separated from me when they attacked our camp. It was deliberate they insisted on giving me separate quarters from you. It's their way of showing their respect to the Gaia-Domes. Do you want to spit on that? Look, they're not our prisoners. Like it or not, we're negotiating on their turf, on their territory. Rebels have never had their own turf before, on a permanent basis. Did you ever think about that? It's a difficult job, and a complicated task, and in spite of what you may think, it can only be handled with delicacy and tact. Not with blunt instruments, understand, but with delicacy and tact."

"You're a dangerous dreamer and a fool," Celsius said. "I won't allow you to show me up in the future."

Lloyd smiled again. "I won't show you up. You have shown me the way. You have shown me the right way to proceed. I know what I need to say to these bedraggled, little rebels—from here on out, rest assured, trust me."

"Remember," Celsius said. "We don't have to admit anything except the superiority of our military and the infallibility of our Gaian religious principles. By the way, you are not to have any private conversations with Iona—understood? If you wish to speak to her in the future, you say what you need to say during the negotiations." Celsius left the room.

Lloyd thought about this. The Gaia-Domes were bent on operating like they had been operating for the last fifty years, but the world was changing around them. Slowly but surely, the planet Earth was healing itself. Against all odds, the survival of Iona was proof of that. Lloyd noticed that the conditions of the environment in the Western Quadrant, at least the limited parts he had seen, were very harsh, but not *devastatingly* so. When he asked Iona to explain this phenomenon at their first meeting, Iona told him that there were parts of the world, parts that were small in size, that were recovering from the climate change and the global warming much, much faster than the rest of the world. But you had to know exactly where to find these isolated places, these tiny pockets of safety, and living in the Gaia-Domes did not afford one the skills to do that.

Iona had explained that that was also a reason why The Unseeing Watchfulness of Gaia should be allowed to survive. "The people in the Gaia-Domes will never know when it's safe to come out," Iona said. "If you allow the descendants of we primitives a chance to act as your guinea-pigs, we'll be able to tell your descendants when it's safe to emerge from the Domes. I'm explaining this to you now, Lloyd," Iona continued, "because the subject will never come up in negotiations. I don't wish to place you in an embarrassing situation vis-a-vis your other colleagues. That's why I mention it to you now. To you alone."

Chapter Forty

THEY MET AGAIN for negotiations. This time the tenor of the exchange changed. Lloyd talked methodically, but he repeated himself over and over again. His message was clear. The Unseeing Watchfulness of Gaia must bow down and submit itself to the Gaia-Domes in the form of a complete capitulation. The negotiators met again the next day. Lloyd repeated himself. They met the next week. Using different words, employing alternative phraseology, Lloyd repeated the same message. Kull grew tired of the repetition but Iona remained strangely unaffected and unperturbed.

When the discussions had grown too repetitive even for Celsius to bear, Iona suggested a break in the negotiations. The excuse she gave was that they wanted to conduct a religious festival in honor of their guests. Kull thought this was a ruse and a hilarious one at that. There were no religious festivals, they had never held a religious festival, *religious festivals had been banned by Iona*. Iona just made up the idea so that they could stall for time. The rebel's implicit adherence to the Gaia-Dome's concept of Gaia, demonstrated in the form of a mock religious festival, also gave Celsius hope in thinking that the negotiations might end in a fruitful resolution.

Lloyd embraced the idea with enthusiasm, speaking to the same effect. Celsius wasn't any the wiser and he found the show mildly entertaining.

Iona devised a ritual whereby the Gaia-Dome's interpretation of the Gaia concept was honored. Lloyd played his part to a tee, but Celsius, no expert on the primitives' concept of Gaia, and its differences with the official Gaia theology, was impressed, if only for a short time.

After the festival was over, they had no choice but to resume discussion.

Lloyd warbled on with the same old tired talk about how each side needed to extend respect toward each other, but in the end the message was unchanged, the rebels were going to have to capitulate.

Toward this goal, Lloyd was running out of things to say. He had an uncanny gift of talking for hours at a stretch and saying very little, but now he was being pushed to the limit. He realized maybe Celsius wasn't going to be recalled after all. Maybe his benefactor, the grandmagister James Clare, and his minority faction on the general council, had been outflanked. It had not been determined how long Lloyd was to wait for Celsius to be recalled. (Indeed, the very logistics of how Celsius was going to be recalled had never been properly worked out. How was a message—or messenger—going to find the rebel outpost? Did anybody back in the Gaia-Domes even know where the rebel outpost was located? Of course not!) Lloyd was kicking himself that he had not insisted that James Clare work these details out in advance before he was sent on this dangerous, and seemingly now even more forlorn, mission. But Lloyd knew that there was a point where he would have to conclude the negotiations, assuming Celsius was not going to be recalled, and that eventuality was becoming more certain as each day passed.

Lloyd surreptitiously threw in a line that was straight out of one of Tom Novak's novels. But Iona did not catch the reference, or acted as if she had not caught it.

Lloyd shot a glance at Celsius. He saw that there had been no reaction to his literary allusion. In increasing desperation, Lloyd grew bolder. He talked about how there were ways of thinking that had existed not only prior to the Age of Gaia, but also prior to the Eleven-Years-War, and how these ways of thinking were held by a number of writers and poets in those pre-catastrophe days when there were such people, gloomy authors of *disillusionment-and-skepticism* literature. Titles like *Memories From Nowhere, Requiem to Illusion,* and *Expression Without Illusion* passed through Lloyd's lips. And then glancing again at Celsius and seeing no reaction, he grew even bolder. "Who was the author of these books? It could have been a man who lived a life of personal austerity and a life of intellectual humility, but a humility that combined with devastating perceptiveness." Lloyd grew so desperate that he tried to reenact in an abridged form Tom's philosophy. "What if someone had come up with the expression, 'All history is philosophy, all philosophy is religion, and all religion is literature, and all literature is art, all art is music, painting, dancing, and all music, painting, dancing are the heart, brain, hand of man and woman, through all of time;' and carefully wrote out the words on an animal's skin, so that they could be preserved for posterity? And that man's philosophy was formed in an earlier part of time. What if that man preached that the self only became itself by throwing everything into doubt and embarking on a quest for certainty? And what if this man, whom everyone loved and trusted, tried to predict the weather, a power he had inherited from his heritage background, but he didn't have enough time to do so? What if he was running out of time? What if he did not have enough time to predict the change in the weather? And he knew the end was drawing near, and he was dying, and he knew that something terrible was happening, so he felt he had to say something? *Anything?*"

Celsius looked like he was ready to fall asleep, at last Lloyd had lulled him into a state of inattentiveness. (Lloyd's multitude hours of dull, boring talk had paid off at least in some way.)

A shock of recognition came over Iona's face. And Kull recognized that Lloyd was talking about something Iona knew about. This hardly constituted a breakthrough, but Iona at least was aware that Lloyd was *desperately* trying to say something to her, something that held a private meaning, without at the same time, incurring the suspicions of his other colleagues.

But without clarification on this hidden meaning, Iona could not be sure. Lloyd knew all about Tom Novak. So what?

When Lloyd realized he did not know what next to say, he broke off the negotiations in a fit of frustration. Celsius wasn't any the wiser but the ruse did nothing to create a breakthrough. How could Lloyd convey to Iona that as long as Celsius was at the table, in the end Lloyd was going to have to tell them that the Gaia-Domes were doomed to destroy them?

The next morning Lloyd found that there was something new in his larder. There was a seven-pound sack of almonds and a five-pound bag of green peas. Lloyd was delighted! He had mentioned in passing to Iona his need for some kind of legume or green in his diet, to ease his constipation and indigestion. Where were they able to find such scarce commodities? Lloyd wondered. He knew that even by the standards of the Gaia-Domes these items were rare and valuable. Iona must have gone to great lengths to procure them.

After wolfing down a pound of almonds during the first day, Lloyd gobbled a half pound of them each morning, mixing them with smaller portions of pinyon nuts. He soaked the peas carefully every night and ate them as a supplement to his supper. He found that the change in his diet had made his digestion much more agreeable.

Lloyd stalled for another week in negotiations but he knew he was running out of time. And Celsius took the time to reiterate to Lloyd that he was forbidden to talk to Iona at any time, except during the negotiations. On this particular point, Celsius had become even more vigilant than ever.

Lloyd did not know what to do. Three times, after the negotiations had been concluded for the day, Iona tried to approach Lloyd on the subject of Tom Novak, but each time Lloyd brushed her off. Lloyd was too afraid of what might happen if Celsius knew he had spoken to Iona outside the parameters of the negotiations on *any* subject. With his five junior assistants, Celsius had spies everywhere.

Lloyd knew that it was hopeless to wait. He couldn't stall any longer. He decided to pick an arbitrary date when if Celsius had not been recalled by that time, he would have to choose whether to sacrifice himself, commit treason and tell Iona and Kull the truth, or break off negotiations. Once his party returned to Glenwood Springs without bearing a signed document with a submission of a complete capitulation on the part of Iona and The Unseeing Watchfulness of Gaia, the Gaia-Domes would attack the rebels. Whether they actually had it in their power to destroy the rebels was a different matter, but Lloyd knew what the future would bring.

Lloyd was on the horns of a dilemma. He decided to pick that evening to decide.

Chapter Forty-One

FOR LLOYD, THE DECISION was gut-wrenching. In anticipation of coming to a resolution, he paced the floor of his hovel all night long. Between his two possible choices, he vacillated endlessly. On the one hand, he could tell Iona the truth, knowing that Celsius would report back to the council his indiscretion, thereby certifying his own death warrant. Or he could save his own skin, wrap up the negotiations, signed document or no signed document (Iona wasn't going to sign any document of capitulation anyway), and return to the safety of the Gaia-Domes. Happy ending for him, anyway.

As Lloyd debated the points inside his head, he knew that the second course of action was the easiest and most prudent to follow. Even James Clare had told Lloyd that if Celsius wasn't recalled, Lloyd should cut his losses and allow The Unseeing Watchfulness of Gaia to succumb to the fate they richly deserved. Lloyd had never had an opportunity to act like a hero before. He was grossly overweight, a man pressed into service, wanting nothing more than to return to his privileges and the solitude of his pampered life, a future that was guaranteed to him back in the Gaia-Domes if he only behaved as he was expected to.

It had been an exciting and adventurous journey going to the Western Quadrant, a great learning experience, but Lloyd could exist there only as long as he was pampered more than anybody else, and that was a state of existence that wasn't going to last beyond the length of the negotiations. The rebels were primitive people. Their beliefs were strange. Their cause was not Lloyd's cause. Why die for something that didn't matter? It wasn't going to change anything anyway. The Gaia-Domes were going to rule forever...*weren't they?*

So it was a choice between life back in the Domes or death. It should have been an easy choice for Lloyd, but he could not decide easily. Morning came and he was shaking in his chair as if he had been gripped by a fever. He had experienced delirium and chills. He had been up all night. He still could not decide what course to take. That didn't mean he was being strong-willed, just the opposite. He was just too cowardly to admit he was going to take the easy way out. He was even too cowardly to admit he was a coward. All he felt was disorientation and shame. He had enough imagination to be valiant, but not enough gumption to make it happen. He was going to allow Celsius to drag him back home—like a dog on a leash—that much he was certain of. After all, notwithstanding Lloyds's capacity for independence of thinking, he was a creature of the Domes, inextricably linked by binding girders of steel to that behemoth.

But by a strange twist of fate, another decision was being made for him. (*The only decision Lloyd made that was the right decision was to wait until that very night to reach a decision.*)

He left his hovel so early in the morning that the air was still cool. He took a long walk and then he walked over toward the meeting shed and paused to sit down on a stump along the way. After he sat for several hours unable to move, Iona came over to greet him.

Standing over Lloyd as he sat on the stump, Iona's head and upper torso effectively blocked the sun as it rose. Lloyd shaded his eyes with his hand anyway, staring up at Iona with the sun's full glare behind her. Iona pronounced, "Celsius is dead."

Lloyd's face was haggard and red. "What?" he said in a rasping voice.

"Celsius attacked us in the middle of the night," Iona said. "He was methodical. At first he attacked and killed Aglaia and Armando.

That must have been easy. He came in the night and strangled them in their sleep. Then he attacked our military adjutant Fiona. That must have been harder, there was evidence of a struggle. Nevertheless, she was found dead with a cord wrapped around her neck. Celsius must have been extremely stealth-like when he moved. Did you know he was an expert at killing people in their sleep?"

"No," Lloyd said, too numbed by everything Iona was saying.

"Well, there are a lot of things you don't know, apparently," Iona said in an irritated voice. "Apparently, Celsius's next victim was going to be me."

"Why aren't you dead then?" Lloyd asked, shading his eyes, looking up with his hollowed face and flushed cheeks. The words came out differently than he had intended, but he didn't bother to change what he said.

"Kull stopped Celsius in his tracks," Iona said. "Shot him. But before he could get a shot off Celsius buried a knife many inches deep into Kull's chest."

"How is Kull now?" Lloyd asked in a confused voice.

"He's alive. Just barely. Celsius's knife missed Kull's heart by an inch. Kull's been paranoid about Celsius since the day he first arrived. Having been raised as a slave on a platform rig, Kull knows how to sleep with one eye open. He also knows how to use a laser gun—at very close quarters—for defense. Difficult angle. For anybody else, impossible shot. Learned that technique when he was fighting with those guerillas thirty years ago. If they taught him anything, they taught him how not to be bushwhacked while asleep. A man who can sleep with one eye open, take several inches of a blade in his chest, still be able to reach for his laser gun—Kull is *both* double-jointed *and* ambidextrous—shoot a man hovering over him at a distance of less than twenty inches, now that's a dangerous man to interrupt in his sleep."

"My God," Lloyd gasped.

"The only mistake Celsius made was going after Kull before coming after me," Iona said. "Coming after me first, Celsius probably would have finished me off. Unlike Kull, I sleep soundly."

Lloyd put his hands in his lap as if in a demonstration of supplication, trying to take everything in.

"I'm convinced that that was Celsius's real mission from the beginning," Iona then added. "Cut down the leadership of the rebellion in one fell swoop. He was not a negotiator on your team. He was a paid assassin—a highly compensated one, although what form of compensation he received, I don't know. It was a suicide mission. He killed three of the five most important people in this camp and came within an inch of killing the other two. They must have given him something special before he came out here. If you couldn't get us to capitulate in the negotiations, he had no intention of going back."

"But that doesn't make sense," Lloyd said.

Iona laughed. "The negotiations were a cover. You, Lloyd Thompson the fourth, grandson of your grandfather, the great and famous grandmagister, were an even more perfect cover."

"But having learned all this, why wouldn't you just kill me now?" Lloyd asked. "How would you know that I was not part of the scheme?"

"That's what I was supposed to do. Kill you. Or rather, somebody in the camp, after I was killed, would kill you. Thereby destroying any attempt to have a fruitful conclusion to the negotiations. And the hardliners back in the Gaia-Domes would have overcome the objections of the minority on the council whose secret agenda was to seek reconciliation with us. *Your secret agenda was to seek reconciliation with us, wasn't it?*"

"How did you know that?" Lloyd asked. "Nobody knows that. Celsius didn't know it."

"I didn't know it. But I guessed at it. When you told me about Tom Novak, imputing that you knew all about Tom Novak, that was the one clue I needed." Iona smiled. "Look. You had two different factions on your council. Each faction was playing off the other with their own secret agendas. Did you ever wonder why the hardliners agreed to these negotiations in the first place? What could have been their motive? When it came to secret agendas, the right hand didn't know what the left hand was doing. And vice versa. Why didn't you think that the secret agenda of the majority faction on the council wouldn't have won out in the end?"

"But even if you had figured all of this out, that still wouldn't have given you enough cause to trust me," Lloyd said. "All those details I mentioned about Tom Novak... All that meant was that something connected to you from your past was connected to me. Not enough reason to trust me."

"True, it was only a connection," Iona said. "And only half a reason to trust you. For Kull, it was no reason to trust you at all. He never saw the negotiations as anything serious from the very beginning. He wanted to kill all of you, or at least kill Celsius, but I forbad him from doing so. If he had done that, it would have saved some lives, but it would have given the hardliners exactly what they wanted and Celsius would not have had to kill anybody. There was another half. All of the smuggler's wives and daughters back in Glenwood Springs were tortured and executed four days ago."

"What?" Lloyd asked. He couldn't believe his ears. He was flabbergasted.

"We got the report last night. Our couriers traveled nonstop in long relays to get that message to us as soon as possible. From Kull's point of view, that message saved your life. I suppose, in a way, saved my life too."

Lloyd was still trying to piece all the parts of the puzzle together.

"Who would want to give the orders to execute the hostages?" Lloyd asked. "What would be their motive?"

"Torpedo the talks!" Iona said in a caustic-sounding voice. "Or perhaps, some other reason. Maybe it was done out of a bestiality of malicious caprice? The Gaia-Domes are capable of doing such dreadful things, for seemingly inexplicable reasons. Does it matter? It was a dangerous mission, almost a suicide mission. Your negotiation bid was a front to get Celsius into our camp. That was the hardliners' secret agenda. Of course, only Celsius knew about their secret agenda. You were supposed to think that the negotiations were worth holding—that they had an intrinsic value—and with your display of earnestness, sincerity and friendship, it would only lull us into a state of incautiousness. The hardliners must have had their own timing mechanism for Celsius's attack as well. With Celsius dead, we can never even guess now what that timing mechanism was."

"What happens to the smugglers?" Lloyd asked.

"They're horror-stricken with grief at the loss of their loved ones. But they have no reason to go back to the Gaia-Domes; all their kin are dead. We'll send them down the Colorado River with the best of hopes. In the end, who knows what will happen to them, but at least they'll have another chance at life. They're tough. Maybe they'll be able to start again."

"And Celsius's five junior assistants? What will happen to them?"

"We'll send them back with you. Why not? They don't do anything. What a useless bunch! Since the smugglers will be gone, our people will get you back to the Gaia-Dome at Glenwood Springs."

Chapter Forty-Two

IONA AND LLOYD spent their last days together talking about Tom Novak. Years later, Lloyd told Iona how he had suspected that Tom Novak knew something about Iona.

"It's amazing," Lloyd said. "Tom Novak alone managed to escape the euthanasia program. After being with you a number of years, he must have survived—living alone—in the desert for several more years. How? That's a mystery. And then to have fallen into the hands of that commander who protected him for eighteen long years? It's truly remarkable."

Iona was eternally thankful to Lloyd for telling her everything he knew about what finally happened to Tom Novak. Iona was flabbergasted that Tom had managed to live to the ripe old age of 103. That could never have been possible without the timely intersession of Lloyd. But, of course, above all, she had *sensed* that Tom had been alive, during those times. It was marvelous that Lloyd was able to explain in detail what had happened to Tom.

Kull proceeded rapidly with his recovery. The knife wound healed quickly. From his mat, he bellowed out in a self-mocking voice, for everyone to hear: "I have wounds everywhere. I have a nine-inch-long wound in the back of my left thigh, I have a three-inch-long wound in the front side of my right chest, I have fifty wounds, some of them eighteen inches long, crisscrossing all over my back. I've got wounds all over my body!"

At one point, Lloyd wanted to ask Iona something that had been bothering him since his arrival. "I'm dying to know the answer to this."

"Go ahead," Iona said. "Ask away."

"The suicide squads that destroyed the water supplies for our army? How did they do that? And then they disabled our helioplanes so that they couldn't be used in an attack against you. Also, how did they do that? Both feats were amazing accomplishments. Their successes were crucial to your victory."

"That's not one question, that's two questions," Iona said. "Besides, they're military secrets."

"Of course," Lloyd said. "I understand. But can't you at least tell me how they were able to travel across the desert undetected? We've never been able to figure that out."

Iona weighed the issue in her mind. Then she decided to share this one little secret with Lloyd—as a small token of their new trust. "Remember the old gas stations from one hundred years ago?"

"Yes, my grandfather taught me about them. His father had been a big man in the oil business. That's how my grandfather made his first fortune."

"They were located along various routes anywhere from a few miles apart, to thirty miles apart, to fifty miles apart. Even out in the desert there were gas stations."

"Yes. So what?"

"We found the locations of the old gas stations from an old map we were able to acquire. Our suicide squads hid in the ruins of the gas stations."

Lloyd was incredulous. "But what ruins?" he asked. "There are no ruins?"

"That's why it worked. True, there are no ruins—*above ground.* Everything above the ground had been swept clean and cleared during the Eleven-Years-War. Back in the old days, they had built underground storage tanks to hold the gasoline. *Below ground.* The cavities in the ground, that's where they hid."

"It must have been incredibly hot in there," Lloyd said.

"Yes," Iona said. "That's what they're trained to do. During the daytime our suicide squads hid in the storage tanks. Clever, no? We knew you'd never figure that out."

"Amazing!" Lloyd exclaimed.

Lloyd grew serious. "Looking back, you must understand, Iona. Tom Novak never once betrayed you. Not once. No matter how many times I pressed him, no matter how hard I interrogated him, he never admitted to the truth that you were still alive. When it came to that, he had absolute resolve. He took your dearest secret to the grave. He insisted on maintaining that you died when you were five years, ten months old—out in the desert of Bolivia—corroborating what had been concluded in the Gaia-Domes official report. To his dying day, he was absolutely insistent on hiding your identity. And he did it effectively. To the very end."

"I'm not surprised," Iona said. "No matter how world-weary, disillusioned, or skeptical Tom may have been, no matter how despairing he may have been about his own future, he still believed in some sort of future. Tom had a vague affinity for Gaia, but, technically, he did not believe in it. He was, at heart, a skeptic. That was his nature."

Lloyd sighed. "Isn't it amazing how all these things happened? Who would have guessed it? It's as if there is a hidden purpose or design behind it all."

"Maybe there isn't anything behind it, just a cruel, or an indifferent, or an unmindful universe," Iona said. "That's what Tom would have believed. On the other hand, maybe there is something to it. *Who can tell? How can we know for sure?* We measure our faith by the sum total of our doubts."

"Spoken like a true student of Tom Novak!" Lloyd exclaimed.

Before retiring for bed that night, Lloyd jotted down some notes for himself. *As a teacher, Tom Novak was an unusual personage, a rare and dying breed. Like your typical (alas, too typical!) early 21st century thinker, a species too frighteningly prone to nihilism, he was a total nonbeliever, except when it came to his weather prediction abilities. But since he was old enough to have known and studied under what was to him 'the older generation' (Tom was born in 1994—his teachers were from the 1960s or even earlier) he was also like the late, obsolete 20th century man in that he was angry and unhappy there is no certainty. The older generation's insular skepticism, passed down like mother's milk to Tom's generation, kept them from seeing the environmental catastrophe that was barreling down on them like a juggernaut. It didn't affect their lives, mostly, but it did affect the lives of their children, their grandchildren, and their great-grandchildren. That legacy turned Tom into the perfect teacher for Iona: who was herself the very product of this age of maximum uncertainty.*

Before Lloyd, accompanied by his five junior assistants, was escorted out of the Western Quadrant by a small party of Iona's advanced scouts, Iona had one last conversation with him.

On this occasion, they held a sort of celebration. Lloyd laughed gaily. "I have one last message for you, Iona. *Not my boss's secret agenda, not the Gaia-Domes' secret agenda, my own secret agenda.* Never trust the Gaia-Domes. Whether you agree to sign a piece of paper with them or not, whether you agree to 'capitulate' to them or not, it doesn't matter; never trust them. You must never trust them. Never let your guard down. If they ever find it within their powers, they will destroy you. If another ambassador comes to visit you, and offers you hope, never trust him. Never. That's all there is to it."

Iona smiled. "I agree. We understand the Gaia-Domes better than I think they themselves understand themselves. And I think you understand that now, too. I think I can say with confidence, we have become friends, Lloyd."

"Yes," Lloyd said. "I think that is true."

"One last thing," Iona said, "before you go, one final thing."

Iona took her time before she spoke. She cleared her throat. "If we could look into a crystal ball and see into the future, and if that crystal ball could tell us that the Gaia-Domes will come to a complete accommodation with us, I would want you to become my most trusted adviser."

"It would be an honor," Lloyd said. "I am complimented and flattered by the thought. It is an entertaining idea. But it will never happen, at least, not in our lifetime. And you know that."

"Well, of course, you're right," Iona said, "it will never happen, at least, not in our lifetime. But take this back with you when you return to your home in the Gaia-Domes. Heroes come in different shapes and sizes. We never think of a person who is a creature of the Gaia-Domes as a hero, or a courageous person. But you could be a hero, or a courageous person. You could be that person. Silently, of course, unbeknownst to anyone. But you could do it just by carrying within you the memory of the truth. Tom carried it with him until the day he died. You could do that, too."

"But what difference would it make?" Lloyd asked. "No one will listen to me in the Gaia-Domes. I've already come close to perishing several times because of my big mouth. You know what they're like."

"You don't understand," Iona said. "Among The Unseeing Watchfulness of Gaia, there is only one wise one left. Of the original twelve, only one now remains: Ambrosia. She is five years younger than me and ten years younger than Kull, but when she dies, who will replace her? And when Kull and I die, who will replace us? We are the last ones who have been defined and shaped by the old forms of literacy and education. We will be the last ones to have one foot in the old world. When we pass on, so much will be lost. We can pass down some of that tradition, but even within the second or third generation, it will become hopelessly diluted. Tom's philosophical quote on the animal skin—the skin so tattered, worn so badly, the text now is barely readable. Some of my followers carved the words onto the surface of a block of stone, so to preserve it for posterity. Our knowledge is going to be transmitted by stone-carvers. But the stone-carvers may not know what the words truly mean. And later generations won't even be

able to read them. The words will be like runes on a stone. *Mysterious.*
Oblique. Indecipherable. Our people are much more primitive than
we'd like to admit. That's the sorry truth."

"If I can preserve the truth in some way, I'll try," Lloyd said. "If
I can find a way. Maybe I can bury the truth in the ground somewhere, maybe in the form of a secretly-written document. Even if
that document could only be discovered by humans in the very distant future. What difference would it make? The document would
be for the future! For posterity!"

Before Lloyd left, Iona pressed two small gifts on him. One
was a one-and-one-half-ounce-size compass—lightweight, dinted
from use. It was the compass Iona had lifted from the corpse of
a Gaia-Domes courier, she came across while she was crossing the
Forbidden Zone, when she was a little girl. During the intervening
years, through periods of seclusion, war and peace, Iona carried the
compass with her around her neck. In spite of it being dinted, the
compass's needle still pointed magnetic north. She took the compass
from around her neck and tenderly folded it into Lloyd's hand.

With her other hand Iona then handed Lloyd a frail, three-and-
a-half-inch high pumpkin.

"I'm sorry to present you with so sorry a specimen," Iona said.
"This pumpkin is pathetic. It's scrawny. In this harsh land, under
such circumstances, we're struggling mightily to make a go of it as
farmers, and it's the best we can do. Two small round things to take
back with you to remember us by."

Chapter Forty-Three

SIX WEEKS LATER, Lloyd returned to the Gaia-Domes without incident. The rebel trackers knew exactly how to get him and his group back safely. Lloyd's party was forced to wear hoods over their heads during the first one hundred miles of the journey so as not to be able to recognize the path. Lloyd was given a horse to ride from the outset, but the rest of the party were also provided with horses for the last two legs of the trip.

Upon his arrival in Glenwood Springs, Lloyd was immediately flown in a helioplane back to New York. He was happy to be back home. He was relieved to be welcomed by all of the members of the world magistrate council. The first thing he did upon his return was wolf down two steak-and-egg dinners and drink a bottle of twenty-six-year-old champagne. During the previous three months in the rebel camp, even though he had been provided with more food than anybody else, he had lost eighteen pounds.

He gave to the council his report and detailed analysis—some of which of course he convincingly faked and fabricated—of what happened during his brief stay at the rebel's camp. Without controversy or debate, the council accepted Lloyd's report. (After all, Celsius was not alive to offer a dissenting or contradictory perspective.)

Lloyd presented to the council the scrawny pumpkin Iona had presented to him, which they all laughed at derisively. Lloyd never showed them Iona's compass.

Lloyd was immediately reappointed to his chairmanship as residential scholar in Hominid and Post-Hominid Studies. As special magister, all of his privileges were given back to him. Did he consider himself lucky? Yes. He did not return with signed documents indicating a capitulation on the part of the rebels. In fact, his mission had been largely a failure. Lloyd did not want to tempt fate by questioning the wisdom and judgment of the world magistrate council, after all, opinion had shifted generally in his favor. Politically, nobody wanted to bring the majority faction's secret agenda up; it was conveniently swept under the rug. Through Celsius's intervention, three important leaders of the rebels had been assassinated, two wise ones and an important military leader, Fiona, although Celsius failed in his task of killing Iona and Kull.

Over time, the Gaia-Domes became increasingly distracted by events occurring in other parts of their empire. In a sense, Iona's gift of the scrawny pumpkin, at least symbolically, had served as a sort of talisman. The message was clear. Why waste precious resources to eliminate a group that posed no direct threat to the Gaia-Domes? The Gaia-Domes had come to the conclusion that they did not have to eliminate all their enemies. If anything, their power had become more secure and concentrated.

The hardliners convinced themselves that the rebel group would probably not survive another fifty years anyway, and Lloyd said nothing to contradict that overly sanguine opinion.

As long as the primitives known as The Unseeing Watchfulness of Gaia never ventured beyond the edges of the Western Quadrant, they were seen as relatively harmless. In security matters, containment—rather than the control-freak's imperative to annihilate anything that moved—had become the new Gaia-Dome watchword. The plan devolved into letting the rebel group die out naturally. Or at least the arguments for inaction outweighed mounting a concentrated attack against a group that was spread out over a large geographical area, always lived in isolated groups, and were constantly on the move and were therefore hard to pin down.

The minority faction on the world magistrate council, led by grandmagister James Clare, had not beaten their more powerful adversaries, the hardliners, at their own game. Rather, they prevailed through the force of *real-politick default*. Whenever anyone raised the issue of attacking the rebels, more pressing issues always seemed to get in the way.

Kull's wound healed quickly. Iona and Kull traveled around the Western Quadrant, never occupying one place for more than three or four months at a time. The decades flew by. Once the threat from the Gaia-Domes decreased, and then seemed to almost completely disappear, Iona simultaneously eased up on the propagation of the Gaia religion. Kull was greatly relieved by this change in Iona. Kull knew that what had started as a liberating phenomenon *could*—in the fullness of time— turn into precisely its opposite. The teachings of Gaia could contain seeds of major reversals. Having been a slave in his childhood, if Kull had learned nothing else from the Gaia Epoch, he had grasped that the more perfect the answer, the more terrifying its consequences. Imperfect improvements were the best they could hope for, and probably all that they should seek.

But if the Gaia-Domes had been wrong in trying to control nature, and by virtue of that fact, evil by default or design, in the near future, or in the distant future, Kull knew that the concept of Gaia could recreate itself into a resplendently beautiful thing again. Who knew what could happen in the future? Nothing could sustain itself forever, not even the totalitarian impulses of the Gaia-Domes. Who knew what the future would bring? But Kull was no fool. He knew that history could be capricious, non-linear, and not necessarily even ultimately progressive. It didn't promise *anything*. The path to truth was always found by improvising in the existential moment, getting to the truth was the goal, but the dilemma was how to make truth live longer than a fleeting moment.

In other words, how could one transfer a necessary truth from

one generation to the next? Was there an overriding ideal that transcended immediate experience that was necessary? Was a Truth,
spelled with a capital T, necessary to keep the smaller, more elusive—
harder to find—truth, alive?

After all, saving the planet was a great and noble ideal, perhaps
the grandest ideal that humanity had yet to come up with. But the
first seventy-five years of the Gaia Epoch had shown what terrible
things could happen when right ideas were implemented by wrong
thinking. Were humanity's solutions always going to be so bestial,
brutal, nasty, and horrifying, Kull wondered?

Once the survival of the group was no longer in question, Kull
saw a change come over Iona. To his satisfaction, Kull noticed that
the Gaia religion was no longer essential to Iona's overriding worldview. Iona had used the religion for both strategic and pragmatic purposes when the group was threatened, or when great sacrifices were
required. But once these factors were no longer operative, Iona's role
as leader of the rebel group underwent a further transformation.

For one thing, Iona ceased referring to herself as a prophetess.
She ceased making predictions. She now lived the simplest of lives.
She no longer presided over subordinates as a leader of a religion.
Rather, she acted as a role model on how to conduct a modest life.
In fact, she no longer saw religion as the necessary glue to bind
people together. She no longer talked about philosophy, religion,
politics, or even that vaguer and more ephemeral thing, *spirituality*. The few occasions when she did speak on weighty subjects, she
spoke sparingly—only a few words.

In the biggest transformation, Iona eventually ceased being a
leader altogether. She gave advice rather than directives, and that
was confined to the most practical matters. When to plant crops and
what crops had the greatest chance of surviving. How to tend one's
garden. How to survive against the elements. How to hunt small

game when available. How to build fires. How to cook food properly. How to find caves to live in and how to find rock overhangs to
live under. How to husband one's supplies. How and when to move
from one region to another area without exhausting resources. How
to travel lightly. How to travel at night in safety and comfort. How
to protect oneself against the perils of sun death. How to pass on to
the next generation the essentials for survival. How to be free from
the burden of attachment to unnecessary articles. How to live.

And to Kull, Iona taught the greatest lesson of all: how to age
gracefully and with dignity.

When Kull turned seventy in Year Gaia Seventy, and Iona at the
same time turned sixty-five, nineteen years after the time of the negotiations with Lloyd, Iona said, "The Earth will take care of itself.
The Earth will heal itself now. All we have to do is get out of the way.
All we have to believe in is 'Everything is interwoven, and the web is
holy.'"

In Year Gaia Eighty, Iona said, "In the context of geological
time, the last three hundred years will mean nothing to the planet
Earth. Even if the next 500 years, or even the next 1000 years—are
a time of great upheaval and dislocation, in the fullness of time, the
damage to the planet will mean nothing. It will be just a blip. For
four and a half billion years the planet has survived continuous and
violent upheaval: mountain ranges rising and falling, great chasms
of oceans opening up and closing, comet and asteroid impacts, ti-
tanic explosions, volcanic eruptions, whole continents bumping up
against each other and grinding. As a people, as a race, as a species,
it is we ourselves who have been damaged. To the planet, it matters
not—we've been here only a brief flicker of time."

In Year Gaia Eighty-Two (2133 A.D.), addressing Kull, Iona
said, "We are not much longer on this Earth. It's time we find a place
to die. I am five years younger than you. I want to find a place where I
can take care of you for the years that remain. We can't keep traveling
from place to place like a pair of *Homo peripateticus*. We must find an
isolated place that is well sheltered where we can reside."

Ambrosia knew exactly where such a place could be found. It had to fulfill two contradictory requirements: be a place where the old couple could live easily, and also be a place that was remote and inaccessible, protected on all sides by a large desert. To Ambrosia, there was only one choice. With the help of fifteen trusted assistants, Iona and Kull were transported there.

The place was located 400 miles to the northeast of the Escalante Plateau, in the middle of the Nevada Desert.

Ambrosia found the perfect valley beneath a lone mountaintop that rose to an altitude of 11,473 feet.

Even with the erratic changes in climate, several storms would blow consistently in wintertime, and heavy precipitation would occur, but only at the highest levels of elevation. Snow would accumulate near the summit of the highest mountains. The sun would melt the snow pack during the hot summer months, *but not during the winter and early spring months,* when the cold would hold the snow in place. Just when the snow pack would all but vanish, sometime in early autumn, the first new storm of the year would blow in just in time, within a matter of weeks, or at most a month, depositing a new pack of snow, and the cycle would repeat itself all over again.

Because of a permanent, well encrusted snow pack tucked in a u-shaped indenture on the side of the mountain—600 feet from the top—unlike what occurred in the majority of cases of other mountaintops above 11,000 feet, this one single snow pack created a tiny stream-base which never ceased running, never completely being depleted as a source of water. The angle, direction and inclination of the u-shaped indenture at the top of the mountain was uniquely favorable to preserve a moderate-size snow pack all year round. The stream ran down from the snow face, flowing continuously all the time, although twenty-five miles from the mountain, the stream rolled down onto the flat surface of the scorching desert, where it disappeared into the sand.

In between the top of the mountain and the desert floor, in a ten-to-twelve-mile corridor, the stream flowed. Several potholes, some of them as deep as six feet, along the water course, held fish and saved them at critical dry times in late summer and early autumn.

There were trout in the stream. There were butterflies in the valley. And overhead, migratory birds passed. It was a marvelous mini-ecosystem, undisturbed and verdant, that had survived the ravages of time.

Go thirty-five miles in any direction and it was dry desert. But within the confines of that snow-fed environment was a unique and extraordinary pocket of life, only ten-to-twelve miles in length.

With the aide of fifteen assistants, Iona and Kull were transported on sleds across the desert. After arriving at their destination, three youngsters were assigned to help them set up accommodations and lay in provisions. These three youngsters stayed on for six months. Once it was clear that Iona and Kull were finally autonomous and could make it on their own, the three left.

Sixty years earlier, Kull had never acquired a taste for saltwater fishing. In fact, he had been totally incompetent at it. But now he learned how to fish. Having acquired this angler skill, Iona and Kull were able to eat trout, and, on occasion, a small-mouth bass. Iona reacquainted herself with her old hunting skills. She carried on her person her bow and arrows at all times. Even in her dotage, Iona was still a relatively-speaking competent hunter. But she never hunted at night (nor did Kull fish at night). They figured at their age not even a large dosage of sun death could do them any harm now. They could live as they wished.

Kull said to Iona: "It's amazing what you have accomplished. Surviving in the Forbidden Zone when you were a thirteen-and-a-half-year-old. Surviving alone in the desert for the next seven years. Getting such a large group of orphans together. Giving them a reason to live. Making the caves work as a place to live in, and to survive in. Making those caves home to thousands of young people for *twenty long years*. Amazing! Winning battles against nature. Then, when we were strong enough, winning the battle against the Gaia-Domes. Defeating the Gaia-Domes, first by hiding from them, then confronting them. Guiding five thousand, then seven thousand, then twelve thousand children and young adults over fifteen hundred miles to the Western Quadrant, fighting battles along the way. Later on, getting the Gaia-Domes to leave us alone. Maybe that was the greatest victory of all, getting the Gaia-Domes to keep their hands off of us so that we could find enough breathing space to survive. Then you quit pushing your own agenda. All that old hocus-pocus Gaia stuff, you let it go. Letting our young people grow on their own, and take on a new life."

Kull was so filled with joy he could barely contain himself.

"I remember what Clive taught me as a boy. He once told me about the arrival of new ideas on the threshold of intellectual change, scientific revolutions, industrial revolutions, but my favorite was the one he told me about bird migrations and the metaphor it provided for us as humans. You'd think, of all the preposterous things, bird migrations! But I recall it as his finest example of storytelling. Clive told me the story about how birds travel thousands of miles, following time-honored routes. Maybe the migration route was a mere hundred miles, but some birds flew exceedingly long distances. Some birds migrated from South America to North America, and, of course, returned. Some birds flew across the Sahara Desert. Some birds flew across the Atlantic Ocean. Some birds flew all the way from the Arctic to Antarctica, over eight thousand miles. These migrations could go on for millions of years. But the Earth changed. In 'normal' times, the Earth changed.

Now this is the special thing that Clive taught me that makes this story about bird migration so extraordinary. Every once in a while, he told me, a bird goes 'off its head,' in other words, gets side-tracked. It happens now and then. The bird gets separated from the group. Maybe the bird's instinctual homing device is fouled up, who knows? Whatever the reason, the bird suddenly turns away from the main group and heads out in a crazy direction, going the wrong way. Before the bird knows it, it's way off course. What happens 999,999,999 times out of a billion is that the bird flies on and dies.

End of story. Happens all the time. But one bird in a billion manages to survive. That one bird—by accident, goes off in the wrong direction, gets swept away on the winds, maybe is driven out to sea, yet instead of dying like all those other luckless birds, it manages to land on land— on a remote, uncharted island. The island is located a thousand miles away from the bird's normal flight pattern. And, by accident, the island turns out to be an ideal spot—the perfect place for that species of birds—for resting, nesting, traveling, *everything*. And the bird gets its instinctual homing device back up and running, and continues on its trip to the next stop, rejoining the flock. Then, the next year, other birds follow this bird to this remote island. And more birds follow the next year. A new pattern is set. The flock grows larger. Finally, an alternate migration route is born.

And the next thing, perhaps one thousand generations later, there are as many birds going on the new migratory route as there are going on the old migratory route. Then the alternate route becomes so popular it overtakes the main route. And what has been accomplished? Diversity! Then the climate changes. A new ice age occurs. Or a 'mini-ice age' occurs. Or some other big natural change occurs. The sun gets hotter. A meteor lands. A volcano erupts. An earthquake occurs, wait, that shouldn't make a difference. Wait, wait, it does make a difference! Along the old route are some old islands in the middle of a lake, the water level drops, a land bridge is created because of the lowering of the water, and the foxes raid the islands and steal the eggs of the birds. Catastrophe! And the original leg of the migratory route is now kaput, destroyed—no longer safe—hopelessly untenable. The birds on the old route are finished. *There's no old route.* There's only the new route. And the new route is *THE* migratory route. The species is saved. Diversity! All because of this one loony bird. All because of you, Iona."

Kull stared at Iona.

"All because of you. You are that bird, Iona. And the new migratory route, for humanity, runs through the Western Quadrant. That's how I see the future shall be written."

Chapter Forty-Four

TWO YEARS PASSED, and it grew bitterly cold one winter night. The temperature dropped ten degrees Fahrenheit below freezing. Iona came into the hut after a brisk hunt. She had bagged only two measly, mangy jackrabbits, which she had already skinned and readied for stew. She found Kull lying on the floor. Only two months before, they had celebrated Kull's eighty-fifth birthday. The body was lying next to the table. Iona was not at all surprised to find Kull passed out. His old wounds had been acting up, troubling him, especially on cold nights. Between the long scar on his left upper thigh and the scar on the left side of his chest, the whole left side of his body sometimes seemed to go numb at night. After several episodes of this, the shine and luster had left Kull's eyes. Now Iona checked Kull's pulse and discovered that he was dead.

Iona washed Kull's body early the next morning and buried him in a shallow grave. At first, she thought of putting his remains on a raised platform so that the birds could come and devour his flesh. Kull once said his parents had remembered that *their* parents had been practicing Buddhists. But they weren't that kind of Buddhists, not Tibetan Buddhists, so she decided against that funeral variation.

Iona knew for certain that Kull didn't want a watery grave, so shipping his remains to the coast was out of the question. Iona remembered Kull saying how much he detested large bodies of water, didn't matter whether he was on the surface of it in a boat, or on a nuclear rig platform. Iona also remembered Lloyd telling her that upon Tom's death the Gaia-Domes would not allow him to dignify Tom with a proper burial. Tom was cremated and his ashes were scattered in the air above the ocean, signifying the ignominious fate of a pauper's grave of an un-Gaia person. Tom's end had struck Iona as sad. She found it funny, however, that it had never occurred to her to ask Kull what she should do with his remains. Now it was too late to ask. So she made the decision for him.

Shoveling dirt upon Kull's remains evoked in Iona memories of his stories of his childhood. Iona remembered Kull speaking of himself as a boy, with stunted physical development, but accelerated mental achievement, caused by his having been a multi-time, trauma- tized child. How he fought within himself over his origin as a slave. And how, many years later, he had turned into a calm, steady, calcu- lating person whose decisions were always based on thoughtfulness and clarity of vision. In his life, Kull had had so much to overcome.

For some reason, Kull's death also made Iona think about Tom Novak, whom she had not thought about for a long time. Suddenly finding herself bereft and alone, Iona couldn't stopped herself from thinking about her old teacher. Then the thought of him made her think of other people from her past. Now Iona couldn't remember the name of the woman who had saved her life when she was thir- teen-and-a-half, sixty-seven years before. Iona had known her simply as the woman doctor. She would always be the woman doctor, even though she had been like a surrogate mother to her.

Iona wondered if Lloyd was still alive. She wondered if he had had a chance to write his secret documents and bury them, as he said he would do. She thought back. It had been more than thirty years since they had played the game of negotiations with the Gaia-Domes.

As she prepared herself, other memories flashed in her mind. Iona could not remember *the image* of her father, Regis Snow. She had last seen him when she was three-and-a-half-years-old, it had been so long ago, she could not remember. She could not remember his face. She tried to but she could not. But she could remember his voice, soft, full, and sad. Iona did remember the face of her mother, September Snow. Iona had been nine-years-old when she had last seen her face. In spite of her age, Iona was still tough, but she was not used to being alone. This was something new. She felt ashamed of herself for feeling lonely. Kull had meant so much to her, but what kind of an example was that to set for others? Had she not taught herself to live for others?

Iona had to come to terms with the fact that she was no longer a sage, a saint, a prophet, a great and outstanding thinker, a leader of a rebel group. She was just a tired old woman. She did not have to set an example for anyone anymore. Those days were over.

Iona decided to do something she'd not done during the wintertime before. She decided to climb the mountain to the edge of the snow pack. It was a risky and dangerous thing for her to do at her age, but she didn't care. She wanted to do it at least once, before she died.

She dressed warmly. She strapped her bow and arrows on her back. She hiked up the mountainside.

If anyone had been there to see it, the sight would have been a strange combination of the heroic and the absurd. To see a woman of eighty years, climbing over boulders, making her way through thickets, ditches and trenches, snaking her way up the winding stream bed, to where the water came right off the snub-nose of the snowdrifts. Many places along the way Iona had to stop and catch her breath, but in spite of her age, her walking was steady and progressive. In the early winter half-light, in the course of four hours, the sun slid down the sky. With the sun's last rays, it turned the gloaming into a crimson fire, but only for a minute or two, and then there was that strange afterglow of velvet and violet. Oh that soft feeling, just before dusk. If Iona strained her eyes it made everything look so sharp, especially for someone who had once been so good at hunting in the twilight and the darkness. It was perishingly cold.

Then she saw it. At first, she thought what she was seeing was an apparition. But the form moved. And the eyes, gleaming, translucent, bold, intrepid, stared down at her. This was no jackrabbit or mangy coyote, half-starved and shriveled, this was a full-grown mountain lion. Being a nighttime predator, and a highly reclusive animal, the beast must have started its hunt early and Iona must have startled it. It was crouching low on a boulder, staring down from a distance of only a few yards. Oh, the glory of it. A chill surged like electricity through Iona's body. She thought of Tom Novak, not just his memory, but of his ghost, of his spirit, *as if he were present with her.* Iona thought of the woman doctor, no, now Iona remembered—Marjoram had been her name—how could she have forgotten! And how proud Marjoram would have been seeing Iona, not a child of thirteen or fourteen anymore, not hunting mice, squirrels, prairie dogs, or other rodents, but sighting a mighty mountain lion!

Then Iona thought of her father, as if scolding her from the distance of seventy-seven years, his voice speaking with a soft, underplayed, under-spoken authority, "A thousand scientists can say the planet is growing healthier, but the sight of a single lone mountain lion found in the middle of nowhere would speak massive volumes!"

Iona remembered where she was. *And with all her bewildering and intersecting thoughts she was alone.*

She had to remind herself that this was a large carnivore crouching in front of her, purring, and there was no morality.

Iona thought, "He can eat me if he wishes. Doesn't matter. But I will not give any aid for me to be devoured. I have as much right to be here as the beast does. And I will die fighting."

Iona reached over her shoulder and grasped the shaft of an arrow from her quiver and symbolically touched her bow and twanged the string and shouted a harsh, warbling, piercing shriek but all the dramatic fanfare afterwards seemed so unnecessary, foolish, and childish in the subsequent hush of silence.

Iona felt almost ashamed at her antics.

From his crouching position the mountain lion turned and slipped away into the darkness, moving so silently and stealthily that even Iona could not tell where he had gone.

THE END

the story continues...

Runes of Iona is Book Two of THE BLESSINGS OF GAIA series
Book One: *September Snow* (June 2006)
Book Three: *Embers of the Earth* [forthcoming]
Book Four: *Auger's Touchstone* {forthcoming}

Book one of the Blessings of Gaia series

"Robert Balmanno's *September Snow* is futuristic fiction at the very top. It can be placed beside Frank Herbert's *Dune*, Aldous Huxley's *Brave New World* and George Orwell's *Nineteen Eighty Four*."

Book one of THE BLESSINGS OF GAIA series

September Snow

In 2051 AD the world changed...

Robert Balmanno

a novel

A Caveat Lector Book

Order yours today on line, on Amazon.com, through the publisher, or at your local bookstore.

ROBERT BALMANNO has worked as a library specialist in a Silicon Valley library for 23 years. He is a trade union activist and served as a Peace Corps volunteer in West Africa, working with cattle in small villages in Dahomey (Benin).

Balmanno earned his bachelor's degree in Political Science from the University of California, Santa Barbara and did post-graduate work at the University of Edinburgh in Scotland and the University of London, King's College.